PROMISE ME

BOOK THREE IN THE TRUST SERIES

KRISTIN MAYER

OTHER BOOKS BY KRISTIN MAYER

THE TRUST SERIES
TRUST ME
LOVE ME
PROMISE ME

DEDICATION

*I dedicate this book to my husband, Paul,
my daughter, Makaela,
and my grandmama, Edna.*

*Grandmama, you inspired the Edna character in this book from the
conversations we had in the kitchen while we baked each time I came to
visit you. I miss and love you every day.*

CONTENTS

CHAPTER
1

Sam

I awoke to the sound of my alarm buzzing as I had an early morning flight to North Carolina. I groaned at how weary my body felt. Guilt and relief simultaneously flooded my mind as I thought about my late-night activities within the walls of Club Envy, the sex club I belonged to.

None of my friends knew this side of me. All those times I'd told Allison I was going to Atlanta to work for the sorority, I'd actually gone to find my release in order to keep my world standing right side up.

Yesterday, with Allison's news of being pregnant, the past had tried to come over into my present, and that was unacceptable. It had shaken me to the core, bringing up long-forgotten memories. That box of emotions had been locked and buried for years, and I had been fine up until then. Everything had bubbled to the surface at once, unveiling the dark place from my past. My Pandora's box had been opened. I needed to find the key again and lock the damn thing shut forever.

The feelings had been too much, and last night, I'd used the only method that worked to keep me balanced since coming to Waleska for college almost four years ago—sex at the club.

Six months ago, I had quit the club cold turkey right after Ben kidnapped Allison. After watching Damien's past come back and haunt him, I'd realized I needed to get my act together. I'd pushed the thought from my head every time I had the desire to go to the club for that detached freeness it brought me.

I'd thought I was better and no longer needed the club as I had gone a couple of weeks without thinking about it. I had been wrong on so many levels. Maybe keeping myself away from Club Envy had been a bad idea.

Club Envy allowed the members to keep their identity hidden if they wanted. No one knew who I was at the club besides the owners. I always made sure to keep my identity anonymous by wearing a kitty-cat mask and a red wig. One of the owners, Adam, was who I would spend my time with while at the club. He knew how to relieve the darkness brewing inside me. He was the perfect fuck buddy.

Since the first time I'd entered the club after hearing about it one night at a bar in Atlanta, Adam had been my partner. The coping mechanism I could find at Club Envy seemed to effectively deal with and tame all the emotions swirling around inside me, threatening to erupt.

My mind went back to last night.

In my car, I continued to stare at the old brick building where my utopia for the night resided. I shook my head, trying to clear the thoughts.

Put the car in drive. Leave, Sam. Get the fuck out of here.

My craving for happiness was supposed to be buried so deep in my soul that it would never surface, bringing these emotions with it. When I'd initially worked up the nerve at Tybee Island, I should have told Allison what had happened that awful New Year's night all those years ago. In the end, I'd lost my nerve from my own insecurities of what she would think. I knew my fear had been irrational.

Focusing my thoughts away from the memories, I looked at Club Envy again. The building called to me in a pulsing manner. I could forget all this the moment the metal door shut, encapsulating me in the alternate universe I had created.

Stay strong, Sam. You don't need this.

I screwed my eyes shut, fighting the pull this place had on me, but then I remembered what it could bring—the hidden identities, the ultimate control, the separation from my mind. This place had been a godsend when I started college as I was barely hanging on by a thread. My mind tried to make my body turn on the car and drive away, but my body just sat there.

Fighting the pull, my fingers were wound tight around the steering wheel, my knuckles turning a ghostly white.

Just one more time. Only one more time.

The feel of leather, the clink of metal, the sound of a whip—that was all I needed in the moment.

My phone chirped.

> Adam: Come on, Kitty Cat. I always have
> what you need. I'll make you feel better.

My head snapped up, and I saw him standing at the entrance with his hand extended. My body took over, shutting out my thoughts. My hands reached out and grabbed my red wig. I put it on, followed by my cat eye mask.

Just one more time. All I need is one more time.

No attachment.

No strings.

No romance.

Just SEX.

His muscle shirt showed all his sexy muscles. His arms were covered in tats. He was the kind of guy girls wanted to make theirs—all girls, that was, except for me.

After I walked up to him, he reached out his hand and led us silently to the side door of the building. The front half of Club Envy was a bar, and most patrons had no idea what went on behind the brick wall where the sex club was.

Right as we entered Adam's office, he turned to me. "Kitty Cat, how rough do you want it tonight?"

Licking my lips, I leaned up on my toes and then ran my tongue across his earlobe. "I want it rough and hard. I want to be fucked ten ways to Sunday against that wall. I want to forget. Do you think you can handle that?"

I bit his earlobe, and he growled.

Grabbing my hips, he pushed me against the wall and devoured my mouth. "What do you need, Kitty Cat?"

"Suck my breasts—hard."

He lifted my shirt, and seeing me braless, he groaned in approval. He sucked my nipple so hard that I knew I would be bruised tomorrow. I threw my head back in pleasure from the pain.

I moaned, "Fuck me hard."

He raised his chocolate eyes up to mine. "I always have what you need. I'm going to fuck you so hard that you'll be sore tomorrow."

My core clenched. I am definitely going to be sore tomorrow. *"After this, I want to tie you up, Adam."*

"Whatever you need, Kitty Cat."

For now, I wanted to stay the course and not go back to the club again. I had my fingers crossed that I would be able to find a healthier way to keep everything in its place, so I could function like a normal human being. Memories of those sexcapades would have to suffice since I was moving today. I had graduated last weekend from Reinhardt College, and I was moving up to North Carolina for the time being.

Focusing on the sound of metal chains snapping from last night, I got up and headed to the shower. As I stepped into the water, Adam's words came back to me.

You'll be back, Kitty Cat. I'll be waiting, ready to give you what you need when you do come back. You're a fun fuck buddy.

We'll see. I wasn't entirely sure he hadn't been right, but distance would keep me from coming back. Preseason football would be starting soon, and I had my dream job. Damien had offered me the chance of a lifetime, creating the Team Relations Manager position for me. It was a multilayered job that involved scouting new talent, re-upping soon-to-be expired contracts, reporting on things that could potentially harm the team brand, and other tasks.

I wouldn't start officially until August, but I was going to use the next two months to get acquainted with everything. Damien and I had decided that it would be best if I lived up in North Carolina at least half of the time. Fortunately, with my kick-ass new salary, I was able to easily afford a place both there and here in Atlanta. My parents felt better about the decision, knowing I would be back home in Georgia some of the time.

Georgia will always be my home.

Turning the water up even higher to an almost scalding temperature, I cleaned myself. Though I'd needed the release last night, the hot water always felt like I was washing away the activities from the club forever, like I was creating a clean slate. I hated feeling dirty, and I would wash my skin almost raw each and every time after going to the club. My flesh was reddened from the harsh scrubbing before I began washing my long black hair.

This isn't healthy. This can't be healthy.

There had been so many times when I almost told Allison about what had happened to me in high school, but after all the you-need-to-go-to-therapy lectures I'd given her when her parents died, I'd felt hypocritical, and I'd sentenced myself to a prison of silence.

I shook my head from those thoughts and continued thinking about today.

Too much dwelling on the past does nothing but lead you right back into the past.

Allison and Damien would be flying out to North Carolina on the company plane later this afternoon. She had insisted on making sure I was settled there. Of course, they had offered me a ride, but I had already booked my ticket. Now, I was thankful for taking the conventional way of flying. I knew I wouldn't have been able to take seeing their happiness, considering how I had mentally reacted to the news of the baby yesterday.

I loved my best friend with my whole heart, and I was glad she had been doing so well after the loss of her parents almost two years ago. I felt like a bitch for reacting to her pregnancy like I'd mentally done, and I needed to get my feelings under control before I hurt her because of my fucked-up past.

The one thing I hadn't been able to get out of was staying at Allison and Damien's new home while I searched for a place of my own. Allison would know something was up if I didn't stay with them. However, a new home for me would be found by the end of the week. I felt bad for having those thoughts, but I had to look out for myself if I was going to drop the sex-club habit.

I finished my shower and dried off. After wiping away the steam, I looked at myself in the mirror, my green eyes reflecting back at me. My eye color was my favorite feature on my body. Only two small bruises had formed on my hips from last night. That wasn't bad, especially with how rough we had been. I had a naturally curvy body in all the right places, and men loved to play with it.

After combing through my hair, I tied it up and went back to my room to finish packing. Looking at the clock, I knew the company car would be here in less than ten minutes to give me a ride to the airport. I threw a few last-minute things into my suitcase. Leaving my brand-new condo in Atlanta was bittersweet.

For a change, I had decorated this condo in a more modern theme. Allison had scrunched her nose at some of my artwork choices, which had made me laugh. She always thought that abstract paintings looked more like the work of a kindergartner. The tables and light fixtures were all chrome, the furniture was purple and red, and all the cabinets were black. It was pretty swanky and different. Allison had been a blessing while helping me get my place here all set up. Without her, I couldn't have gotten it all done while I'd been in school. She was always there for me in the exact capacity I needed each time.

Looking out the window, I saw the car waiting for me. After grabbing my bags, I headed down to start my new post-college adventure. As I crossed over this milestone, I knew my life was never going to be the same.

I welcome the change.
I embrace it.
I hope to hell it will be enough.

The plane ride had been uneventful, and I was glad to finally be arriving at Allison's new home. Zipping through traffic in my new company car, a red convertible BMW, was an exhilarating feeling. It was apparently part of my bonus from re-signing players. I'd had no complaints when I was told what I was getting. I respected Damien for how he ran his company. He was always fair to his employees, but his expectations were high. I liked that in a boss. I had no problem earning every penny I would be making.

My phone pinged. It was Allison.

> *Allison: Landed. I'll be there shortly. I'm so excited for you.*

> *Me: Me, too. Sounds good. See you in a few.*

I pulled up to the three-story brick mansion in my little red car. Allison had said it was smaller than their Atlanta home, but it was still a magnificently large one. She was always a humble person. The house sat on a vast estate with a perfectly manicured lawn.

As I approached the gate, the guard came out to greet me. "Miss Matthews, a garage spot is waiting for you around back."

"Thank you."

He went back into the guardhouse and pushed a button that caused the huge gate to start moving. After giving him a wink, I pulled through and headed around to the back of the home. I loved that my down-to-earth best friend hadn't changed from being around money. She was who she had always been. If she had her choice, she would wear yoga pants and a T-shirt every damn day of her life. No one would ever know she was worth millions by looking at her.

Hell, it could be billions for all I knew.

Since the incident last fall with Ben, Damien had still kept some security around. Now, that had been a seriously messed-up situation. Ben had been completely crazed and obsessed with Damien, and that had led to an obsession with Allison. I'd known she was keeping something from me with how withdrawn she had become. Balancing a new marriage, media frenzies, a crazy stalker, plus everything else in her life had to have been incredibly difficult. I had been deeply hurt that I was kept in the dark all that time about such a significant event in my friend's life, but I'd understood when it all came to light. I couldn't hold it against her too much, considering the secret I had kept since the incident my senior year.

Making my way to my room at Damien and Allison's place, I started to mentally go over everything I needed to do in order to find a place, stat. All the rooms in each of their homes were warm and inviting. My room here was decorated in green and gold with a hint of cream. My body instantly felt tired from not getting enough sleep last night. Just as the thought of taking a short nap entered my mind, I heard my best friend's voice from down the hall.

"Sam, are you here?"

"I'm in my room."

A few seconds later, Allison's head popped around the door, and she was peering inside. She had no idea how beautiful she was, and her cluelessness drove men even wilder. Her dirty-blonde hair was thrown up into a messy ponytail, and she had on a cute, little blue sundress. She looked tired. My eyes went to her stomach for a brief moment as I thought about the pregnancy. Damien was going to go all alpha-like on her when he found out about the baby, wanting to keep his family safe. Allowing someone that much control over me would never happen, but it worked for them because he loved her.

As she entered the room, I was frozen in place with the glow emanating from her. It had only been yesterday when she told me she was pregnant.

Forcing my feet to move and knowing I had to act excited, I walked to her and embraced her in a hug. I was glad to see her. "Congratulations! Good to see you, bestie. Where's that crazy-ass, barbaric husband of yours?"

She rolled her eyes and gave me a sweet smile. "Thank you. Bane dropped Damien off at the office, so he could sign some paperwork. A car will be sent back for him. He'll be here in an hour or so. Anyway, it'll give us some time to catch up since you've been so busy these last few months. I've missed you. You know you can stay here for as long as you need to, right?"

Bane was their badass security guard, who had played an essential part in killing Ben.

While I continued to feel the happiness emanating from Allison, I prayed that the unwanted emotion from yesterday wouldn't come back. "I know. I appreciate it. You guys are too good to me, but I'm ready to find a place and get settled in. So, little mama-to-be, is Wales over-the-moon ecstatic?" I wagged my eyebrows up and down for added effect.

She giggled, but then she huffed and lay down on the bed with her arm across her face. "He still doesn't know."

Shocked, I responded, "What? You know, in eight months or so, baby Wales will be making his or her debut in this world, so you might want to let Daddy know before then. Did you have any idea?"

She sighed in frustration. "No, but Damien and I had already decided I was going off the pill. Yesterday was my yearly checkup. I wanted to talk to my doctor and get mentally prepared. When I told her I hadn't been feeling well, she did a pregnancy test. I'd gotten pregnant even with birth control. Sam, I'm so happy. It's a lot to take in. I wasn't prepared."

I could hear the stress in her voice.

I was trying to think of what to say to support her, when she continued, "I was about to tell him, but then Katie started chasing the horses, causing a ruckus. By the time all that was settled, Damien was sweaty, filthy, and tired. I didn't want to just say, *Oh, by the way, I'm pregnant.* I want the moment to be perfect."

I gave her a small chuckle at how this must be rocking her perpetual planning habit.

It was time for a subject change to something less stressful for both of us as I said, "I love that dog. Katie is the best gift Martin and I could have ever gotten Damien."

That caused us both to smile. I started thinking about when Martin and I had figured out what to give Damien as a just-because gift. Martin and I were always giving Damien a hard time.

Martin had been Damien's best friend from childhood. After the death of Damien's sister, Rebecca, Damien and Martin had caused each other wounds, and they were now healing from them. Since I had met Martin on Tybee Island, he had become one of my very dear friends and a big part of our group. Martin and I were each other's sidekicks when it came to giving Wales a hard time. Martin was a blast and so funny.

"Sam, what the hell are we going to get Wales? It can't be some boring-ass gift. We have a reputation to uphold."

Leaving the fifteenth store, I racked my brain for what to get Damien. It couldn't be just anything. With the shit we gave him on a constant basis, this had to be epic. Just then, I heard some whining. I turned my head and saw the most adorable black lab puppies. Martin was still walking when I grabbed his shirtsleeve to stop him.

"What the hell, Sam?"

A devious grin spread on my face as an idea formed. I pointed toward the puppies. "Maybe we should get Damien a practice baby. Do you know how much shit we could give him every time the dog did something bad or good?"

Martin grabbed my hand and started pulling me toward the pen. "You pick which one, and I'll pay. You're a genius."

Picturing the endless fun this was going to provide had me laughing.

Throwing her hands out to the side and rising from the bed, Allison continued, "I feel awful because I've known about being pregnant for over twenty-four hours without telling the father."

Obviously, Allison isn't ready for a subject change.

Coming to sit beside her, I grabbed her in a half-hug. "Allison, just belt it out. He's not going to care one way or another how you tell him. We all know how badly he wants one. Plus, he's had a lot of practice with Katie. He's more than prepared."

She gave me a small smile. I was sure she was thinking about all the crap Martin and I had dished his way when it came to Katie.

Allison's phone rang from her purse on the dresser. It was Damien's ringtone. The dreaded look on her face made me laugh as she marched toward it like it was a death sentence.

"Shut it, Sam. It's not funny. Damien's going to think I'm upset. I'm so happy. I was just shocked."

She grunted in frustration as she picked up the phone, which caused me to laugh even harder as she answered the call.

"Hey, Damien. Yes, I made it. Okay—"

All of a sudden, the phone was pushed into my face before Allison ran to the bathroom and closed the door. It appeared that my best friend was having her first bout with morning sickness.

What the hell am I going to say to Damien?

Putting the phone to my ear, I spoke, "Hey, Damien. It's Sam. Allison had to go to the bathroom?"

Way to sound like I'm covering something up.

"Sam, is she okay? What's wrong?" His concern came through the phone as he rapidly fired questions at me.

I was at a loss for what to say. As I looked at the bathroom door, I responded to his questions, "I think so? Um…doesn't feel well?"

Why am I talking in questions? In my stupidity, I threw my palm to my face. *Allison is going to kill me for not being my usual suave self.*

From the bathroom, I heard retching. I needed to get in there to help my friend.

Damien continued, "Sam, I don't know what's going on, but I'm on my way."

"Okay. She's okay, Damien. I've got—"

The phone disconnected before I even finished. I rolled my eyes, thinking about what my ever-concerned brother-in-law was doing to everyone to get here immediately. Well, Allison was about to have to let the proverbial cat out of the bag. She was going to be irritated beyond belief at my less-than-suave manner.

I walked through the bathroom door as my poor friend dry-heaved into the toilet. After grabbing a washcloth, I wet it and squeezed out the excess water. This was what my mama had always done when I was sick, and it had seemed to help.

Removing Allison's hair from the side of her face, I handed her the damp cloth. "Do you need anything else, sweetie?"

She shook her head as another round of dry heaves racked her body. I hoped she wouldn't have this for too long. It looked awful.

Finally, after what seemed like forever, she collapsed on the floor and wiped her face. "Ugh, not fun. I need to brush my teeth."

I helped her as she wobbled up onto her feet.

She pulled out a new toothbrush from the bathroom drawer. "I'm too lazy to go to my bedroom right now." She leaned on the counter, obviously exhausted from what baby Wales had put her through.

I got a new washcloth and went to the other sink to wet it. Folding it on the counter, I told her in my no-nonsense tone, "Once you're done, let's go lie down for a few minutes. You're looking a little ashen."

She nodded as she made her way to my bed and lay down. I needed to keep her distracted from remembering that Damien had been on the phone with her before the marathon puking began. Making that task easier for me, Allison closed her eyes, clearly exhausted.

"Thanks for helping me, Sam. You're the best."

"Oh, I can remember a few times in the beginning of college when you held my hair away from the porcelain throne. It's what best friends do."

Allison gave a weak laugh, and her eyes fluttered shut.

All too soon, I heard commotion, and Damien's voice was calling for her. My head snapped over to the door as Allison bolted upright in bed, trying to fix herself. We looked like we had as kids when we had gotten caught doing something wrong. Our eyes were as big as saucers, and our bodies were as stiff as boards. We had definitely lost our touch today.

Right on cue, Damien marched through the door, looking at both of us. He took in the still sick-looking Allison, and he was by her side in a minute. Totally consumed by her, he brushed the side of her face, and my chest tightened infinitesimally as he looked at her.

Ah hell, I need to get out of here, stat. I got up from the bed and walked to the far side of the room.

Worried, Damien said, "Baby, what's wrong? You look like you've been sick. I'll have the doctor come."

"I'm fine, Damien. Just had...I mean, I'm...oh geez, this is not going how I planned it in my head." Allison looked down at her knotted fingers.

Reading my best friend was easy. I imagined Allison was internally battling with herself on whether to tell a little white lie or blurt out the truth. I wanted to belt it out and save her the hassle of digging herself out of this one, but I remained silent while observing it all.

"Alli..." His voice became commanding.

Allison looked into his eyes before he continued.

Control—he had it with Allison, and she gave it to him freely.

"What is going on? You're scaring the hell out of me with how sick you look. Tell me what's going on, baby."

Automatically, she started rambling, "I was going to tell you yesterday, but then Katie caused that ruckus. I wanted it to be perfect because everything you do for me is perfect." She took a deep breath and raised her hand to stop Damien from speaking. "Just know that I'm ecstatic, and the only reason I haven't said anything is because I wanted it to be magical when I told you. When I went to the doctor yesterday, I told her I wasn't feeling well, and she did a test."

Allison stopped breathing as Damien's eyes lit up. There appeared to be hope in his features, but Damien didn't say a word as he waited for her to continue. My legs were frozen as I took in the scene. I could feel the same emotions that had led me to the club yesterday starting to surface.

A smile spread across Allison's face. "I'm pregnant, Damien. I'm about five weeks along."

His lips descended on Allison's in adoration, and a pressure in my chest increased to where I felt like I was suffocating.

Damien pulled away and put his hands on her stomach. "We're having a baby. Alli, you have made me the happiest man on earth. I'm going to be a dad!"

Triumph and joy radiated from them both. As I took in this scene, my world started to unravel. I slowly moved to the door. They were talking to the baby when I slipped out of the room, undetected.

This was their moment. Images of the dreams from my past started flooding my head, and I drew an iron curtain to stop my mind. When I thought I was out of earshot from Allison and Damien, I took off like a bat out of hell, needing to regain control of this emotion that kept popping up.

CHAPTER
2

I hopped in my car and started to drive. I had gone without using sex as a coping mechanism for six months.

Six months!

And I had needed it for the last two damn days. *Why am I losing so much control all of a sudden?* It was unacceptable. All my well-constructed walls were starting to shift and become weak.

I looked at my phone, and a thought started to form. I picked it up and dialed the number. I needed something to take the edge off. People had casual sex all the time. Maybe that was my balance instead of going to Club Envy. I had already had sex with Mark a couple of times, so it wouldn't be adding another notch to the belt.

The phone rang a few times while I nervously tapped my fingers against the leather steering wheel.

"This is Robertson."

He didn't recognize my company number. He had tried to contact me on my personal line on several occasions, making it clear he'd wanted more. The couple of times I'd hooked up with him were phenomenal. He was one of the few who I had gone back to for seconds—and now, apparently, thirds. However, when he had mentioned the word *date*, I had gone running in the opposite direction. I didn't date, but right now, desperation was running through my blood. I would be up-front and make it clear that I just wanted sex.

Only sex. Nothing more.

"Hey, Mark. It's Sam. Where are you?"

He was momentarily stunned as silence filled the line. "I'm finishing up my workout at the stadium. Then, I need to hit the showers and grab a bite to eat."

"Great. I'll be there in a minute."

I hung up before he had the chance to respond. I knew he didn't have a girlfriend. I had to follow information like that on all the teammates in case it could hurt the team.

I drove like hellhounds were chasing me. After screeching into the back entrance, I threw my car into park and looked down at my appearance. I was in jeans, wedge sandals, and a fuchsia silk tank top. It wasn't my finest ensemble, but it would have to do. I opened my purse and put a condom in my pocket.

Quickly, I jogged inside and headed down to the locker room. In the past few months, Mark and I had seen each other in team settings, but I would disappear right after, not wanting that awkward tension between us because of how I had left things.

Mark was the only guy from the team who I had slept with. Our first time had been in Vegas after the gala. The second time had been when I'd re-signed the kicker for Wales' team. After the kicker had left, Mark and I happened to be at the same bar. After I'd snuck out of the room, leaving Mark behind for a second time, I'd made a vow to keep my sexual encounters away from any personnel on Wales's payroll. I didn't want to be the team whore. Since I had already hooked up with Mark prior to that self-imposed rule, I figured I could still sleep with him for my needed release.

I came into the locker room, and I was thankful to find it abandoned. No one was in the showers or the locker area, not even Mark.

Damn it, I told him to wait.

Just as I was about to call him, I heard cabinets opening in the physical therapy room. Through the small window, I saw Mark looking through the cabinets, and he pulled out a tube of cream. I assumed it was probably for his sore muscles. I slipped in the room and quietly closed the door. When the lock snapped, Mark's head looked my way.

"Sam, what are you doing here? I was surprised to hear from you. It's been a few months."

He was the perfect specimen of a man. His muscles were flawlessly sculpted, and his short blond hair was a sweaty mess. My sex started to throb in anticipation, wanting a release. I couldn't wait to be on top of him again.

He set the tube of cream down and leaned against the counter. Folding his muscular arms across his chest, he waited for me to speak first. I started to walk his way with enough sway to be on the seductive side.

"I haven't seen you in a while, and I thought I should say hello since I'm about to officially be a North Carolina resident." I stopped right in front of him as I licked my bottom lip. "I thought you'd want to personally welcome me to the city."

My blood roared as my hormones took over. His athletic shorts were hanging low on his waist, showing that muscled V that I loved on a man. I knew it was dangerous, coming back to him when he affected me on such a primal level, but I would control it.

His skin glistened with sweat from what had to have been an intense workout. "Well, welcome, Miss Matthews. Now, if you'll excuse me, I need to go shower."

I leaned against the counter, blocking his path. "That's not a very neighborly welcome." I batted my eyelashes up at him.

The moment his eyes dipped to my breasts, I knew if I played my cards right, I would be in the homestretch.

He cleared his throat. "How about a cup of coffee?" His voice was smooth.

I shook my head as I inched a little closer, and our eyes locked in a lust-filled trance. Hopefully, he wanted me as much as I wanted him in this moment.

We had been hot as sin in the bedroom together.

I bit my bottom lip as my hand reached out and traced the top of his shorts. His muscles quivered under my touch as we continued to look at each other.

Mark pressed on and asked, "What about dinner then?"

"Oh, Mark, I was thinking more of a joyride."

I dipped my hand underneath his waistband and brushed the tip of his erection. *Mark Junior is ready to come out and play.*

A light hiss escaped between his teeth. "Sam…"

I put my index finger to his mouth and then stepped back. His gaze followed me. I pulled my silk tank top over the top of my head and then shimmied out of my jeans. Mark's knuckles turned white as he gripped the counter.

Using my authoritative voice, I said, "Take off your shorts if you want me to ride you on the chair over there."

Mark actually looked torn about what to do.

What the hell?

The asshole countered, "Let's go get dinner, and then we can go for a joyride."

What is he trying to pull?

"No deal. I'm sure I can find someone else to welcome me properly if you're not up for the task."

I hoped he couldn't tell that I was bluffing. My pulse hammered with uncertainty. I needed this now to right my control for a bit. To further sell my charade, I bent over to give the impression that I was about to get dressed. Instead, I was actually grabbing the condom from my pants, and I also wanted to showcase my sheer red thong. His intake of breath gave me the hope I needed.

Bingo.

"Damn it, Sam."

I felt a hard body come up behind me as hands grabbed my hips, pulling me against his erection. I grabbed the condom out from my pants.

He whispered in my ear, "You're not going somewhere else, but we are having dinner together."

No way in hell is he going to take control over this situation.

"Mark, you either want this, or you don't. I don't do strings and attachments. You should know that by now. This is purely sex, and from what I remember, it'll be great sex."

I stood up slowly, grinding into him, and then I opened my bra from the front hook. I moved my hands down to his, and I slowly guided them up to my breasts that were heavy with need. He grabbed them and stood there.

Holding the condom up, I asked, "Are you gonna pass or play, Sport?"

One hand took the condom, and the other instinctively started kneading my breast. Small erotic pulses started jumping to my groin. I loved this part of the game—the buildup to get to the finale. The telltale sign of ripping foil caused my core to clench. I tilted my head to the side, and he accepted my invitation as he began nibbling up to my ear.

"Hell, woman, you drive me crazy. I'll play."

I smiled at the victory. I turned around and pulled his shorts down, and then Mark kicked them to the side. Pointing across the room, I said, "On the chair, Sport. I want my joyride."

Before conceding, he took my mouth with his, wrenching my body close. Slowly backing us toward the chair, he kissed me, and I met his tongue stroke for stroke. My skin inflamed, and my desire skyrocketed to a whole new level. As his body lowered to the chair, he brought one finger down the middle of my chest to my navel, slowly making his way to my underwear.

I continued to take control as I said, "Rip them off."

Without hesitation, he tore my panties from my body. He took in my Brazilian-waxed sex, and his groan of approval was all I needed to move closer. I straddled him, barely hovering above his throbbing erection. Our eyes locked as want emanated from both of us. In one fluid motion, I slammed home and moaned at the sensation, loving the stretched-out feeling that was on the verge of pain because I hadn't primed myself.

"Fuck, Sam. You didn't give me a chance to work you up. Are you okay?" Mark asked, concerned, as he grabbed my hips to stop my movement.

He was trying to dislodge me while I reveled in pleasure.

I hushed him. "Shh…"

I started to ride him, and he snapped back into the moment, letting my body go, as he moved faster and faster. He was one of the few who could stroke that spot deep inside me.

"Bite my breasts, Mark. Bite them hard."

His hand went to my breast and started to squeeze my nipple hard while his other one went back to my hip. Mark's mouth found the other nipple and sucked it into his mouth. I was building so fast, and he wasn't listening.

I screamed, "Bite me, Mark! Now!"

He listened and bit down, and I moaned in delight.

"Harder."

He complied, and it caused me to fall off the edge. Mark climaxed in return.

That was incredible and just what I needed. Ah…

The relief coursing through my veins was a drug, and for the time being, the aftereffects of the orgasm sedated those unwanted thoughts from before.

I started to dismount when Mark grabbed my hips.

"That was unbelievable, Sam. Have dinner with me?"

"I can't. You know that. Let me up."

He immediately released me. As I started to get up, his gaze dropped to my hip. "Did I do that to you? Shit, Sam. I didn't mean to grab you so hard."

I looked down at the bruises on my hip from last night. When Adam had taken me hard from behind, his grip had been intense.

"No, it's fine."

Something dark passed over Mark's expression as he took my face in.

"Who did that to you then?"

I didn't like where this conversation was going, and I began getting dressed. He had no need to know. It wasn't his business. Mark donned his athletic shorts, and then he was right behind me, hovering in my space, as I slipped on my shirt.

He whispered in my ear, "Sam, you're crazy if you think I'm going to let you disappear on me again."

I refused to pay attention to his serious tone. My body was trying to respond, but I reined it in. Casually, I replied, "I'll be around. I live here now, remember?"

Grabbing my ripped underwear from the floor, I turned and tossed them to him. "Thanks for the welcome, Sport. You were quite the joyride."

As I began to walk out of there, feeling a hundred times better, he yelled after me, "Sam, you've met your match this time. Be prepared."

A shiver ran down my spine. I ignored it as I left without a word. He had no idea how strong my walls were. Commitment and I did not go together.

CHAPTER
3

A few days had passed, and I had finally found myself a condo. Waking up in my own place was nice. It had cost a little extra, but I'd had the essentials—such as a couch, bed, and table—delivered immediately. I had decided to go with the contemporary decor for this place, too.

My emotions had seemed to balance out, and the need for a release seemed to quiet down—until last night. Dinner with Damien and Allison had brought all those feelings I'd been experiencing right back to the surface.

At Damien and Allison's home, we were having a celebratory dinner for my move and the baby. Damien and Allison were both beautifully glowing at the impending arrival of baby Wales. It hurt like hell, knowing I would never have this. The buried memories began to arise all over again. The way Allison kept looking at me told me she knew something was eating at me, but she never pushed.

I took a large swig of wine before I asked, "So, when are you making the public announcement?"

The last thing I wanted to talk about was the pregnancy, which made me feel like such a bitch. I swallowed my feelings and prayed I could make it through the meal like a normal person. I was happy for my best friend, but being around them right now made me feel restless.

She sighed. "We're still talking about it. I'm thinking around twelve weeks."

Knowing that sweet, crazy-ass husband of hers, he'd want everyone to know immediately so that the public would further know Allison was his.

Allison bit her lip. "If we delay it, I'm hoping that security won't have to go up until people know."

Taking her hand and looking at her with more love than I had ever seen, Damien responded, "That is nonnegotiable, baby. I need to know you and the baby are safe all the time."

The word safe always did it. It was Allison's kryptonite. Damien never relented on her safety.

They were locked in a trance, and I was beginning to feel more and more uncomfortable.

Clearing my throat, I asked, "So, when are you guys heading back to Atlanta? You know Mama and Dad are going to want to see you guys as soon as you tell them."

Damien's hand glided to Allison's stomach as he looked at me. "Tomorrow morning. I want to get her to the doctor to check everything out. Then, she wants to go see your parents this weekend and tell them."

She calmly responded, "Oh, Damien, I'm fine. I just went."

He gave her a look, and she laughed. My stomach knotted at the love unfolding in this scene.

Images from that night in high school tried to seep in. I needed to get away. Hopefully, sleep would ease these emotions. After Mark's parting sentence, I didn't want to go back to him if I could help it, but at this point, he was better than finding another club.

As soon as it was possible, I left and drove as fast as I could to my condo.

I felt guilty for feeling relieved because Damien and Allison were headed back to Atlanta today, but I needed to regroup and get control over all these emotions. My skin hummed, and my mind kept going back to Mark. He had been the perfect release the other day.

I needed something to take the edge off prior to going to the team dinner this evening. I refused to break my rule regarding sleeping with anyone else from the team. However, with how keyed-up I was, I needed to take precautions. That much male testosterone could test the virginity of a nun, let alone someone who loved sex—no, someone who thrived on sex.

I picked up my phone and sent Mark a text. He hadn't called or contacted me since our locker-room hookup. I had taken that as a good sign that maybe he would be a good booty-call guy after all. My thoughts kept jumping from one extreme to another when it came to him.

Me: Where are you?

Mark: Just finished my morning run.

That wasn't a response, and he knew it. He was so frustrating.

Me: Yum. Hot and sweaty—my favorite combination.

Mark: Well then, I'd be your favorite treat right now.

Me: And where would I get my favorite treat?

Mark: At a coffee shop.

I groaned out loud. He was trying to play me.
What is wrong with him? Most guys loved wham-bam-thank-you-ma'ams.

Me: Enjoy your coffee. I'm off to get me a snack of my own. See ya.

Eventually, he was going to call my bluff. Yes, I'd had my fair share of sexual conquests, but I'd also kept them in check. I wouldn't get sucked in to coffee or dinner.

My phone rang with Mark's number flashing across the screen. I smiled, smelling victory in the air.

"Hello?"

"Damn it, Sam. Where are you?"

He was all kinds of agitated with his roughened voice, and my desire surged.

"My new place. About to get ready." It wasn't a total lie. I had plans to get ready at some point today, but currently, my hair was up, and I was in my black silk nightie that was slightly sheer at the top.

"Where's your new place, Sam?"

The sensual tone in his voice had my libido jumping into overdrive. I needed a release, and he was the perfect choice to give me what I wanted.

"Same condo complex as you—unit number nine nineteen."

"I'll be there in five. Don't go anywhere."

"You'd better hurry then, Sport." I hung up, smiling.

For about thirty seconds, I debated whether or not I should change. If he was working up any kind of resistance, like he had in the locker room, I needed whatever assets I could flaunt on my side.

Sheer-top black nightie is staying on.

Exactly five minutes later, I heard a knock on my door. I walked over there slowly and sexily said, "Who is it?"

"Sam…"

I chuckled at his scolding tone. Normally, that was a turnoff for me, but with him, it worked. I opened the door, and his eyes raked over my body.

"Shit, someone might see you."

He pushed me farther inside, trying to cover me in case someone happened to walk by, and then he closed the door behind him.

Mark pulled back, clearly concerned. "You'd better not be opening the door like that for anyone else." He stared at me, trying to freeze me in my place. His blond hair was sweaty from his run, and his arms still had a slight glisten on them.

Giving a noncommittal shrug, I moved farther into the dining room that adjoined the kitchen. Of course I didn't usually answer the door that way, but I wanted to keep him on edge and me in control. Turning around, I was momentarily stunned. He was delicious-looking in his soaked-through tank top and running shorts. With the way I responded to him, I definitely needed to keep him off-balance and not give him any sense of power over our sexual relationship.

"If you hadn't come, someone else would have."

A growl emitted from his throat, but he stayed put.

"Are you going to the dinner tonight with the team?" he asked.

"Yes, of course. Why?"

"Go with me." He was absolutely serious.

"No." I didn't like where this conversation was going.

It was frustrating how he kept pushing an outing together.

He stepped toward me, wrenching his shirt off the top of his body. "Explain why not."

I licked my lips as I started to step back while he continued to prowl after me.

"I don't do strings, Mark. We've been through this. If this is not your thing, we can stop."

"But you'll go elsewhere?"

I stopped retreating, remembering myself, and I stood my ground. "Yes, I will."

He needed to know the score and where I stood on things. He continued to walk right up to me, looking straight into my eyes. He had the most gorgeous eyes. They were green like mine but speckled with brown.

He studied me for a minute, thinking something through. "So, you want me to fuck your brains out and then leave?"

I swallowed. Hearing that hard, raw sensuality had me climbing before we even started.

"Yes. I like it hard and rough and simple."

His eyes dipped to my hips, and I remembered him inquiring about my bruises the other day. I had no idea what Mark was thinking, but he was probably wondering who had put those bruises on me. I felt dirty from having those marks from Adam.

That thought caused me to blurt out, "I'm clean. I'm tested often, and I always use protection."

Something battled over his features as he stepped into my space. Instinctively, I started to lean into him before I caught myself and stopped. He saw my slipup and smiled at me.

Bastard.

"Sam, I'll give you what you want today, but if you want this again, know that I'll have requirements of my own."

I stepped back, but he caught my hips and pulled me to him.

I pushed on his chest, giving me a little space. "I don't do commitments, dating, or the girlfriend thing. I want you to understand that."

Bringing his lips only millimeters from mine, he said, "I'm not asking for that. It's not worth discussing unless we get together again."

With that, his lips crashed down onto mine. The explosion of scents, his sweat and pheromones, invaded my nose, and I moaned at the savage way he was kissing me.

Pulling back, he sexually whispered against my lips, "I'm about to fuck you hard and fast. Is there anything else you want?"

"No."

He palmed my ass and picked me up. He walked us over to the kitchen island, and then he grabbed a condom from his shorts. Barely dropping them low enough to free himself, he sheathed his dick in latex. Wham-bam-thank-you-ma'am was about to happen, and I loved it.

"Spread your legs, Sam. If I'm too rough, I want you to tell me."

"You won't be." I locked my eyes with his as I complied. "I promise."

He looked torn as he grabbed my legs and pulled me to the edge of the granite countertop. He poised himself at my entrance, and in one swift movement, he slammed home. I arched off the cool surface. He was one of the largest men I had ever been with. He pounded into me over and over again. I felt myself approaching my orgasm faster than normal. He turned his hips, and as one finger found my clit, he sent me flying. He pumped into me a few more times, massaging out his own orgasm. Then, he swiftly withdrew, and I lay on the counter, boneless. The condom was discarded, and his shirt was on in less than a minute. I rose up on my elbows, and he gave me a good-bye kiss on my forehead.

"I'll see you this evening, Sam."

Next, he walked out the door without a second look back. *Perfect.*

I'd been out of sorts all afternoon since Mark left after our quick fuck. Right now, I was resorting to pacing my condo to and fro, back and forth. He had given me exactly what I had asked for in spades, but I still felt off.

What is wrong with me?

I wanted sex with Mark again—but without strings. I needed that freedom of not feeling trapped.

Hopefully, my outfit tonight would lure little Marky out to play. I was wearing a fitted black cocktail dress that dipped down into a low V on both the front and back. Tall bright-red heels and jewelry took the attire from boring to attention-grabbing. In the end, I left my hair down in bouncy large curls because I'd had no patience to put it in an updo.

I needed to calm myself down and reel in my nerves. There was no way I could contact Mark this soon. Minimally, I had to wait at least three days before I called him again, so he wouldn't think he had any hold over me. I could always find someone else, but I knew I wouldn't be satisfied until Mark was out of my system.

I drove to the team event being held at a local upscale steak house. Normally, I liked to arrive late, but I needed a damn drink.

Damien and Allison were supposed to attend, but he had been anxious to get her back home to have her normal doctor check her and the baby. Damien needed triple verification that morning sickness was completely normal. I wished she were here to keep my mind off of what I really wanted—sex with Mark.

Shutting off my car, I mentally slapped myself to pull it together. I was going to make Mark come crawling back to me, not the other way around. He pulled in moments later in his pickup truck, and our eyes locked as we both sat in our vehicles. Images and memories from our encounters flashed across my mind, and my body temperature rose higher and higher. Shaking my head to break the connection, I jumped out of my car.

As I approached his vehicle, I gave a sexy little grin. I walked past his truck door and toward the entrance. Behind me, the vehicle door opened, and I increased the sway of my hips. I was pulling out every trick I knew to get him to come to me first. Seconds later, I heard footsteps following me.

Right as I hit the sidewalk, Mark came up and said, "You look beautiful tonight."

He was closer than I had thought he was.

"Thank you." I continued walking without missing a step or looking back even though I wanted nothing more than for him to take me here and now.

As we approached the doors, Mark grabbed my waist and moved us past the building and brought my back against the wall.

"Sport, what the hell are you doing?"

"Just saying hello to the new neighbor."

His lips pressed against mine, and I yielded to let him in. He had pursued me, so there was no reason not to play just a little. One hand slinked up my inner thigh under my dress and grazed my clit through my barely there sheer thong. It was enough to have my want ratcheting to all new levels. Instinctively, I moved my hips, trying to deepen the touch, but he pulled away.

His voice was low as he said, "Let me know when you're ready to hear my requirements, and I'll give you what you need anytime you need it." With that, he turned and left.

Bastard. I threw my head back against the wall and heaved out a breath as I closed my eyes. *This is getting way off track fast.*

Slowing down my breathing, I mentally pulled myself together and walked inside the building with my head held high. He was not going to get the impression that he had gotten the best of me. He would have to crawl back to me for that incident. Immediately, I spotted Mark talking to some of the football players and one of the cheerleaders, Missy. It was obvious she wanted him badly. She appeared almost desperate with how she was trying to get his attention.

Shit, who wouldn't with the way that Mark's green dress shirt and black dress pants were hanging on him perfectly?

To make matters worse, I knew what was underneath his clothes. *Nothing but bliss.*

Mark's eyes briefly met mine as I headed to the bar. I broke eye contact first as the bartender started speaking to me. I plastered on one of my sexiest smiles.

"What can I get you, gorgeous?"

"Gin and tonic with extra lime, please."

The clean-cut bartender gave me an appraising smile as he fixed my drink. He wasn't bad-looking, but I felt no pull to him. My mind went back to Mark.

Double shit! Stop thinking about him. I needed something to take the edge off, and alcohol was going to have to do for now until I figured out what his game was. *What kind of requirements would he have for me to get laid by him on a regular basis?*

My thoughts were interrupted as the bartender slid over my drink and a cocktail napkin—with a phone number on it. As I went to get some cash from my purse, I glanced at his name tag, reading the name Jack.

Jack touched my arm. "It's on the house, gorgeous. I hope I get that call later."

I gave a small smile to Mark and threw back half my drink. The burn of the gin helped take the edge off.

I turned around and was about to walk off when Jack added, "Hey, don't forget this."

As I looked back, he was waving the napkin with his number on it.

Maybe he and Missy should hook up.

He had given me a free drink, so indulgently, I grabbed it, not wanting to insult the poor guy.

I'm not a total heartless bitch.

When I turned back around, my eyes locked with the muscled blond jock who had my wits a mess in the first place this evening.

Payback time.

I saucily smiled at him as I opened my clutch and ceremoniously put the napkin inside. His eyes widened, and his smile dimmed. Putting my finger to my chin, I tapped it, like I was contemplating whether or not I should call the bartender.

Finally, one point to me. It's about damn time I won a round.

My inner power started returning as I worked the room and talked with everyone. I loved events like this where I could flirt freely without it leading to sex. It was a sort of escape when I got to leave my head and be in the moment, feeling weightless. Before I knew it, I had been given three more numbers, and each and every time I'd added them to my stash, I'd known that Mark was watching. In fact, I'd made sure of it. His eyes had grown darker each time he saw me put one in my purse, which had caused me to smirk at him.

The room was buzzing with preseason excitement.

A man came to the door and announced, "Dinner is served."

The mumbles of approval filled the air as we started walking toward the double wood doors. Finally, we were going to eat. I was starving for some real food. The agenda for tonight was to go over management changes, expectations for the upcoming preseason, and general housekeeping announcements. From living with Damien and Allison at the beginning of the week, I knew what all was going to be said, but I wanted to show my support. I needed to start melding more with the team since I would be around a lot during the season.

I saw Monica, the head manager of the PR team. I knew her well, so I started heading toward where she was standing in the middle of the room at a center table.

A hand wrapped around my hip bone, and a mouth appeared at my ear. "You'd be much happier over in this other seat."

Oh, that teasing voice had the alcohol burning away and my sexual desire running to the forefront.

Mark was leading me to the back of the room.

"I'm not so sure about that, Sport. I won't be able to mingle back here."

He didn't respond but kept taking us to the farthest corner of the room.

I'm letting him do this. I am still in control.

Whatever cologne he had on was so manly that I wanted to bury my head in his chest to envelop myself in that scent. That alone had me interested to see where he was going with this, so I didn't press.

After taking my seat, Mark scooted my chair in, and at the last second, he angled it toward his chair before taking a seat himself. Moments later, Missy joined us. She took the seat right across from us. Her outfit was lower cut than mine, which added more of a slut feel to hers.

She licked her lips. "So, Mark, are you coming out with all of us afterward?"

Casually taking a sip of water, I watched the exchange between them. *Has he slept with her?* For some reason, I didn't think so. She was acting too desperate to get him with how she was bouncing her breasts and twirling her blonde hair.

He responded coolly, "Not tonight, Missy, but thanks for the invite."

She pouted her lips as people laughed and began ribbing Mark about going. Even back in the corner, the star quarterback received the most attention. Two other cheerleaders joined us, and I internally groaned. At this point, Monica was looking like a much better option to sit with. Shifting in my seat, I was about to make my move.

Right as dinner was being served, Mark leaned in and whispered, "Don't leave. Please. I'll make it worth your while."

Those words had me wanting to straddle him and ride him to oblivion. Giving him a sassy wink, I smiled and turned my attention to eating. This small exchange caused the three bimbos at the table to focus their attention on me. By the looks in their eyes, they apparently viewed me as competition. I wanted to gloat and say I'd already won, but I refrained and continued eating. They wanted answers and clarification though.

The cheerleader to the right, April, asked me, "So, how do you know Mark?"

Sweetly, I replied, "We met at a Vegas gala last year. Since I'm new in town, he took me for a ride yesterday. He's been very welcoming."

Mark almost choked on his water, but all three cheerleaders had relief in their eyes.

Idiots. I wasn't sure why I'd said what I had. It had honestly just slipped, but they had seriously started to irritate me, and I didn't understand why.

When I spared a glance at Mark, he gave me a panty-dropping wink. That alone might require me to go to the restroom and make myself come quickly before dessert.

The cheerleaders continued to flirt with Mark, giggling at his every word, but I worked on trying not to let it bother me.

By the time presentations were about to start, I was on my third glass of wine and feeling good. The lights dimmed, and the microphone was turned on, giving that initial squeak sound that had us all moving our heads back. Everyone at our table turned toward the podium, giving full attention to the managers.

Frank, one of the team managers, scratched his head and said, "Good evening. Glad you all could make it."

Cheers erupted, and after the right amount of pausing, he continued, "We hope you had a good dinner. We have a lot to get through tonight. Let's get started, shall we?"

Several agreements filled the room. I took another sip and focused on listening. As the wine glass left my lips, I felt a hand caressing my thigh, and I slightly jumped in surprise. My head snapped in Mark's direction. He was grinning a devilish smooth smile in almost a challenge. His thumb stroked my inner thigh, and I opened my legs in acceptance, giving him my answer. He had no idea how semi-exhibitionism turned me on.

His hand moved slowly up my leg, and I opened as wide as my skirt would allow. When he reached my soaked thong, he sucked in a quiet, harsh breath, and his eyes met mine. It was my turn to smile back when he realized how turned-on I was.

Mark mouthed, *I like you wet.*

In return, I mouthed, *I like to be wet.*

He groaned in approval as his fingers dipped beneath my barely there thong and started stroking my cleft. I wanted to lean back and moan, but I kept my eyes trained on the speaker, hearing nothing of what he had to say. First one and then two fingers penetrated my core. Mark's thumb began stroking me, building me. It was a slow build, and I knew this climax was going to rock my world with how sexually tense I was.

He wouldn't send me over the edge, and I was right there—so close yet so far away.

How long has this been going on? It was the longest build I had ever had, which meant it was going to be a strong orgasm. Just when I thought he was going to finish the deed, he withdrew his hand, and the lights flicked on. Being pissed was the biggest understatement of the year. The night had concluded, and Mark had played me.

Bastard.

Guys never played me.

The group at the table was talking about going to a bar, but I wasn't able to focus exactly on what they were saying because my insides were shaking so hard. I was reeling from what had just happened.

How did he get the upper hand in this situation?

I had let my guard down, and he had taken control.

Arrogant asshole.

Someone spoke from across the table.

"Sam, are you coming out with us?"

Anger boiled and simmered my blood. Paybacks were a bitch, and I was about to exact my revenge.

"I wish, but I have a date tonight." I gave a wink and shook my clutch, hoping Mark got my drift. I wanted him to think I was going to call one of the numbers I had collected tonight. "You guys have a wonderful night. I'm really excited to be a part of the team."

With that, I left the table to head straight home to relieve myself, but I reveled in the fact that I'd left Mark wondering who would be in my bed tonight. The phone numbers had proven useful after all. I hadn't waited to hear about Mark's plans or to see his facial expression.

The main doors were jammed with the entire team trying to leave. Not caring and needing to get out of here pronto, I headed out another exit door leading to a red-carpeted hallway with mahogany walls. Getting outside was my goal, and one of these doorways had to lead the way. My pace was clipped, and I was getting close to an exit sign when familiar arms came around my waist. Faster than I thought possible, I was pulled into some kind of supply closet.

Mark started the exchange while his arms were still wrapped around me from my backside. "Where are you going?"

"To get satisfaction," I spit back. I was pissed.

"Sam, I'm sorry. I should have gotten you off. I need to get some things straight between us first, but I can't keep my hands off of you when I'm around you."

"Let me go."

I tried to get out of his hold, but his hands held me in place.

"Wait, hear me out."

For whatever reason, this heated exchange was causing me to get hot and bothered all over again. It should have had the opposite effect and dissipated any growing desire, but I was worked up. I maintained my stance though, not giving any indication that I was sexually aroused by him.

"What could you possibly want from me?" I asked.

"We both know we burn for each other, Sam. It's evident. All I want is exclusivity with you, Sam."

"We're not dating, Mark. I'm not the girlfriend type."

My eyes were beginning to adjust to the dark, and I made out some shelving along the wall.

"I'm not asking you to be my damn girlfriend. I heard you the first fifty times when you said you didn't do that. Call it whatever you want, but we will be exclusive. When one of us ends it, it's over. I'm not a booty call for when you're in between men, Sam. I'll keep you satisfied, but you'll exclusively be mine to satisfy anytime."

My core melted into lava at the words *satisfy anytime.*

I needed to confirm what he'd said. "No strings, no expectations. Just great sex with only each other."

He grabbed my hips tighter. "Yes, but if we have an event, then we go with each other. I don't care what you tell people. We aren't going to do this bullshit of sleeping with each other but taking someone else out to the different obligations we have."

His breath was warm against my ear.

"But—"

He cut me off. "That's my offer. Take it or leave it. If you leave it, know that I'm closing the door on us."

His tone had such a finality to it that I knew he was serious. He was basically offering me exactly what I wanted, except for the escorting-each-other-to-events clause.

We'd more than likely both be going anyway, so what's the big deal?

This would at least keep me out of any local sex clubs, especially while I learned to work through these emotions that had been brought on by Allison's pregnancy, unearthing long-forgotten dreams.

Without another moment's hesitation, I responded in the dark, "Deal."

He spun me around and hiked up my dress in one movement. He unzipped his pants, freeing himself, and then he picked me up and put my back against the wall. "Good decision, Sam."

My legs wrapped around him, and he pushed deep inside me, causing a moan of contentment to escape me. His hardened length inside me felt warmer and more intense than normal. He had me so worked up.

A hand came down on my mouth as he softly said, "Shh…"

I didn't care as the sensations continued to rock through me. He pumped me harder. My muscles started to quiver. He moved his hand and covered my mouth with his lips as the orgasm went through my body. After all the sexual buildup, my mind was a complete fog. As the high still coursed through my body, giving me that release I craved, I heard Mark cursing lowly.

"Fuck, I can't believe I did that."

He was still hard inside me, and I was pinned against the wall of the janitorial closet.

"Sam, I swear…I've never…I'm clean, too. Damn it to hell."

He hadn't worn a condom.

Shit. My blood ran cold. It was no wonder why it had felt warmer and more intense.

"Please tell me you didn't forget, Sport."

"Sam…"

I knew he hadn't done it on purpose, but that was a hard, fast rule for me. I disengaged, and he immediately released me.

I was lost in thought as I said, "Shit, shit, shit."

I paced as I felt another crack forming in the wall of the fortress I had built around me. I'd liked having him raw inside me. I'd loved squeezing my inner walls around his dick as he'd gotten harder, but these rules had been made to keep me safe.

"Sam, this is—"

I interrupted him, not even wanting to know where he had been going with that sentence, "I'm on birth control."

There was an audible sigh of relief in the dark.

Does he think I'm stupid?

I stopped pacing when I felt something warm start to slowly trickle down my leg. "Where's the light?"

I heard him wrestle with his pockets, and then a light from his phone popped on. I searched and found a clean paper towel to wipe away the cum dripping down my leg.

"Well, there's no question about your virility, Sport."

He grabbed the towel from me and hastily wiped in between my legs before pulling my skirt down. "My place or yours? You pick."

"What?"

"Sam, I don't have condoms on me, and after seeing that, I want you now." His voice was gravelly.

Breathily, I responded, "Yours."

He grabbed my hand and yanked me from the closet. It made me smile that my body could drive him crazy.

This agreement is looking better by the moment.

We both lived in the same upscale, gated condo complex. Each unit had a garage, and the floor plan was as big as a medium-sized house but without all the upkeep. It worked well for me.

We pulled into our condo parking lot, parked our vehicles, and ran up the stairs to his condo door. The moment the door closed, clothes went flying as we devoured each other. Mark picked me up, and I wrapped my legs around him.

"Mark, fast and hard. Don't fuck around with making me orgasm this time."

He lifted me higher and sucked hard on my nipple. I loved the intense pressure. Mark didn't say a word as he continued walking, and then he tossed me onto the bed. He pulled a condom out of his drawer, put it on, and walked toward me. Next, he grabbed both my legs and brought me to the edge of the bed. Finally, he entered my body deep.

"Yes. Faster. Harder. Faster," I said.

He complied without a word as he nearly fucked me into oblivion. He was like a well-oiled machine. The stamina was incredible. The friction against my inner walls caused that delicious pre-orgasm feeling to build until I touched my clit, and then I went to the blissful place I loved.

I have definitely met my match in the sex department.

Mark collapsed and then rolled off of me. We were both panting hard.

"Shit, that was hot, Sam."

I was still out of breath. "You are quite the fuck buddy."

He stared at me for a second and then smiled. "I'm going to take a shower. Do you need anything?"

"No, I'm good."

I admired his fine ass as he walked to the shower. The moment the water started, I took it as my cue, and I left.

It was the wee hours of the morning, and I was excited for my head to hit the pillow. I walked through my door, locked it, and then started to strip as I headed to my bed. I noticed that he hadn't called or texted, which made me smile. Most guys would try to be all cavalier about me getting home safely. That spelled relationship, and I wanted no part of that.

My head hit the pillow, and I crashed, finally satiated.

It had been a couple of days since I had left Mark while he was showering. Neither one of us had called or contacted each other, which made me smile. Hopefully, Mark had gotten the point, and he was now only in it for a sexual partnership, like I'd wanted. All my mind could do was try to figure out when I should contact him again for a booty call.

Needing some fresh air, I headed to where I'd seen a deli a few blocks from the condo complex. Under a blue-and-white striped awning, the word *Edna's* was written in cursive on a big glass window. I walked through the door, and the inside was cute, warm, and inviting. The smell was heavenly. Round bistro tables with blue tablecloths were placed around the dining area. I took a seat, and a waitress approached to take my order. While I waited for my food, I stared out the window. My food arrived, and I was midbite through a turkey sandwich when the chair next to me moved.

"Hey, stranger. Is this seat taken?"

I looked up, and my mouth instantly watered at the sight of Mark. He was the epitome of a fine man. He had on dark jeans and a T-shirt that outlined his finely toned body when he moved. His blond hair was all messed-up from the wind.

I gave him a sexy smile as he looked at me.

"It is now."

I took another bite, forcing the conversation back in his court. He casually glanced around and then back at me. He wasn't staring at me with lust in his eyes. He was looking at me like I was a friend who he'd had a good time with. My heart plummeted a little bit because I wanted him to want me.

He nodded to someone at the counter as he said, "I come here a lot. Edna makes the best cookies in town."

As he was finishing his statement, a waitress came up with some sort of hot sandwich and fruit. "Hey, Mark. Here's your usual, sweetie. Let me know if need anything else."

I took a look at the older woman, who appeared to be the age of a grandmother. She was adorable with her gray hair in a bun and her frumpy midsection.

"Thanks, Edna," Mark said.

She stood there, looking from Mark to me and back to Mark again.

When it was evident what Edna wanted, Mark said, "This is a friend of mine, Sam. Sam, this is Edna, the best sandwich and cookie maker in town. She owns this fine establishment."

She looked at him adoringly and patted him on the head. I giggled.

She turned to me next, smiling a kind smile. "Aw, Mark, she's a beauty."

I smiled at her. She had one of those addictive auras that made people want to love her immediately.

Next, she addressed me. "Hey, Sam, nice to meet you. You've got yourself a nice man here."

I started choking.

Between coughs, I sputtered, "Oh, we're not dating. We're just friends." *Friends with benefits.*

Edna knowingly looked at me. "If you say so."

She then patted me on the top of my head and walked off. Mark was laughing at me now.

Bastard.

"Not funny, Mark."

"If you say so."

I laughed at his mock country tone. He started to lean in to give me a pat, but I swatted his hand away.

"I promise, Edna doesn't mean any harm. She loves to meddle. So, are you all settled in at your place?"

I was glad to move on from Edna's comments. As long as Mark and I knew where we stood, I would try not to let the musings of an elderly woman bother me.

After taking a small sip of water, I responded, "Just about. The rest of my furniture was delivered yesterday, and all I have left to get are some things for the guest bathroom and a few things for the kitchen. I don't officially start until the preseason, but I wanted to have time to get settled."

He finished chewing and gave me a friendly smile. "Well, it just so happens that I need a coffee pot myself. How about I show you around town? I wouldn't want to be accused of not being neighborly again."

His green eyes sparked as we stared at each other. Memories of what had happened in the locker room flashed through my mind. He continued eating his sandwich, and I swallowed hard, remembering his words.

Sam, you've met your match this time. Be prepared.

It seemed like he had been asking truly as a friend, but my guard was up, just in case.

He paused midbite, looking at me, confused. "If you can't, don't worry about it. I thought I'd offer since I was heading that way, too."

I finished the last of my sandwich and mulled it over. This seemed innocent enough as I watched him continuing to eat his sandwich. He appeared not to really care if I went with him or not.

"I think I will take you up on that, neighbor. It would be nice not to use that damn GPS for a change." I hated that thing. It constantly spouted off directions and then made that awful racket if one itty-bitty wrong turn was made. That voice was becoming my nemesis.

"Great. Is your car here?" He finished the last bite. He had nearly inhaled his sandwich.

I shook my head as I answered, "No, I walked here."

"We'll take my truck then." He pushed back from the table and rose. "Shall we?"

"We shall, but I'm warning you...I get veto power over the radio selection."

I pushed my chair in and happened to catch Edna watching our exchange. My heart started to sputter as she looked at us. *What is she thinking?*

"Hey, Sam, you ready?"

I turned and Mark was watching me impassively, but he seemed a little stiffer. His words were smooth, but his rigidity put me on edge again. I was starting to doubt my decision.

He continued as he looked at his watch, "Hey, we better get going. I have a team meeting this afternoon."

Oh, that's what's bothering him. He's afraid of being late.

Instantly, I relaxed. "Let's go, but I can take myself if it's a problem."

He instantly smiled. "No problem at all. Let's get going."

Swinging the door open, he motioned for me to go out first, and I complied. After we cleared the door, he put his hand on the small of my back. My body instantly warmed, and I wanted to lean into the touch, which led me to pull away. I looked over my shoulder, and his face was blank as he stared toward his truck.

It's a friendly gesture, that's all.

Stop overreacting, Sam. You're being neurotic!

I was starting to feel better and better about hanging out with Mark. Unless we were sleeping together, he'd really only shown a friend kind of interest in me. It was exactly what I'd thought I wanted, but I felt myself wanting to have other thoughts, and I immediately stopped them.

We made it to his white pickup truck. It was high off the ground, and it required me to use the side rails to jump in.

He got in on the driver's side and started the beast up. He put the truck into drive and began making the way to our destination. "What exactly do you need for your bathroom?"

"Towels. Nice, big fluffy towels."

He chuckled at my dreamy tone. "I think we can manage that. Some other time, I'll point out some good shops, restaurants, and hangouts for when you're out and about. Because of time, I'm going to take the quicker way today."

"Sounds good."

We were in the bath section of the store, and our cart was filled with a few kitchen gadgets for me and a coffee maker on steroids for Mark.

I was feeling the different towels when he came up behind me.

"What are you doing?"

"I'm feeling the springiness of the towels. I like my towels soft and fluffy."

His arm came around me, reaching out to touch a towel, and of course, his smell permeated all my senses. I wanted to have him right here on the bed displays.

"A towel is a towel. Why are women so picky?"

I closed my eyes, forcing myself to calm my sexual tension. When I regained my control, I opened my eyes again. "Well, a woman doesn't want to be sandpapered to death when she gets out of the shower."

"Good to know." His breath tickled my ear, and then he pulled away and started feeling some other towels. "Hey, these feel nice."

I walked over and felt the towel. It was nice.

He gave me a wink. "See? Aren't you glad you came with me? I found you the perfect towel, soft and springy."

He patted my head, and then he went to stand behind the cart again. Mark chuckled as I playfully scowled at him. I turned my attention back to the towels he'd picked out, forcing my thoughts away from what I really wanted—Mark.

Stop it, Sam.

I grabbed eight black towels and set them aside. These were going to be perfect in my lime green bathroom. I was in the midst of grabbing some washcloths when two giggling bimbos approached Mark. My bitch mode kicked in, and I had to beat it back with a stick. I didn't want those women talking to my fuck buddy with lust in their eyes. They had obviously unbuttoned their shirts two buttons too low, and they'd hiked up their skirts indecently high on their legs.

One of the blondes giggled and asked, "Hey, you're Mark Robertson, aren't you?"

Momentarily, his green eyes flashed to mine, but then they returned to the avid fans. "Yes. What can I do for you ladies?"

The other one giggled as she thrust a Sharpie and a piece of paper into his hand. "Your signature and your phone number would make my dreams come true."

I wanted to gag, but I busied myself by recounting the hand towels I had in my hands. My ears though were highly tuned into his response.

"Thanks, ladies, for your support. I'm not currently on the market with the season coming up, but I hope you can make it to some of the games."

My eyes connected with his, and we smirked at each other. Images of our times together flashed through my mind.

Sorry, ladies. His body is exclusively mine for now.

They followed his gaze to mine, and I could feel icy glares from the bimbo sports junkies.

Mark was about to say something when I addressed them, "Save your hate for someone else, ladies. We're just friends."

They relaxed and tried to continue the conversation. I dumped my gathered towels into the cart. Mark chuckled and smiled at me, and I gave him a sassy wink.

We started to walk off, and I heard one say, "Whoever gets his heart and sleeps in his bed at night is one lucky bitch."

Well, I don't have his heart, but I have him at my disposal. I chuckled to myself at the thought.

We checked out and began driving back to the condo complex. The radio was on low, and Mark seemed content to just drive.

As he made a left turn, I asked, "Do you go home to Colorado often?"

Where the players lived in the off-season was common knowledge among the team.

"As often as I can. My lake house is near my parents and sister. It's peaceful and quiet."

Sitting there, I tried to picture his home. The picture in my head was remarkable. Part of me wanted to go see this place, but I pushed that from my mind. "It sounds lovely. I've never been to Colorado before. I grew up in Homerville. My mom and dad are retired and old-fashioned. We have a small house on a few acres."

He laughed. "Well, my family is not what you call traditional. They're loud and in everyone's business, but they're family, and I love them."

The look he had on his face told me he was reliving memories with them. His family seemed wonderful.

We arrived back at my place in what seemed like seconds. He helped me carry my purchases to my door.

We were depositing the last of the bags on the counter when Mark said, "Thanks for letting me show you around town. I'll see you soon. Holler if you need anything. I've got to head over to the team meeting."

"Will do."

After that, he left.

What the hell have I gotten myself into?

He'd only touched me in a friendly manner a few times at the store, and I wanted him again. After being in his presence all day, I needed a release and pronto. I sat down and huffed. Normally, I wasn't this affected by guys. In fact, I had never been affected to the extent that I would go out of my way to try to get one. Well, it had seemed he understood the boundaries. This was a consensual sexual exchange. We were adults.

I dug out my phone to text Allison as a plan started to form in my head.

Me: Is Damien conferenced in for the team meeting?

Allison: Yes. What are you up to?

Me: Oh, you know me. Where's he at in the meeting?

Allison: Let me check. Hold on.

I waited a few minutes as my knee bounced.

> *Allison: Sorry. Had to walk out to the stable office. They're halfway through, so there's less than thirty minutes left from what I can tell. By the way, we'll be up this weekend. Damien wants to take everyone out since he missed the last meeting. You'll be getting the announcement shortly.*

> *Me: Thanks. You're the best.*

> *Allison: No, you are.*

> *Me: Xoxo*

> *Allison: Xoxo*

Well, I had completed step one of the plan. Now, I had to implement step two. I giggled to myself and pulled up Mark's number.

> *Me: Has the team meeting started yet?*

> *Mark: Yep.*

Ugh, the one-worded answers drive me crazy.

> *Me: When is it going to be over?*

> *Mark: Not sure.*

> *Me: Sigh…too bad…*

> *Mark: Why? What's up?*

> *Me: Well, I was thinking you'd be the perfect guy for the job, but I guess I'm going to have to rely on my BFFF.*

> *Mark: BFFF?*

Me: You know, my Best Friend For Fucking—aka my vibrator. Maybe next time. Toodles.

Mark: Wait for me. I'll be at your place in half an hour, regardless if this fucking meeting has ended or not.

Me: Better hurry. My BFFF can be very impatient when he's been taken out of the box.

Mark: Damn it, Sam. Wait. It'll be worth it—for you and your BFFF.

Me: Oh, it's starting to purr for me. You've got thirty minutes, Sport. Timer started. Door unlocked. Turning off my phone now.

I threw my head back and laughed. I loved foreplay with Mark over text messages. It was exhilarating for some reason. I sprang into action, going back to my room to change. I found the perfect thing to wear—open-crotch red lace boy shorts. A top wasn't needed tonight. I let my hair down to trail over my breasts, and then I added some sparkly sheer red lip gloss. After grabbing my BFFF, I positioned myself on my purple satin sheets.

It didn't take long before I heard the door opening and the lock clicking behind it. Those sounds alone had my heart racing faster. I turned on my little friend and started rubbing it against my cleft.

Ah...

The vibration felt good. I gave a little moan as he walked through the door, and then my eyes locked with his.

"Fucking hell, you're gorgeous," he said.

I stroked the vibrator along my clit, causing my body to bow a little off the bed, while I closed my eyes. I heard the rustle of clothing as I rubbed it a little farther in, reaching the entrance to my core. I was about to push it inside when a hand stopped my progress.

"Let me."

Mark's hand wrapped around my BFFF, and I let go. He dragged it slowly up my cleft. When he hit my clit, pleasure shot through my body. My eyes opened, and my breath hitched. Mark was poised above me. His erection was already sheathed in a condom, and it was stiff between his legs as he took me in.

"Can we play with the BFFF later? I want inside you."

His words caused goose bumps to appear on my skin as I stretched my hands above my head, arching my back. His gaze drifted.

"My mechanical best friend understands. However, he'll want attention later."

He tossed my BFFF to the side, leaned down, and sucked on my neck. He moved his lips up to my earlobe, nibbling. "Good."

At that, he pushed into me all the way. He took my mouth. We were both desperate as we moved like animals. I met him thrust for thrust, feeding the fire, as I absorbed the feeling of the friction provided by the enlarged head of his length.

He moved his hips slightly, and I screamed, "Mark!" as my body soared sky high.

He pumped into me three more times, massaging out my orgasm, and then he found his release before collapsing on me. My body absorbed his weight, but he pulled out from me and rolled to the side. I moved with him until my head was lying on his arm.

"Fuck, Sam, that was fantastic."

I turned toward him, breathless, and waggled my eyebrows. "I'm glad I waited. That was much better than my BFFF."

He palmed my ass and brought me to him. "I like your vibrating friend."

I giggled as he pulled me closer.

"And I love these shorts."

"Mmm…me, too, especially now." I wiggled into him for added effect. "I'll have to get more surprises to debut for you."

He groaned. "You're going to be the death of me."

Then, he took my mouth with his and gave me a slow kiss. My mouth opened, and I kissed him back. The mint flavor of his mouth was addictive. His hand came up to my cheek, and his thumb began to stroke it. It was a loving gesture. When that thought registered, I froze.

We are fuck buddies, not a loving couple.

I disengaged and started to back off the bed, pretending I needed to turn off the vibrator. I knew the touch probably hadn't been meant as a loving gesture, but I'd felt my heart melt a little. I had no right to feel that way.

We are just friends with benefits. Anything else would be complicated.

"Sorry, Mark, but it's late. I should probably get to bed. Thank you."

What the hell? Did I just thank him for sex?

He looked at me, confused. Then, he quietly got up from the bed and started to grab his clothes. After dressing quickly, he came over and gave me a chaste kiss that had me wanting him again, but I refused to give in to the temptation as I fisted my hands at my side.

"Until next time, Sam. Lock the door after me."

I gave him a salute as he marched backward out the door, smirking at me. I knew I had read too much into him touching my cheek.

Damn it, I could have had multiple rounds if it wasn't for my idiotic brain malfunction.

Breathing a sigh of relief, I changed into my T-shirt and boxers and lay down on the bed. It seemed like Mark had truly accepted this for what it was—a fuck-buddy relationship.

Why does that not seem like enough all of a sudden?

A couple of days had passed, and Allison and Damien were coming in today. The team dinner was tomorrow. Originally, the plan had been for them to come in right before, but Damien was worried about exhausting Allison and the baby, and he wanted her to have a day to rest.

My phone rang. It was Allison.

"Hey, Allison. Did you guys land?"

"Yes. Oh geez, Damien is outside with Bane, talking about safe routes to take. My sweet, overprotective husband is about to get a reality check with all his Neanderthal ways regarding this baby."

My snicker couldn't be helped at her voicing the thoughts I'd had on numerous occasions.

She giggled. "Oh, Sam, be quiet. So, are you bringing anyone to the team dinner tomorrow night?"

Shit. Are Mark and I going together? I have no idea.

Allison had been rooting for Mark since Vegas last year. I didn't want to make it out to be more than what it was. Damien was Allison's one and only. Casual sex didn't make sense to her. I wasn't ready to share what Mark and I had been doing. At times, when we had been together, it had felt like more than sex buddies, and that had scared me. I refused to let it continue that way. Plus, Allison had no idea about my past or the sex club.

"Mark and I might go together. I'm not sure. He's been nice and shown me around. You know, he's just being friendly, that's all." *Yeah, I like the way I stammered through that. I am losing my touch.*

Her singsong voice came through as she said, "Oh, that's nice. Hey, gotta go. Damien is getting in the car, and I need to get some ground rules straight with him before he goes completely insane."

"Bye, bestie."

"Bye. Muah."

Damien had definitely met his match when it came to Allison. They were perfect for each other.

Resuming my walk to the kitchen, I was reading an email about proper equipment usage. Even though my job wouldn't officially start for a couple of months, I already had my email set up from the previous work I had done regarding the contracts, so I was trying to get acclimated on the front side.

My phone beeped.

> *Mark: Where are you?*

I giggled that Mark was using one of my starting lines.

> *Me: In my kitchen, reading about the proper usage of equipment.*

> *Mark: I think I need to stop by and demonstrate it. I hear hands-on learning is much better than reading.*

> *Me: I think the stick goes right here…*

I was laughing at our juvenile exchange when there was a knock at the door. Wondering who it could be, I scurried to the door, wanting to get rid of the stranger, so I could go back to the sexual-foreplay texting. Opening the door, the smile that emerged on my face was unstoppable.

"I hear you need some equipment serviced."

Mark, sweaty from a run, was standing in the doorway in a tank top and running shorts. His muscles were taut from the strenuous exercise. My mouth wanted to taste him, and my body wanted him inside me. I started to laugh, but I reined it in as I took in his cocky smile while he was holding his phone, about to finish sending me another text.

Mashing my lips together for a few seconds, I put my arm up on the door and leaned in at a seductive angle, showcasing my curves. "I called a serviceman to help me with my equipment issue, but he hasn't shown up. I might require self-servicing."

"Oh, he must not have told you. I'm the handyman, and I'm well versed in all equipment issues."

He gave a little hip gyration, and it sent me over the edge. Laughing, I slapped him on the chest.

He continued, still staying in character, "Ma'am, it could be a real issue if it's not serviced properly." A devilish grin emerged on his face.

I grabbed him by his tank and pulled him into my condo. I was still laughing as we stumbled through the doorway and fell to the floor. Our lips united, and our hands began roaming all over each other's bodies. There was something irresistible about him after a hard workout. Just by a simple touch, he worked me up faster than anyone ever had.

Right as his hand reached underneath my shirt, I heard a gasp from behind me, and both of our faces looked back to see Allison standing in the doorway, holding a container of bakery cupcakes. She was turning redder than a beet.

She gave a small wave. "Oh geez. Hey, you guys. I was surprising Sam with some, um…I'll be going now."

Allison hastily laid the cupcakes inside the door on the floor. She was biting her lip, smiling, and not making eye contact. She was embarrassed and amused at the same time. I was completely horrified and frozen.

Mark looked at me and then jumped up as Allison was about to turn and dash. "Hey, Allison, don't go. I was helping Sam out with a problem when she fell."

Allison stood there, motionless, as she eyed him and then glanced my way. Mark casually smiled.

Hell, he's better at keeping a cover than I am.

I started to sit up, and nonchalantly, I pulled down my shirt. She caught the gesture and was trying to keep it together at the obvious cover-up. Her lips were pressed so hard together that they were turning white. Mark looked at me to help him sell the lie, but I was totally tongue-tied.

Allison walked over and so sweetly gave him a little pat on the shoulder. "Glad you were able to be so neighborly. That's really nice of you."

With Allison's response, I totally lost it as I was sprawled out on my entryway floor, remembering the conversation Allison and I had just had. Mark started laughing, too, and Allison gave us that knowing smile. It was funny that all of us were acting so juvenile when we were adults.

Turning to me, he said, "Sam, I'll see you later. Allison, it was good seeing you."

Allison looked at Mark. Still being just as sweet as can be, she said, "I'll text you when I'm leaving in case she needs help again."

Mark winked at me and replied, "I'd appreciate that."

He turned and made his exit. Before he was out of earshot, Allison started laughing, and then I started laughing all over again. We were near tears. Chortle boxes were officially turned on. After today, I was never going to be able to give her shit again about that kiss she had given Damien on the football field.

As we began to settle down, she leaned against the wall and fanned herself for effect. "Girl, the heat coming from that floor scene I walked into…"

Damn it. That was exactly what I had done to her after that damn kiss on the football field. Right now, I wanted to slap myself for everything I had teased her about. *Paybacks are a BITCH.*

"What? He was only helping me out." I busied my eyes on the floor as I lifted myself up, trying to look innocent.

"I guess it could be considered help…if you define it as his P helping your V." She started laughing again as she picked up the discarded cupcakes. "I hope you realize all the paybacks that will be coming your way from all the shit you've given me."

"Be nice, or I won't share my cupcakes with you. Just so you know, his P does fit very nicely into my V."

Having her here eased my tension. I needed this girl time more than I'd realized.

We giggled all the way to the table where she laid down the cupcakes. It took no time at all for me to show her around my modernly decorated condo.

When we finished, Allison gave me a big hug as she said, "I love the place. It's perfect."

"You think?"

"I do."

I went and grabbed the cupcakes, and then we settled into the black leather sofa. Trying to ignore the big elephant in the room, I focused on the cupcakes. I took one out, unwrapped it, and took a big bite.

Around a mouthful of frosting, I said, "Mmm…these are delicious. Thanks for bringing them. Do you want one?"

Allison scrunched up her nose slightly. "You're welcome. No, thanks. Food and I aren't on the best of terms. I'm basically forcing myself to eat at this point. Damien is a little worried. I eat ginger thins to help with the nausea."

She looked at me expectantly. I was practically shoving the rest of the cupcake into my mouth to avoid talking.

Of course, Allison didn't let it die. "You know, I'm dying over here for the details about you and Mark. You never go back after you've walked away. Don't get me wrong. I think he's a wonderful guy. I'm just surprised."

I knew this was coming. She wasn't judging me or even questioning my decision. She was truly curious. Honestly, I would have been, too, if she had a history like I had.

It would be best if I went with the simple truth. "We hooked up right after I got into town. He seems to get that I'm not the dating type, so with that understanding, we are continuing to *help* each other out."

"Is it exclusive?"

"Yes, it is exclusive. I never sleep with more than one guy at the same time. You know that."

She smiled and bit her lip, trying to suppress her smirk. "I was just wondering."

"Allison, there is nothing going on." I was stressing the words to her, almost pleading. The last thing I wanted was for anyone to get the wrong idea.

Without pause, she shrugged. "I didn't say there was. I was just asking. Take a chill pill, my friend."

I watched her closely, but she was smiling contentedly, not accusingly. I was so on edge. Allison wasn't trying to put me there, but my mind kept wanting to go somewhere I didn't want it to go when it involved Mark. I wanted to change the subject. An idea formed that would help decrease the amount of talking.

"No more talk of boys. How about we pop some popcorn and watch a chick flick, like old times?"

"Sounds like fun."

We made our way to the kitchen to make popcorn. Allison always knew what I needed as a friend, and I loved her for not pressing or teasing me about the Mark thing. I felt bad for all the shit I had given her.

We started the movie and snuggled underneath the blankets. We were halfway through our movie when I looked over and saw Allison fast asleep. Her phone was beeping, and I quickly grabbed it to silence it.

Of course it's Damien.

It made me smile to know she had found her other half. They were truly perfect for each other.

> *Damien: Just checking on you two. Are you still at Sam's?*
>
> *Me: Hey, it's Sam. She's asleep over at my place.*
>
> *Damien: Thanks, Sam. I'll be by in a bit.*
>
> *Me: Sounds good. She's out cold.*

Damien: Thanks. She's been tired a lot lately. Doctor says it's normal.

Me: You're funny. Of course it's normal. She's creating a life. Stop worrying so much.

Damien: I can't. I love her too much.

Those last words struck a chord within me. The truth was, I wished things had turned out differently. I wished I wasn't so tainted, that I could be whole for someone. *Someone like Mark.* I wished I could go back and erase that night from existence.

I stopped my train of thought.

It wasn't possible. My hand in life had been dealt, and it was what it was.

As Allison's mom had always told us, *There's no reason to cry over spilled milk, girls. It's already been spilled.*

I had made the best of the situation, and now, I was coping.

I continued watching the movie. As I sat there, my mind raced back to that night…after I had been raped.

Tears streamed down my face as I ran like hell away from what had to be a nightmare. Adrenaline was the only thing keeping my body going.

He was supposed to be there for me. He'd said he would wait for me forever…until I was ready to give myself to him. He'd said I was his everything. We'd had dreams of having a family together one day. I had wanted to be the mother of his children when we got older.

At the party, my worst fears had become my reality. Greg, my high school boyfriend, had robbed me of my purity. The images flashed over and over again in my head. The pleas I'd made echoed in my ears before I blacked out.

I jumped at the sound of Allison's phone vibrating in my hand.

Damien: I'm here. Don't want to knock if Alli is still sleeping.

Me: I'll be right there.

I got up from my couch and collected myself before I let Damien in. *The past is the past.*

Before I opened the door, I plastered a smile on my face and pushed the ugliness back down, deep inside me. Still in his dress shirt and slacks, Damien must have come straight from the office.

He gave me a brotherly hug. "Hey, Sam. Good to see you."

I pulled back. "Back atcha, Wales."

I was glad we had been able to move past our disagreements regarding Allison. When she'd had her meltdown last year, no one would listen to me. I'd seen my best friend slipping away again, like she had after her parents died. Damien had said that he knew I was looking out for her, and that had made him love me even more as a brother.

Damien was taking in all his surroundings, and then his gaze lingered on his wife. He looked at her adoringly. "Nice place. Do you mind if I wait here while she rests some more?"

I quietly laughed. "Thanks, and of course not. Let's get a beer and stay in the kitchen where we can actually talk instead of whisper."

"You read my mind."

He followed me into the kitchen where I pulled out a couple of beers from the fridge and handed him one. We both casually leaned up against the counter on opposite sides of the room.

After taking a swig, he raked his hands through his black hair as his blue eyes darted around the room. "How are you liking it here so far?"

"Great. I'll be ready to start when it's time, but it's been good to have a few weeks to settle into my new surroundings."

He arched his brow. "Let me know if you want me to push up your official start date."

"I'll let you know. It's nice to have a break."

He nodded.

"So, how many times has Allison had to tell you to stop worrying?" I took a sip to hide my grin.

He started rubbing his forehead. "She's been so sick and tired."

He really was worried as his hands progressed to his hair again, and he moved his fingers through it several times.

Normally, I would give him a hard time, but I felt the urge to try to comfort him with words. "Wales, she's pregnant. It's normal. She's healthy, and you have the best doctors looking after her."

He gave me a slight smile.

"She couldn't be happier, so just enjoy it," I said.

Letting out a breath, he replied, "Thanks. I'll try. I'm ready for January to hurry the fuck up and get here." He was strung so tight.

"Hey, she'll be fine." Then, my mind went a different direction. I stood erect. "Has the doctor said something? Allison said everything was fine. Damien, if something is wrong, tell me."

He started shaking his head. "No, the doctor says she's perfectly fine. I started reading one of those baby books, and my mind has been a clusterfuck ever since. She's still doing everything she was before. I would put her in a bubble if she'd let me."

That earned a snort from me, thinking about how Allison would not stop living. Since she had gotten her life back, she had been living it to the fullest.

"Hey, Allison is going to be fine. You could always call my mom and see if Allison's mom had any problems. That might ease your mind."

I relaxed my posture again. Me being tense would only make him tense. He was being his normal worrywart self about Allison.

His eyes lit up at the suggestion. "You don't think your mom would mind?"

"Are you kidding me? Mama can talk babies for hours. Be prepared after baby Wales gets here. She'll probably move in with you guys." I tipped my beer in his direction.

He chuckled, and some of the tension left the air. "Thanks. I'll do that." He eyed me for a second. "You seem to be doing better yourself."

"Of course. I'm always fine." I didn't like where this was going.

He pressed on. "You know, Alli worries about you. She'll never push you, but she knows something is eating at you."

He was staring at me in that business way he does for measuring a person to see how he or she responded. Sometimes, those blue eyes were like spears when they targeted on something.

I nodded, but I had to ask one question before I closed the door on this subject. "How did you move on? How do you live with it, day after day?"

From what Allison had told me, Damien had a wild past also. When his grandparents died, he began sleeping around. Shortly after that, his sister was murdered which further sent him on a downward spiral to filling the emptiness with other extracurricular activities that were not healthy. Allison had brought him from that dark sordid past and into the light.

Leaning back, he put his hand up to his chin. "I learned the past is the past, and I needed to live in the now and look to the future. I should have dealt with my past before it started fucking so much with my present. I'm a lucky bastard because Alli loves me so much. If I had to guess, you need to find a way to forgive yourself. Alli helped me find that through her unconditional love."

I didn't know how he had figured out that I was fighting my own internal struggles. He had always known. From what I had been told, which was probably only a small piece of the story, he'd had a wild past himself.

My grip on my beer bottle was so tight that my knuckles were white.

I was about to respond when a raspy voice sounded from the other side of the bar. "Hey, you two. Sorry, I fell asleep. What are you guys doing?"

Damien immediately walked over to Allison's side and kissed her hello. "Sam was telling me not to worry so much about you and the baby."

His hand went to her stomach, and my chest tightened. *Why is it so painful for me to be around them?*

I was happy for them. I had been around this for months. It was like the baby was a trigger to a ticking time bomb inside me. It was so intimate, witnessing their love on a depth I knew I wanted but didn't deserve.

Yes, I want what they have. Fuck.

She gave him a hug as she responded, "Well, you should listen to her. Don't we have dinner plans tonight with Frank?"

She looked exhausted. Babymaking was really taking it out of her.

"I postponed it. You're tired. Let's get home."

Damien was totally consumed by her, in tune with her every need.

She rolled her eyes. "Sam, I might call you hourly to remind him not to worry."

"Baby, I don't think that would help," he said.

We all laughed as they left.

Is forgiveness the key to all of this? I have no idea.

I had so much on my mind that I turned off my phone and went to bed.

CHAPTER
7

I had missed the team dinner, claiming I didn't feel good. Allison had not been happy with me.

With all the realizations that had been streaming through my head, I couldn't go to the dinner.

I want Mark. I don't deserve Mark.

This is the closest thing to happiness that I will ever achieve.

There was no way I could let Mark see that after what we had agreed to. I would have to be fine with being fuck buddies.

So, instead of confronting the issue, I had taken the pansy-ass way out of going to the dinner. I kept replaying that night over in my mind.

I needed to get out of the dinner. The pressure of attending with Mark was too much. I texted Allison.

> Me: Not feeling well. Going to skip the team dinner.
>
> Allison: Bullshit. I'm on my way to your place, and if you're lying, I'm dragging you there.

She is going to come over. I knew it.

Picking up my phone, I called Damien.

"Hey, Sam."

"Hey. Allison wants to come check on me, and I'm not feeling well. I decided not to go tonight because of the baby, and I would hate to get her sick."

"Thank you, Sam."

"Anytime."

That made me feel even shittier, but I needed time to come to grips with everything.

Moments later, Allison texted me.

> Allison: You don't play fair. I'm worried about you.

> Me: Don't be. I just need some time. Please. I promise, I'll be fine. I always am.

> Allison: That's what worries me, sweetie. I'm here when you need me.

> Me: Thanks, bestie.

Laying back on the couch, I mentally confirmed that I needed to avoid Mark for the next few days. What was wrong with me?

I was in a funk and needed to pull myself out of it. After putting on my baseball cap and sunglasses, I hastily walked to the deli. Because of my social hiatus over the last few days, I was out of food. The deli wasn't too crowded, so I was able to snag a bistro table in the far back corner.

"Hey there, Sam. You just missed Mark. What can I get you?"

I looked up to Edna and gave her a weak smile. Her news was both relieving and disappointing at the same time. I missed him, and that scared me to death.

"Just a turkey sandwich on wheat and a lemonade."

I put my head down, not wanting to continue talking. She took the hint and left.

Thank goodness. My emotions had been all over the place.

My conversation with Damien had struck a deep nerve. He had gone through hell and back, and he'd still been able to find his version of happily ever after.

Maybe there is hope. Sam, stop being stupid. This is your life.

A plate was set down in front of me.

Without looking up, I responded, "Thanks, Edna."

Then, the chair started to scoot, and Edna sat down beside me.

Oh shit, here we go.

Edna asked, "Is everything all right?"

"Yes, thanks. I've had a lot on my mind."

What the hell? Why am I sharing all this with a stranger? I still refused to look up even though her presence did comfort me.

"I see. Man troubles?"

"You could say that, I guess."

I sounded pathetic, even to my own ears. I was too tired to pull out my inner self that acted as if nothing was wrong. Everyone knew me as the happy-go-lucky person. For some reason, I felt like I could let my guard down with Edna. It was refreshing. I glanced up to her face, and she was looking at me so lovingly.

"Well, Sam, the best thing you can ever do is follow your heart. What's your heart telling you?"

The napkin in my hands was being shredded to smithereens. "To try something I don't deserve."

"Oh, we all deserve happiness. Most of us are just too scared to really go after it." She had the kindest voice, one that was perfect for reading bedtime stories. "Take it slow. Don't rush it."

A few tears slid down my cheek, and I hastily wiped them away. I felt like I was on a cliff, ready to jump, and I was scared to death. "We'll see."

"Eat up. Take each day as it comes." She patted my hand and gave it a little squeeze.

Reminding me of my mama, who always wore aprons in the kitchen, Edna's blue gingham apron made me want to crawl onto her lap and cry.

"Also, remember that whatever you're doing now isn't making you happy. So, what do you have to lose? The worst that could happen is that you would still be unhappy."

My heart started pumping a little faster as her words set in. "Thanks, Edna."

"Anytime. My deli is always open to you. Remember, one day at a time."

I nodded and started eating my sandwich as she walked away.

Slow...I need to take this slow. I raked over all her words with a fine-toothed comb.

Hell, I made it so clear to Mark that I wanted no entanglements, and now, I potentially want to have a few. He's going to think I'm delusional. What if he only wants me as a fuck buddy?

After finishing my lunch, I left enough money to more than cover the meal and the tip. As I walked by the counter, I gave Edna a little wave, and she winked back at me. Taking a deep breath, I headed out the door. I was about to make a left when I saw Mark casually leaning up against his pickup truck right in front of me. He was in jeans and a loose-fitting T-shirt. He gave me a smile, and I smiled back. Unsure of myself, I started kicking around a rock on the sidewalk as I shifted my gaze to pavement.

"Hey, stranger. I saw Allison at the stadium yesterday, and she said you were sick."

"Yeah, it's been a rough couple of days."

Nervously, I adjusted the baseball cap on my head and tucked back a few pieces of hair that had escaped. The silence caused me to look up as he pushed away from his vehicle before he walked over toward me.

He grabbed my hand and started rubbing it. "Hey, why don't you take a drive with me? I have a few things to pick up, so you can get some fresh air."

I swallowed. "Sure." I felt so stiff around him now.

We got into the vehicle and proceeded to pull out of the parking lot. The truck was quiet, and my nerves were on edge.

We were coming to the entrance of our condo complex when I blurted out, "Why don't you drop me off at my place?"

He looked over at me as I rubbed my sweaty palms down my jeans. My mind was frazzled, and I was scared to voice what I wanted.

"Sure, Sam." He pulled in and parked the car.

I jumped out. "I'll see you later, Mark." I bolted up the stairs so quickly.

Damn it, I chickened out again.

I was stepping through the door when hands snaked around my waist. Mark pulled me to his front, and my body conformed to him. He walked us both inside my condo, and then he shut the door behind us with his foot.

"What happened? Why are you pulling away from me again? I've given you exactly what you wanted. I'll take you however I can get you. Talk to me."

I took a deep breath. Barely above a whisper, I said, "What if I want to try for a little more?"

He spun me around and grabbed my face. "What are you saying, Sam?"

I stood there. Our green eyes were darting back and forth across each other's features. My mouth wouldn't work as all the moisture left it.

"If you want more, I'm ready to give you more. Just tell me what you want," he said.

"Yes, I want to try for more."

Then, he sealed his lips on mine. I was relieved not to talk anymore right now. I had already said so much. We went for each other's clothes, stripping down.

I sucked on his neck as I pulled him towards the living room. As I leaned back on the arm of the couch, he skimmed his hand down my stomach and dipped his finger into me, massaging the walls of my core. "Shit, you're wet."

I moaned at the sensation as I pulled us both backwards, tumbling onto the couch. Within seconds, he spread my legs and impaled me. I wrapped my legs around his waist, pulling him into me deeper, harder. I needed it like this in order to forget what I had said. We were moaning as we were climbing in a desperate way. We were both totally lost in the sensations.

"Sam, wait. Stop. I forgot a condom again. Shit."

I groaned as he disengaged to go find his jeans. He was taking forever—or maybe I was that horny.

"Hurry the hell up, or I'm getting my BFFF."

He was back, sheathing himself, before he slid into me again. We were even crazier for each other, and it took no time before I was screaming out incoherent moans while the rush flowed through my bloodstream.

That was exactly what I needed.

Mark lay beside me. We were both panting, lying boneless from our release, on the couch. It was always satisfying with Mark, each and every time. He kissed my forehead and cuddled me closer. My ingrained reactions kicked in, and I started to pull away. He let me as he sat up with me. My high from my orgasm ebbed, and I was a nervous wreck again. I jumped up and put on his T-shirt, needing a shield, and then I sat down by him again, keeping a few inches of distance. Sex was easy for me, but feelings and emotions were hard.

"Talk to me, Sam. If I misunderstood what you wanted...shit...I fucked up, didn't I?"

I turned to him and put my fingers on his lips. "I wanted that, I promise."

Pulling my fingers away, I started worrying the hem of his T-shirt. I refused to look him in the eye. "I do want to try for more, but I need to take it slow." I let out a slow breath. "I'm not the kind of girl you take home to your mom. I have my quirks and my problems, but I do want more with you. I just don't know how much I can actually give."

He said nothing. I was starting to get nervous because I had not felt that raw and exposed in a long time. I looked up to him finally, and he was smiling at me. I smiled in return, and a little of the nerves started to fade.

Finally, he said, "I'll take whatever you want to give, Sam. I need you to promise me that if I push you too hard, you'll tell me."

Can it really be that easy? I thought about his words for a moment. "Okay, I'll try, but I'm not good at this, Mark. I've never done this."

He was still grinning like a damn sexy buffoon. My heart was leaping with a joy I didn't recognize.

He put a cautious hand on my knee as he asked, "So, does *more* include being public about us seeing each other?"

I took another deep breath. "Um...I guess, if you want that."

Without hesitation, he responded, "Yes, I want that."

I let out the breath I had been holding. *Who would have thought this would be so hard?* This was exhausting.

There was a knock at the door. I started scrambling for my pants as Mark leisurely put on his jeans. My nerves returned in full force, and I had no idea why. I tossed him the T-shirt on the floor and then dashed to the front door. Part of me welcomed the distraction and distance a visitor would bring, so I could regroup.

When I opened the door, I wished I had pretended not to be home instead of trying to escape the awkward conversation I was about to have with Mark. Allison was standing there, trying to look furious with her scowl, but the glow from her pregnancy hindered her significantly.

"Sam, you've been ignoring me for too many days. What is going on? I know you're not sick."

A hand came down on my shoulder, and it felt nice. I refused to let my fear overreact on such a small gesture.

Mark was right there with me. "Hey, Allison."

"Hey, Mark."

Allison looked down at my shirt and then at Mark. I followed her gaze when I realized I had on his T-shirt, which meant he must be shirtless.

Ah hell, I threw him my shirt.

Allison's eyes got wide. "Oh my gosh, how do I keep doing this? I'm never dropping by here unannounced again."

She went to leave, but then she pushed through us with her hand over her mouth, running toward the bathroom.

Poor thing. I knew the nausea was getting worse and worse.

I looked up at Mark. "I'll be right back. I'm going to see if she needs my help."

"Is she okay?" He was a gentleman through and through with how worried he sounded.

"Yes, she's okay. I'll be right back." I was not about to break the news of her pregnancy to Mark without her consent.

For the time being, Damien and Allison were being careful with who they told.

I ran after her to the bathroom. I closed the door as I found her cleaning her face and pulling out a new toothbrush from her purse.

After brushing her teeth, Allison leaned against the counter and pinched the bridge of her nose. "I'm getting to be a pro at this. I'm hoping it gets better during my second trimester." She threw away the toothbrush she had used.

"Can I get you anything?" I had no idea how to help her.

"I'm good. I've got some crackers." Allison started wagging her eyebrows up and down. "So…"

I was shocked at how fast she was able to bounce back after being so sick. She was fine now, so there was no reason to treat her with white gloves.

My finger went in the air, pointing at her. "Okay, l don't want any shit for what I'm about to tell you. Mark and I have decided to officially start seeing each other."

"Good. I'm glad." Her voice was so calm and nonchalant, but her smile was huge.

I knew she was on the verge of jumping up and down, but she was resisting the urge. I smiled back, finally trying to allow myself to be happy about this.

Allison held out her hand as she said, "Shall we? Hanging out in the bathroom for a long time might look a little weird."

"Okay." I eyed the door cautiously. *This shit is about to get real.*

"Hey, don't worry. I won't make a big deal even though I'm really excited about it."

I finally moved to open the door, and we made our way back to Mark, who was still shirtless.

Shit. This is awkward.

He walked toward us with concern etched on his face. "Hey, Allison, are you feeling okay? I let Damien know you were sick."

She groaned, and his brows pinched in confusion.

"He's probably on his way, isn't he?" She fished out her phone and started typing out a text, probably trying to halt Damien from leaving work.

I was sure that was a regular occurrence these days. Part of me wanted to laugh as Mark tried to piece together this situation.

He responded, still confused, "Yes, I think so." He had no idea he had fed Damien's need to ensure Allison was okay every second of the day.

Her phone pinged.

"Geez, women have been having babies for centuries. A little morning sickness isn't going to kill anyone. I'm going to get some water real quick."

I wasn't sure if she was talking to herself or Mark. In a huff, she left the room.

"Is Allison—"

I didn't give Mark a chance to finish his question. As soon as she left, I wrenched off his shirt and threw it at him. I found mine on the back of the couch, where he must have laid it after I threw it to him, and pulled it on.

Mark was smiling at me. "Sam, it might help if you put it on the right way."

I looked down, and it was inside out and backward. I started fixing my shirt while he laughed at me.

Bastard. "Not funny."

He was calmly sliding his shirt back on. Just as I finished righting myself, Allison came back in the room with her crackers and water. She still wasn't showing at all in her T-shirt and jeans. She looked at both of us and smirked, but she didn't say a word. Mark was at a loss for words as he stared at her while she moved to sit on the couch.

Allison looked over at Mark and sweetly said, "I'm sorry I got irritated with you earlier. To clear it all up, I'm pregnant, and Damien is in total overreaction mode. I might have him committed before this is over with."

"Congratulations. When is the baby due?" Mark asked.

He came and stood a little closer to me, and it made my insides feel gooey for some reason. I had no idea what was proper protocol for being a girlfriend.

Allison took a small sip of her water. "Thank you. We're beyond excited. We're due at the beginning of January. Please don't say anything to anyone. We're waiting a few more weeks until I'm out of the first trimester."

She was so adorable, munching on her crackers.

"Won't say a word." He did some little cross thing over his heart.

"Thanks. Plus, if you do, I'll sic Sam on you."

She gave a little shrug and a wink, and Mark smiled.

There was another knock on the door, and I went to open it. Damien came straight in, greeting everyone, while trying to look over Allison without being crazy about it. He failed, of course. Even though she was irritated at his overreactions, she smiled the moment her eyes made contact with his. That action alone spoke volumes of how she really felt. They had true love.

We all took our seats, and Damien's hand automatically went to Allison's stomach. He remembered himself though and tried to casually take it back. I was surprised others hadn't already caught on.

Also noticing what he was doing, Allison piped up, "I told Mark since he's dating Sam now. He also got to witness my spectacular bout with morning sickness."

The smile on Damien's face was glorious.

Mark squeezed my knee. "Congratulations. Allison says the baby is due in January."

I thought Damien was going to explode from joy because someone else knew the news.

"Thank you. Yes, we're excited," Damien responded with pride in his voice.

For the first time, the thought of them having a baby didn't cause me to panic, and I was able to enjoy it with them. Emotions were a bitch when they weren't cooperating, I had found out.

I tried to settle in next to Mark. Our relationship felt different now.

"When are you guys making the official announcement regarding the baby?" Mark asked.

He put his arm around the back of the couch, and my body started to slowly relax.

Allison responded, "When we get back from the guys' rafting trip in Colorado. I would rather announce it than have people think we are hiding it. I don't want the press to start hounding us again."

Shit, I forgot about the trip to Colorado.

It had been in the works for a while now with Damien, Allison, Martin, Nina, and me. Nina was Martin's girlfriend, and it'd appeared they were serious about each other. The guys were going on a rafting trip, and the girls were going to hang together.

Allison asked, "Sam, are you still going with us?"

"Of course. Why wouldn't I?" I wanted to smack my forehead. My heart started pounding because I wasn't used to having a significant other at all. *How do I handle this? Should I invite him?*

A relationship wasn't going to stop me from doing things. I needed to talk to Allison about how to handle this kind of stuff when Mark and I were in public.

Being the best friend that she was, she completely bailed me out. "I didn't want you to feel pressured with everything you have on your plate from the move. Mark, you're more than welcome to join us. We leave this Thursday. Damien and his friend Martin are doing a one-to-two-day rafting trip."

Damien interjected, "One day."

Allison rolled her eyes and continued on, "Well, there's a rafting trip. The timeframe is to be determined. If you want to fly out there with us, you're more than welcome. I believe Martin is meeting us out there with his girlfriend."

I was definitely going to get pointers from Allison on how to do this relationship stuff while we were in Colorado.

Mark smiled and gave me another squeeze. "Sounds like fun. We can stay at my place. There's plenty of space there." He turned to Damien. "Plus, it's already secured from the public eye, which would make it easier on your security. My family is also right there."

Damien didn't even hesitate. "We had accommodations at a lodge, but I'd prefer your place since you're offering. It's more isolated. Thank you."

Allison started clapping. "Oh, girls' time is going to be so much fun!"

Damien blanched, and I started laughing.

"Wales, don't worry. I was only thinking a few strippers and maybe some body shots."

Mark was chuckling behind me as Damien stated, "Definitely only a one-day trip."

Allison stood. "We probably need to leave, so I can get ready for dinner." She turned back to Damien. "Don't even think of canceling." She then walked over to me to give me a hug as she whispered, "I'm so happy for you. Love you."

My chest tightened at how much she loved me as I whispered back, "Love you, too."

Damien was smiling at his wife, which meant he had probably been about to cancel. She definitely knew him well. They made their way to the door as I followed them, and we said our good-byes.

After closing the door, I mentally breathed a sigh of relief. I had survived.

When I turned, Mark was casually leaning against one of the tables. "What do you want to do?"

"What about running those errands that you needed to do this morning?" I responded.

He walked up to me and gave me a small kiss. "I can do that another time."

Fidgeting, I responded, "I'd like to do that though. It seems normal. Isn't that what couples do?"

Without hesitation, he grabbed his keys. "Then, let's go be normal."

I smiled at the thought. Me, boys, and normal had never been in the same sentence prior to today.

Looking down at my appearance, I said, "Let me change real quick, and then we can go."

We can still mix in a little not-so-normal throughout our day.

CHAPTER
8

I had changed into a yellow sundress with some wedge sandals. As the girlfriend of a famous quarterback, I would not go out in public looking like a disaster. So far, we had been to the dry cleaners and the hardware store, and we were now headed to pick up some suits.

Mark parked in the upscale store's parking lot, and I jumped out. He had been trying to open my door for me all afternoon, but the act had made me nervous for some reason. I knew I was being ridiculous, but every small thing he had done seemed magnified all of a sudden. With his hand around my waist, we walked into the store and went straight to the men's area.

A salesman came up and greeted us. "Mr. Robertson, we have your suits ready. Please follow me to a dressing room."

We followed the impeccably dressed salesman to a private dressing room that had several chairs with a platform for fittings and a heavy curtain separating the actual changing area.

The fairly attractive salesman gestured to the chairs along the wall. "Please have a seat. We'll get your suits and refreshments."

We took our seats, and my legs began bouncing in a fidgeting mess. Mark gently laid his hand on my knee, and I took a deep breath. The calmness I felt from his touch was amazing.

A few minutes later, the sales staff returned with some suits.

The salesman pointed to the fitting room as one of the staff passed by to hang up the clothes. "Mr. Robertson, if you would, please try these on to make sure no additional alterations are needed."

A woman came in and set a tray with two flutes down on the table as the salesman said, "Here is some complimentary champagne for you and Miss…"

Part of me wished it were shots at this point.

I stood from my chair. "Sam. Thank you."

I grabbed a flute and started drinking as the man's eyes lingered on my breasts a little too long.

Mark must have noticed because from out of nowhere, he said sternly to the salesman, "I'll let you know if we need anything."

The man coughed, ducked his head, and exited the dressing room. Something inside me liked seeing Mark slightly jealous.

I walked up to him and gave him a kiss. Just as it was about to intensify, I pulled back and said, "Are you sure you want to try on your suits, Sport?"

His gaze heated as I went to sit down in the chair. As I crossed my legs, I was sure to give him a peek of what was hiding underneath my dress. He watched me heatedly. Mark started toward me, but then he looked at the door and then at me as if he were torn.

Damn it, why isn't he taking me here?

Finally, he sighed, grabbed his suits, and disappeared behind the red velvet curtain.

He is not going to shy away from my needs just because we are in a dressing room or because I'm his girlfriend now.

The moment he closed the curtain, I quietly sprinted to the door and put the lock into place. I pulled off my dress, leaving on my white lacy underwear and bra. I grabbed my glass of champagne, a condom from my purse, and went to sit on the raised circular box used for the tailoring process in front of the mirrors. My legs were crossed at the ankles as I leaned back on one arm and casually drank my champagne with the other. I felt at ease doing this, but throw emotions into it, and I would fold like a cheap suit.

Mark came out, looked at the chairs, and then started moving toward the door.

He was almost at a jog when I said, "Hey, where are you going?"

He froze and slowly turned. The gray suit fit him perfectly, and he was gorgeous. I slowly licked my lips.

"I'm one lucky fellow, Sam."

As he watched, I unsnapped the crotch of my underwear, allowing for easy access, and desire sparked between us.

"Lucky is an understatement," he added.

I finished my champagne and then replied, "You're about to get real lucky, Sport."

I tossed the condom to him, and he caught it. As he stalked toward me, he unzipped his pants, freeing himself, and then he rolled the condom on. He was on me in two seconds, and we consumed each other's mouths. He dragged his erection down my cleft, and I bucked into him to feel the friction. There was nothing like that zinging sensation pulsing between my legs in anticipation of the plunge. He pulled me to the edge of the raised platform as he pushed into me. I closed my eyes at the sensation.

I loved how he took me. He started sucking my nipple through my sheer bra as he continued moving in and out of me, faster and faster. Reaching the spot that caused me to dig my nails into his ass, our bodies connected on a nuclear level. My hands went underneath his suit jacket, and I moaned when his other hand came up and pinched my nipple hard. It was a race to the finish as we both exploded. Lights danced across my closed eyelids as our breathing calmed down.

Between gasps, Mark groaned, "Fuck me."

"I just did." It was all I could get out with how hard I was panting.

He raised his head and smiled down at me before giving me another kiss. "Yes, you did—perfectly, I might add. I like how responsive you are to me."

I kissed him.

We were both starting to respond to each other again when he pulled back. "Sam, we need to get out of here."

"Yes, hurry."

He pulled out of me and discarded the condom before bringing my dress to me. I hastily pulled it on after snapping my underwear back into place.

"I love those. Where the hell did you find those?" he asked.

My high came crashing down. Images of all the knowledge I had gained from the sex club flashed across my mind.

On the spot, I saucily responded, "A girl has to have her secrets." I winked, keeping up the charade, but I felt dirty inside. Although these panties were new, I still knew about all this stuff from Club Envy.

He barely knows me.

I resumed my position in the chair. Mark tried on all three suits, and the sales staff checked the different hems and lengths. I hardly paid attention.

He doesn't deserve someone as tainted as I am. He wouldn't want me if he knew about how ugly I really was on the inside.

Mark's voice brought me out of my thoughts. "Hey, are you ready to go?"

The associates handed him a bill, and he signed it. The entire time, he kept one eye on me, and I tried to look normal.

"Yeah. Your suits look great."

His eyes continued to search mine. "Thanks. Let's go pick up some food and eat back at my place. Does that sound good?"

"Sounds perfect." My voice sounded normal, but my insides felt like they were shattering.

He pulled me into his side as we left with the suits slung over his shoulder. The employees had tried to insist on carrying them out, but Mark had adamantly and politely refused their offers.

My mind was trying to tell me to end this here and now even though my heart didn't want to. I kept going back to Edna's words, *One day at a time.*

We picked up food and brought it back to his condo. I was pushing around my spaghetti in a circular motion, eating every so often. On probably the fiftieth rotation, a hand came down on mine, stopping the continuous movement of my food on my plate.

"Sam, what's going on in that beautiful head of yours?"

I looked up and gave a smile. "I'm good."

"Listen, I don't mind you saying you don't want to talk about it, but don't lie to me. Don't feed me that bullshit you feed everyone else about being good when you're not. I don't want to push you away, Sam. You're shutting me out though when you should be talking to me."

His voice was stern enough to force my mind to snap off of autopilot and start responding.

After taking a deep breath, I tried to warn him. "I don't think you know what you're getting yourself into by dating me."

I looked down as I started pushing my food around again, and a finger came underneath my chin.

His green eyes penetrated me as if he were looking deep into my soul. "Let me be the judge of that. Let's take this slow, okay? There's no rush. I'm not on a timeline here, Sam."

"Okay."

My emotions started to lighten up as we finished dinner. I needed to get control of all these ups and downs. As we were cleaning up in the kitchen, I realized that bedtime was coming soon. I knew that Mark had an early training session with the team.

I was about to go grab my purse and head home when he asked, "How about we watch a movie? You can pick."

Internally, I jumped for joy that he wanted me around more, but I also became nervous because bedtime was approaching. I wasn't ready to stay all night. I had never stayed the night with a guy. I normally fucked men and left them. However, I needed to keep this light. We'd had so many heavy moments today.

"Hmm…I should pick some super hottie to watch." I tapped my index finger against my lips as I thought about it. "A definite super hottie." I gave him a wink.

"Whatever gets you in the mood."

The seductive tone he'd used caused a flame to begin low in my abdomen, and it needed stoking. Finally, my mind was turning off, and my body was taking over.

Much better.

I leaned in a little closer, and he mimicked my movement until we were only a few inches apart.

"Some of those hotties can really get me going. Are you up for the challenge?"

"I think I can manage."

I loved the calm cockiness he exuded. It wasn't over the top. It was just the right amount to ooze sex appeal.

"I think I'll be the judge of that, Sport."

As we talked, the space between us slowly closed. Lust filled the air. Mark leaned down, and the moment our lips touched, they crashed together. We were lost in each other. Clothes started coming off until we were sprawled together on the kitchen floor with me on top. He was feeling around the floor with his hands, and I was getting frustrated. My body needed attention.

"What are you doing? I'm right here."

"Condom. I can't find my damn jeans. Those fuckers are really getting in the way."

Taking control, I stopped the kiss, sat up, and reached for his jeans. He laid beneath me with lust filled eyes as I pulled a condom out of his jeans. I scooted down to take him in like a lollipop. The moment I touched his hardened length, all confusion vanished from his face. I created a tight suction as he pushed into my mouth. He was big, but I kept taking him until he was buried in my throat, and then I began a low hum.

"Fuck, Sam. Shit, don't stop."

I continued until he was almost ready to go. That was when I stopped. I quickly put the condom on him and slid him inside me. The initial stretch was the best part. Then, the frenzied hard ride started as he thrust into me. It was almost painful, but the pain-pleasure mixture got me off. We both started screaming at the same time as we fell off that cliff of ecstasy. Our bodies were covered in a fine sheen of sweat as I collapsed on him.

"Woman, you are incredible."

"You're not so bad yourself, Sport. I think you have me ready for the incredibly hot movie star men now."

He laughed and smacked my ass as I stood up. We walked to the living room, and I perused through his DVDs until I saw the perfect choice. I handed it over to him, and he laughed out loud.

"*Unnecessary Roughness*? No chick flick?"

"Nope," I said as I popped the P. "I prefer my hotties to be sports jocks."

He smacked my ass again at my sarcastic purr, and he put in the DVD, still naked in all his glory. Sitting on the edge of the couch, I wasn't sure how we were supposed to watch this together. He came and lay down behind me, and then he pulled me to him. He put a blanket on top of us, and he wrapped himself around me. Soon, the warmth completely took me under, and I succumbed to sleep.

Waking up, startled, I was completely disoriented. I was in a bed, but it wasn't mine, and I had an arm draped across my body. *Mark*. Somehow, I had ended up in bed with Mark. I remembered the movie, being exhausted from all the happenings of the day, and then nothing. Fear crept up in me. I had never stayed the night with any guy.

My chest tightened as if I were suffocating, and I couldn't get enough air. *Home*. I needed to get home before he destroyed all the barriers I had built to protect myself. He was getting inside my heart way too quickly. I slowly extricated myself from his grasp.

My clothes were still in the kitchen. I headed in there and dressed quickly before I headed out the door as quietly as possible.

After entering my condo, I saw the clock, and it was after midnight. I found my yoga pants and a T-shirt, and I crashed on the couch. The memory of me in bed with Mark was still vivid in my mind. Tossing and turning, I felt bereft of the warmth I had just had. This was so frustrating how nerve-racking all this was.

At some point though, exhaustion claimed me, and I went into a restless sleep.

CHAPTER
9

I woke up to pounding on my door and my name being shouted. My head felt like it had been hit by a truck as I tried to right myself.

Mark was yelling through the wood door with panic lacing his voice, "Sam, are you in there?"

Did something happen?

I opened the door to find Mark in his sweats with no shirt and no shoes. My body still wasn't functional, and I squinted against the morning sun behind Mark's body at the door. The look on his face caused my adrenaline to rise, and it overpowered my fatigued muscles. He rushed through the door and started looking me over.

My voice came out dry from not speaking yet this morning as I asked, "What's wrong?"

"Where did you go? Shit, you scared me. What happened? Why did you leave?" he questioned.

The questions were coming so fast that I had to focus to catch it all. He was rubbing his hands along my shoulders and arms as his eyes searched mine.

"After I woke up, I came back home. I knew you had an early morning, and I didn't want to disturb you."

He let me go and began pacing in front of me.

Why is he agitated?

He stopped and then turned to me, obviously struggling with what to say. Irritation had apparently won out.

"Sam, don't lie to me. Like I said, you can decline answering, but don't lie."

It was too early to be doing this. "I did come back home, and you do have an early morning. I didn't lie. I might not have shared it all, but I didn't lie. Back the fuck off, Mark."

He backed down his demeanor. "Damn it, Sam. I was worried when I saw you were gone this morning with no note or anything. You've run away like that from me before. When we were together in Vegas and then again on that night about six or seven months ago, you slipped off in the middle of the night. I didn't see or hear from you for months after the last time you did that. This morning, I slipped on the first thing I could find, and I ran over here. I needed to make sure you hadn't vanished again."

My pulse was racing. This was too much, and part of me wanted to call the whole thing off. As I focused on his stressed-out face, my heart started melting at the realization that I'd caused him to worry. Detachment was normally easier for me, but it wasn't as fulfilling as being in his arms last night, and that was what kept me from uttering any words of finality.

He is only worried. He's not trying to control me.

"I get it. I'm sorry. I was a little off-kilter from waking up in your bed."

Mark squatted down to bring his eyes level with mine. "Then, just tell me that, and I'll bring you home. I'm not asking for anything you're not willing to give. Just the fact that you're willing to give us a shot is all I want."

The sincerity of his voice rang in my ears. I'd never expected him to be this understanding.

It made me want to give him a sliver of truth. "Okay, I wasn't thinking. I panicked. I've never stayed with a guy before."

He let out a breath and pulled me to him. "I have to leave for the team workout. Just promise to tell me next time. There's no pressure on how fast our relationship progresses, Sam."

"I promise."

I brought my arms up to him, and he hugged me closer.

He kissed my lips softly and pulled back slightly. "I'm not trying to smother you, but I also want to know that my girlfriend is okay, regardless of where you are. Are you going to be around this afternoon?"

I bit my lip. I wanted to believe everything he was saying, but my brain was still having problems reconciling with the fact that he had gone from being fine with us being fuck buddies to now wanting something with me.

"I should be. I'm not sure what I'm doing, but give me a call or a text."

"Okay, go back to sleep. You look exhausted."

After he broke the hug, I gave him a salute and a kiss on his lips. He left, and then I went to my bed and flopped down. My brain needed to be put on mute, so I could get some sleep.

How do people do this every day?

Close to lunchtime, I woke up and decided to make my way down to the deli for a sandwich. I was hoping to see Edna again. She had put it so simply the other day, but it was not simple. It was complicated.

Am I doing it wrong?

When I walked in, Edna spotted me. "Hey! How's it going?"

I shook my head. "It's going."

"I see. Let's go grab a table in the back. I'll be there in a sec."

I walked over to the same table where I had sat yesterday. *What a difference a day makes.*

I smiled as Edna set down a plate of cookies and a glass of milk for me. Her apron had been removed.

When I took a bite of a chocolate chip cookie, my mouth salivated, and I died and went to heaven. The way the chocolate was still soft told me these were fresh out of the oven.

"So, what's troubling you?"

"Honestly, I don't know why I keep finding myself here, wanting to talk to you."

She bit into a cookie and laid it back down. "The way I look at it is that it's better to get it out than to let it fester."

She has a point. Maybe she can help me put it all into perspective again. "I don't know what I should do. I feel at odds with myself."

"Do you feel at odds with yourself or at odds with what you think yourself should be?"

She got right to the subject with no dillydallying. I liked that—no fluff and straight to the heart of the matter. The way she had worded it made it seem like a rhetorical question, and I didn't have to answer if I didn't want to.

"I don't know." I sat there with the glass of milk in my hand as I tipped it from one side to another, watching the coating of the milk on the inside of the glass vanish. "Something happened to me a long time ago…" I stopped myself from going on. What had happened didn't matter. I was broken, and now, I needed to figure out how to mend myself the best way possible in order to continue seeing Mark.

"I see."

I looked up as she studied me. She had soft features, but her eyes were knowing as the powder-blue irises stared me down.

Edna took another bite of the cookie and chewed for a minute. "You've put a lot of barriers up to protect yourself, and you're now finding them starting to come down. Sometimes, the past matters more than we think it does."

How the hell did that sweet, innocent lady sitting next to me figure it out so quickly?

My mind had been trying to tell me that, but I'd kept shutting it down for self-preservation. "It's only been twenty-four hours since we made it official, and I'm a complete mess." I laid my head in my hands and tried to shake out all the confusion.

Edna patted my arm. Her words were soft. "That's good. It means you're doing it right."

I laughed as I looked at her in confusion.

Before I had a chance to respond, she asked, "Do you know how to bake, Sam?"

This was insane in the best possible way. "I do. I bake all the time with my mama when I go home."

Part of me wanted my mama, but talking to her about relationships was hard because I'd never told her what had happened. She thought I was waiting for Mr. Right to sweep me off my feet, like Daddy had done with her. My parents were old-fashioned, to say the least.

"Well, why don't you come with me to the kitchen? I always find that baking helps me get my thoughts straight. I'd love some company. It's an open invitation, if today doesn't work."

She started to stand, but I put my hand on her arm. Immediately, a connection formed, like a grandmother-granddaughter feeling. I had lost my grandmother when I was ten, but being with Edna made me feel the way I used to when I was with my grandmother. I was drawn to Edna. She felt safe. I'd never trusted someone this quickly, but I wanted someone to talk to. I needed it. I was desperate. I wanted to talk to someone without having to deal with all the questions.

"Edna, you really think it's supposed to be this way? Messy?"

I needed her confirmation one last time. I wanted to stay the course with Mark. It felt right.

She patted my shoulder. "I know it is. Stop thinking so much, and listen to that heart you've been ignoring for a long time. Now, if you're free, I'd love some help."

Relief flooded me as I allowed myself to believe that I wasn't absolutely horrible at this relationship thing. I wanted to spend some more time with Edna. She calmed and reassured me without needing the details of my sordid past.

I wanted to hug Edna. Her gray hair was still in a bun, and her blue plaid shirt only added to the perfect grandma persona.

"I have some free time now."

"Great. Let's get to baking."

I followed her into the kitchen where I spent the next few hours baking and laughing with her. We talked about what type of flour she had bought and which one of us had the better stirring technique. She was such a funny woman.

I was putting my apron up and heading for the front door as Mark was coming in.

I gave him a shy smile. "You're always showing up while I'm here. I'm going to start thinking you're stalking me."

He didn't seem surprised to see me. It was almost as if he had known I would be here. I looked back at Edna, but she was busying herself with some mediocre task.

Mark walked up to me and gave me a sweet one-second kiss on the lips. "You have become my favorite obsession. I was going to get us some sandwiches for a picnic this afternoon. I wanted to take you out on an official first date."

He looked back at Edna and gave her a small nod, and then he refocused his attention on me.

"I think you can bypass the trying-to-swoon-me phase. Last I checked, I was pretty much a sure bet."

His hand went down my cheek. "I'll never take you for granted, Sam. I think it'll be fun. I want to take you to a place I go sometimes."

"I'm a mess from baking this afternoon. Can we swing by my place, so I can change?" I started smacking away all the caked-on powdered sugar.

He gave me a sweet smile. "Sure. I'll drop you off, and then I'll pick up a few things from my place. But you're beautiful the way you are."

I gave him a get-real look as Edna walked up. She winked at me as she handed Mark a picnic basket. Like the kind seen in movies, it was an old-fashioned brown wicker basket with a lid that flipped up.

Mark gave Edna a hug. "Thanks, Edna. I appreciate it."

"Anytime. You take care of her. She's a keeper."

I blushed and smiled at the fact that Edna approved of me. From my conversation with Edna, I knew she and Mark were close. Her approval meant a lot to me because she knew I had a past. She gave me another wink and then walked back to the kitchen, disappearing to finish icing the dozens of cookies that had just come out of the oven.

I turned my attention back to Mark. "So, where are you taking me?"

"It's a surprise."

We walked out the door, and once in his truck, we made our way to the condo complex.

I'm about to go on my first official date.

As I was getting out of the car, Mark said, "Dress comfortable."

"Will do." I gave my salute and went up to my condo.

I needed a shower. Running and stripping at the same time, I practically fell face-first as I tried to shimmy out of my jeans. I showered in record time, quicker than flash lightning. I ran to my closet and started looking at my clothes. I needed something comfortable and not over the top, something simple and cute. In the end, I went with a knee-length cotton skirt and a plaid sleeveless shirt with ruffles going down the front with the buttons. It seemed outdoorsy, but it was still adorable, and it showed off my assets at the same time. I put my hair up into a ponytail with a hair tie, and I did my makeup in more of a natural look. After grabbing my purse, I headed for the door to wait for Mark in the parking lot. When I opened the door, there he was, standing with a bouquet of wildflowers. I loved them, and I gave a shy smile since I hadn't expected this.

He handed them to me and said, "You're gorgeous."

"Thanks." I brought the flowers to my chest and smelled them as we walked to his vehicle. "Wildflowers are my favorite."

He squeezed me tighter to him as we made it to the truck. My insides were all jittery. It had been a long time since I received flowers from a guy.

My curiosity of what he had up his sleeve got the best of me. "When do I get to find out where we are going?"

"When we get there."

Gah! His state-the-obvious routine was utterly annoying at times.

He helped me into the vehicle and gave me a kiss before closing the door and getting in himself.

I decided to try to play dirty. "I should probably tell Allison where I'm going. She'll be worried."

"Taken care of. I talked to her this morning."

My mouth dropped open, and then I closed it. I was at a loss for words.

"Sam, you're mine this evening."

That statement alone had desire blossoming inside me.

We drove for an hour, and his calmness made me feel more and more like myself.

"So, Sport, tell me about your family."

He smiled fondly. "I have a sister who's three years younger than me. My parents were high school sweethearts. My dad was actually drafted to go pro-football, but he had an unexpected knee injury. I think that's where I get my love for the game. I've been throwing a ball since I was a toddler."

"Do they come here to visit you often from Colorado?"

"Yes, some. Mostly during the season to attend the games. We're a close-knit, all-in-each-other's-business kind of family. They'll be excited to meet you."

I wasn't ready to delve too deeply into thinking about meeting his parents. I had never met someone's parents as a girlfriend. The thought terrified me, so I buried it for the time being.

As Edna had said, *One day at a time.*

Mark interrupted my thoughts, changing the subject, which I was thankful for. "So, how did you and Allison meet?"

"Our parents were friends, so it was pretty much a requirement. Good thing we actually liked each other. We got into a lot of mischief together. She actually taught me a thing or two."

Mark gave me a surprised look. It was funny how everyone pictured Allison as the sweet little girl and could never imagine her instigating most of the things we had gotten in trouble for.

"Yes, Allison has a mischievous side."

He looked at me endearingly. "I'd say you were right there with her."

"Damn straight I was."

We drove up a mountain and then pulled off the road. It was bumpy as we traversed the rougher terrain. There wasn't much room between the truck and the brush. The foliage was lush green, and it felt like we were entering another world. The road ended, and a small path was in front of us. We got out of the vehicle, and Mark grabbed the picnic basket and quilt.

Reaching for the quilt, I said, "I can carry that."

He handed it over and pointed to the little path I had noticed earlier. "This way. I want you to see the sunset. I like to come up here. It reminds me of being home in Colorado."

The path got thicker and thicker with underbrush, and it felt as if we were passing through another dimension. Our pace was slow as Mark moved branches out of the way for me to pass by, unscathed. The forest smelled of earth and life, causing me to take cleansing deep breaths. I loved clean air.

A few minutes later, we walked into an opening, and we were standing on a ledge, looking over the entire city. Birds chirped in the distance while leaves rustled in the wind. It was a stunning sight with everything being a radiant green at the beginning of summer. Mark grabbed my hand and interlaced our fingers.

I whispered, "Thank you."

Mark squeezed my hand. "I'm glad I was able to share this with you. I've imagined this moment."

I wasn't sure what to say, so I squeezed his hand back. *This is what a perfect moment feels like.*

He set the picnic basket down and then turned me to him. He bent down and gave me a kiss as the sun lowered, casting bright orange rays all around us. When he pulled away, we dopily stared at each other.

No, I was wrong. This is what perfection feels like.

He spread out the quilt as the sun continued to set. The magnificent hues of oranges and purples were electrifying. We sat and ate until I couldn't take another bite. This morning, Allison had mentioned talking to Mark, and I hadn't paid much attention to it. I now knew why they had spoken. She must have given a list of all my favorite foods because he'd had all of them in that basket—chicken salad sandwiches, deviled eggs, and chocolate cake.

It was nearly dusk as Mark began putting all the remnants of food back into the basket. While his back was turned, I unbuttoned my shirt and left it open as I slid off my shoes. I was not getting totally naked without a partner in crime. If we were to get caught, we would get caught together. I unsnapped the front clasp of my bra and leaned back on my elbows. He was turning to grab the last container when his eyes caught a glimpse of me, and he froze.

"See something you like, Sport?"

"You're a dream come true, Sam."

I stood up and walked over to him in his seated position. As I knelt before him, his right finger lightly grazed my nipple. From that small touch, my desire ratcheted up tenfold. I unzipped him, and I was about to free him when he grabbed my hand, halting my movement.

"Shit, Sam. The condoms are in the truck."

I looked back for my purse and remembered leaving it in the truck. *Shit*. Closing my eyes, I took a deep breath. "I'm clean and on birth control. We can go back to the truck, or we can stop using condoms. It's up to you." I pulled away for a second. I didn't want his decision to be made because of lust.

"I'm clean, too, I swear it. As long as you are absolutely sure with this, I would love nothing more than to have no barriers between us. I've already felt you, and it was the most incredible feeling I've ever had."

I leaned back in and finished freeing him. When I unsnapped my panties, a groan came from Mark.

"I fucking love those panties."

He was driving me insane with his barely there touches on my breasts. I crawled up onto his lap, straddled him, and then positioned his erection to where it almost breached my entrance. Repeating this little movement, I took him in a little more each time. I could tell I was driving him mad as his touches began to turn into full-out groping. I reveled in the sensation and closed my eyes as I moaned. The moment my eyes closed, he pushed into me all the way.

That caused me to open my eyes. "Yes, please, Mark. Take me…take me hard. I need it rough."

He stood up, still fully inside me, and he brought my back to the nearest tree. The bark scraping against me created another sensation to my already sensitized skin. He began pounding into me, and I took it.

Love it.

Need it.

Want it.

"Yes, Mark. Fuck me to oblivion."

He started pushing in deeper, causing me to rub against the tree harder. He bent down and bit my nipple hard, making me scream. I was clawing at his back as my body was overloaded with sensation. Fast, rough, and hard made sense to me. He hit my G-spot one last time and had me screaming for more as I flew into my orgasm. He released himself into me as he said my name. In this moment, it felt as if he possessed me.

"I love being inside you like this," he said.

Having him in me brought us closer together. Even though we had already been together like this, this time felt as if we were sealing a bond between us. We both sagged to the ground while he was still semihard inside me. He kissed me, cherished me, adored me.

"Thank you for bringing me here. It was the perfect first date." I nipped his lip.

Pulling away, he said, "You're more than welcome. It was the perfect first date. I swear, I'm going to treat you right, Sam. Will you stay with me tonight?"

Taking a deep breath, I mustered up the courage I knew I had in me somewhere, so I could try to take this step. "I'll try. I can't promise I'll make it through the night, but I'll try."

He stroked his finger along my jaw. "Just tell me if you need to go home, and I'll take you. No questions, no pressure. I'll take you home immediately. Promise me though that you'll tell me if you need to leave."

"I promise."

CHAPTER
10

Damien, Allison, Mark, and I were leaving for Colorado today, and honestly, I was exhausted from this week. My schedule was beyond screwed-up at this point.

Each night, Mark had taken me on some sort of date—movies, dinner, and a hot-air balloon ride. They had been wonderful, thoughtful, and filled with off-the-charts, hot, wild monkey sex. Since I'd said I would try the relationship thing, it was more than sex at this point, but nevertheless, the sex had still been incredible. My mind had kept trying to reduce it to a fuck, but I'd known it was more.

I had barely slept since I started trying to stay the night at Mark's place. Needless to say, I was making progress at a turtle's pace on the length of time I'd stayed there after going to bed. He must have been as exhausted as I was from my erratic behavior, but he never complained. Not feeling pressure from Mark helped and encouraged me to keep trying.

I remembered back to how the movie date following the picnic had ended.

We were pulling into the condo complex. He parked his truck outside my condo and turned my way.

"Will you stay with me tonight? I'll take you home the moment you ask to go home."

I took a deep breath. Last night, after the sunset picnic, I had barely made it into bed before I was asking to go home. "I'll try, but it'll probably end up like last night."

Mark put the truck in reverse and then pierced me with his green eyes. He stopped the truck again and grabbed my hand, forming a connection between us. He brought it to his lips. "Sam, stay as long as you feel comfortable. As of right now, I'm grateful for each extra minute I have with you. There's no pressure, no expectations. I want to spend every moment I can with you."

Taking a deep breath, I responded, "Okay. I'm not good at this."

He countered, "I think you're perfect at this."

I gave him a small smile, and he put the truck back in reverse. He drove to his condo across the parking lot. We made our way up to the door, and my mind was in a haze as Mark talked about our evening. I tried to smile and squeeze his hand in agreement. He probably knew I was nervous, and he was trying to calm me. My nerves were working a number on me.

Walking into his room, he asked, "How do you want to sleep tonight?"

"T-shirt."

I needed a barrier to protect myself if I was going to try to sleep through the night with Mark. Normally, being naked with Mark was more freeing, but it terrified me right now. If I was naked and he touched me lovingly, it would cause panic to rise inside me. He had the power to hurt me emotionally, and it was unsettling to give someone that type of control. He handed me one of his T-shirts, and I put it on and then crawled into bed. He left on his boxers and lay beside me, making himself comfortable. His hand drifted to mine, and our fingers wove together.

"Thanks for trying, Sam. I like having you in my bed."

I squeezed his hand back. "Thank you. Night, Mark." I wasn't sure what else to say. I sounded so lame and not romantic at all.

This was beyond uncharted territory for me. I was determined to show progress even if fear was starting to filter into my mind more prominently. I wanted to stay in his bed for as long as I could. I had already made it longer than last night, and that little victory made me want to shout from the rooftops.

I took deep breaths as I lay there, looking at the ceiling, counting the seconds. Each time I would think I was getting sleepy, my mind would start running a marathon.

What if I have a nightmare that I haven't had in years, and he hears me screaming? What would he think? What if I can never stay the night? What if he gets tired of waiting for me?

I feigned sleeping, and I knew the minute Mark was asleep. His hand instinctively moved up to my waist, and it caused my breath to hitch. This was so intimate.

Would he want this connection if he knew how dirty I am? I can't do this.

I need to go home.

But I don't want this to end with him.

I sat up, and Mark immediately woke up.

"Please take me home, Mark. I'm sorry."

He looked at me and smiled. "There's nothing to be sorry for, Sam. I have you, and that's all that matters."

We got dressed, and holding my hand, he walked me to my door. I gave him a hug and buried my head in his chest. He smelled so good.

Muffled, I said into his chest, "I'll keep trying."

He lifted my chin to meet his eyes, and then he gave me a loving kiss. "Don't stress about it. Sleep tight. Call me if you need anything. Thank you for telling me."

"Thanks for being patient with me."

"There's nothing to be patient about, Sam. You're worth waiting for."

The following night, we had gone to dinner, and it had ended the same way. Even after returning to my bed on both nights, I hadn't fallen asleep until I'd received the text from Mark saying he was headed to training. I'd tossed and turned each night, wondering what would have happened if I had lasted five more minutes.

Would the panic have lessened? Honestly, I don't know. Is my past impeding me from moving on with my future?

Last night, after the hot-air balloon ride, I had felt determined to stay with him in his condo all night.

I awoke from a light sleep, and I felt panic starting to consume me.

I had fallen asleep on the couch as we watched TV, and Mark had carried me to bed. This seemed to work best because my mind could focus on the movie and not being in his bed.

Mark woke up. I looked at the clock and realized I had made it three hours in his bed.

Sleepily, he asked, "Sam, sweetheart, do you want me to take you home?"

Trying to calm down, I responded quietly, "No, I'm going to go sleep on the couch."

It was dark, and he was rubbing my hand. He gave me a small kiss on the hand, and I could feel him smiling.

He started to sit up as he stretched. "I'll take the guest bedroom. You stay in here. This is a better mattress."

The thought of being in his bedroom without him terrified me more. My body jerked into an upright position. "That's okay. I can just go home."

He dragged a hand down his face. "I'm sorry. I'll back off. If you want the couch, it's yours. If you want me to take you home, I will."

I felt bad for being so dysfunctional. "I'm sorry."

His finger came underneath my chin. "Sam, don't be sorry. I shouldn't have pushed. I'll take you however I can have you."

"I want to stay here. I'll sleep on the couch."

He grabbed my hand and kissed it. "Sounds good. Let me get you some blankets."

I had succeeded in staying at Mark's place the entire night even if it was on the couch, but I'd tossed and turned all night. My body would yearn for him when we weren't together, but my mind would always step in and be the voice of reason, saying I was too messed-up to deserve him. The two needed to get on the same page before I lost too much more sleep. I was considering medicine to help me before I became an insomniac.

Edna was a godsend. She'd helped me keep it all in perspective. I had gone to see her a couple of times this week.

Yesterday, after going on four days, including the night of the picnic, with limited sleep, I had traipsed through the deli doors, and I practically collapsed on a table.

Edna came out in her little blue gingham apron. "Get in here, missy. We have some cookies to bake."

Dragging my ass, I headed into the kitchen for cookie therapy.

"So, what's the matter? You look like someone stole your puppy."

Leaning on the counter, I absentmindedly stirred some sifted flour. "Mark has been asking me to stay at his place, and I only make it a little while before I panic and leave."

She pulled a few more ingredients out of the cabinet. "How long did you make it the first night?"

"The night of the picnic, I had to leave the moment I woke up. I fell asleep on the couch and Mark carried me to his room. I woke up panicked and left without telling him. We had a fight, but I agreed to tell him going forward when I needed to go home. When we went to the movies, I made it about five minutes after getting into his bed before he took me to my place. After our dinner date, I made it one hour, laying in his bed. Last night, after our hot-air balloon ride, I slept around three hours before I had to move to the couch."

It was embarrassing, talking to Edna about sleeping with a guy since I wasn't married. My parents would go through the roof. They were so traditional that it was almost extreme at times.

Edna was taking it in stride, and it hadn't seemed to faze her. "Can you add the eggs and sugar to the flour?"

Without thinking, I added them and stirred.

"Now, add the vanilla."

I complied and stirred absentmindedly.

"Can those cookies be baked as they are right now?"

Sometimes, she is crazy. Looking at her, confused, I responded, "No. They're still missing the chocolate chips and that tidbit of almond extract you add."

She smiled. "But you've made a step in the right direction to get to chocolate chip cookies."

My eyes went to hers.

"You see, any step forward is a step in the right direction, regardless of how far you still have to go."

A few tears escaped as I went to hug her. "Edna, you are so special to me."

"You are to me, too. Now, grab the missing ingredients and finish my cookies."

She swatted my ass with a dish towel as I made my way over toward the last two ingredients.

I truly love that woman.

That piece of advice was sticking to me like glue as I repeated it over and over and over again.

I was also clinging to something Allison's mom had always said. *All we have is today. Yesterday is the past, and we aren't guaranteed tomorrow, so live your life for today.*

That was easier said than done, but I was trying.

I had invited Allison over for breakfast this morning. I knew there was a team meeting, so she would be alone at her house anyway. Plus, I needed to talk to her. She was such a calm force for me, and my mind was such a swirl of emotions and chaotic thoughts.

My phone beeped as I was setting the glasses of orange juice out. It was Allison.

> *Allison: It's me. I'm at the door and taking precautions since the last two times have scarred me for life. Bleaching my brain might be required since I can't get the images out of my head.*
>
> *Me: Funny. I'll be right there.*

I opened the door, and she was standing there, wearing a cute little blue summer dress. She was pleased as punch with her text message. At least she was holding a steaming cup of coffee from my favorite coffee shop.

She was giggling. "Morning, sunshine. I'm not taking any chances since you two can't seem to keep your hands off each other." She nudged me lovingly.

"Morning to you, too. Is that for me?"

I went to grab my sweet nectar, as I'd sometimes called it, but she pulled it out of my reach. I gave her a dirty look.

"Maybe."

She was keeping it just out of reach as she gave the cup a slight teasing shake.

Damn it. After living on no sleep for three days, I needed my caffeine fix pronto. I adopted my mama's no-nonsense tone as I said, "Allison, give that to me, or I'll tell Damien you're inhaling caffeine."

"Traitor." She playfully gave me the cup.

"I know you're eating basics, so I got some plain bagels this morning. Damien said that you've also had luck with mangoes."

"You're the best, Sam."

She made her way to the kitchen counter and started fixing herself a bagel.

Ah, I would crawl to the ends of the earth for a vanilla latte. I took a sip, and my body started to feel rejuvenated.

Allison perched on the edge of a seat and started nibbling slowly on her bagel. Right before she took another small bite, she said, "Oh, I have a few updates that transpired this morning. Martin's girlfriend can't go to Colorado because of a last-minute photo shoot, but Martin can still come. He had to change it to a one-day trip because of some hotel emergency he's having. Damien tried to cancel, but I threatened to tie him to the damn boat. I think Damien somehow bribed Martin to have a crisis, so it would be changed to a one-day trip. Oh, you and Martin are both on my shit list. You guys group-texting Damien about what a good idea it would be for you to take me to a strip club while he is on the rafting trip nearly sent him over the edge."

Allison gave me a wry look, and I laughed.

"Remember payback is a bitch," she said.

Between laughs, I responded, "I don't know why giving your hubby one hell of a time is so much fun."

She rolled her eyes and chuckled. "He can be a tad overprotective at times, but I love him." She sighed and then went back to picking at some fruit on her plate. "So, how did the hot-air balloon ride go last night? I've always wanted to have sex in one."

The sincerity in her voice made me laugh again. Allison was probably a wildcat behind closed doors. However, those were details I would *never* need. Oddly enough, I had thought the same thing, and I'd been disappointed when we were told we had to have someone with us.

"There was someone in there with us. Despite that fact, it was wonderful, like the rest of the dates. He held me as we watched the sunset while floating in the sky. He goes out of his way to make me feel special, but he isn't overbearing about it, if that makes sense."

She smiled. "Oh, I'm sure he goes out of his way to make you feel special." She wagged her eyebrows up and down for added effect.

"Shut it. On another note, thanks for the coffee. You're my fave, especially when you come bearing gifts in the form of caffeine." I raised my cup a little in a salute.

"I couldn't have you irritable for the inquisition. Just wait though. The overbearing part will come. It might not be as drastic as Damien, but I wager that Mark will have his moments."

I took a seat next to her, building the courage for what I wanted to ask. She had provided the perfect segue to the topic I wanted to discuss.

"Does it bother you when Damien is overbearing?" I tried to busy myself with some fruit on my plate, so eye contact wasn't needed.

She stopped eating, noting my serious tone, as she turned my way. "No. To everyone else, I'm sure it seems like madness, but why he is that way makes sense to me. I would imagine every relationship is completely different. I think as long as it's healthy, then that's all that matters."

I scrunched my brow in confusion. My first instinct was to withdraw from this conversation and say something sarcastic, but Allison was the safest person to discuss these matters with. I knew she would tell me the truth and not judge me.

Pushing the lump down in my throat, I continued on, "What do you consider healthy?"

She took another bite, mulling over my question. She was probably thinking about the wording more than the answer itself. After taking a sip of orange juice, she responded, "Healthy, to me, is having complete trust and loving each other unconditionally. You don't start off right at that spot, but as long as you keep building toward that, I consider that healthy."

My appetite was gone, and I turned to her, giving her my full attention. "Do you and Damien know everything about each other? Is that what you consider trust? Does it bother you that he's had multiple partners?"

She mirrored my movement. "I don't know everything about Damien, and I'm sure I've forgotten to share some stuff about myself. As you know, he has a bit more of a colorful past than I do. However, if I wanted to know something, he would tell me, and I think that's where the trust lies. I don't need all the details of his past, but before I married him, I needed his willingness to share any details. Because of Ben, Damien had to share more graphic parts of his past that I would have rather not heard about. Do I like the fact that other people know how wonderful my husband is in bed? No, but I can't change it, and it wouldn't stop me from being with him. It's part of who he is. I have his present and his future, and that's what matters to me. As my mom always said, 'The past is the past. It's over and done with. Look at the now and the future. That's where the new chapters of life lie.'"

I allowed her words to permeate my brain. "Do you think there are any exceptions to that?"

Her tone was gentle as she responded, "Sam, that's just my opinion. I think you and Mark will define what works for you. I know that if I had slept with someone prior to Damien, he would want every single detail. I don't need that from him."

"But do you think a relationship can last without disclosing everything?" I prayed she would give me the answer I needed.

She took another bite. I was grateful that she wasn't just answering off-the-cuff and that she was giving it to me straight.

Taking a deep breath, she looked at me. "Only you and Mark can decide that. Only the two of you can decide what works and what doesn't work." She laid her hand on my shoulder. "I'm here when you want to talk about what happened, Sam. I'm here for you. I always have been. It might help for you to share now that you're ready to give this part of your life a chance."

A tear streamed down my face, and I hastily wiped it away. "I know, and I'm getting closer, but I can't…yet."

"Hey, sweetie, I'm not putting you on a timeline. Just promise me one thing even if you never tell me…"

"What's that?" My voice slightly cracked as I spoke. I worked to regain my composure.

"Try to forgive yourself for whatever it is you're blaming and tormenting your mind with." She gave me a gentle squeeze and maintained eye contact. "The past can eat you away until there's not much left."

"You don't know that it's not my fault." I looked down at my knotted fingers.

"I know you, Sam, and that's enough for me to be certain that it's not your fault without you ever telling me."

I didn't know what to say. She loved me so much. I grabbed her and hugged her tight, and she returned the hug.

Pushing me back slightly, she looked me in the eye. "I think Mark is good for you. When your instinct tells you to run, stay and talk it out. Okay?"

"What makes you say that?"

"I tried to run from Damien, and a very good friend of mine helped me stick it out. Now, thanks to her, I'm happily married to the man of my dreams."

She gave me another squeeze, and I smiled. It made me feel good, knowing I had helped her out with her relationship even if I was terrible at having one myself. It gave me hope.

I tapped my chin. "Hmm…maybe I can convince Wales that we're even again, so he can quit holding that damn bet over my head. I still can't believe that he got you to understand sports and not mind attending the events. I tried for years. I just don't get it."

Shaking my head in disgust and irritation earned me a little giggle from my dear friend.

Allison knew I was ready to move on from the serious conversation. She knew me more than I gave her credit for sometimes. Not pushing me to tell her what had happened made her a saint in my eyes.

"Oh, Sam, it's the power of the P. You never had a chance."

And with that, she took a big bite, and I giggled.

We arrived in Colorado in record time. Flying in a personal jet, especially one with a bedroom, had definitely been the way to travel. Before even boarding the plane, Allison and I had decided that we were commandeering the bedroom and taking a nap. If I didn't get my sleep schedule back on track soon, my nights and days were going to be reversed. I was officially starting my job in a few weeks, and I needed to be on top of my game.

Damien and Mark had stayed in the main cabin and worked. I had heard Mark ask Damien about suggestions regarding PR announcements, which caused that flip-flop motion in my stomach to occur. At this time, I was going to ignore the upcoming announcement of our relationship until it actually happened. Our relationship going public in the media was too much to think about right now.

We were driving to Mark's home, and Allison and Damien were in a separate car in case Damien needed to leave unexpectedly. Security was with them, and I thought Allison had probably insisted on that since they could be overwhelming at times. I needed to be as calm as possible.

My phone pinged with a text message.

> Allison: *We are going to stop off at a place I saw. We'll be about thirty minutes or so behind.*
>
> Me: *Sounds good.*

I knew she was giving me a few moments alone with Mark, so I could acclimate myself to being at my boyfriend's place without other people. *I love her.*

My nerves were a little frayed. Mark and I had not talked any more about my erratic night behavior. Mark was something I definitely wanted, but the toll it was taking on me mentally was exhausting. I knew his parents were nearby, and I wasn't sure if I was ready to meet them.

As we continued on the drive, I felt like I needed to say something, but I didn't have the nerve. I hated how insecure this made me feel. The world saw me as an outgoing girl without a care in the world, but the inside of me was a totally different person.

I stared off into the distance at the beautiful mountains, trying to calm myself. There was a residual snowcap on the highest of the mountain peaks. We were leaving a quaint town, and at the base of the mountain, we turned off onto a road. The coloring of the green foliage was amazing. Trees surrounded us on both sides of the roads. It felt like I was passing into another world, my own fairy tale.

We drove through iron gates and entered a driveway. His house was incredible. It was a stone and wood mixture with a modern and rustic feel. A huge iron light fixture hung from the front porch. Trees were all over the yard, strategically placed to add to the ambience. It wasn't what I had expected, but it felt like Mark at the same time.

He placed a hand on my moving leg, and I startled slightly. "What do you think?" His voice was low.

I looked over at him, and he actually seemed nervous.

"It's beautiful. I love it."

He smiled, seeming truly relieved. "I'm glad. My parents live across the lake behind the house. My sister and her husband live halfway between our places. We aren't going to meet them this time around. Maybe next time."

The fact that he wanted there to be a next time made me smile. I was also relieved that I wouldn't have the pressure of first impressions with his family, and I relaxed some.

"Okay. Do you guys have the entire lake?" I looked back out the window and noticed the water behind the house for the first time.

"We have all but one section. We bought the tracts when they became available over the years. It gives us some isolation. My dad did well with his investments, and I haven't done too badly with the team. Between the both of us, we've been able to buy land as it becomes available. Let's get out, and I'll show you around."

I opened the truck door and took in the smell of cedar. It was rejuvenating. The mountains in the background created one of those settings seen in paintings. Mark grabbed me from behind and pulled me to him.

He kissed the back of my head as I murmured, "Thank you for bringing me here."

He turned me around, and he looked at me for a moment. It was as if he was about to say something, but he decided to kiss me instead. It was slow and the most loving kiss he had given me yet. He pulled back and looked in my eyes again. His green eyes sparkled in the light. He grabbed my hand and pulled me toward the house.

As we walked up the stairs, I worked on squelching that earlier fear, remembering Edna's confirmation to me that messy was right. Mark looked at me so tenderly, and I reveled in it, pushing aside those other unpleasant feelings.

We walked inside, and Mark began showing me around the place. Wood beams lined the ceiling. The house was done in browns and reds. I instantly felt at home with the warmth, and I pictured myself curled up by the fireplace while snow fell outside. It had just enough of a modern edge that made it eclectic. We were in the kitchen, and Mark was pouring me a glass of wine when my phone chirped. It was Allison.

Allison: We are almost there. Just trying to save my eyes from another unwanted visual.

Me: Shut it. I don't want to have to call you the B word.

Allison: I'd rather be called the B word than walk into P-and-V action.

Me: Funny. Biotch.

Allison: Muah! Xoxo

Me: Xoxo

I couldn't help but chuckle. I wished she hadn't walked in on Mark and me at my condo because she was never going to let me live that down.

"They're on their way."

"What's so funny?" His brow quirked up as he finished pouring his own glass of wine.

We clinked glasses as I responded, "Allison refuses to walk in unannounced anytime we are alone."

"Smart girl."

Mark put down his glass, and I followed suit. He started to prowl toward me, and I knew what was on his mind.

"No, no, no." I started to round the island, keeping it between us. "You stay away."

He continued to stalk me as I laughed nervously. If he touched me, my body would ignite, and all normal reasoning would be gone. My mind was craving a hard, fast release.

"I mean it, Mark. We have tonight."

He stilled for a moment, but then he continued on, and I kept going around and around the island, keeping him on the opposite side.

"If you don't stop, I won't show you what I brought for this evening," I said.

That made him stop dead in his tracks. He put his hands up, surrendering this game, and slowly walked to me.

"What do you have for me tonight?" he asked.

His hands moved to my hips and he pulled me against him. I felt his breath on my lips. My stomach quivered at the thought of what his lips had done to me on numerous occasions.

"You'll have to wait to find out."

We both slowly inched our mouths together, and our breaths mingled. The moment our lips touched, they fused together, like two magnets drawn to each other. His tongue swiped across my lips for entry, and I granted it to him immediately. His hands were slowly moving down my backside, leaving a trail of fire in their wake. My libido came roaring to the front.

I was about to suggest taking this to his bedroom when I heard, "Holy hell, you guys. I even gave you a warning that I was coming. Seriously?"

I disengaged and saw Allison with her hands on her hips. Even agitated, she was still adorable.

"You guys, there are some things that cannot be unseen," she said.

Mark obviously wasn't going to respond. *Traitor.* Though, in his defense, I'd left him completely on his own when he tried to be all suave the time she caught us spread out on the floor of my entryway.

Damien strolled into the room, put his hands on Allison's shoulders, and looked at all of us.

Here we go.

Speaking to his wife, he asked, "What's going on? Sam looks like she's about to die of embarrassment, and you look like you've seen something out of a horror show."

Being the intelligent man Damien was, he quickly caught on and gave one of those cat-ate-the-canary grins at Mark.

Boys. My face heated even more, if that were possible. I wasn't sure why I was getting embarrassed and not embracing it and playing it off like I normally would. If it had been me with an easy conquest, I honestly wouldn't have given a damn, but being with Mark made it all different.

Allison looked up at Damien and saw his smile. She gave him a light smack on the chest and simply responded, "Do not encourage them."

Smiling her sweet smile, she turned back to Mark and me. I pleaded with my eyes for her to change the subject.

She answered my request when she asked, "What are the plans for dinner?"

I gave her a wink, and she smiled.

I knew I was actually getting off easy compared to the shit I would be giving her, and she knew it. It was obvious what she was doing since she was still only eating the basics.

Becoming the gracious host, Mark joined the conversation. "I had the house stocked with meals, or we can go into town and eat. Whatever the ladies prefer."

I looked at Allison, and we both blurted out, "Here," in unison. We looked at each other and laughed.

I guessed we both wanted a peaceful night in. With everyone's hectic schedules, it was actually a treat to be able to relax and dine.

Mark gave me a kiss on the cheek. "I'll get dinner ready if you want to go freshen up."

After offering to help Mark, Damien kissed Allison. The love I felt in this room caused my heart to clench in pain. I wanted that myself, but I knew it wasn't likely.

I scurried out of the room before Mark could see my face.

Dinner had been delicious, and we were now sitting on the back porch, sipping wine on the love seats, with the exception of Allison, who was having juice.

She yawned, and Damien rose, holding out his hand.

"I think we are going to turn in for the evening. I guess we'll be leaving in the early hours, if we're still going," Damien said.

Allison stood. "There's no option. You guys are going. Period."

She gave a sweet little smile to Mark and me before heading to the room with Damien.

Mark pulled me closer, and we stared out onto the lake on this clear night.

"Do you see that clearing over there?" His finger pointed to a place to the left of the house.

"Yes."

"That's where I plan on building a guest house this spring. It would be a smaller version of this place. I'd like to show you the plans sometime to see what you think."

I laid my head on his as I yawned. "I'd like that."

"Why don't you head upstairs to the bedroom while I lock up? It's been a long day."

Standing, I stretched. Refusing to let fear enter my mind, I replied, "Perfect. See you upstairs in a few."

He gave me a loving kiss, and I tried to walk nonchalantly into the house.

My heart started beating faster as I climbed the stairs. I refused to think about the fact that I still hadn't slept an entire night with Mark. When he couldn't see me anymore, I bolted up to our room to get ready for bed. I had purchased lingerie as a surprise for him, and I was nervous that he might not like it because he had only seen me in more provocative clothing. The white ruffle-tiered chiffon nightie had a satin ribbon that tied below the deep V lace cups. The nightie hit just below my ass. It was sophisticated but had some flare to it at the same time.

I ran my hands through my hair a few times, adding volume. Hopefully, this would get Mark in the mood. I liked dressing up. Plus, I needed the distraction. I needed that feeling to keep all my other thoughts at bay.

I can do this tonight. I will stay the night with him.

After putting all my stuff back into my bag, I headed into the bedroom. Mark was pulling the pillows off the bed. He looked to be deep in thought. It all seemed so domesticated, like we had been doing this exact same thing in this house for years. My throat tightened as I saw a life I wanted.

Mark glanced behind him as if he was checking to see if I had come out yet. He saw me and stopped pulling the bedspread back. He stood there and stared, not saying a word. I began to wonder if I had taken it too far, getting this type of lingerie versus my more crazy, seductive outfits.

As I was right on the verge of turning around, Mark said, "You're gorgeous...unbelievably breathtaking."

I smiled. "Thanks. I was hoping you would like it."

I gave a little turn, and before I completed it, I was up in his arms. My legs automatically locked around his waist, and our mouths connected. The rush to finish took over as we started devouring each other.

He walked me back to his bed, and his hands began to roam. He finally made it underneath my nightie and groaned in approval when he found I had chosen to stay bare. We crashed onto the bed. He pulled back and practically ripped off his clothes, not giving me a chance to help. I loved his wild abandonment that caused all my chaotic thoughts to disappear. In moments like these, my raging hormonal fire took over, consuming everything else in flames. The freeness that I felt when I had an orgasm was what drove me to these moments, caused me to want these moments, and kept me seeking these moments over and over again.

I was sprawled on the bed as he stood there, staring at me for a millisecond, and something changed. He reached for my foot and slowly began moving his finger along the arch and up to my calf and then to the inner part of my thigh. It left a wake of goose bumps, causing me to moan. I wanted him inside me. He repeated the motion on my other leg.

Why the hell is he taking his time? We never take our time. I was getting frustrated, needing that relief that made my mind blank out and leave reality.

I looked down. He was hard, and I knew he wanted me badly. His erection jumped each time he touched me. He slowly climbed on the bed and began kissing my leg where his fingers had left off. He kissed to the apex of my thigh. As he made it to my core, his tongue came out and tasted me thoroughly. His mouth went to my cleft, giving each centimeter of me equal attention. As he made his way back up to my clit, two fingers slipped inside, and he began to suck me harder. It felt so good, having the constant pressure on my sensitive flesh, while he stroked my walls. I was incoherently moaning as the tingles began to take over my body, signaling I was close to my release.

He slightly nibbled on my nub, and it sent my body over the edge as my body was consumed with euphoria. While I was still on the high, his hands started to move up my legs to my stomach. He worshiped my body as his lips went to my breasts.

"You're incredible. I could taste you all day."

"Please, I need you."

My mind froze when I realized what I had said. I had never admitted that I needed someone before. Mark came over to me and was smiling sexily at me, satisfied with my admission, as his green eyes raked me in. His stomach muscles were taut, and I reached up to run my fingers along them. His body trembled beneath my touch. His mouth slowly came down to the exposed section of skin between my breasts, and he started kissing me there. I wanted him to rip the clothes off my body, but he did the opposite as he made his way to my nipple and sucked it into his mouth. I had just had an intense orgasm, but I needed another one.

One hand snaked around my back as his mouth continued to suck each of my nipples. He lifted my arms, and he slowly removed my nightie, leaving me completely exposed. I had been naked around him countless times, but this time felt more intimate. Before I had time to process, he laid me back down, and his mouth sought mine, his tongue slowly exploring. Our tongues danced together, fully tasting and appreciating each other. The heat of his body, the touch of hands, the feeling of his tongue had my brain completely scrambled.

I felt him slowly slide into me. The slow and sensual feeling was exquisite. We found our rhythm, and it was intense. Our hands were memorizing each other as we fit our bodies together.

I was on the brink of a cataclysmic orgasm. Mark must have been right there with me as he pulled back and locked his eyes with mine. He continued to build me as he pumped into me. The moment our eyes met, I felt the heat spread as my orgasm took hold, like a wave building toward the shore. Mark reached his point of no return at the same time I did, and we maintained eye contact as he spilled himself into me.

"I'm never letting you go, Sam."

Those words caused my world to snap back into reality. I smiled, but I knew it was tentative.

Mark and I had just made love. We hadn't fucked. We had made love. I had never made love with anyone before, and I thought my heart was going to seize in fear.

CHAPTER
12

I lay there for what seemed like an eternity while my heart hammered a million beats a second. Mark had a near death grip on me, and he hadn't let go since he had slipped out of me and pulled me to his side. I wasn't able to speak. Shocked was too simple of a word to express how I was feeling right now. My mouth refused to work, so I stayed silent. Without a word, he pulled the covers on top of us, and I closed my eyes. Like a coward, I pretended to fall asleep after his admission of never letting me go.

I now understood all of his slow movements. He had slowed it down and kept me drugged with want. Realization of what we had done had not happened until after we made love, and my heart had split in two. I wanted him to never let me go, but I knew I would never be what he deserved.

Finally, his grip loosened, and his breathing evened out. Mentally, I sighed and slowly extricated myself from him, moving a centimeter at a time until I was freed. After the week we'd had, he had to be exhausted.

Quickly, I went to the bathroom and slipped on my boxer shorts and a T-shirt. I tiptoed faster than lightning as I flew down the stairs to the patio door. I fumbled with the lock and ran out onto the back porch. Leaning against the rail, I sucked in air as tears streamed down my face.

How did my world totally change in such a small amount of time? How did I let this get so out of control? How did I fall so hard and so quickly?

It made no sense, but I knew I had to end this immediately. Only heartache was in store for me since I could never be the person Mark needed, and I would never be worthy of having him. The thought left me cold. The old me seemed lost after these couple of weeks with Mark. She was gone and replaced by someone who wanted more, someone I wasn't familiar with.

Where do I go from here?

"Sam?"

I spun around and saw Allison standing on the doorstep, holding a glass of milk.

She started walking toward me and then set the glass down on the table. "What happened? What's wrong?"

I sank to my knees, facing the lake, and I started to sob. Immediately, she was at my side, stroking my back. Needing the comfort, I turned to my best friend and sobbed four years' worth of crying that I had stuffed in the very bottom of my soul, not letting it out until now.

"Shh…it's okay, Sam. I'm here."

I worked on getting my sobbing under control.

As I was quieting down, Allison asked, "What happened, sweetie?"

In between unladylike sniffles, I whispered, "Mark made love to me."

I looked up to see her response. Her brows scrunched as she continued to rub circles on my back, which was oddly enough soothing me.

"Did he hurt you?"

"No." I looked down and started playing with my nails, keeping me from making direct eye contact. "I've never made love to anyone before. I only fuck them, Allison. I've never allowed myself to be close to anyone. He's broken through all those walls."

"Sweetie, isn't that a good thing?"

I was thankful beyond belief that I had Allison in this moment. Her motherly voice was comforting. I wanted to purge myself from all the ugliness. I wanted a normal life.

I let down the gates that had kept me guarded and safe for so long, and I felt so exposed. My voice was barely above a whisper as I said, "Not when it makes me realize that I'll never be able to have him. I don't deserve him. He deserves someone who isn't tainted."

"Why do you think you're tainted, Sam? What happened? Talk to me. I'm here for you. Regardless of what it is, I'll still be your best friend afterward."

She squeezed me, and I clung to her like my life depended on it. I swallowed. Part of me wanted to push the truth down, and the other wanted to extricate it from my system forever.

The truth shall set you free.

"Do you remember that New Year's party you told me not to go to our senior year?"

She thought about it and then nodded.

I started playing with the hem of my T-shirt. "I went anyway, and I never told you."

I looked up and waited for the judgment to pass over Allison's features, but it didn't. I only saw compassion, which spurred me to continue.

She continued to rub soothing circles on my back as I kept talking, "That night, Greg was heavily drinking. I'd had a few drinks, but I wasn't drunk." The tears started to fall again. The wind caused the water tracks to be cold, and I focused on that sensation as I told the next part. "The party was out in the Webster's field near my parents' place. I was dancing, and Greg asked for me to come with him. His speech was slurred, and he wasn't acting right, but I went with him anyway. We went to the abandoned barn on the property. When we walked in, we started making out, getting to that point that we would always get to. We were right on the verge of having sex. I always stopped it prior to getting there, and we would get off in other ways. Greg had said he would wait for me to be ready to have sex with him. We were supposed to get married and go to college together. I didn't want our first time to be in a dirty barn. It didn't seem like him because he'd said that when I was ready, he would make it special. I knew something was wrong with him. He wasn't just drunk. When I went to stop our progression…"

I took a deep breath and started again. *This is tough.* "When I went to stop our progression, Greg pinned me to the floor and told me he was tired of being played. He was cursing at me. You know Greg had never raised his voice at me. He was normally so kind and gentle with me. Something was wrong with him, and I wanted to leave. When I tried to stop him, he slapped me a couple of times. It was so hard that it caused me to black out momentarily. My head was already spinning from the alcohol. When I woke up, he was savagely ripping through me. I started screaming for him to get off of me, but no one could hear me with how loud the music was from the party. He was beyond drunk, nearly out of his mind." More tears ran down my face, and my voice became thick. Having to live through this shit again was wretched. I hadn't thought about this night in detail in a long, long time, but it would always be seared in my memory as if it happened yesterday.

Taking a deep breath, I pushed through. "He said some horrible things about me being a tease as he continued raping me. When I kept screaming, he held his hand over my mouth. He didn't stop until he collapsed on me and passed out. I shoved him off of me and ran home."

Leaning into Allison, I started sobbing as she stroked my back.

"Allison, I promised myself I would never get attached to anyone after that night. Greg had promised me the world and then took it from me, ruining me forever. I had trusted him, and he had used it against me. After that, I was able to keep my sexual interaction with guys to sex, no feelings…until Mark. I feel so much for him, but I don't deserve him. I'm tainted."

My sobs racked my body, and I thought I was going to split in two from all the hurt pouring out of me. The ugliness had surfaced, and I wasn't worthy. Allison rocked me and soothed me until I was completely cried out. Finally, I looked up at Allison, and she had tears in her eyes.

"Sam, being raped is a horrible thing. It would affect anyone. Sweetie, you're not tainted, and you deserve to fall in love like anyone else. You need to go to the police to—"

I pulled back. "I'm not going to the police. I've dealt…or I'm trying to deal with that piece of my life. Don't, Allison.

Mark and I won't last, and things will go back to the way they were."

I understood why she wanted me to go to the police, and that was the exact reason I hadn't wanted to tell anyone.

She backed off. "Okay. I'm sorry. I shouldn't have pressed. That's probably why you haven't told me all these years."

I nodded, trying to stop the new flow of tears.

"You're a beautiful person, Sam, inside and out. Don't throw your relationship away with Mark. You deserve him as much as he deserves you."

I started to respond when a familiar voice, deep and husky from sleep, sounded from the house.

"Don't throw us away, Sam. I'm in love with you, past and all."

Allison and I both spun our heads around to the voice. Mark was standing there, bare chested and in his lounge pants, in the shadows casted by the lights in the kitchen. He looked nervous and pained. His muscles were strung tight.

My palms were instantly sweaty as I asked, "What did you hear?"

He stood there as he raked his hands through his blond hair. He didn't say a word. I was terrified that he now knew my dirty little secret.

Shit. Shit. Shit.

Allison gave me a hug and whispered, "Talk to him. Let yourself be happy. You deserve it, too. We all do."

I didn't say anything in response as she got up. Part of me wanted to make her stay with me, and the other knew I needed to have this conversation with Mark—alone.

As Allison was crossing the threshold, she leaned up to Mark and whispered something. Right on cue, Damien appeared at the bottom of the steps, looking for her. She patted Mark on the shoulder and then hastily made her way to Damien. She knew I wouldn't want Damien seeing this clusterfuck of a mess I had gotten myself into tonight. Damien looked out onto the back porch as she pulled him back up the stairs.

I sat there and watched Mark at the threshold as he stared at me. He slowly started making his way toward me as if I was a skittish animal ready to run, and in a way, I was. Exhaustion consumed me, and I wanted to get this over with.

We are finished.

There was no way he had said what he just had a few moments ago and not heard what I had told Allison. When he reached me, he held out his hand, and I silently took it while biting my lip to the point of pain. He pulled me close to him, wrapping his arm around me, and he led us off the patio and toward the water. My mind memorized the way I felt when I was in his arms, and I enjoyed these last few minutes I had with him.

We were both barefoot, and the wet grass felt cleansing against my damp, sweaty skin. We approached a dock. At the end, a covered area had plush outdoor furniture that created a seating area. He walked us to the couch, and we sat next to each other. He tried to pull me into him, but I scooted away. I sat on the edge of the cushion, needing some distance. Being that close while he broke up with me would cause me to be weak. My pulse was hammering like a sledgehammer as the end of us approached. I wanted him badly, but I wouldn't fight to keep him if he wanted out. He deserved to be free of me if he wanted it.

His hand came to my back as he spoke softly, "I heard it all, Sam. I walked up to the door right as Allison sank to the floor and started consoling you. I should have let you know that I was there, but I had to know. I had to know if I was the one who had hurt you. I had to know why you kept pulling away from me when I could feel you had feelings for me. I had to know why you disappeared on me for all those months."

I felt defeated. My voice was barely above a whisper as I said, "It wasn't you. I understand what you must think. I'll save you the trouble and end it for us."

He spun me around so quickly and pulled me on his lap. "What the fuck are you talking about? Damn it, Sam. I'm not letting you end us like this. I want you regardless. You're not broken or tainted. You're perfect. I could kill that bastard for touching you like he did. A man should never get to the point that he doesn't have a fucking clue what he's doing to someone. I know you're not ready to say it back, but I'm in love with you. I've been in love with you for a while...ever since you came to the game last year. I knew if I waited, I would get my chance to see where we could go."

Tears started to stream down my face again, and I gave up trying to wipe them away. I thought maybe the first time he had said the L word was because Allison was sitting there, and he hadn't wanted to be a douchebag in front of her, but now, he had said it twice.

I had to double-check though before I hoped too much. "You don't want to end us? Even after finding out how tainted and ruined I am?"

His thumb came out and stroked my cheek. "You are the most perfect person I have ever met. I want to make love to you every day. I want you to give us a chance to find our way. I can't lose you right after I've finally gotten you. Please give this a chance. You're not tainted. You had something horrific happen to you. You're strong, you're courageous, and you're mine." His voice was laced with sincerity, possessiveness, concern, and love.

His eyes sought mine in the moonlight, looking for my confirmation. When I hesitated, only because I was caught up in the moment, he tightened his grip on me as if he was afraid I would bolt.

The pressure caused me to speak. "If at any time my past gets to be too much, I'll understand."

"Sam, it won't. Please don't try to doom us before we begin. I'll never blame you. You need to forgive yourself and allow yourself to be happy...allow us to be happy, together."

"I don't know how you worked your way in, but the thought of walking away from you is impossible now. I've never let myself be this close to anyone, and I'm scared. I'm petrified. You deserve so much better."

He hugged me to him. "I only want you. We'll figure this out together. Don't run. Stay. Promise me, you'll talk to me first, regardless of what it is."

I pulled back and looked into his eyes. He was sincere.

Searching my heart, I looked to see if I could make that promise. I thought it through and then said simply, "I promise."

With that, he brought his lips to mine and kissed me slowly as if he was sealing the pact between us.

"Will you come back to bed with me to sleep? I need to have you close right now. If staying in the bed with me makes you nervous, I'll sleep on the floor, or I'll hold you on the couch. I'll do whatever you need."

"Mark, it's not you. It's me. I'll try."

His thumb traced my lips, and I leaned into the touch.

"Just talk to me if it gets to be too much," he said.

"Okay."

He stood and led me back to the house. I liked the fact that he wasn't trying to carry me or treat me like an invalid after learning about my past. He held me close, not letting me go. I knew we weren't done discussing what had happened with Greg. Mark must have known that I was emotionally exhausted from revealing the rape.

After what seemed like an eternity, we made it back to his bedroom.

The bed loomed in front of me, and my palms started to sweat again. I closed my eyes and took a deep breath. *I can do this.* I kept repeating that in my head over and over again as I got underneath the covers.

When I opened my eyes, Mark was watching me from the other side of the bed. "Do you want to go back downstairs?"

I shook my head. He looked like he was ready to run after me if I decided to leave. We both got into bed, and he slowly brought me to him. His movements were gentle and loving, and I started to relax.

I wanted this. I wanted to be with him. I wanted to be free of my past. I hoped my past wouldn't fight to cling to me. I closed my eyes and prayed that I was free from all this baggage now, but I had a feeling that my past was still going to linger around and haunt me.

"Just hold me, Mark."

"Always."

CHAPTER 13

There was rustling and clicking that caused me to stir. Peeking my eyes open, I saw the clock read four in the morning. First, relief flooded through my veins as I had made it through the night in his bed. Mark had one arm wrapped around me as he continued to click away with one hand.

Groggily, I asked, "What are you doing?"

He looked at me and smiled sexily, which I sleepily returned.

"I'm texting Damien. We're thinking about canceling the trip."

His arm pulled me closer to his body, and I wrapped my arm around his waist. I was still reveling in the fact that I had made it through the night, and I didn't feel panicked.

"He says Allison had a hard night, and he wants to stay with her. I told him I thought it was a good idea."

Smiling into his chest, I liked that he didn't want to leave me after everything that had happened. The truth was that part of me wanted him to stay. The other part of me knew they needed to go, and I also needed a little downtime from all of this.

"I liked waking up in your arms."

He smiled and was about to say something when my phone pinged, and I blindly reached for it. It was Allison.

> *Allison: Damien is going on that trip, regardless of whatever he's telling Mark.*

I closed my eyes and held in my giggle as Mark's phone pinged.

"Damn it. We're going now."

To be a fly on the wall in Damien and Allison's room would have been hysterical. I would have loved to watch her put her foot down.

"You guys will have fun." I yawned.

He leaned over and kissed me. "We'll be back as soon as possible."

He got out of bed, and then a few minutes later, I felt a finger trailing on my cheek as sleep started to claim me again.

"Sam, last night was the best night of my life. I loved having you in my bed." He kissed me again.

As he pulled away, I whispered, "I loved being in your bed."

"Sleep tight. We'll be back soon."

Blissfully, I sought my pillow and went back to sleep. I was amazed that he'd treated me as if I was normal and not tainted.

The bed started bouncing, and my best friend began obnoxiously singing a cheery made-up tune I had never heard before.

"Good morning, good morning to my very best friend.

You're being a sleepyhead, and you have to come help me blend.

Good morning, good morning. No more sleepy time for you.

Wake up. Rise up as the day is starting anew."

Ugh. That was beyond annoying this early in the morning. I wished I could shoot this song like how people shoot roosters in the movies when they cock-a-doodle-doo in the morning.

After she finished, she continued in her singsong voice, "It's time to rise and shine. If you don't get up, I'll have to sing the second verse, and it's the same as the first."

I mumbled into my pillow, "Good thing I'm not naked."

"Oh, your nakedness doesn't bother me. It's you being enthralled with another man to the point of nakedness that forever scars me."

She was giving the bed the tiniest of bounces.

Damn, I want to push her off.

She was laughing, and she knew she was irritating me.

Swatting in her direction, I said, "I'm coming, I'm coming. Please don't sing that song again."

When Mark and I had come to bed last night, I hadn't changed out of my shorts and T-shirt. Mark had stayed in his lounge pants and held me all night long. It had been perfect and exactly what I'd needed.

Allison and I headed downstairs and pulled out some fruit and pastries that Mark had told us about last night at dinner. We were sitting at the bar when my phone and Allison's beeped at the same time.

> *Mark: Hey, we are about to hit the river.*
>
> *Me: Hey, Sport. Save some of the rough-water riding for me.*
>
> *Mark: Damn it, Sam. I do not need to be hard with a bunch of guys in the raft.*
>
> *Me: I like you hard. It makes me wet.*
>
> *Mark: We are going to paddle the hell out of the river today, so I can get back to you.*
>
> *Me: Until then, I'll see what kind of trouble I can get into. Hmm…did I bring my BFFF?*
>
> *Mark: Fucking hell. You're killing me. I've never been more jealous of a vibrator in all my life.*
>
> *Me: Paddle hard.*

I looked over at Allison, and she was watching me, having already put her phone away. With our hair piled on top of our heads and wearing yoga pants and T-shirts, we both looked like we'd had rough nights but for different reasons.

She was smirking. "Please do not tell me you were sexting right beside me after everything else you have put me through."

"I wasn't sexting." I tried to act all nonchalant, but my damn cheeks flushed, like I was a teenager getting caught sneaking in past my curfew.

She playfully pushed me. "Liar."

"Well, you asked me to tell you that, and I did."

"Geez, Sam, you've got it bad."

"Is that bad?"

I knew she was playing, but I didn't want to be one of those crazy, possessive girlfriends who clung to her boyfriend like he was the air she breathed.

She matched my seriousness. "No, I didn't mean it like that. You just get a sweet, gooey expression when you're texting him. It's a good thing."

"Oh, okay." I looked down at my plate. "I'm new to all this. I don't want to screw it up."

She grabbed a bagel off the plate. "I remember feeling like I wasn't good enough for Damien, like he was going to wake up from whatever fantasy he was living in and leave me. I was scared that I was falling too hard, and I'd be left heartbroken."

Taking a bite of my pastry, I forced myself to eat to calm my stomach. "It was obvious Damien never felt like that. Anyone who saw how he looked at you knew how crazy he was for you. I knew it from the first time I met him at the bar."

"Sam…"

I stopped scooping the bowl of berries onto my plate and looked up. "Yeah?"

She looked me straight in the eyes. "The way you saw Damien looking at me is exactly how the world sees Mark looking at you. Enjoy your relationship. Don't spend so much time, like I did, wrapped up in self-doubt. Remember, my mom used to say, 'Enjoy the road you're on. Don't worry about where the road leads as long as you are staying true to yourself.'"

It all clicked in that moment. Mark knew my past, and he'd accepted it. He still wanted me. Letting my best friend's advice take root, I smiled as I started to believe the fact that he really wanted me. There would be obstacles in our relationship, but I wanted to give it my all. I wanted to give myself over to him completely, to share my life with him. I wanted to let go of that horrible night.

"Allison, thanks for always being there for me exactly in the way I needed it."

She leaned over and gave me a squeeze. "There's nothing you can do to get rid of me. If you don't want to talk about this, let me know."

I nodded, not sure where she was going with her line of questioning.

She continued, "How are you doing with all this? How did it go last night after I left?"

Pushing the berries around on my plate, I thought about how I felt. "I've been keeping it buried for so long that it was cathartic to let it out. The first time I had sex after the incident, I was apprehensive, but there was a release that it provided for me. From there, I thrived on having sex with no strings, which seemed to keep me in balance. I know it wasn't healthy, but it kept the crazy feelings at bay. I was always safe, and I know it sounds as if I had hoards of partners, but that is not the case. I've had a lot but not hoards."

She thought for a moment. "I haven't personally gone through it, but I know Damien used sex as a means to forget things that had happened. The only thing I wish is that you didn't have to carry that by yourself for all those years. I don't know how either you or Damien did it without talking about it. Why didn't you ever report it or tell anyone? Will you ever consider going to the cops? I'm not pushing. I'm just asking, trying to understand why you kept it to yourself." She held her hands up in surrender to emphasize that she wasn't pushing.

She is adorable.

I knew this was coming, but it still made it hard to talk about. "Greg wasn't himself that night. You remember seeing us together. He was always so attentive to me. He put me ahead of everything. We were both drunk that night, and I think he had taken something else. After I broke up with him, he tried reaching out to me over and over again. He begged and pleaded for me to give him another chance. Greg thought we broke up because I had found out he cheated on me. He told me about how he'd woken up naked in the barn that morning, but he couldn't figure who he had been with. He was so sorry for being unfaithful and said it would never happen again. He loved me. He wanted to marry me. With the way he groveled, I couldn't tell anyone. He had a scholarship to a university, and if he knew what happened, Greg would have turned himself in. He needed that scholarship. He wouldn't have been able to go to college without it. By telling anyone what had happened, all it would have done was ruin more lives. I couldn't do that. Our parents didn't know we were dating, so I figured it could all be swept underneath the rug and forgotten."

"Sam—"

I held up a finger, cutting her off. She needed to see my point in this.

"Right, wrong, or indifferent—it's my choice. I don't want to dwell on that part. I don't want my life scrutinized and combed through like I'm the suspect. I don't want my dirty laundry aired in front of my parents and complete strangers. When you were nearly raped after being drugged by Brad, I knew in that moment I should have come forward when Greg raped me during our senior year. At the time, I was scared of getting into trouble for going to that party. I didn't want my life turned upside down. Stupid, I know. That was why I started the awareness program and emphasized the part of telling someone. I should have told someone then. Being raped still royally fucked with my head, but I'm dealing with it the best I can. It might make me a hypocrite, but I'm the one who has to be okay with my decision, not everyone else."

She was about to say something, but I cut her off again, wanting to drive the point home. "I'm not condoning what he did. I know anyone from the outside looking in would criticize my decision. I'm at peace with my decision though, and ultimately, it's my decision to make even if everyone else thinks it is the wrong one. I want my life back. I want to leave the past in the past."

She put a hand on my shoulder. "Sam, I was going to say, I support you. I'll always support you. Just make sure you have truly dealt with the past. Otherwise, it has a way of coming back to the present and forcing you to work through it. Speaking from experience with Damien, that's generally the harder way to deal with it. You remember my mom always said, 'Never judge someone's decisions until you've walked in that person's shoes.'"

Regardless of how haggard we looked, it felt good to decompress. Breakfast had all but been forgotten at this point.

"Thanks, bestie. Two regrets that I'll always have are not talking to someone and using sex as an unhealthy coping mechanism. My relationship with Mark might have started out with only sex, but making love to him last night rocked me to the core and shattered all those defenses."

"Just remember, I'm here if you need to talk. I love you."

I knew that she was truly going to support me in whatever I did. She wasn't judging me. She was just being my best friend.

I reached for my glass of juice, feeling relieved. "I love you, too. You'll probably get tired of all my questions."

For some reason, I had made this thing with Mark into something big, scary, and terrifying, and it was the exact opposite.

Allison genuinely responded, "Never. I'm here anytime you need me. Enjoy the relationship, and remember to talk it out. I think people get into trouble because they don't say what they are really thinking, and it causes things to fester. Then, a big misunderstanding happens, and it just blows up from there. A lot of heartache could be avoided if everyone stayed true and honest to themselves."

"You're starting to sound like your mom with all that poetic advice."

Allison smiled as she thought about her mom. I knew Allison missed her mom each and every day. I knew it was hard being pregnant and not having her mom to talk about it with. She had called my mama a lot, and I was glad, but a mom can never be replaced.

"Thanks, Sam. I hope so. I miss them. Damien and I went last week to the cemetery to tell them about the baby."

I squeezed her hand, and she gave me a smile that was laced with sadness as her other hand went to her stomach. We all had sad parts in our lives, but each and every day, all we could do was make the best out of the moments we had. Allison had lost her parents tragically, but she had welcomed love when it found her in the end.

I put my free hand on top of hers as I said, "I'm glad you've found a way to keep them in your life. You're going to be a wonderful mother."

"Your mom has been great. She's helped Damien a lot, too."

Her phone beeped, and by the smile on her face, I knew it was Damien checking in on her again.

We had both showered and dressed and were now on the back deck, laughing. Mark's place provided peace and comfort to me, like we were on a deserted island all by ourselves.

"Sam, I swear, I might not survive this pregnancy with my husband. He's going completely overboard. He already has the route planned to the hospital with five backup contingency routes."

I was mid-sip of my orange juice when I snorted, and it came out my nose. "Shit."

Grabbing a napkin, Allison laughed at me while I cleaned myself. I could picture Damien having it all planned with road maps in case all technology went down. The image was too damn funny.

"So, have you ever had anal sex?" Allison asked it as if she were asking me how I liked the weather today.

I was mid-gulp again, and then I was choking for air.

"Geez, Sam, you all right?"

I was still trying to recover. "Shit. No."

Allison was up, patting my back. Finally, I recovered from my second near-choking experience in a time span of less than five minutes.

"Just took me by surprise. I prefer to keep the party in the front. Why? Have you?" I gave her a nudge with my foot.

"No." She actually seemed a little disappointed.

Roar, Allison.

She huffed a little and continued explaining as I raised my eyebrow, "Damien said he wanted to a while back. I brought it up to him recently, and you would have thought I was asking to bring another man into bed with us. Needless to say, I don't foresee it in our future anytime soon."

I loved having girl time with Allison. It had been a long time since we had talked.

"If he wanted to take the party to the back before, he'll want to after the baby is born. I bet he's being more cautious with you overall." A giggle escaped as I thought about how much more open Allison was about sex.

"Yes, oh my gosh, I want to scream sometimes." She slapped her chair. "I won't break."

"Horny much there, dear?"

We both started laughing.

Four out of the five security guards, including Bane, had been left here to watch us. Three of them were currently patrolling the perimeter, and I caught sight of them. Allison seemed to have adjusted to their presence, or she forcefully forgot they were around. I had to admit that it was very distracting to have them constantly watching, roaming, and talking into those damn ear things.

"Before the baby is born, I think it would be fun to do a girls' night sometime," Allison said.

I was about to respond to Allison's statement about the coronary she was going to cause her husband when we heard the sound of an approaching boat. The security team was in place and ready to go.

Bane was at the dock with two security guards as Jeremy, another security guard, walked toward us.

"Ladies, would you mind stepping inside while we see what's going on?"

Allison responded, "Sure, Jeremy."

She was used to this behavior now and rolled with it. We stepped inside and went to the study while he stood guard at the entrance. From in here, there were no windows that allowed us to see outside. I sat my phone down on the table. Even though I knew we were safe, my heart was speeding up. Allison was cool as a cucumber as she sat down on the couch.

"Does this not make you nervous?" I asked.

She crossed her legs. "No, not instances like this. It's probably one of Mark's friends or family members, and they don't realize the extreme measures Damien takes. When we are in public places, then yeah, I get a little more nervous because of the whole Ben incident, but I refuse to let it rule me. The therapist helped a lot with that. Damien would have me in isolation if he could, so the compromise is increased security for peace of mind. You probably haven't noticed how the security is when we are at functions, but this is pretty standard." Allison's phone beeped, and she smiled. "It's Damien. He said Mark's mom and sister are here to say hi while the boys are gone."

She typed something back as my stomach plummeted.

"Holy hell, what am I going to do? I wasn't supposed to meet them on this trip. I'm not ready for this. Shit." I was mortified about meeting his family. "Do you think they know about me?"

Allison came up to me and grabbed my shoulders. "I'm sure that's why they're here." She gave me a wink.

Not helping.

"Hey, just be yourself. I can't imagine Mark having a house close to them if they're crazy. Plus, it really can't get much worse than my in-laws, and hey, I'm still standing. You can do this, Sam. I've met them once at a game, and they seemed nice. You've got this."

I let out a nervous laugh as I rubbed my hands on my yoga pants. Allison had been dealt a pretty bad deck when it came to her in-laws.

"Get your big-girl panties out, Sam. You can do this. You're living in the now, remember?"

She arched her eyebrow as if challenging me, and it calmed me.

"At least you're not being debuted on live television, like I was."

I laughed, and I was about to rib her again for that kiss she had given Damien for millions to see, but Bane walked into the office.

"Mrs. Wales, Mark's mother and sister are here to see you ladies. Mr. Wales has been informed. Would you like to see them? Mr. Robertson has said you can turn them away if you would like."

In return, Allison looked at me for the decision. For a second, I stood there, frozen. It would be easier to send them away and stay hidden behind Allison's security guards.

Shit. Okay, no more hiding. It's what you've been doing for years.

Finally, I answered, "Yes, Bane. We'll come back outside. Thanks."

Bane excused himself and walked back out toward the terrace. Now that we had visitors, I wondered if security would stay closer in proximity and more visible. As we crossed the threshold, my suspicions were confirmed as they had already moved their posts closer to us. I smiled.

We were greeted by two ladies who shared so many similarities to Mark that it was unnerving.

A blonde woman who I assumed was Mark's mother asked, "Sam?"

As I stepped forward, they both pulled me into a hug and then released me after nearly squeezing the life from me. His mom kept her arms on my shoulders as she smiled at me. She was blonde, slim, and tall, and she had the same shade of green eyes as Mark.

His mom didn't give me a chance to say anything as she continued, "I'm so glad to finally meet you. Mark told me not to bother you girls today, but I couldn't keep myself away."

"It's nice to meet you, Mrs. Robertson. I believe you've already met my best friend, Allison Wales," I said.

I was glad my mom had ingrained my manners into me to the point where they were second nature. I was nervous, wondering what they thought of me.

"Please call me Annie." She briefly turned to Allison, who was outstretching her hand. Letting me go, Annie shook Allison's hand. "Nice to see you again, Allison."

"Likewise, Annie. Sorry for the greeting. My husband is a little overprotective." Allison motioned to the security detail.

Annie waved her hand dismissively. "Oh, I get it. We should have called first, but I had to meet Mark's dear Sam. He speaks so fondly of you." She pulled me in for another hug and then motioned to who I assumed was his sister. "This is Mark's sister, Sabrina."

His sister was identical to their mom, just a younger version. We exchanged pleasantries, and she was as sweet as his mom. They seemed down to earth and kind—not super obnoxious like Mark had lovingly described them.

Allison remained standing as we took our seats. She politely smiled with her hands folded in the front and said, "I hate to leave you guys, but I have to get some photo edits done for the team that are due at the beginning of the week. It was good to see you both again."

She gave me a wink, and I knew what she was doing. She had finished those edits last week. She wanted me to have some alone time with his family. I didn't know if I wanted to hug her or strangle her. I was going to trust her—for now.

Annie responded, "It was nice seeing you again, Allison. We didn't mean to interrupt your girl time."

"Nonsense. We giggled ourselves out this morning."

We all laughed as Allison said one final good-bye. As she walked out of the room, I prepared myself for the inquisition I was about to receive.

Mark's sister and mother were absolutely amazing. We fell into conversation and didn't stop for what felt like hours. We laughed as Annie told me stories of Mark's childhood. I shared stories about my family and my love for cooking and sports. They were both laid-back and down to earth as we talked. They weren't measuring me to see if I was good enough for Mark. They truly seemed happy to meet me.

As she refilled her wine glass, Sabrina asked, "Did Mark ever tell you about having to play Annie in the school play in junior high?"

I started choking on my wine as I began giggling. "No, he's failed to mention it. Do tell."

She took a sip of her wine before continuing, "He's going to kill me for telling you this, but I have definite bragging rights. He never bet me again after this. We were outside, playing and running. Mark was taunting me about how slow I was. Anyway, I bet him that I could climb a tree faster, and if I did, he would have to try out for the play they were doing at school, *Annie*. He took the bet, and I smoked him up the tree."

She paused, and I bit down on my lip, preparing for what was ahead.

Mark as Annie? Shit, I hope they took pictures.

"Anyway, we all went for the audition. He came out, dressed up like the little redheaded scrapper from the movie, and he lip-synced the entire song of 'Tomorrow.' Funniest thing ever."

I busted out laughing. I was practically snorting.

Sabrina started chortling also as she barely got out, "We have it on video. I'll show you when you come to my house. He was the cutest Annie ever."

"I have to see it."

We were in the middle of recovering from laughter as Mr. Annie himself came strolling out. He looked slightly tense as he took in the scene.

He came to sit next to me. "Hey, I've been trying to reach you." His voice was low and urgent. It was as if there wasn't anyone else in the room but me.

I looked and remembered leaving my phone in the study. "Oh, I left my phone in the study when security had us move in there before your family arrived."

I searched his eyes as he searched mine. I was wondering what was causing him to be on edge.

His mom broke our staring stance. "Mark, it's good to see you. We couldn't stay away, knowing your Sam was here. We've had the best time, talking this afternoon."

His Sam?

He hadn't stopped staring at me, but then he looked at his mom. When he looked back at me, he started to relax a little bit, but he was still tenser than what I was used to seeing him as.

What the hell has him so on guard?

He sat back and threw his arms around my shoulders, pulling me to him. He was trying to exude calmness, but I could see his pulse jumping in his throat at a galloping pace.

"Glad you girls had a fun time."

I snuggled into his side as I asked, "How was the trip?"

"Long, long, long." He scrubbed the hand not holding me over his face that was shadowed with blond stubble.

I looked at him, confused, but his sister and mom seemed like they knew exactly what was going on.

Gah, this is frustrating.

Sabrina chimed in, "We weren't expecting you guys back for a few hours. We were going to take Sam to dinner. We can all go now as a family."

He scrubbed his face again and tiredly asked, "Can we do that another time? I haven't seen my girl all day."

Sabrina looked disappointed.

Annie answered, "I bet you're tired. Will we be able to see you guys tomorrow?"

Mark shifted uncomfortably. "Mom, probably not. I'm not sure what time we're leaving. Let's plan a trip where you guys fly out to North Carolina, and we can all hang out there."

His mom smiled at us. "That sounds great. You guys probably need some time alone."

He exhaled a long, quiet breath. He looked exhausted and seemed a little edgy. I could feel his muscles flex around me. Damien and Allison walked out onto the patio. She was playfully hitting him, and he looked triumphant.

Damien wrapped his hand around her waist as he asked the group, "I'm going to take Alli into town for some dinner. Would anyone like to join us?"

She had mentioned this morning that she wanted to go out to dinner tonight before their big announcement tomorrow. Things always seemed to get hectic for them in public for a while after any major changes. Damien was about to have them on lockdown, and Allison knew it. The public was in love with her. Hoping to lower the appeal of the story, Damien and Allison had moved up the announcement, so it could be done at their discretion.

All of us declined, and they headed out.

Annie was the next to rise. "We're going to head back. Your dad is probably starving. He wanted to come with us today, but I figured you would for sure kill me if I brought everyone."

Sabrina spoke next, "Yeah, Mike, my husband, has been texting me, asking when I'm coming home. He's threatening to come this way shortly and devour your fridge."

Mark stood. "Well, you guys have had her enough today. I'm not sharing tonight."

He sounded playful, but I knew he was serious, and I could hear the underlying warning tone not to push it any further this evening. His family obviously knew him well as they followed suit. Standing, I joined him, and he put his hand around my waist.

His mom came up and enveloped me in a hug first. "It was wonderful finally getting to meet you. I'm sorry we crashed on you like we did, but I had to meet the girl who has made my boy so happy. We'll plan a trip out to North Carolina soon."

I smiled. "Sounds wonderful. I'll hold you to that."

Sabrina was next. "I'm glad I got to meet you, Sam. We have heard so much about you. Thank you for making my brother so happy."

What all has he said to them?

Next, they moved to Mark, giving him a hug, and then they left toward the dock on an illuminated path as they called out one last good-bye. We both stood there and waved, and I realized that we were home alone for the first time since arriving. I took the moment to enjoy the peacefulness, the completeness I felt.

Mark was stiff beside me. I looked over, and he was watching me warily.

"What's wrong, Sport?"

"I'm sorry about them bombarding you this afternoon. I told them to stay away."

I grabbed his face and kissed him, which forced him to stop speaking. The boat was far away from here at this point, and an idea struck me to lessen his stress.

I pulled back. "Hey, I loved it. I had a wonderful time."

He still didn't believe me as I stepped out of his grasp and into the yard. I slipped off my flip-flops and felt the cool grass beneath my feet. It was just after dusk now.

"What are you doing?" he asked.

He was starting to walk toward me as I ripped my shirt over my head, causing him to stop midstride. I shimmied my pants down, leaving me in nothing but my undergarments.

"Sam, you're beautiful."

I did a little flirty turn as I took off my bra and panties in the sexiest way I knew how. He gave me an appreciative groan as he started to come after me, which spurred me to take off at a run toward the water.

He called after me as I ran to the shoreline, "Sam, I will catch you, make no mistake."

A shiver ran up my back as I neared the water's edge, and I laughed. He was on my heels, but I made it first since he had to stop to strip himself. The water was cool and refreshing as I ran full speed, splashing into it, and then I swam until I was standing in water up to my shoulders. Keeping my eyes closed, I listened for him to enter the water, and then I waited to feel the water move around me, signaling he was near. Before I knew it, his hands snaked around the front of my stomach, and he pulled me to his front where his erection pressed hard against me.

"I missed you, Sam."

"I missed you, too."

I grounded my ass into him, and he pulled me tighter to him. One hand slowly moved up my body toward my breast as he began sucking on the part of my neck right before my shoulder starts. I felt desired. His other hand made its way down, and he started rubbing my clit in a circular motion that had my body temperature rising, even in this cool water. Mark began rolling my nipple between his fingers, hard. I whimpered at the conflicting sensations my body was feeling. It was exquisite—a little pain mixed with pleasure. He pressed down on my clit, causing the orgasm to take over. It was quick, but it relaxed my muscles as I sank into him.

"I think it's time you were inside me, Sport."

There was no need to say that twice as he spun me around. Immediately, my legs wrapped around his, and he lined up and entered me. He walked us up into shallower water until my breasts were above the water. His mouth descended on my nipple, and he sucked it hard into his mouth. He continued pushing us both higher. Water caused the friction of him inside me to be raw, which in some ways I loved, but I couldn't prolong the build as long as I would have liked. He pulled me back down on him, hard, and the ecstasy took over. He was right there with me, and we both said each other's names as a prayer.

Walking slowly to the shore, he continued pulsing inside me. We were kissing, and he nipped my lip.

I asked, "What had you so tense when you first got back from your trip? You were in serious need of a distraction."

He rubbed his nose along my chin as he responded, "When Damien got the call that my family had arrived, I was worried they would scare you off. They can be a bit much at times. My family doesn't do boundaries very well. I tried reaching you, but I didn't receive an answer. I actually had Damien check with his security to make sure you hadn't left."

That statement caused me to look down at the water. "Were you ashamed for me to meet them? I didn't even think about that. I should have—"

A finger came under my chin, and he brought my eyes to meet his.

"I will never be ashamed of you. I was nervous it would be too much, too fast. I just got you, Sam. I'm afraid you're going to bolt, and I'm trying to make you feel secure in us."

My stomach twisted sourly as I asked, "Did your view of me change last night when you learned what had happened?"

"No. Hell no. I want to pummel the bastard."

The conversation was intense as we maintained eye contact and spoke to each other. It was intimate, and I felt connected to him.

I pressed on. "Does it bother you that I've had multiple sexual partners through the years?"

His grip tightened on me. "Do I like the thought of another man touching you? Fuck no. Do I understand that we both have pasts? Yes. We can sit here and list it all out, but I don't see what that would accomplish. As long as you're completely mine, that's all that matters."

I let his words sink in as I played with his hair. We had never once wavered in looking at each other, and it felt like it was strengthening our bond with each second that passed.

"I want you, too. I never wanted this before. I'll probably royally suck at it, but I want it. I want it with you. I just need you to be honest with me if my past becomes too much. I don't want to worry about if you think I'm broken because of it. It probably has fucked with my head a little bit because I kept it buried for so long, but I swear, I'll communicate with you."

"Sam—"

Cutting him off, I said, "Mark, I need that. It'll help me keep at bay all the self-doubt that I've been carrying around. You have to promise me. I think I can focus on us if I know you'll tell me."

He didn't even hesitate as he responded, "I promise, Sam. It doesn't matter, but I swear, I'll tell you."

I smiled up at him. "Please take me up to your room and make love to me."

He walked, kissing me the entire way. The moonlight bathed us before he carried me into the house. As soon as we hit the bed, he did exactly what I'd asked for.

Boneless, I lay on the bed, wrapped up in the sheets with Mark. I was lying on my stomach, and his legs were on top of mine. He was trailing his fingers up and down my exposed back. I felt complete and whole.

He nuzzled my neck. "What are you thinking about?" His voice was gravelly from sex.

I turned onto my back, and he covered half of my body with his.

My hand went up to his face. "I was thinking about how good this felt."

"Just tell me if I'm pushing too hard. I've wanted you as my girlfriend since the Vegas gala last year. You ruined me the moment I had you. I knew there would never be anyone like you again."

My throat started to tighten, but I took a deep breath. He was watching me closely, and I finally managed a genuine smile.

"Thanks for continuing to pursue me."

He looked triumphant as he pushed some of the hair away from my face.

"You, Miss Matthews, are worth the pursuit."

I gave him a kiss, and he kissed me back.

"How about I get us something to drink and gather our clothes from outside before our guests return?" he asked.

"Probably a good idea. You better put on some pants in case they come back early. I'd rather your manly bits stay for my viewing pleasure only."

I wiggled against his manliness, which earned me a lustful look.

He pulled me to him and kissed me hard. "Manly bits?"

"Mmhmm…"

"Bits? I think they're bigger than just bits."

I giggled as he pulled himself off me.

"You've been warned. When I get back, I'm going to spend the rest of the night showing you how non-bit-like they are."

I pressed my lips together as I tried to stifle a laugh. "I look forward to it, Sport."

He sauntered into his closet and came out in some gray sweatpants. It was incredible how defined his muscles were. They flexed as he moved and walked.

"You like what you see?" he asked.

"You have no idea."

He walked out of the room, giving me a very nice view of his back, as he lifted his arms in a pose that had me swooning at how toned he was. I lay back and closed my eyes, reveling in the feeling of being wanted and accepted. The door opened, and Mark came back with a champagne bottle, two glasses, and my phone.

"Your phone was beeping in the study. Thought you might want to check it. Also, there was a note on the counter addressed to you."

He handed the phone and note to me, and then he busied himself, opening the bottle before pouring us two glasses. There were a few missed calls and texts from Mark.

Mark: Sam, you don't have to visit with my family if you don't want to.

Mark: I'm sorry they came over without warning you. Please talk to me if you need to leave.

It was incredible how much he truly cared about me and had wanted to ensure I was okay. Next, I opened the note. It was in Allison's handwriting.

Sam,

We are headed to our California home this evening after dinner. This was set in motion prior to the boys getting back, but I wouldn't allow Damien to tell anyone. It's what we were texting about when Mark's family showed up this afternoon. I needed to pack discreetly, and you needed time to see that his parents liked you for you.

You and Mark need your time together. You guys need time to grow into your relationship and love for each other. Damien has arranged for you guys to go home first class since we'll have the plane. I just had to make sure you were okay after last night, but now that I know you are going to be more than okay, you guys need your space.

Open your heart, Sam. You deserve this more than anyone I know. I love you, and I'm here anytime you need me, regardless of how small you might think it is. Enjoy each phase of your relationship—the fun, the exciting, the hard, and the sweet times. Each one will strengthen you in ways you never knew possible. They all are part of building a beautiful, lasting love.

I love you more than life itself.

Xoxo,
A

I smiled at my bestie. She was an amazing person. I opened my text messages and sent her a text.

> *Me: I love you, too, Allison. Thank you. I'm turning off my phone now and taking the advice of my best friend.*

I smiled as I turned off my phone. When I had been in the sorority, I remembered hearing stories about how girls would forget their friends when they met a new guy. I had vowed never to do that, but it all made sense now why Allison had basically disappeared when she met Damien. Allison had still been there for me, but I was used to her being around all the time. I felt like an ass with how it had probably looked like I'd been trying to come between them and undermine Damien at times. I'd just missed her, but I thought they had both known that and understood it. Damien was perfect for Allison in every way.

I took her words to heart, and I was excited about my journey ahead.

We were on our flight back to North Carolina. Damien arranging a first-class ride home for us had meant he'd booked the entire first-class cabin. He was an over-the-top bastard, but I loved him like a brother, and I was appreciative for the alone time. Mark had let the stewardess know we were not to be disturbed, and we would buzz if we needed anything.

I was looking through a magazine, leaning on Mark's shoulder, as he was reading a playbook.

There were some red fuck-me heels I was thinking were a must-purchase when Mark said in a low voice, "Sam, in the next few weeks, when the preseason starts and then the season, my life is going to be a little hectic for a while."

Closing my magazine, I looked up at him. "I know. I'm not going to be one of those clingy women. I understand the life. I have a career starting that I'll need to focus on."

"There are going to be photo shoots with cheerleaders, fans tend to be a little more expressive, and rumors get started, especially when the player is dating someone."

I honestly hadn't thought about how much our lives were going to change, but I should have. Even though it had been short, I was getting comfortable with our current setup. *As long as we stay levelheaded, we'll adjust.*

"As long as it stays strictly business, then you have nothing to worry about. I get the PR factor. You have to remember, too, that I'm going to be with players in meetings and at dinners, selling them on the team. But that's all they'll be—a job, nothing sexual. You know rumors circulated about me when I signed Dyn-O-Mite so quickly, but I'd been with you that night. You're the only person I've slept with on the team. Fidelity is not an issue for me." I gave him a reassuring smile and a light kiss.

He smiled. "That was an unforgettable night. I knew I'd have to find a way to make you mine when I walked out of the restroom, and you were gone. Fidelity isn't an issue for me either. I only want you, Sam. Just remember to talk to me if you don't like something, and we'll work out some sort of compromise."

"I'm glad you didn't give up on us."

I nestled into him, and he stroked my arm as he said, "Me, too."

I loved these moments of complete peace when my inner storm calmed and let me be.

We were in Mark's truck on the way back to our condo complex when his sister called. His phone was synced to the truck.

Mark looked over to me and said, "I want you to see how much they like you, Sam. I'll let them know you're with me in a minute. I know you've been worried about what they think."

I nodded and smiled as he connected the call.

"Hey, Brina," he said.

There was squealing on the other end that caused me to try to shy away from the noise. My eyes grew a little wider at this change in his sister. His sister and mom had not been this obnoxious the other day.

Finally, Sabrina started talking, "Mark, I love Sam. I mean, I love her. Hey, hold on, that's Mom."

The line was silent for a minute. Mark grabbed my knee that had started to bounce, and he squeezed it. I stopped the movement and grabbed his hand, giving it a reassuring squeeze back.

Sabrina came back on the line. "Hey, Mark. I've conferenced Mom in, too."

His mom spoke next, "Mark, we want to come see that sweetheart again as soon as possible. Can you give me Sam's number, so I can discuss some plans with her? She's absolutely perfect for you. We all can sync our schedules this way."

Sabrina chimed in, "You can't be selfish with her this time. I want to go out with her. Maybe we can do manis and pedis together."

They seemed to like me, but it was throwing me a little off-kilter with how much they wanted to get involved in my life after only meeting me once. Mark looked at me, and I smiled. I knew I was probably overreacting with my response, but part of me wished he would take the phone off speaker. I kept telling myself that they were just being nice.

Mark went to speak, but his mom picked up right where Sabrina had left off. "We'll text you some dates. Mark, I do hope you two are practicing safe sex even though I wouldn't mind having a grandbaby."

My eyes instantly bulged, and Mark looked right at me

"Mom, gotta go." He disconnected the line.

Shit. Oh shit.

She said the B word—well, not the B word exactly, but a word that contained the B.

The B word…

The blood was slowly draining from my face, and I was reeling from what they had said. His description of his family was making more sense after that little exchange. I hoped they stayed more docile with me for a bit until I had time to adjust. It was overwhelming, to say the least.

We were pulling into the condo complex and then stopped at the stop sign. Mark grabbed my hand, causing me to look at him.

"Damn it. I am sorry. My family is a little forward. They honestly don't have filters sometimes. I wanted you to hear how much they liked you. They've been group-texting me nonstop about wanting to spend more time with you."

Instead of freaking out, I playfully slapped his leg. Neither one of us was ready to talk about the B word, but it sure made me want to reinstitute condoms in our sex life.

"I'm fine. I was shocked by the openness. Hell, my mom is going to have a coronary because I'm dating, period. My parents are very traditional, so no freaking out if she mentions the M word."

He leaned in and gave me a kiss. "The M word?"

"Yeah, that big scary word men normally run from. It's about as scary as the B word. So, trust me, it'll all be evened out after you meet my family. I suggest we impose a no-freak-out rule when it comes to the parentals. Plus, you're gonna have your hands full with meeting my dad, considering I have never mentioned the word boyfriend to him or brought a significant other home. He might chase you off with a shotgun after he's had his fan moment."

Mark laughed at me as a car honked behind us, obviously irritated that we had chosen this stop sign to stop and have a conversation. An emotion passed over his face that I wasn't able to place, but it was gone just as quickly.

"Fair enough, no-freak-out rule imposed. My place or yours tonight?"

"Let's do mine tonight."

He turned right and parked the truck. I wondered if we would start staying with each other most of the time. I was going to let it happen as it was supposed to. I was not going to try to define parameters. All I needed was exclusivity and to feel safe at this point.

After getting our bags, we walked up to my place. It felt good to be home and not be as tense as I was prior to leaving for our trip.

He was walking back from my bedroom as he said, "Hey, Sam."

I looked up, waiting for him to continue, as I pulled some ingredients for sandwiches from the refrigerator.

"I want the PR group for the team to do a release about us. I want everyone to know I'm off the market. Are you okay with that?"

"When do you want it to release?" I liked the idea of being totally committed, even in public, which shocked the hell out of me.

"As soon as you give the go-ahead."

He joined me in the kitchen and started pulling things out that he wanted to add to lunch. It was amazing how normal this felt.

Tapping my fingers on the counter, I responded as I tried to tame my nerves, "Okay, I need to tell my parents first. I don't want them surprised by it since I've basically avoided the big R word for as long as they can remember."

We had stopped what we were doing and were discussing this like a real couple. I reveled in that thought and enjoyed it. *I'm normal.*

"You and your letters." He was clearly amused at me. "When are you going to tell them?"

This is going to be tough. Finding my courage, I answered, "I can tell them now, but I'm going to get a million questions, and they will want to know when I'm bringing you to meet them. I know you'll be busy with the preseason soon, but having someone in my life is going to shock the hell out of them, so I'll need to give them some kind of an idea of when we can go, even if it's a month from now."

He walked up to me and turned me to him, taking this conversation to a whole new level of seriousness. "Let's go this weekend. I want your family to be comfortable with me prior to the start of the season. I want them to see how much you mean to me before all the chaos, so they aren't wondering who the hell you are with."

His green eyes penetrated mine as we stared at each other.

"Okay, let me call them." I took a deep breath as I decided that it was best if we went ahead and chose a date for me to meet his parents as well, so they weren't trying to sync me to death via my mobile. "Why don't you see if your family wants to come the week after, so we can have a few weeks alone before the season starts?"

I was surprised at how calm I was at the prospect of breaking the news to my parents. The thought of spending more time with his family was freaking me out a little more at this point.

"Sounds good. It'll get Brina off my ass."

I laughed as he sent a text to his sister, and I grabbed my phone. I took a deep breath as I dialed my parents.

My mom's cheery Southern voice answered on the second ring, "Hey, Sam. How's North Carolina?"

"Hey, Mama. It's good. Are you sitting down?"

I was never good at prolonging things or easing into it. It drove my mom crazy how I'd put it out there without all the suaveness a situation sometimes required. I turned down the volume of my phone. The last thing I wanted was for Mark to hear a bad response from my mama.

"I am now. Don't tell me you're moving to California. Sam, that's way too far."

The cautionary, scolding tone made me smile. My move had been hard on them.

"Mama, calm down. I'm not moving again. I was going to come home to see you guys this weekend."

Mark was watching my exchange carefully as he continued to fix us sandwiches, which made me a little nervous.

She gave a little sigh of contentment. "Oh, that's wonderful. Your dad will be so glad. He's missed you terribly. He'd never say a word, but he's missed having you so close."

Here goes nothing. I cleared my throat and went for the big splash. "I miss you guys, too. Hey, Mama, I'm bringing someone home with me this weekend."

"Oh, good. I can't wait to see Allison. Is she showing yet?"

Of course my mom would assume I was bringing Allison because I hadn't brought anyone else home since leaving for college. I wanted to facepalm myself.

"Mama, I'm bringing my boyfriend home. We've only been dating for a couple of weeks, and I want you guys to meet him."

Something dropped, and then I heard some rustling and murmuring.

Did she drop the phone in shock?

She came back on the line and said, "Sorry, I dropped the phone. Did you say *boyfriend*?"

Part of me wanted to laugh at how I had stunned her. "Yes, Mama."

She was shocked, and I didn't blame her.

Sweetly though, she said, "That's wonderful. Tell me all about him."

"He's the quarterback for Damien's team. His name is Mark Robertson, and he's wonderful. He's sitting right here, Mama, so I'll talk to you later about the rest."

That earned me a raised eyebrow from Mark, but I was not going to go into detail with him standing right there. In response, I stuck my tongue out, and he smacked my ass before he took a seat at the bar.

My mama was so caught up in the moment that she wasn't paying attention to what was happening on my side.

"Lordy mercy, your father is gonna have a heart attack."

"That's why I called you, so you could tell him. Gotta go. I'll let you know when we are coming in."

"Sam—"

"Bye, Mama. Thanks for telling Dad. Love you."

I hung up the phone as she was continuing to sputter. Letting her break less palatable subjects to my dad was one habit of mine she did not find amusing.

Mark slid a plate over to me, and I started eating my sandwich. I knew he wanted to know what my mom had said, but I decided to stay quiet for a few minutes as I took a couple of bites. Honestly, she was probably still trying to get her head wrapped around it all. My parents were huge advocates of abstinence until marriage. It was one of the reasons I'd never told them about being raped by Greg. I hadn't wanted them to think less of me. That was the last thing I needed to be thinking about, so I focused back on the topic at hand.

In between a full bite, I mumbled, "You sure know how to make a good sandwich, Sport."

He arched an eyebrow at me, and I sweetly smiled back.

"Thanks. Is there anything else you want to tell me? Maybe what your mom just said?"

"Nope," I said it with a loud, playful pop on the P sound. I didn't know why I was teasing him on this.

"If that's the way you want to play it, babe." He shrugged and took another bite.

I looked at him and fluttered my eyelashes. "I have no idea what you're talking about."

The glint in his eyes told me he was up to something.

What is he planning?

We finished eating, and I put away the plates from lunch.

As I was bending over, finishing loading the dishwasher, his mouth was right at my ear.

"I was thinking about going to the deli and getting some dessert. What kind of cookies would you like?"

The seductive tone in his voice had me instantly wanting him. I loved this type of foreplay. I started to stand, but he held me in my bent-over position.

"Whatever she's just taken out of the oven. Tell her I'll be by soon. I—"

He bit my ear. "I'm glad you didn't tell me what your mom said. This is going to be a lot more fun."

Oh, this is bad.

He was going to win this game, and he knew it.

Wanting to play but not be tortured forever, I decided to tell him, "Before you go, I'll tell you everything my mama said."

He chuckled as he pulled me to a standing position and gave me a light kiss. "I like my plan better. I'll be back in just a minute."

Trying to regain some control in this conversation, I sassily replied, "Have it your way. You might be missing out on some really juicy details."

He nibbled on my lips. "I'll take my chances."

Shit, I'm screwed.

Our breath mingled, and my pulse continued to climb as I thought about what he was going to do to me when he returned. He kissed me hard and left me in a sexual tizzy.

Shower. I need a shower. The moment the door closed, I went to wash off the traveling grime. *Maybe it will also tame my libido and help me keep my wits about me in this little game we started.*

Five minutes was all I needed, and I would be out before Mark got back. After stripping down, I turned on the shower. The water was nice and hot as I stepped in and reveled in the feeling of the heat. I washed quickly.

As I was getting out, the sound of the front door opening and closing reached me in the bathroom. This showdown required comfort, so I found tight boy shorts and a T-shirt. Not wanting to fight totally fair, I left the girls floating free in my nearly see-through T-shirt.

Perfect.

"Sam?"

The smell of fresh cookies wafted through the air. Rounding the corner, I didn't have a chance to respond before he continued, "A batch of peanut butter cookies just came out of the oven, and Edna sent some of the chocolate dipping sauce you love with it."

"Oh, boy." I jumped up and down.

His eyes went to my chest.

One point to Sam.

Trying for extra credit, I gave him a little shimmy to emphasize their free, bouncy nature. As his eyes grew more lustful and his body posture changed, I wanted to shorten playtime and get him inside me sooner rather than later.

"Do you want to know what she said, Sport?"

He was pulling off his shirt, and I wanted to pass out at the sight.

"Go on."

A finger went to my nipple as I tweaked it, he groaned.

"She's telling my dad, and it's okay for us to come."

He smiled. "Do you trust me?"

I licked my lips. "Yes."

He walked up to me, and I stood my ground. His finger came up and started at my chin. He gently grazed my neck, working his finger down achingly slow to my left breast. I closed my eyes and absorbed the tingling feeling that caused that sensual flip-flopping in my stomach.

"Sam, can I take control for a bit?"

My eyes went to his as his finger traced the underlying curve of my breast and continued working its way to my navel and then farther down south. I thought he was going to continue to the top of my boy shorts, but instead, both hands slowly went up my torso.

My breathing had picked up slightly as he maintained eye contact.

"I'll try." My voice was softer.

My sex was beyond wet at this point with the slow, teasing movements. As he slowly pulled my shirt up, I put my arms straight up in the air. When the shirt was covering my face, I felt the tip of his tongue come out and flick my nipple. He sucked it in his mouth, hard. As he finished pulling my shirt off of me, he blew on my nipple, which caused it to stand erect. Mark's finger then trailed down my neck and in between my breasts, slowly making its way to my navel and then to the top of my shorts. I shivered at the sensation.

Next, he pulled my boy shorts down ever so slowly. As they went down my legs, his fingers barely grazed my clit, and I emitted an involuntary whimper. I wanted him more than I had ever wanted him. His fingers skillfully touched all the right places on the inside of my thigh and continued their trail as my boy shorts made their way to my ankles, and I kicked them off.

His hands slid back up my body to my hips and then across my breasts. The heat emitting from our bodies could start a forest fire.

"You are the most beautiful woman I have ever seen. You're about to scream for me to give you that release."

I barely whispered, "Please."

The devilish grin that spread across his face had me thanking my stars that he was mine. He grabbed my hand and led me to the kitchen. I was curious about what he was going to do with me in here, and I remembered the time he had taken me on the kitchen island before. Prior to this, I had never given a guy this much control. It was a little daunting, thinking about it, but I took a deep breath. Mark could be trusted.

He grabbed the nape of my neck, brought my lips to his, and roughly kissed me. Feeling his chest slightly against my breasts was amazing at this point. Any small touch sent my body up in smoke. One of his denim-cladded legs came between my legs and began rubbing me. I was building, and I started meeting his grind. On my second rub, he pulled away while I was practically panting. He stepped back and began to strip out of his pants. His erection stood at full attention, and I bit down on my lip at the sight. He started pumping himself a few times. I loved watching Mark touch himself.

"Hop on the counter, Sam. You're about to become my new favorite treat."

I obeyed. I believed I could handle giving him a little control, knowing he would stop at any minute I became uncomfortable. The cool granite counters brought a new sensuality to my body. Mark went to the bag from Edna's deli and pulled out the chocolate dipping sauce that I loved.

He walked back over. "Lie back and close your eyes."

I did as he'd asked. Warm dollops of chocolate landed on my nipples and slowly dripped across my body. Between the cold countertop and the warm fudge, I felt a mixture of all different kinds of sensations, which heightened all my senses. More warmness was drizzled between my legs. His tongue started tracing the inside of my thigh, following the chocolate trail to my core. He was moaning appreciatively as he licked up my cleft.

"Please, Mark."

"Not yet. I haven't had you near enough. You earned a penalty, and you have to serve the sentence."

He dipped his tongue into me, and he had to grab my hips to keep me from coming off the counter. He licked, sucked, and worked me up to a near explosion and then stopped. I groaned in frustration, and he chuckled.

Bastard.

My dominant behavior took over, and I went to rub myself. He grabbed my hand and then climbed up on the counter, putting himself between my legs.

"Not yet, Sam. I'll give it to you but not yet. I won't ever deny you. Let me pleasure you."

"Please...I want you inside me."

He spread my legs farther and positioned himself right at my entrance. His mouth came down and devoured each of my nipples, lapping up all the chocolate. This was going to be an off-the-charts orgasm. His dick played with my entrance, acting as if he was going to enter, but he didn't. My body was strung so tight. I needed him. He pushed in all the way, stretching me. He knew I had reached my limit, and he was true to his word and didn't deny me.

I screamed, "Yes! Oh, yes! Finally."

He started moving, and I was meeting him, trying to get as much friction as humanly possible. He was keeping the strokes long and hard, soothing a deep ache that had been building since the last time we had sex. His hands held mine above my head, and we were both breathing hard. I was so close. He was right there with me as I could feel him getting harder inside me. On the next stroke, I erupted into a million pieces of pleasure, and I screamed incoherent words. He came and continued massaging both of our climaxes out until they had dissipated.

As we both slowed our pulses, I murmured, "Holy hell."

"You were made for me, Sam."

He was gazing at me, and my heart was becoming his, but I wasn't ready to admit that...yet.

"Back atcha, Sport."

He pulled out of me, and I sat up on the counter. Looking down, I saw I was a mess with remnants of chocolate all over me. When I looked up, I saw it had also rubbed off on him.

"Ah, Sport, looks like you are going to have to take a shower with me to clean up your mess."

Mark gave a devilish grin as he responded, "It's a tough job, but someone's got to do it."

He picked me up, and I wrapped my legs around his waist. He kissed me the entire trip to the bathroom. I had a feeling it was going to be a while before I actually got clean.

We were driving down to my parents' house. We had flown into Atlanta around lunchtime. We were now only about an hour away from Homerville, and I was about to introduce my boyfriend to my parents. I was a nervous wreck with sweaty palms, a racing heart, and a ball in my stomach. My body was fidgeting in every way possible. This was hard since I wasn't sure how my parents would take me having a boyfriend. I knew they would be nice to him.

But what will they think of him?

I hoped they didn't delve too deeply into our relationship because in their minds, they believed in the days of *Little House on the Prairie*.

Mark squeezed my knee, and I jumped.

"Hey, Sam. Why don't you go ahead and call your parents? I have that phone interview in just a few."

He let go of my knee, and it started bouncing on its own accord as if it had consumed twelve cups of coffee.

His hand rested on it again as he said, "There's nothing to be nervous about. We have each other, and that's all that matters."

Mark seemed laid-back and at ease with all this, which lessened my nerves some.

Why isn't he nervous?

Rummaging through my purse, my knee that wasn't being held captive by Mark's hand started to bounce. "You're right. Good idea. I'll call them to let them know where we are. It'll be okay. We'll be okay. It'll all be fine."

Before I hit their preprogrammed number, Mark grabbed my hand. "Sam, I promise you, it's going to be fine. Even if they have a hard time with us, it will be fine. I'll be there for you, and nothing will change that. Regardless, they won't change my feelings for you. That's why I'm not nervous. We are in control of our relationship, and no one else."

I let out a deep breath and nodded. "Thank you."

"Anytime. You and me—that's what matters."

"You and me."

I hit the speed dial and called home as I said a silent prayer for this weekend to go smoothly. I wanted my parents to approve of Mark.

The phone rang, and then a frantic voice answered, "Hello?"

"Hey, Mama."

There was a vacuum noise in the background.

"Hey, honey. Where are you guys?" She sounded like she was running around crazy.

"We're about an hour away."

The phone made some noise, and then she was yelling at my dad, but her voice was muffled. "Dean, hurry up. They're almost here."

I heard more shuffling.

Then, her voice was clear again as she said to me, "Sounds good. Can't wait to see you guys."

The tone alone of my mom's voice signaled she was a nervous wreck. Part of me wanted to laugh and tell her, *Welcome to the club*, while the other part wanted me to call the whole thing off. Normally, going home was easy and not stressful. This time though, it felt like the real me was coming home for the first time. Since the night I'd been raped, I always wore my façade. To them, I was the perfect daughter, waiting for Mr. Right to sweep me off my feet.

I was silent for too long as my thoughts infiltrated my mind when my mama said into the phone, "Sam?"

"Sorry. Can't wait to see you either. Don't stress. It's fine." I was speaking so fast.

She let out a breath. "I know. It's not every day we get to meet our daughter's boyfriend. Be safe."

"Will do. Love you."

"Love you, too."

She was hollering at my dad again before she hung up the phone. My poor, poor dad was going to have a hard time with this. The phone call to him had been interesting.

While Mark was at training, I needed to call and talk to my dad. It had been two days since I had told Mama about my boyfriend. I wasn't sure how me breaking the news of me having a boyfriend to my dad was going to go down, and I wanted to talk to him when Mark couldn't hear me. I was afraid Mark might get the wrong impression of my parents. Digging deep, I marched over to my couch, sat down, and called home.

"Hello?"

"Hey, Mama. Is Dad there?"

"He is. I'm glad you called to talk to him, Sam."

I took a deep breath and lied through my teeth, "Me, too."

"Let me go get him. He's in his office."

Her voice was approving. I hated disappointing my parents, and I knew the way I had handled telling them was shitty. I wasn't ready for questions they wouldn't like the answers to, like if we were having sex or not. I knew I was a grown woman, but I hated confrontation with my parents. Anyone else, it was fine. With them, it felt like my fragile world was falling apart.

"Here he is."

The phone made a rustling noise, and then my dad's voice came through the phone. "Hey, Boo Bear. I heard you're coming home."

I took another deep breath as my dad greeted me.

"Hey, Dad." I closed my eyes. "I am. I'm excited to see you guys. Did mama tell you that I'm bringing my boyfriend home?"

Silence.

More silence.

Even more silence.

I was starting to get nervous, and then my dad spoke again. "Just remember your morals, Sam. Don't let him talk you into anything you don't want to do. I know this boyfriend thing is new to you, but don't jeopardize who you are for a guy."

This was the hard part with my parents. I loved them, and they loved me, but they weren't approachable at all on certain subjects.

"No worries, Dad. I'm about to go bake some cookies."

"Bye, Boo Bear. Love you."

"Love you, too, Dad."

I hung up the phone and immediately went to the deli to see Edna. I needed her advice and some cookie therapy.

Mark brought me out of my daze as he asked, "Did it go okay?"

"Yes, they can't wait for us to get there." I gave him a small smile.

He looked over at me again. "I need to dial in to this conference call. Are you okay? Or do I need to cancel?"

I squeezed his hand. "I'm fine. I'll be okay. Just a little nervous."

He looked at me questioningly, and I worked on reassuring him.

"I promise. Make your call. It's a big PR moment for the team."

My phone pinged again as Mark called in to the conference call. Looking down, I internally sighed. It was Mark's mom and sister again, doing the group-text thing with me. They never stopped. His mother and sister kept going like that damn rabbit on the battery commercial.

> *Sabrina: When we get to North Carolina, I think we should get pedicures and manicures done prior to going out that evening.*

> *Annie: That sounds great. I'm also starting to plan our family vacation after the football season. So excited Sam will be with us this year.*

> *Sabrina: Oh, this is going to be so much fun. Maybe we should get a limo?*

> *Annie: I'm on it. Sam, where are you and Mark going to be for Christmas this year? We'll need dates, so we can plan everything. I'll also need the size of*

sweater you wear, so I can get you one that matches the family.

Sabrina: At our afternoon tea we've booked, I think we should plan a girls' weekend away.

I quietly sighed and peeked over at Mark. He was focused on the phone call.

Maybe we should have spaced out the family visits between mine and his?

This was much more intense than I'd thought it would be. My parents were polar opposites from Mark's family, and I felt like I was getting ping-ponged back and forth as I went from one extreme to another. Mark's family had confirmed they were going to arrive midweek. At times, it had become a tad overwhelming with his mom and sister group-texting me nonstop like this. Mark's description was becoming more and more accurate as the seconds ticked by. Before my phone continued to spasm in my hands, I typed out a quick response.

Me: Not sure what we are doing for Christmas. I wear a small. Thanks. I won't be on my phone much while I'm at my parents'. You guys have a great weekend, and we'll see you both next week.

Immediately, my phone pinged as if they were tigers waiting to pounce.

Sabrina: Oh, we have to see you at Christmas! I can't wait to meet your family.

Annie: Me either! I can't wait for next week!

Sabrina: What are you wearing for our night out?

Annie: I think we should all go shopping for new outfits. Sam, keep me posted if you need me to bring anything for our trip.

I was beyond overwhelmed with Annie and Sabrina at this point. I was trying to catch my breath and adjust to it all. I only responded part of the time to their onslaught of texts, and I never shared my feelings with Mark on it because I knew they were only being friendly. His sister was extremely enthusiastic about everything, and I wanted his family to be more laid-back, like they had been in Colorado that afternoon. He was only letting his family stay for two days at his condo, which was a relief.

Forty-eight hours—hopefully, my nerves would last.

While Mark continued his phone interview, I thought about the conversation I'd had with Edna to calm my nerves earlier this week.

The moment I walked through the door, she knew Mark and I were officially together, and my heart leaped at seeing her excitement and approval.

We were in the kitchen, baking, like we always did, when I asked, "So, does every couple fight? Mark and I haven't fought yet."

She continued kneading the dough as I sprayed the pans. I was covered in flour, and she was perfectly clean with her gray hair in its neat little bun.

"Yep. You know that kudzu vine that grows in Georgia and covers everything in its path, swallowing it and keeping the plants from the light?"

I nodded, smiling, as I wondered how she knew so much about where I was from.

She continued, "You know it was brought over to help fight erosion, and over time, people stopped tending to it once the erosion problem had been fixed. Now, it covers anything in its path, and they can't stay ahead of it. Same thing goes for relationships. When you stop tending to things, they tend to get obliterated by something unnecessary."

There's so much that goes into relationships. *"So, fighting is healthy? Is it bad that we haven't?"*

"No, it's not bad. When it needs to happen, it will. It clears the air and keeps it all clean. Plus, it's a necessary part. Without fighting, you'd never be able to make up."

My cheeks reddened at the innuendo.
"Take it day by day, Sam. Follow your heart."

I loved that woman. She kept it all in perspective, providing me with a solid base. Allison was wonderful, too, but I liked talking to someone who wasn't one hundred percent loyal to me.

Mark was still on the phone, doing his interview with the show, and I started listening to him. The national radio show was spotlighting several members of the team. He looked my way and gave me a half-cocked grin. There was no telling what the radio guy was asking him.

I received my answer when he responded, "Yes, Sam and I will be traveling together some during the season. I'm looking forward to us being able to spend time together on the road."

He gave me that seductive look, and I knew exactly what he was referencing in regard to spending time together. I put my hand over my mouth, stifling a giggle, as I looked away. He was too damn adorable sometimes. They moved on to different topics regarding game plans and expected performance while I focused on the green foliage before the Georgia summer sun turned everything crispy.

He was ending the call as we were pulling into the driveway. "Sorry about that. I didn't know it was going to take so damn long, or I would have pushed up the time even more."

"Don't sweat it. It's part of building hype and getting ticket sales. You ready for this?" My head nodded to my house as I rubbed my hands on my legs while I took a deep breath.

He was watching me closely, like he always did during tense situations for me.

"Yes. I hope your dad doesn't kill me on sight." His brow was quirked, and he was smiling.

Just like always, his calming voice relaxed me, quieting those terrifying voices that constantly circled in the back of my head.

"Well, as long as you don't tell him the things you've done to me, you should be safe. Don't forget that they are very old-fashioned. Also, don't forget about the sleeping arrangements. And—"

He put his fingers to my mouth, stopping my rant of reminders. He glanced down at my mouth before his eyes darted to the door, and then he looked back at me. My parents were probably waiting outside. My mama had probably been camped out by the window for the last hour.

"Sam, it'll all be fine. It's me and you."

"Me and you."

I knew he wanted to kiss me, but he reeled it in. Immediately, he got out of the truck and walked to my side. We were going to have to find a way to be alone this weekend. It was going to be hard with how my parents would probably be stuck by our sides, maximizing as much time as possible with us. He opened my car door, and I got out. I grabbed his hand, and he gave it a little squeeze. My heart felt like it was stuck in my throat as I anticipated what I was going to say.

My mama was adorable. She was standing up on the porch, watching with a loving expression on her face. I had ended up looking like a combination of my parents. My mama was shorter and rounder around the middle while my dad was tall and lean. In the middle of the two of them, I was curvy. My mother and I had the same eye color while my dad and I both had dark hair. His was peppered with gray now. I could tell by her smile that she was so excited, and my dad looked like he was uncomfortable but trying to smile under my mom's orders.

They love me. They will love Mark. It will all be okay.

"Hey, Dad. Hey, Mama."

Mom took that as her cue to come down and hug us both at the same time. "Oh, so glad you little darlings made it safely."

She pulled back as I introduced everyone. "This is Mark. Mark, this is my mama, Chandra, and my dad, Dean."

My dad joined us on the driveway.

"It's a pleasure to meet you, Mr. and Mrs. Matthews."

My mom gave him another hug as she said, "Oh, please, Mark, you call us Dean and Chandra. Welcome. We are so glad to finally meet you."

When she pulled away, Mark then shook my dad's hand. My dad said, "You had a hell of a season last year, son."

"Thank you."

One of my favorite things about Mark was how humble he was regarding his incredible talent as a football player. He never gloated about different things he had done, and he seemed to be embarrassed when people would praise him too much.

My mom took over the conversation again. "How was the flight from North Carolina?"

"It was good, Mama. It's good to be home."

She gave me a squeeze. "It's good to have you both here. We've missed you. Let's show you to your rooms once you guys get your bags."

As we climbed the stairs, I thought back to when I had warned Mark about the sleeping arrangements at my parents' home.

We were in my bedroom, and I was packing for our trip to my parents' this weekend. Mark was working on his laptop. I was nervous about telling him how traditional my parents really were.

"Hey, Mark?"

He stopped working and looked up. "What's up?"

"So, I need to warn you about this week. My parents are more traditional than the average parents."

Mark sat his laptop to the side, stood up, and walked toward me. When he got to me, he put his hands on my hips. "What is it, Sam? Talk to me."

My leg started fidgeting. "My parents don't believe in a couple sharing a room, living with each other, or sleeping together until marriage—like, at all. It's just...they just...shit..."

"Sam..."

I was chewing on my lip and bouncing my leg. Finally, I looked up.

Mark continued, "Are you okay with how our relationship is going?"

"Yes."

"That's all I care about. It's going to be a long couple of days, not having you in my arms at night, but we'll be fine. I have you, and that's all that matters."

I blew out a sigh of relief. He's so wonderful.

Mark had been great, but I knew this was going to be tough. We were both getting accustomed to sleeping with each other, and it was going to be hard being apart. The words *abstinence* and *Mark* did not belong in the same sentence with me.

What the hell am I thinking, having us stay here?

Mark was ever the gentleman. My mom was eating out of his hand, and my dad was being nice but on the quiet side, taking in the whole scene. Mark was helping my mom move something in the kitchen, and I was giving my dad a hug.

"You know, he doesn't bite, Dad."

He returned the hug, squeezing me. "Boo Bear, I think you should sleep with your mom tonight, and I'll take your room." His tone sounded worried beyond belief as he stared back at me with his chocolate eyes.

"Dad, don't be ridiculous."

"Boo Bear, it was pretty hard to watch Damien look at Allison the way he did since I feel like she is my daughter, too. It is damn near unbearable seeing a man look at you like that."

My poor dad was reeling from the whole situation, but only elation flowed through me at his words. Maybe I had been waiting for someone to say that to me besides Allison.

"He looks at me the same way Damien looks at Allison?"

He gave me that don't-be-ridiculous look, and I clapped and bounced on the couch like I was thirteen again.

My dad mumbled, "You should definitely sleep with your mom tonight."

I gave him a kiss on his cheek and scurried into the kitchen to make sure my mom hadn't gone overboard on telling Mark stories. I heard my dad groan. I turned and blew him a kiss, which he caught and held to his heart.

"Don't be silly, Daddy. I'll always be your little girl."

He smiled as I went to find the man who looked at me with love.

The world started to come into focus as I stretched from chasing away the last of the sleepy fog. I missed Mark beside me in bed, which brought a smile to my face. Just over a week ago, I hadn't been able to make it through an entire night with him without freaking out. I giggled, thinking about our texts from last night.

We were all climbing the stairs together. At my door, my parents gave me a hug. Mark had no choice but to settle for a kiss on the cheek, and then he practically shoved me through the door before closing it. Moments later, I received a text from him.

> Mark: Sorry for pushing you through the door, but it is taking every bit of willpower not to come get you to have you next to me tonight.
>
> Me: I could come to you once my parents fall asleep.
>
> Mark: Your dad left their damn door open. No way am I taking that chance.
>
> Me: Spoilsport. I can be quiet.

Mark: Damn it, Sam. Quit tempting me. I'm trying to do the right thing here, and you're making it impossible.

Me: How about we go back to my place in Atlanta tomorrow?

Mark: You just made a man desperate to have you very happy.

It was hard going to sleep without Mark by my side. The whole thing was comical, especially with our age, but I fell for him even harder with him not wanting to take a chance that my parents would wake up and walk in on us.

Hell, I don't think I could have gone through with it anyway.

Tonight, the plan was to go back to my place in Atlanta after we had dinner with my family. I wanted Mark to see my other place, too. My parents seemed to act oblivious to anything that wasn't happening right under their noses or that couldn't be officially confirmed.

I climbed out of bed and threw my hair on top of my head to go see where everyone was. The smell of my mom cooking breakfast in the morning was heavenly. Biscuits and gravy with sausage was my favorite when I came home.

Walking into my mom's yellow sunny kitchen, I smiled at her cooking at the stove.

I gave her a hug from the side. "Morning, Mama."

"Mornin'. Coffee is in the pot. Vanilla creamer is in the fridge."

I gave an appreciative noise as I started preparing my caffeinated fix for the day.

"Where are the guys?"

She continued adding milk to the gravy mixture, which made me salivate, knowing it would be ready soon.

She responded, "Oh, Mark was about to go for a run when we came out. Instead, he and your dad took off."

"Oh geez. Dad didn't have his gun, did he? I hope I get my boyfriend back."

I was only half-joking, not sure how my dad was handling the fact that I had a boyfriend.

After stirring the creamer in my coffee, I took the first sip as I watched my mom continue to cook in one of her little gingham aprons.

I smiled as she spoke over her shoulder, "I made your father promise to deliver Mark back in one piece. Your dad will never admit this, but he likes Mark. I like Mark, too. I'm worried you're going to rush things with him. Wait until marriage, and grow in your love with each other."

All the blood drained from my face. This was what I had been afraid of. I wasn't prepared to tell my mom anything descriptive about our relationship. I didn't know what to say.

She sighed as she slightly turned toward me and gave me a sweet look.

Why didn't I sleep in longer?

"Oh, Sam, I know what it's like to have a gorgeous boy looking at you like you're the air he needs to breathe while your hormones are out of control. Just don't give away what you've been saving for that special someone."

My heart dropped. There had been nothing saved for Mark. It had been ripped from me.

Putting on my façade that I was used to wearing, I comforted my mom. "Mama, don't worry. Mark is ever the gentleman." For some reason, I needed some approval from my mama, so I asked, "Do you think relationships can move too fast or too slow?"

"No, love doesn't have time limits—as long as it's love and not lust that's driving the relationship."

I sat there and drank my coffee as I thought about it all. She pulled the biscuits out of the oven, and I grabbed the little one she always made for me with the leftover dough. She gave me a loving smile, watching me do something I had done since I was a child.

She continued with her questions, "Are you nervous about the season starting and how that's going to affect the relationship?"

I shrugged. "Not really. I trust him. Plus, I'll be traveling with the team some because of my job, and we'll get to see each other. The press and the pics—it's all hype that happens for the fans. You know how it is from seeing how Allison was exploited, and things get turned upside down for a bit."

"Oh, I know. I was just checking. You've always been grounded, but I wanted to make sure you were okay with it all. I have a feeling that he'll be getting you to travel with him more times than not even if he has to call someone's certain best friend to convince a certain husband it's necessary."

She went to the cabinet to pull out the glasses as I giggled.

"I'll get the glasses, Mama. You've been cooking all morning."

I took the glasses out and set them down on the counter near the refrigerator. While I was filling the glasses with orange juice, I decided this was the best time to nonchalantly break the news. "Oh, and after dinner tonight, Mark and I are going to go to Atlanta to stay at my place."

She arched her brow, knowing I was telling her so that she could tell Dad. I gave a little puppy-dog face, which earned me one of those mom looks. She was about to say something, and I was sure it would be about me telling dad or about having enough linens for the guest bed, but I was saved as the screen door to the kitchen opened with my two favorite men coming through.

The moment Mark and I left, my parents would become oblivious again, and they would assume we'd be sleeping separately.

Mama smiled at the door and took the gravy off the stove. "Perfect timing, you two. Breakfast is ready."

Mark came over and gave me a kiss on the forehead. "Morning. How'd you sleep?"

I wanted to say miserable because he wasn't with me, but that might be a tad awkward with my dad sitting there, watching our exchange. "Okay. You?"

Mark's back was to my parents, and he gave me a tortured look, but he happily replied, "Good."

Mom brought over the rest of the meal, and we all took our seats and began eating. I'd missed my mama's cooking.

Mark was the first to speak, "Chandra, this is delicious."

"Thank you, Mark. This is Sam's favorite. I've been cooking this for her once a week since she was a little girl."

I smiled in between unladylike mouthfuls as I devoured my meal.

During breakfast, I texted Allison and asked about taking Mark out to her parents' farm to have some alone time. Damien had bought the farm back for her as an engagement gift after she was forced to sell it when her parents died. She had never wanted to part with it, but she couldn't maintain it while going to college.

As we were cleaning up breakfast, my phone pinged with a response from Allison.

> *Allison: I've notified the Andersons that you guys will be out there. Damien had four-wheelers delivered out to the place a while ago. Your dad has a key to the shed we had built out there. Feel free to use whatever.*
>
> *Me: You're the best.*
>
> *Allison: Xoxo*
>
> *Me: Xoxo*

"Who was that?" Mark asked.

He was standing right behind me, almost close enough to touch, but he was maintaining a couple of inches of space. I turned around and caught my dad watching us. He reminded me of one of those chaperones at high school dances who wanted at least three inches of space separating the teenage couples at all times.

I watched my dad's response as I answered Mark, "Allison. I'm going to take you to her farm and show you some of our old stomping grounds you've been hearing about."

Mark smiled, and I turned to my dad. "I was hoping we could go eat at The Harvester House tonight. Does that sound good to you, Dad?"

I'd say anything to get my dad's mind off of me going off with a boy. Plus, I had missed Darlene's home-cooking. She was the owner of The Harvester House.

My dad look pleased that I wanted to go to town this evening. "Of course. Darlene will be glad to see you. I'll let her know you're coming, so she makes sure to keep some of your favorite peach cobbler aside for you before it sells out."

I gave a little happy dance, which had both Mark and Dad smiling. They seemed to be getting along, and that made my heart soar.

I smacked Mark on the chest. "Get changed, Sport. I'm about to show you some fun out in the country."

I walked over to my dad and gave him a hug. "Where's the key to Allison and Damien's shed? They said we could borrow their four-wheelers."

Dad got up, walked over to a small drawer, and handed me the key.

I grabbed it and gave Mark a kiss on the cheek. "Meet ya back down here in five."

After that, I raced upstairs to change. I threw on a pair of skinny jeans, a form-fitting V-neck T-shirt, and my older cowboy boots. I came running back down to meet Mark at the front door. He was in jeans with a button-up shirt that had the sleeves ripped off. I swallowed.

Holy hell…

He made my mouth water.

I called out, "Bye, Mama. Bye, Dad," and then we headed for the truck.

As we got into his truck, my heart was hammering with what I was planning on doing at some point today. I was ready to take the next step. I didn't know how I was going to do it…yet.

CHAPTER
17

Mark and I had spent the afternoon having fun as I'd shown him the places where Allison and I had learned that cow-tipping wasn't possible, had rolled in circular hay feeders down the hill, and had sworn an oath of sisterhood, among other things.

We were racing back on the four-wheelers as the wind whipped through my hair. Mark was slightly ahead of me since he'd taken a turn better earlier. Little clods of dirt were being thrown up from the wheels. It felt good to relieve some of the stress I had over what I was about to do. He came sliding to a stop and then jumped off in one smooth movement. He put his hands in the air, cheering and jumping in front of the shed. Stopping my four-wheeler near him, I gave a pouty face and crossed my arms over my chest. He came up to me, pulled me off, and let me feel all his hard muscles as he brought me closer. I needed him. It had been too long since I had had Mark inside me.

He kissed my nose. "Don't be a sore loser. You won one, too."

To accentuate the pout, I jutted my lip out, and he leaned down and nibbled on it. He was starting to kiss me, and I knew where we were heading quickly. It was time to tell him what I was feeling before we made love again.

As he moved to my neck, lightly trailing kisses on it, I breathlessly asked, "Can I take you somewhere else before we go home and get ready for tonight?"

"I want to take you here."

His hands were starting to roam, and he began this sucking thing that drove me wild. I knew I didn't have long before I lost all willpower, especially after not having him close to me last night. I pushed him back lightly on his chest, and he responded by taking a half-step back. He looked confused as I'd never pushed him away.

"Mark, I want you, too, but I want to take you somewhere. It's important to me."

"Then, it's important to me, too, Sam, but I need you, so let's go."

After locking up the four-wheelers, he grabbed my hand and pulled me to the truck. He practically threw me into the vehicle and ran to the other side of the truck. He got in, slammed the door, and fired up the truck.

"Are you in a hurry there, Sport?"

"Which way, Sam?"

He sounded like a man on his last leg. I looked down and could see a hard bulge pressing against his fly, waiting to be freed. I giggled.

"Which way, Sam?"

He was growing more impatient, and I loved that he wanted me so badly.

"Take a right out of the driveway."

He gunned the vehicle, and I laughed.

"I haven't been close to you in almost a day. I need you. I've become dependent on having you, so yes, I'm in a fucking hurry."

I bit my lip and smiled. I directed him to the spot. I had never seen him this frazzled before. He was so calm and collected normally. Per my instructions, we had pulled off on a side road and emerged at the pond's edge before putting the truck in park.

There wasn't anything special about this place, but it held its own beauty for me. Pine trees were broken and lying in the pond. The water was murky with green moss growing on the top. The world was quieter here and accepted anyone.

Mark was alternating between staring at me and the scene in front of him out of the truck's windshield, trying to piece together the reason I had brought him here. My ears were ringing with anticipation now that we were here, and I was about to lay it all out on the table.

Not taking my eyes from the stagnant water, I started to explain, "I used to come here all the time to think and make important decisions. I know it doesn't have a surreal beauty to it, but I love it here. It's a hidden gem. A little TLC, and this place would be a fairy tale. I felt like I could relate to this place, like it understood me. I was so ugly on the inside, and I wanted to be beautiful. I wanted to be loved. By loving this place, it gave me hope that I might be loved one day. It was important for me to share this with you."

I turned to look at Mark, and his green eyes were penetrating me, absorbing all my words. He went to say something, but I leaned over and kissed him, needing to finish.

Pulling back after silencing him, I continued, "When I met you, I was terrified because it felt like you saw all the hidden beauty in me and wanted me for who I was, past and all. I never believed that was possible. You've told me that you have fallen in love with me, and you've been patient and not pushed for more. I wanted to bring you here to a place that no one else knows about to tell you that I am completely and totally in love with you."

I took a deep breath after giving that speech. A smile slowly spread across his face. He jumped out of the truck, and I mirrored his actions, meeting him at the front. This was our moment, and it was perfect.

He pulled me to him and kissed me slowly. I opened my mouth to him the moment our lips touched, and it felt like my heart opened as well. My nerves had dissipated the instant he took me into his arms, reaffirming his feelings for me. He pulled back slightly, and I could feel his breath on my face.

"Say it again, Sam. Tell me again."

Time stood still as I said, "I love you. I love you. I love you."

"I'm in love with you, too. I'm so in love with you, Sam. I'll never tire of hearing that from you." He pulled me to him again and held me like I was his lifeline.

I murmured into his chest, "Make love to me, Mark. Please. I want to make love to you here."

It was far off the road, and with all the underbrush, someone would have to be looking for his truck to see it. He picked me up and carried me to the back of the truck where he set me in the bed. In one movement, he was up and over the side of the truck and next to me. We slowly began taking off our clothes, stripping one piece off at a time, until we were both naked, staring at each other in the afternoon sun.

"You're it for me, Sam. You're everything I've ever wanted. You're everything I'll ever need."

He brought me to him and laid me down on the rubber-matted truck bed. His body was half covering mine, and I could feel every inch of him. It wasn't the most comfortable thing, but it was perfect at the same time.

Looking him in the eyes, I let my true feelings out as I said, "I feel the same way. Just please be patient with me. I'm scared I'll never recover from this if something goes wrong."

"You own me, heart and soul, Sam. I'll give you whatever you need."

He trailed kisses from my shoulder to my lips and kissed me slowly as our bodies automatically started to align with each other. We were like puzzle pieces that naturally fit together. My hands reverently explored his sides and back. We possessed each other, consumed each other, owned each other. Right before he pushed into me, he pulled back, and our eyes locked as he oh-so slowly entered me. Our eyes never wavered from each other as he continued inching in and out, which multiplied the intimacy of this moment. A tear streaked out of my eye.

"Don't cry, Sam. I can't stand to see you cry."

I pulled him to me, and right before our lips met, I said, "I never knew I could be this happy."

His lips came down on mine as we slowly climbed to our release. The walls of my core began to tremble, and he pulled back to look at me again. The look in his eyes alone started the orgasm that was slow and intense. It was glorious.

Exhausted and spent, he rolled to the side, and I interlocked my legs with his. His arm wrapped around my body while his fingers trailed a pattern on my back. My head was on his shoulder, and I was tracing a pattern on his abs, thinking about how this amazing man was mine. We both continued to lay there, letting the significance of the moment absorb, take hold, and deepen our connection.

He sighed, and it sounded like contentment, but I wanted to know exactly what he was thinking.

"What was that sound about?"

"I'm not scared shitless that you're going to leave anymore. I feel like you are truly mine."

I snuggled deeper into him. "I am, and you're mine."

We lay in each other's embrace for a while more while the sun was getting lower in the sky.

"We better head back to see my parents for a bit if you still want to go to my place after dinner tonight."

He tightened his grip on me. "After this afternoon, there's no way I can't have you in my arms tonight, Sam. I need you."

I loved hearing that he needed me.

"I feel the same way. It's like I've found the missing piece to me that I've been looking for my whole life."

He kissed me again as we bathed our bodies in the sun.

Sometime later, we were dressed and heading back home. I sat next to him on the truck bench, not wanting any space between us. The revelation of the afternoon and what we had done played through my mind. There was a peace that had seemed to settle on our relationship. It felt right, and it didn't matter how fast this had moved.

We were sitting at dinner at The Harvester House, waiting for our meals to arrive. It was an old-fashioned restaurant that had antique tools hanging on the wall. The old wood tables had individual wood chairs.

My mom was definitely in her planning mode as she began to drop hints. "Mark, we'd love to meet your parents sometime. During the season, maybe we could pick a city where you'll both be, and all of us could meet there."

Just the mention of his parents had all of the group-texting coming to the forefront of my mind. There were so many expectations. My parents would probably need to be sedated after an afternoon with his family. I was on the verge of needing narcotics.

Our dinner arrived as Mark responded, "They'd love that. They're coming to North Carolina to spend some time with Sam and me this coming week. You are more than welcome to come up there, too, if you want."

I was amazed at how at ease he was with my family after less than twenty-four hours.

My mom gave Mark a smile. "Thanks, Mark, but we'll let them spend some alone time with you guys. I wouldn't want to cheat them of the same time we've gotten. Plus, we are so much closer, which will make it easier for us to see you guys."

Thank goodness. I wasn't sure I could handle everyone together at the same time yet. I would for sure be committed.

"Then, we'll definitely work something out while I'm on the road," Mark said.

I gave his knee a squeeze, loving how he was treating my family. It made me feel guilty for having the thoughts I'd had about his. Mark looked at me adoringly. My mom watched us and smiled.

I excused myself to the restroom. As I exited the stall, I looked in the mirror and smiled. *The day has been perfect. The night is going perfect. My luck is finally turning around.*

As I was walking back to the table, I bumped into someone and murmured, "Excuse me." Then, I continued on my way.

"Sam?"

I stopped, my blood turning ice cold at the sound of the familiar voice. I closed my eyes, wishing I were dreaming.

"Sam, is that you?"

Fuck. No such luck. Why the hell does he have to be here? Shit.

Keeping my back to the voice, not wanting the face in my head, I responded, "I'm having dinner with my family, Greg. Please don't."

I started to walk off, and I heard him say behind me, "Please, Sam. Just two minutes. Please, can we talk?"

Momentarily, I stopped, still facing away from him. His pained voice was discernable.

I wasn't sure why I paused, but he took this as an opportunity to continue on, "Sam, I know I messed up all those years ago. I still don't know who I slept with. I wish there was something I could do to help us work past this. I've never stopped thinking of you. I tried reaching out to you, but you threatened to report me to the college for harassment. You know I couldn't lose my scholarship. My family was depending on me to get through school to help them. I just graduated. Please, talk to me."

My pulse was racing like a racehorse, and I felt light-headed as images from that night flashed across my mind. Our first semester of college, I had threatened to report him to the dean when he kept trying to contact me. Every time I'd seen him, I'd remembered the slap and how he had raped me.

I peered at him, and he looked completely lost, but there was nothing to say, especially here. We were inside the entryway, and Mark would be able to see us from across the room. The last thing I needed was a scene.

Facing forward again, I responded, "Good-bye, Greg. Please let the past be the past." My voice was cold.

Greg was better off not knowing what had happened. At least, that was what I kept telling myself. On my way back to the table, I kept my eyes focused forward and refused to look back. My features were tense, and my muscles were ready and coiled to run.

Why the hell did I choose to come here tonight of all nights?

When I was halfway back, Mark made eye contact with me, and he knew something was wrong. He started looking around the restaurant.

Fuck.

He was about to get out of his chair when I infinitesimally shook my head from left to right, and in return, he relaxed. Making it to the table, I pulled all my nervous energy and focused it into making the façade I was accustomed to showing everyone. My stomach knotted with a heavy ball of some sort. I pushed the food around on my plate, forcing myself to take a bite every so often, and that only added to the weight building in my abdomen. Mark's hand came to rest on my knee, but I refused to look his way.

The waitress sat Greg a few tables over from where we were seated. He had positioned himself right in my line of sight. I made the mistake of making eye contact, and Greg gave me a sad smile. My fork missed the potatoes I was aiming for and made an awful screeching noise. Of course, my action caused Mark to become hyperaware of me, and he noticed the direction where I had been looking. My mom was prattling on about some change happening in her baking club that was causing an uproar. I thought Mark and I were being obvious that something had changed, but apparently, my parents were not seeing the difference. I said a silent prayer of thanks. I loved it when they were oblivious. Mark was looking straight at Greg, watching his every move.

Shit.

Darlene, a heavy-set middle-aged woman with graying hair, came up to our table with a scratchy Southern voice, revealing she had smoked one too many cigarettes. "Ah, I was nervous, too, the first time I brought my beau home to meet my parents. Don't forget that a boy likes a girl with some meat on her bones."

Mark's hand came to drape around my shoulder, and I let his love ooze into me. I tried to use it to calm me. It was only mildly working at this point.

I mustered my usual chirpy voice, "Thank you, Darlene. I won't forget. Thank you for saving me a piece of your famous cobbler. That'll for sure keep meat on my bones. You can ask Dad. I've been dying to have a piece."

"Well, sug, I brought this just for you." She swapped out my plate with a huge bowl of cobbler and two spoons. "It's the last piece, but I figured you'd be sharing with your beau."

"Thanks. You're the best."

She patted the top of my head as if I were still five years old. "Anytime, sug." Her wrinkles were more pronounced with her smile.

Darlene walked by and gave Mark a pat on the shoulder before she returned back to the kitchen. He scooted a little closer, and I gave him a smile as I offered him a spoon. He took it and started eating the cobbler with me. I felt safer, the closer he was to me. Mark was eating the majority of the cobbler as I was trying to force down the few bites I could manage to take.

My mom asked, "Oh, Sam, isn't that Greg? It's been years since we've seen him or his family after they moved."

That was all I could eat of the cobbler at the mention of his name. More memories of that night flooded my mind—the slapping, waking up to him savagely raping me, the smell of his drunken breath, the way he'd held my hands above my head, the force he'd used. I swallowed hard, trying to maintain my grip on reality.

"Yes, Mama. It looks like they're enjoying their dinner, so there's no need to bug them." My voice was slightly rude as I responded.

My mom raised her brow at me.

Double shit.

The last thing I needed was a lesson in manners right now.

In a semi-scolding tone, she said, "Sam, they were good friends of ours, and if I remember correctly, you and Greg were the best of friends, too. He would have done anything for you. I still don't get what happened with you guys."

It all clicked in that instance for Mark, and he realized who Greg was. His fingers were white-knuckled on his spoon, and his hand had started to cut off the circulation on my leg from how tight he was squeezing my thigh. My body shifted uncomfortably, which caused him to release my leg.

When my mama turned toward Greg, I looked at Mark and mouthed the words, *Please don't. Not here.*

He was pissed. Next, Mama waved at Greg to come over to us. He looked at me and gave a genuine smile. The memory of him ripping my shirt tore through my mind, and I shuddered. Back in the day, he had been considered hot with his dark brown hair and light brown eyes. After all these years, he had stayed in shape from playing football. Once upon a time, I had worshiped the ground he walked on but not anymore. As I looked at him, none of those feelings came back. Instead, I was only filled with sadness from what had been taken from me.

Hesitantly, he walked up to the table. "Good evening, Mr. and Mrs. Matthews. It's wonderful seeing you. Sam, it's good to see you."

The moment Greg had started this way, Mark had possessively thrown his arm around the back of my chair. My dad had noticed, and a small smirk had played on his lips. If my dad knew what was driving this, he'd be reaching for his gun.

I nodded and returned to pushing the remnants of the cobbler around on the plate, not looking up.

My mom stood up and hugged Greg. "Oh, it is so good to see you, Greg. I remember a time when you and Sam were inseparable. Are your parents in town?"

He responded, "No, ma'am. I came here to see some friends. "

From the corner of my eye, I saw Mark looking regretfully at me.

My mom continued on as if we were all getting together for fun, "That's a shame. Hope they are able to visit soon. Sam lives in North Carolina now, so it's a wonderful coincidence that you happened to be here while she was here with her boyfriend, Mark Robertson."

Mama was beside herself with excitement when clearly half the table was not feeling the same way. She wasn't self-absorbed by any means, but I thought she fell more on the naive side of things.

His eyes widened at the recognition of Mark's name. Greg kindly said, "It's nice to meet you. I'm a big fan. Sam is a wonderful person." He extended his hand toward Mark.

It was the first time I had seen Mark be anything less than welcoming to one of his fans as he said, "Thanks."

Mark ignored Greg's extended hand, and my dad chuckled. It was a good thing my dad was attributing this to the jealous-boyfriend column.

Mark looked at his watch. "Dean, Chandra, it was a wonderful weekend. We probably should get on the road, so we don't get into Atlanta too late."

My mom turned her attention from Greg to us as we rose. "Oh, I loved having you guys. Come back soon."

Greg never took his eyes off me as he looked at me pleadingly. He remained quiet. Greg looked sad, but there was no way he and I had any type of a future together, even as friends.

There is nothing left between us.

Mark saw Greg watching me, and he made sure to stay in between Greg and me the entire time.

Hopefully, this is the last time I run into Greg.

I gave my parents each a hug.

Mark managed to keep his calm as he told my parents good-bye. "Thank you, Dean and Chandra. I'm glad I got to meet you."

"I hope you come back really soon." My mom had a slight mist in her eyes. It was always hard on her when I left home.

I jumped in, "We will, Mama. Love you both."

With that, Mark put his hand around my waist and calmly walked us toward the exit. I felt the fury rolling off of him in waves. All the emotions from the memories were brewing inside me. I was a ticking time bomb, waiting to go off.

As we left the restaurant, Mark asked lowly, "Are you okay?"

I nodded, not wanting to have a breakdown. Right now, I wanted to curl into a ball and disappear.

He opened the truck door for me, and I got in. I needed a few minutes to collect myself. He must have known that because he didn't say a word as we drove to the highway. I was staring out the window, watching as the twilight started to claim everything. I wished it would swallow me up right now.

Mark was calm when he asked, "Did they know you guys were together?"

I kept my eyes looking out on the passing landscape, focusing on the whirling shapes whipping by. "No. I was dating him behind their backs, which added to the reasons I didn't tell them."

"Do you really think he was drunk beyond reason? Will you ever report what happened to you? Have you checked into the statute of limitations?" His voice sounded like a mixture of emotions.

I couldn't look at him yet. Taking a deep breath and closing my eyes, I said, "I have to believe that he didn't know what he was doing. I'm not going to the cops. I'm not dragging you—"

He cut me off, letting me know exactly where he stood, as he practically spit out, "Fuck me or what you think you would be dragging me into. You need to do what's best for you, Sam. I'll weather any of it with you. I'll be by your side for whatever you need."

I knew his anger wasn't toward me. I turned toward him and grabbed his knee, hoping the connection calmed him down, calmed us down. His possessiveness was shocking, but I had been warned. I liked it though because it showed the depth of his feelings for me.

"Mark, this is my decision. You might not agree with it, but I'm not changing my mind. It doesn't change what happened. Did you really get a creepy vibe from him? Even tonight, he was still asking if we could talk. He has no idea, none. He couldn't talk to me in college because I threatened to report him for harassment, and then he would lose his scholarship. His family couldn't afford to send him to college, and I knew it. He just graduated."

"Are you defending that asshole now because it's clear he still has some sort of feelings for you?" His voice was rising. His hands were grabbing the steering wheel so tight that I thought he would pull it off.

I raised my voice in volume. "I'm not defending Greg. I'm apparently having to defend *MY* choices to you, so back the fuck off. Just because I said I love you doesn't give you any right to rule over me or dictate to me how I should handle things that have happened to me. It didn't happen to you. You have no say in this."

"Damn it, Sam. I had to play nice with the fucker who assaulted you, and you want me to do nothing about it?"

We were practically yelling at each other, but I was not budging on this. He needed to understand the boundaries on this topic.

Laying my hands on my legs and flexing my fingers, I tried to calm down. "I was the one who was assaulted, and it was before we met. You're not here to defend my honor. That was long gone before you even came into the picture."

His voice softened as he said, "Well, maybe if someone had been there for you, you wouldn't have felt you were worthless, and I wouldn't have almost lost you countless times."

"Please just stop. Please." My eyes were closed, and I pinched the bridge of my nose, trying to calm myself down as a couple of tears escaped. I laid my head back, not wanting to continue this right now, as I was emotionally wrung out.

We had just had a major fight, and my world felt out of whack. My eyes stayed closed. I drifted off in order to avoid figuring this all out.

CHAPTER 18

Mark's voice brought me out of my sleep. His earlier anger was gone, replaced with a soft, loving voice. "Sam, we're here. What do I need to do to get into the gates?"

There were two condos to each building. The lower floor had storage and a two-car garage for each condo, and then the living space was upstairs. It was a gated community with only ten buildings total. There was no need to respond as the security guard came out saw me and then pushed the button to let us in.

Mark pulled through and then asked, "Which condo are you in?"

I responded and sounded detached, "Building five, down on the end, condo ten."

Mark pulled in, and I pulled up an app on my phone that allowed me to open the garage door. My little red car sat there in the garage as he pulled in next to it.

Mark got out of the truck and grabbed the bags. I exited the vehicle without a word, tired and ready for bed since it was after one in the morning. I wanted my pillow. Mark was following me up the stairs. The quiet tension between us felt awkward.

Maybe this is how it's supposed to feel after fighting with a boyfriend. I wanted to go back to our moment in the back of the truck this afternoon. *Tomorrow—there's always tomorrow to sort all this shit out.*

We entered the condo. I proceeded to make my way back to the bedroom. My progress was stopped when Mark grabbed my hand.

He quietly said, "I need to get things cleared up between us."

"Mark, please. I'm tired. Can we argue about this later?"

When he didn't respond, I looked back at him. He looked wrecked, which broke my heart.

He walked slowly up to me and grabbed my other hand. "Let's talk in bed. We'll talk, not argue, I promise."

Bowing my head in affirmation, I led him back to my bedroom. Without saying a word, I stripped down and went for one of my T-shirts in my drawers when Mark's hands came on top of mine.

"Will you leave that off? I want to talk with no barriers. I think being able to feel each other will help us keep it all in perspective."

Dropping the T-shirt back in the drawer gave him his answer, and he shed all of his clothes, too. Reaching for each other's hands, we made our way over to the bed where he slid in first, and I followed, fitting into his side.

He started this intimate conversation as he said, "I don't want to fight with you. You're right. It's your decision. When I actually saw him tonight and it clicked who he was, I damn near lost control. You're the most precious thing in my life, and the fact that he caused you all that pain..." He took a deep breath. "Let's just say that I was ready to take whatever consequence there was just to pummel his ass."

I let his words absorb as I wrapped my arms around his waist. He had been right. Not having anything between us did help.

"I get it. I do. I haven't seen him in years. Like I said, when college first started, I threatened him with harassment charges if he didn't leave me alone. Since then, I haven't had any communication with him. His sister tried to schedule a lunch with me last summer. I was supposed to meet her the day I took Allison to the airport for her Miami trip where she met Damien, but I backed out."

Appearing to be lost in thought, he was drawing lines on my skin. Finally, he verbalized his thoughts, "Is there any chance in talking you into reporting this? Don't get pissed off again. I'm just asking. I don't want you to be worried about tarnishing my career because I don't care about that."

I hugged him closer. I loved having this contact while we talked.

"No, I'm not going to change my mind. You know I started that sexual assault awareness program in college, and I realize how hypocritical that was. Should I have reported the rape? Yes. But I honestly don't think he even knows. Greg has a life now, and all of a sudden, I'm going to come in and pull the rug out from underneath him? I can't do it. I won't do it. If it had been a case like when Brad had intentionally attempted to rape Allison, then yes, I would have."

I gave his chest a kiss, hoping that my little speech gave him an understanding of where I stood on the matter.

"I don't agree, but I'll support your decision. That bastard better keep his distance. You're mine, Sam. I'm never letting you go. I love you too much."

"Good. You're stuck with me. I love you, too."

"I want to make love to you again, Sam, but only if you want to."

Scooting up his body and sealing my lips on top of his, he got the answer he was looking for, and we began consuming each other.

Edna had been right. Making up was the best part of fighting.

Stretching my arm across the bed, I searched for my love, and I came up empty. It was after ten in the morning when I glanced at the clock. There was a thud coming from the living room, and I heard two voices talking.

What the hell?

I grabbed my silk robe from the door, put it on, and cinched the belt tight. I walked out of my room to see that Mark was in his boxer shorts, and he had Greg pinned up against the wall.

Fuck.

Mark was harshly talking to Greg in a low voice, "Why the fuck are you here, asshole? How did you find her place? How'd you get past security?"

This has to be a dream. The scene unfolding before my eyes stunned me into silence. I was rooted to the ground.

Greg was talking fast, and I was having problems hearing it all.

"I told Sam's parents I was heading to Atlanta, and I wanted to see you guys. They gave me the address. The guard let me in after Sam's mother let him know I was coming. Then, you answered the door. I need to talk to Sam. She needs to know how I feel and how sorry I am for cheating on her."

Mark pushed Greg harder against the wall, starting to cut off his air. "You're going to stay the fuck away from her. You don't rape someone while you're intoxicated, drugged up, or whatever the hell you were on, and keep trying to fuck with her head. She's mine, you bastard, and I'll be damned if you're going to keep hurting her."

I gasped, which caused both heads to turn my way. Mark minutely loosened his grip on Greg. My eyes were as large as saucers, trying to get the scene unfolding before my eyes all connected in my head.

Greg is in my condo. Mark told him about that night.

Mark positioned his body between Greg and me.

Greg was white as a ghost. "Is that what happened, Sam? Did I…I thought I cheated on you." He closed his eyes. "Please tell me I didn't do that to you. Please tell me he's mistaken. Please tell me I slept with someone else. Please."

Tears started streaming down my face as I finally had the confirmation I needed. The fact that he didn't remember what had happened gave me a small amount of peace. I had still been raped, but it helped knowing he didn't remember.

I asked, "Why are you here after all this time?"

Greg pleadingly looked at me. "Can I talk to you by myself for a minute? I swear, I won't hurt you. I never meant to hurt you. I need you to hear this before—"

Mark interrupted him, pushing him tighter against the wall, "Fuck no. You aren't getting near her alone."

My voice came out soft, "Mark, let Greg go."

Mark looked at me incredulously, his eyes tight, muscles taut.

He was about to object when I began talking in a normal, calm voice, "Let him go, and come stand by me." Turning to Greg, I continued, "If I agree to talk to you with Mark present, you have to agree to leave me alone forever after this is all over. I want to move on with my life."

Greg looked at me like he had when we dated as if he was trying to see into my soul. That look used to let him in, but the connection was gone. In the past, I'd melted each time he looked at me like that, but there was nothing now. He looked like his heart was breaking, and a lump formed in my throat. Regardless, Greg had been my first love, and this was tough. I was standing in front of the man who took so much from me but looked more apologetic than anyone I knew.

Beseechingly, Greg said, "Forever is a long time, Sam. Don't ask for that. Please."

I stood there, staring straight ahead, swallowing hard. There was no hope for us. To give him hope was cruel, and anything less than my request would give him the impression that I would be open to more one day. The last thing I wanted was to rehash this same conversation for years. We both needed to move on. I needed to heal from my past.

Finally, Greg relented, "If that is what it takes for you to hear me out, then my answer is yes. Sam—"

I held up my hand for Greg to stop. "Let me change, and I'll be right back."

Doing this only in my silk robe was not a good idea. Walking to my room, I tried to prepare myself for what was coming. I went to the bathroom and splashed water on my face. As I changed, I focused on taking deep breaths. Allison had been right. The past did have a way of coming back and haunting the present. Hopefully, getting what had happened with Greg out in the open would put the past in the past.

I want to live for the now and the future…with Mark.

Less than five minutes later, I came back in and noticed my hands were shaking a little bit. I needed to sit down in order to have something to tether myself to. Mark was by my side, and both guys were eyeing each other. This was the very definition of a clusterfuck mess.

I motioned to the chair across from the couch for Greg. This made sure there was distance for all parties involved. We all took our seats. I sat all the way back in the couch, and my leg started bouncing slightly. Mark stayed halfway perched on the end with his hand on my knee. Emotionally, I was worn out.

After taking a deep breath, I asked, "What do you want to talk about, Greg? Why are you here after all this time?"

"Is it true, Sam? That night at the Websters'…did I force myself on you? That has to be the night it happened. It's the only time I don't remember when I know you were around."

Greg moved to the edge of the chair, and the sincerity in his voice started stirring sorrow deep within me. His chocolate eyes were pained.

I had to break eye contact, and I looked down at my fingers as I whispered, "Yes."

Mark's hand moved from my knee to my hand and began rubbing it soothingly. Greg started running his hands through his hair in a distressed manner. He went to stand up.

Mark interrupted his movement, "Sit the fuck back down, or this ends, Greg. Don't push me, not when it comes to Sam."

Greg sat back down on the chair on command. "Shit. You have to believe that I don't remember any of it. The guys had gotten some pills, and we had all taken them. I took a few, wanting a good buzz, and then I began drinking. The last thing I remember was us dancing. Then, I woke up in the barn by myself the next day. There was blood, but I thought I had slept with someone else. I had no idea. I swear it. I loved you. I was ready to wait for you as long as I needed to. I never stopped loving you. I had to wait until college ended to come and figure out what happened. My sister helped keep me updated, and I knew you weren't seeing anyone through college. She tried reaching out to you." When he spoke, it was pained.

To focus my nervous energy, I shook my foot rapidly. "I never said anything to anyone. I didn't think you knew what had happened. I was fucked-up for a while, but I'm doing better."

"Why didn't you tell me? At least then, I would have known and could have gotten you help. We could have salvaged us. I could have tried to make it right." Greg looked down, not knowing what else to say.

An old crack in my heart resurfaced. This was painful. Memories of the Greg I had dated were trying to break through into my mind. Clearing my voice, I asked, "Why are you here? It's been four-and-a-half years." My voice cracked, which had both men looking at me.

Greg looked like he was forcing himself to stay seated, and Mark continued to try to comfort me as much as he could in this situation.

Greg responded, "I couldn't take a chance that you would actually follow through with the harassment charges when I was in college. I had to have that scholarship. It was my only shot to go to school. I had two classes I had to take the first part of the summer to finish up my degree. I officially finished three days ago. That's why I went to Homerville—to find out where you were in order talk to you about what happened to us. After you guys left the restaurant, your mom went on and on about how she thought you were in love with Mark, and he could be the one. I knew I had to talk to you as soon as possible."

I started massaging my temples. My head was pounding. "It's over, Greg. I'm in love with Mark. Even if Mark wasn't in the picture, you and I could never go back. I could never go there again. Anything we had together shattered that night. I should have told you, but my mind was such a mess."

I was on the verge of tears with all the pain I felt from reliving that night, especially now seeing Greg's heart laid out. I never wanted that kind of pain to be inflicted on anyone, regardless of what had been done to me.

"For what it's worth, I'm sorry." Greg ran his hand through his hair again. He started talking again, "We were good together, Sam. We planned our lives out together, our future. I'll always regret messing up the best thing in my life. Just know, there will always be a piece of me that loves you. Please don't close the door on us forever. We could start slow and build from there. We could try. I would give you the world, like I promised."

This was the Greg I remembered dating. Images of us being together were forced to the forefront of my mind—Greg taking me fishing, us four-wheeling together, me lying in the pasture as he read to me.

"Greg…" Mark's tone was laced with acid and warning.

Greg turned to him. "If you only had one more chance to talk to her, wouldn't you want her to know what she meant to you, regardless if it made a difference or not? Can you imagine what it would feel like to make one decision that fucked up your entire life, keeping the one thing you wanted since grade school out of your reach forever? I have no memory of what happened. You will have the only girl I have ever truly loved." Greg turned to me. "I hope you can forgive me."

His speech had stunned Mark into silence and had my eyes filling with tears. I blinked and felt the cool trail on my cheek. Greg and I both had suffered in different ways from that night.

"I forgive you. I believe that you don't remember what happened, and I do remember what we had together, but our time has passed. I love Mark. Please, go live your life, Greg. Forgive yourself, and forget me. You deserve happiness." I hoped my words freed him from his feelings for me.

I stood, and Greg followed suit. He started walking toward me.

Mark stepped in front of me, barely keeping his irritation in check. "Don't try my patience anymore."

At this point, after hearing all this, my body was a few seconds away from a breakdown. Greg and I would have been happy, and Greg knew that. But the moment I had met Mark, fate had started pushing us together, and I saw a brilliant future with Mark that outshined what I'd had with Greg.

Greg took a hesitant step forward. "Please, Sam, let me at least hug you one more time."

Mark went to speak, and I turned to him, which halted whatever he was going to say.

Standing on my tiptoes, I whispered in his ear, "Mark, I need to do this for closure for me. I need this. Please understand. I love you."

Mark looked torn, and I hated that I was hurting him because of Greg. His grip tightened on my hips. He searched my eyes long and hard before letting me go.

Allison's mom had always told Allison and me, *Decisions you make today can have a ripple effect. Live your life, girls, but make good choices.*

That night at the Websters' had had a tsunami effect on my life. It was time to forgive myself for all the blame I didn't deserve. I needed closure, and though it caused my stomach to drop, I knew I had to do this in order to move on forever.

I turned and took a deep breath as I slowly walked to Greg. When I got within a few feet, he closed the gap and enveloped me in a hug. It was familiar to be in his arms, even after all these years. He squeezed me tighter to him, and I remembered the first time he'd told me he loved me.

We were sitting on the bank of the river. It was right after Christmas, and we were all bundled up and on a blanket. Greg was wearing jeans and a faded blue coat.

He stood, grabbed me by the shoulders, and pulled me up. He took me in a hug and whispered in my ear, "I love you, Sam. I know we're young, but you're it for me. After New Year's, I want to tell our families that we're together. I want everyone to know you're my girl."

I squeezed him harder. "I love you, too. Let's tell everyone New Year's Day when my family comes over for dinner."

The Websters' party had been on New Year's Eve. I had pretended to be sick the day after, and my mama had canceled lunch. Regardless of the past, our hands had been dealt.

I was now in love with another man.

I needed to end this and give Greg and myself closure. I whispered, "Good-bye, Greg."

He squeezed me tighter and then pulled back to look at me. The look on his face would forever haunt me. It was as if I had held a sword and stabbed him.

"Please don't do this, Sam. Just give it some time. Let's go back to being friends."

That did it as my body pushed out the first sob. "I can't. I'm so sorry. Please understand."

And with that, I turned, pushed past Mark, who looked like I had kicked him, and I ran back to my room before shutting the door. In this minute, it felt like I was empty inside as my body flung across the bed, ending up in a heap. I was raw, exposed. I let the dam bust open, purging all the emotions I was feeling.

The door clicked behind me. A body cocooned me as my body was consumed with grief. The years of pain that night had caused were immeasurable.

Mark's arms banded around me, cuddling me close to him. "He's gone, Sam. He said he would leave you alone as he promised." His voice was low and cautious. After a few more minutes of me crying, he broke through my breakdown, "Sam, are you okay? He's clearly still in love with you."

That stopped me, and I sat up and faced him. "I'm s-s-sorry."

He mirrored my action and pulled me to him. I wrapped my legs and arms around him like a vine. I focused on taking deep breaths, so I could talk normally to him. I never wanted Mark to doubt my feelings for him. When my sobs subsided, I looked up into his eyes. He looked hurt.

I wiped my face. "I don't love him anymore. I did once upon a time, but you're the only one who has my heart."

"Sam—"

My fingers went to his lips and silenced his protest. "I only love you. I always hoped he didn't know what had happened, and when he confirmed it, his confirmation brought more emotions I had buried a long time ago to the forefront. Then, he started saying those things about what we were in the past, and it was hard to hear. Tonight was the closure I needed."

"What do you need from me?" His eyes searched mine as he waited for a response.

"Just hold me, and never let me go." My emotions were spent, and I wanted to be loved and cherished.

"I promise, Sam. You're mine forever."

The smell of baked goods greeted me when I walked through the doors of the deli. This was the first chance I'd had to see Edna. We had been back from Atlanta for two days, and Mark's family was coming into town tomorrow. After meeting my parents, the mess with Greg, and the continued hyperexcitement from his family, I needed help grounding myself.

As I entered, Edna cheerily greeted me, "Hey, I missed my baker."

"I've missed you, too. What are we making today?"

I gave her a huge hug that she returned in a grandmotherly way. After grabbing my apron off the hook, I made my way to the sink to wash up.

She was pulling things from the shelves. "Oh, I figured we would do some lemon sugar cookies, so you could give Mark his favorite cookies."

"With the lemon icing?"

"He'd have my head if I sent anything else."

"Yes, he would," I said, chuckling.

Mark could eat almost an entire dozen of the cookies if left to his own devices. He lost his willpower around them, which was funny.

She popped me with the towel as I was drying my hands. "We have twelve dozen to make, so get your tokus in gear and start mixing."

After I gave a noise of elation, I began mixing ingredients together. This was the best kind of therapy for me. The stress of the last few days started leaving me as the beaters went around and around.

We were icing the fourth dozen that had just come out of the oven when Edna asked, "So, you survived your first fight?"

"How'd you—"

She gave me that look that says, *I know all.*

"Never mind. Yes, we did. We worked through it, but I feel like there's something bothering him. He's been more uptight than normal, but because of his schedule, we haven't been together a lot since we got home. Plus, his parents get in tomorrow, and I'm a little on edge, thinking about how overwhelming they can be. Don't get me wrong—I like them. They are wonderful, but they are making assumptions about Mark's future with me, things Mark and I haven't even discussed yet." Focusing on the beaters, I added, "Things I'm not ready to discuss yet."

She picked up a cookie and started to ice it. "Have you talked to him about any of it?"

"No. I don't want to come off as being insecure, and I don't want him to think I'm hinting at the big M word when it actually terrifies me. I don't even want to talk about it. That's what his sister and mom dance around with the Thanksgiving and Christmas plans they make. He has enough on his mind with the upcoming season."

The cookie was iced, and she pulled it away. "Right now, this cookie is moist and delicious. It's ready to eat and enjoy. If I store it and freeze it, it will keep until I'm ready to eat it. If I leave it out on the counter, it'll dry up, be brittle, and break at the touch."

I smiled at her analogy and gave her a salute, reading her loud and clear.

She continued, "Don't let things go too long without being preserved. They have the ability to become fragile."

If I ever move, I'm kidnapping Edna and taking her with me.

My whole world was righting itself again as I walked through my front door, exhausted from my afternoon of cooking with my favorite deli owner. I was sad, thinking about how I would be working full-time in a few weeks. It would be harder to work in these baking sessions, but I would figure out a way. It was too important to me. Mark was out with the boys tonight, doing some male-bonding team thing.

After fixing a sandwich, I sat down on my couch, relieved to get off my feet.

The last few nights, Mark had been busy with various team functions that were for the players only. After what we had just gone through, I thought it made Mark nervous to be leaving me so much. It had been fine with me as it had given my mind a chance to continue healing from the whole Greg incident. I liked having time to myself. During college, I had stayed busy every part of my day to keep myself distracted.

We had been staying at my place for the last few nights. Each night, I would text him while he was out, and I'd ask which place he wanted to stay at. I would receive a reply, saying, *Whichever you prefer. Just let me know. I just want to be with you.* In the middle of the night, he would then slip into my bed and make love to me until the early morning hours.

My phone beeped.

> *Mark: It'll be late when I get back. After dinner, heading out for a few drinks with the team. I hate that it's been like this all week. I'm sorry.*

> *Me: I promise, it's fine. Going out is part of building the team. I understand. You're still there for me because the BFFF hasn't been broken out yet. My place or yours?*

> *Mark: Mine.*

That was short. He was grumpy. Normally, I would at least get a, *Damn it, Sam,* which always made me smile.

There's no need to get riled up about it until we talk this evening. Then, I could ask him what was going on with him and also let him know how overwhelmed I was feeling with his family.

After cleaning up, I got my stuff together to go to Mark's, and then I headed over before it got dark.

Later, my phone beeped again with a picture text. It was from Missy, the head cheerleader who had been hanging all over Mark at the steakhouse. All the team had my number because of my job.

Opening the text, I saw a picture of a girl hanging on Mark. His face was clearly not interested as he looked like he was trying to sign something.

Poor guy.

Missy had probably stalked them there and waited for the perfect opportunity to take the picture.

Can we say desperate?

I knew she wanted him, and as long as she kept it to this kind of stuff, we wouldn't have any problems even though it pissed me off that she was trying to start shit.

Time for some fun. I hit Forward and sent the picture text to Mark. I wanted to warn him about his entourage.

> Me: *Looks like you are having fun with more than the boys there, Sport.*

Almost immediately, I got a text back.

> Mark: *Who the fuck sent that to you? It was an autograph. That was it. I'm trying to get home to you as soon as possible, but it looks like it's going to be a while.*

> Me: *I know. Geez, I'm not accusing you. It came from Missy. She's stalking you tonight, it would seem. Where are you guys?*

> Mark: *We are at The Hound. Shit, she's a bitch.*

> Me: *Is there a past there I should know about?*

> Mark: *We'll talk about it later, but it was nothing.*

*Me: Okay. Not worried. Have fun. See you soon.
Love you.*

Mark: Love you, too.

My heart sank, thinking about him with another woman and how irrational that made me. Hell, we'd both had past relationships, and I wasn't mad. It pissed me off that regardless of what he had done with Missy, she was trying to stir a nonexistent pot. An idea emerged, and I ran back to my condo and changed. Missy was going to get the picture of where Mark and I stood loud and clear.

I pulled into the parking lot and gave myself one last look in the rearview mirror. I added one final sheen of lip gloss. After locking my car and adjusting my nightclub dress, I walked into the bar. My dress was a loose scoop neck, halter red dress with a low V-cut back, and the length hit mid-thigh. It hugged my body perfectly. My hair was down and full. By the looks I was receiving on my way into the club, I knew Mark was going to flip his shit in a good way. My red fuck-me heels alone would have him inside me in no time.

There was a line outside the club. Hoping my looks would get me in versus having to let my boyfriend know I was here, I walked up to the bouncer, and he undid the rope and let me in. I gave him a little wink, which earned me a smile. Upon entering, the music coursed through my veins. I saw Mark seated across the bar with some of the other guys, and of course, women were behind them, waiting for the chance to score a player this evening. The smell of lust was heavy in the air.

Lust away, ladies. He's mine.

Missy made eye contact with me and darted her eyes to Mark.

Bitch.

By the look in her eyes, she was probably wondering if I was going to throw one of those hissy fits because of her text. She would understand this evening when Mark came to me, not the other way around, that he was mine. I gave a little wave, which confused the hell out of her, and I continued walking to the dance floor, passing by Mark. He didn't see me as he was facing the bar, talking with the bartender.

I received a couple of catcalls as my body moved to the music. I knew the best thing was to always ignore them as I let the music take me over. My hips swayed, and my hands went up in the air. The third song started playing, and a light gleam of sweat coated my skin. Some unwanted bodies had tried to get close to me, but I knew how to keep my distance from strangers without losing my rhythm. It was freeing. I was lost in the beat when familiar hands came around my front. I knew it was Mark.

His mouth came to my ear. "Hey. Wanna dance?"

Mark pulled me to him. Our bodies joined, and we began moving together. His head came down and kissed the exposed part of my neck, and I tilted to the side to give him full access. The crowd had thickened and was pressing in on us. The pulse of the music drove us. We moved until we were both a hot mess, and neither one of us had said a word through multiple songs of the most hip-grinding, dirty dancing I had ever done.

After nibbling on my earlobe, Mark said, "Let's say bye to the boys, and then I'm taking you home. I think all these assholes got the picture of whose bed you belong in."

Turning to face him, I kissed him hard as his hands stroked my back. His leg went between my legs, and we started moving again. Our hot tongues danced with each as our bodies moved as one. We were both sweaty and hot. We were about to be a sexual explosion out here if we didn't leave soon.

Pulling back barely, our lips still touching, I responded, "Now, all the girls who were hanging around, hoping for a shot with you, know who you're taking to bed tonight."

He grabbed my ass, bringing me closer to him, and it only increased my sexual need for him.

Mark bit my lip and then said, "I like you a little jealous. Let's go before I lose my remaining bit of self-control."

He turned and pulled me through the crowd. As we were walking, he must have noticed someone looking at me because he shifted me in front of him and walked us to the bar.

We were approaching some of the players as he whispered in my ear, "Give me your keys. We'll get your car tomorrow from Gavin. He rode here with me. I won't survive the car ride without being able to touch you."

The sexual innuendo caused me to shiver. After I swiftly retrieved them from my red wristlet, he snatched them from me right as we pushed through the throng of waiting women to the bar.

Mark spoke hurriedly to his teammate, "Gavin, here are the keys to Sam's car. We're going to head out."

Gavin was the running back for the team. He was lean and muscular with dirty-blond hair that trailed right below his ears in a crazy, unrestrained sort of way.

"Sure thing." Gavin turned his eyes to me. "Good to see you again, Sam. Nice to see that someone tamed this fucker."

He punched Mark on the shoulder, and Mark gave a look of triumph as he pulled me closer.

With an exaggerated wink, I responded, "I do what I can. I do what I can. If you're looking for someone to tame you, Missy is right over there."

That caused Gavin to choke on his drink, and I laughed.

He sputtered, "Fuck no. She's crazy."

I gave a sassy smile, and Mark pushed the keys closer to Gavin. Mark was obviously growing impatient with our little banter.

My mouth started to open to say something else when Mark cut me off, "See ya later. Thanks, man."

Gavin chuckled. Before he had a chance to respond, Mark turned us from the bar and started pushing me through the crowd and out to the truck. We were practically running through the parking lot as he dragged us to his vehicle. The air felt cool compared to the club, causing my nipples to bead as it hit my dampened body. When we made it to the truck, he turned to me, and his eyes went to my chest.

I pushed my chest out, slightly accentuating my pointed nipples, as I asked, "You didn't want to stay for drinks with your friends?"

"You're funny, Sam. Get in the damn truck."

He pulled me to the passenger side of the truck, opened the door, and put me in the front seat. Mark went to his side of the truck, climbed in, and turned the key. The truck roared to life before he peeled out of the parking lot. My right hand slowly trailed down his body until I made it to his groin. When I squeezed, he momentarily closed his eyes and groaned. The club was about fifteen minutes from our condo complex.

Torturing him the entire way there is going to be fun.

I unbuttoned the top of his jeans and slid the zipper down. I leaned in toward his ear, barely tracing his lobe with my tongue. "I'm about to have my merry little way with you the entire way to your place."

His arms flexed, and I moved slightly back in order to untie my halter dress, letting it fall, exposing myself to him. I sat up a little and slid it down the rest of my body, ensuring to rub against him as much as possible. It worked.

"Fucking hell, woman. Someone might see you."

"Don't stop, and they won't see me."

I left my red stilettos on and lay slightly back against the middle of the bench seat.

"Sam…"

The false warning in his voice let me know I had already won, and he wanted this. However, it was still fun to play with him.

"I'll take care of myself real quick, and no one will see me."

He groaned and had a hard time keeping his eyes on the road. One of my legs was on the truck bench, and one was dropped off onto the middle of the floorboard. As I moved one hand down to my nipples, my other found his released cock and began to stroke it. I arched my back as I made my way down to my clit in order to give him as much visibility as possible. I rubbed my clit, building my orgasm quickly. I wanted a quick release while he watched me come. Flicking my clit had that drug I craved releasing through my system.

The truck made a hard left, forcing the tires to squeal, and then we came to an abrupt halt. I barely had time to look out the window to see that we were in a dark alley before Mark tackled me to the bench. He pushed his pants barely past his ass, and then he was entering into me.

"Fucking hell. I need you, Sam."

"Please, I need it hard. I need you."

He started really moving then, and all I could hear was the raw slapping of skin, our heavy breaths, and moaning. He lifted my ass, giving his dick a better angle to hit that perfect spot, and I was coming, screaming in bliss. He followed suit and bit my shoulder as he was rubbing out the last of his orgasm.

"Fuck, that was hot," he muttered.

"Hmm...I'll have to remember that."

We both breathlessly laughed as we tried to slow our pounding hearts.

All of a sudden, he rose and stroked the side of my face softly, searching my features. "Move in with me, Sam?"

"What?" My breath caught in my throat. *Shit, this is a serious step.*

"I want you to move in with me. I had this elaborate plan to ask you tonight when I got home, but I need you with me."

He continued holding my face lovingly, even when I tried to break the intense connection. There were no barriers between us. I was raw and exposed. My mind raced as I thought everything through.

I tried to stall, giving an answer without answering, "I am with you every night."

He was persistent. "Not the same. I won't pressure you, but I want this. I don't care which place we move into as long as it means we're together."

I breathed in deep, searching for what I wanted. When I had asked Edna if it was going too fast and if we needed to slow down, she had simply responded, *Let your heart be your guide.*

In the dim light, he searched my face, waiting for my answer.

My mind spun in a million different directions. "What if—"

He kissed me to stop my train of thought.

"Sam, this is forever. We can go at whatever pace you want. It doesn't change anything if you say no for now."

"It's all so fast. You've been so tense these last few days."

My heart knew exactly what I wanted, but I had to be sure that he really wanted this and that he wasn't just asking me in some sexual bliss haze.

He pulled back slightly and gave me an earth-shattering stare. "I was tense because I was nervous about asking you to do this. This isn't a spur-of-the-moment decision, Sam. We started building this last year in Vegas, and once we finally got our shot to be together, it all snapped into place quickly. This feels more than right to me. It feels perfect. How does it feel to you?"

I sidestepped his question one more time, checking one more time, needing confirmation one more time. "Do you really want this? It means dealing with all my stuff and makeup and craziness."

"I'll happily take it all." His eyes were growing with excitement.

I arched my brow, and he grabbed me closer to him.

"I have a condition then," I said.

"Anything."

"You have to help me break it to my parents."

He didn't hesitate as he stated, "Deal. All that matters is that I have you. I'll take any other consequence."

With that, he sealed his lips to mine, and then this time, he made love to me in the dark alley.

CHAPTER
20

"Yoo-hoo! We're here!"

I stirred and groaned, trying to retreat into the warm body next to me from that awful racket that was penetrating my blissful slumber.

"Mark? Sam?"

That voice was so familiar. *Where have I heard that voice before?*

Reality hit Mark and me at the same time as we clambered into the upright position.

"Shit, my family is here. They must have taken an earlier flight. They have a key."

He threw the covers over his body and started scrambling around the room. He put on some sweatpants and a T-shirt while finger-combing his hair. My dress from last night was on the dresser mirror. There was no denying what had happened in this room repeatedly.

Shit, did we leave anything out front?

They weren't supposed to be here until this afternoon.

There was a knock at the bedroom door that caused me to throw the covers over my head as I lay back down, trying to disappear.

Surely, they wouldn't come right in.

"Hey, Mark. We got on an earlier flight because we were so excited to see you guys. Are you awake?"

I heard the door handle start to turn, and then Mark's hand pushed the door shut.

Double shit.

"Mom, I'll be out in a minute. I'll meet you in the kitchen."

Being buried underneath the covers, I heard the stress in his voice.

His sweet, little persistent mother pressed on. "Is Sam here?"

"Mom, I'll meet you in the kitchen."

I was motionless under the covers, horrified, when I felt the bed dip as Mark sat down.

His hand rested on my leg as he said, "Sam, I'll go out there and get coffee started while you put on some clothes before joining us."

I threw the covers back slightly, exposing my face only. I whispered harshly, "You've got to be joking. I am not going out there to see your parents while I look like I've been fucked senseless all night long. I'm not trying to tell you what to do in your place, but I'm not going out there until I've had a shower."

"You mean, *our* place."

He actually looked irritated at me and not at his family who had walked in, unannounced, practically barging into what was *our* bedroom.

"Regardless, I'm not going out there like this."

Still under the covers, I crossed my hands over my chest for added effect even if he couldn't tell what I was doing. My irritation was getting the better of me at how he'd reacted. I didn't want to fight with his parents in the other room.

I continued, "Just think about it. Would you want to meet my dad for the first time after coming out of my room, looking like you had your wicked way with me all night long?" Softening my voice, I added, "I've never met your dad before. I don't want him to get the wrong impression of me. Plus, this is so awkward right now. They know I've been sleeping in your bed."

My parents would have flipped, and the fact that his parents expected me to be here was causing my head to hurt from all the confusion. I knew my parents were one end of the spectrum, but I hadn't thought ahead on how his parents would react.

Shit, I look like a slut.

He ran his finger down my cheek. "I get it. I'm sorry. My family is really open, and they are probably thrilled at the fact that you stayed the night. They want us to be together, Sam." He continued watching me. "Give me a few minutes, and I'll send them somewhere."

Exposing more of my face, I lowered as I said, "You don't have to do that. It's a little overwhelming this early in the morning."

Mark gave me a kiss. "Take your shower when you're ready. I'll be back in a few."

Before I had time to respond, he walked out the door to the awaiting craziness in his kitchen. I groaned. We had never talked last night about how I was feeling about everything, and all this was adding to the building shit pile of my anxiety. My ears strained to hear anything, but I could only make out some murmuring.

I was still hidden underneath the covers when Mark came back in the room. He looked at me cautiously. Honestly, I was afraid his mom would sense I had moved, and then she'd come in to offer to help me get ready. That was how overbearing his family seemed right now.

"Sam, they're gone. They'll be back in an hour. Is that enough time? I can text them and tell them to give us longer."

Ugh, what is wrong with me? Everyone is trying to be nice. "Mark, it's going to be so awkward now. You told them I needed an hour? Maybe more? Hell, I am so terrible at this."

I threw the covers back over my head.

He was at my side, pulling the covers back and bringing me into a seated position. "I told them that they caught me a little off guard, and I had something planned for this morning, so I was the one who needed an hour."

I threw myself at him, and he chuckled. I was relieved that he hadn't made me out to be a bad guy to his family.

I had to tell him how I was feeling. It was the only thing keeping me tethered in all this. "You're perfect for me. I love you."

"Love you, too. There isn't anything I wouldn't do for you. And just so you know, they're beyond excited to get to be around you more. All of them are. That's why they changed their flight. You're not terrible at this, Sam. You're perfect for me."

His look of what seemed to be pure love had my anxiety edging slightly.

Taking a deep breath, I tried to get ahead of all the mental pressure that was building. "Okay. Let me go get ready."

His body shifted, and I cut him off, knowing what he was thinking. "No, you cannot join me in case they get back early. Go to the guest bathroom to take your shower."

I scrambled off the bed and to the bathroom. I closed the door before he had a chance to seduce me into letting him join me. In the bathroom was a note taped on the mirror.

SAM,

REGARDLESS OF WHICH CONDO WE CHOOSE TO LIVE IN TOGETHER, I WANTED YOU TO HAVE PLENTY OF TOWELS THAT DIDN'T SANDPAPER YOUR BEAUTIFUL BODY. I GOT SOME EXACTLY LIKE THE FIRST ONES YOU'D PURCHASED WHEN WE WENT SHOPPING AT THE STORE TOGETHER. I WAS ALREADY IN LOVE WITH YOU THEN, AND I'VE DREAMED OF THE DAY WE WOULD ACTUALLY HAVE A HOME TO SHARE.

MARK

It was such a small gesture, but it was the sweetest, kindest gesture I had ever received. I opened the door, and Mark was standing there, looking at me with a little smile.

I jumped into his arms. "I love you. If you promise to make it quick, you can shower with me."

He was already walking us toward the shower before I'd even finished my sentence.

We were dressed and headed into the kitchen for coffee. I watched the clock tick down the hour until his family would return. I felt awful, having those feelings. I was beyond nervous at this point, considering how much they had changed since Colorado.

I opened up the fridge and saw my beloved favorite vanilla creamer. There was a note taped to it.

FOR MY FAVORITE GIRL...

YOUR FAVORITE CREAMER.

I pulled it out and eyed it thoughtfully. "You noticed what kind of creamer I use?"

He came up behind me as I stood in front of the fridge, and he wrapped his arms around me. "I notice everything about you. Have you decided which place you want to keep for us? I honestly don't care. I just want to be with you."

I leaned my head against his chest. "Your place is bigger with the two extra bedrooms versus my one, but it doesn't matter to me. Plus, we'll have our place in Atlanta if we go there."

He kissed the top of my head. "My place it is then."

I poured the creamer in my coffee, and we took a seat at the bar.

After taking a sip, I said, "I need to ask you something prior to your parents getting back."

It seemed like the things we needed to talk about were stacking up, and we needed to get some of them out in the open before it caused an implosion. Edna's words about the kudzu vine echoed in my mind. It might not be the best time, but I was plunging forward.

"You can ask me anything, Sam. I don't have any secrets with you."

He grabbed my free hand, and I looked at him. He still had that freshly showered look with his wet hair.

"What were you and Missy?" I held up my finger to stop whatever he was going to say. "I'm not upset by any means. Girls like that are manipulative bitches. I need to know if she's going to be a problem and know the score, so I can prepare accordingly."

He rolled his shoulders. "We never had sex. A couple of years back, we were both really drunk at a party one night, but I stopped before she took her shirt off. She's been after me ever since. After our display last night, I'm not sure how she'll react. She's been trying to land a couple of the teammates for a while, so I hope she focuses on them more." He combed through his hair and eyed me a little warily, which increased my nerves slightly. "I found out last night that Allison is doing a photo shoot in Atlanta soon with a few key players and cheerleaders for promotional stuff. It completely slipped my mind the moment I saw you out on the dance floor. Missy is going to be there."

The thought of Missy and Mark in a picture together caused unfounded jealously to bubble up even though I knew there was nothing going on there. *Stay calm, Sam. There's nothing to worry about. Don't let this bitch get the best of you.*

"When are you headed there for it?"

"It's next week. I figured *we* could go since you still haven't officially started yet, and your schedule is open—or I was hoping that would be the case."

He gave me a warm smile that had my heart instantly melting. I was glad that we had taken one thing off the list of things to talk about. It felt as if I was able to breathe a little bit more, like some of the vines were being cut away that were strangling me.

"Sounds good. And *we* have a place to stay there."

I gave him a wink as there was a knock at the door. Just the sound and knowing what lay on the other side of the door had me a tad antsy after this morning's incident.

Hopefully, wherever they went, they took some chill pills.

Mark went to the door, and his mom, sister, and dad came into the condo. His dad had the same body build and face structure as Mark, but his dark brown hair and brown eyes made him the odd man out in the group.

He came toward me like we had known each other for years. "You must be Sam. These two women have been talking nonstop about you. I'm David."

"Hey, David. It's nice to meet you."

David brought me in and gave me a big hug. This was one of the touchiest families I'd ever met. I had a friendly family, but this family blew mine away with all their enthusiasm.

Deep breaths. It is all okay. They are just being friendly—nothing more.

Right as he let me go, Annie and Sabrina took me into their grasps. I felt like a rag doll being passed from person to person.

"You guys, give her some breathing room," Mark said.

I smiled in relief at Mark as his family took a step back. It was wonderful they liked me so much, but I felt claustrophobic. Mark came up behind me and guided me into the living room. His family followed. Annie and Sabrina were talking a mile a minute regarding everything we were going to do in the next forty-eight hours. I was exhausted at hearing all the additional plans they had packed into our schedule that hadn't been mentioned in the hundreds of group texts that were sent to me.

Sabrina started, "So, I was thinking that we could leave in about thirty minutes for pedicures, manicures, and shopping. We needed to change the appointments a little to fit everything in."

Annie answered back, "I agree. That will be fun. Hair and makeup is this afternoon before going out tonight. The limo is picking us up at six to take us to dinner. Then, I have a tea scheduled for mid-morning tomorrow. I wonder what chick flicks are playing at the theaters. We might be able to squeeze in a movie."

My head was spinning slightly—no, it was actually spinning really fast as I tried to keep up. *Is there even going to be time to sleep?*

Even though I had spent the entire afternoon with them in Colorado, I felt like I was interacting with complete strangers. If anything, Mark had understated how hyper his family was.

When am I even going to see Mark?

Mark seemed to sense me tensing, and he pulled me against him. I tried to relax into him, but I felt like a rigid stick against his warm embrace. There was so much to take in that their voices were becoming blurred as I focused on breathing.

Sabrina broke through the fuzzy noise of voices when she asked, "So, are you going to keep us waiting? What did she say? That's why you made us leave, wasn't it? We're dying to know."

Mark looked uncomfortable and nodded. His mom and sister started doing this little clapping and squealing thing. I was not going to survive this visit. It was as if I had been teleported back to middle school on a continual basis with them.

What did I miss?

He hadn't asked me anything. He'd told me about the photo shoot, but that could not cause this much excitement, even from these two.

Puzzled, I asked, "What is so exciting?"

I looked around, confused, and the attention focused acutely on me.

Oh shit.

Sabrina piped up as she continued to bounce, her blonde hair swaying, "That you agreed to move in with Mark. He's wanted to ask you. We're practically sisters now, especially once he gets a ring on your finger. Then, you'll be married before we know it. Hopefully, it's soon before the season starts. Maybe we should look at some wedding dresses today to see what you like. Oh, I hope it's a short engagement. Then, you can make me an aunt. Oh, I can't wait until we have a little baby in the family."

I felt light-headed as the blood drained from my face. *What the fuck?* My world felt like a colossal train wreck, and my mind started to retreat and shut down. *Too soon...this is all too soon.* I was adapting to the L word and living together. *Shit. Fuck. Holy hell.* I needed to get some air. I needed space. I needed to collect my thoughts.

Standing abruptly, I muttered, "Excuse me."

I ran to Mark's bathroom and locked the door. *They'd have to break it down to get to me now.*

It's too much, way too much. Ring? Marriage? Oh fuck, this is going too fast. Where was the Rewind button?

After turning on the faucet, I splashed my face with cold water, and then I took deep breaths. *I need to calm down. How did things spin that out of control so fast?*

Taking family vacations together would be a walk in the park compared to that huge elephant they had parked in the room.

Someone knocked on the door, and my breath caught, wondering which person was at the door. I turned off the faucet.

"Sam, can I come in?" It was Mark—*thank goodness*—with concern lacing his voice.

I responded, "I'm okay. I'll be out in just a minute." My damn voice broke at the very end. *Way to be convincing, Sam.*

"Sam, it's just me. I want to talk."

He had that determined sound in his voice. I reached over and clicked the lock open. Then, I took a position on the toilet with my head in my hands.

He came in and locked the door again before taking a seat on the rim of the Jacuzzi. "Sam, I'm so sorry. They're just...I don't know. Shit, this is why I was nervous in Colorado. They can be overwhelming."

Looking up, my eyes started to fill with tears. I hated being so fucked-up. "I'm sorry I freaked out. I'm not ready to...I don't want to—"

He was in front of me in two seconds. "Hey, it's not your fault. Brina gets carried away. I shouldn't have told them about me asking you to move in with me. We talk about everything, but you can be damn sure I'll keep it in check in the future. Just don't let it change your mind about moving in with me. Don't run, Sam. Talk to me." He knelt before me and cleared my tear-streaked cheeks with his thumbs. "We'll figure this out."

Sitting there, I kept trying to calm down from that monstrosity of a conversation his family had unleashed on me. It was time to lay it all out on the line. The implosion had happened, just like Edna had said it would since I hadn't preserved things.

I tried to look down, but Mark put his finger under my chin, as I spoke, "It's so much to take in with Thanksgiving and Christmas and the family vacations they're talking about. The group-texting is overwhelming. Your mom actually already asked me to start calling her mom in one of the texts. The next forty-eight hours is completely planned, and you're not slotted to be with me at all. I thought the point of this was to be with both of us. Then, out there, that was more than talking about me moving in. The R, E, M, and B words were mentioned. It's just...a lot to take in. They must think I'm a freak with how I reacted." I took in a deep breath after nearly saying all that in one breath.

Just saying the letters had the words floating in my head—*ring, engagement, marriage, baby. Fucking hell. That is a load of letters.*

My shallow breaths started again.

Mark grabbed my face to make me focus back on him. "Sam, it's you and me, only you and me. We won't do anything we both aren't ready for. I'll never push you. Take deep breaths, baby. Deep breaths."

I started breathing in deeply and releasing slowly, mildly calming myself.

He continued, "Keep breathing. My parents don't think you're a freak. They love you, Sam. They love you because I love you, and I've never loved anyone besides them, and they know it. Trust me, my mother and sister realize how much they overstepped their bounds. They aren't normally this…excited. They got caught up in us and the excitement of me having someone in my life. You are what matters to me. Why didn't you tell me how overwhelmed you were feeling?"

I looked down at my finger tracing a pattern on my knee. "I want them to like me, and I didn't want to disappoint you. I'm afraid they'll think I'm not good enough for you. What if I don't fit in with them ever because of how fucked-up I am?"

"Sam, you could never be a disappointment to me or them. Hey, look at me."

I raised my head.

"I don't care what it is. When something is bothering you, talk to me. You're perfect at this because it works for us. That's all that matters, not what everyone else thinks. You are my first priority. I thought it was all okay because you guys were group-texting. It's no excuse for what happened. They look at you like you're one of the family. And regarding the R, E, M, and B words, don't worry about them. All that matters is that we know where we stand. This is our story to write, no one else's."

I bit my lip and nodded before muttering, "This has been a bad day from the start. I want a redo."

We were staring at each other as his thumb started to stroke my cheek, and then I closed my eyes and leaned into his touch.

"Where is everyone?"

"They're in the living room. They offered to leave."

I shook my head. "No, I don't want them to leave. I really do like them. They're wonderful. It's a lot to take in. You've met my parents. This is a different world to me. Hopefully, we'll find a way to meld. I want it to be us, not just me, hanging out with them. Down the road, we can do girl excursions, but not right now."

"Done."

He pulled me down onto his lap, and I snuggled into him.

"Sam, if it gets to be too much, squeeze my hand twice, and I'll make it stop. Whatever it is, I'll make it stop. I hope you understand how important you are to me and how much I love you."

"I do. Thank you. I love you so much that it hurts at times."

"Me, too, Sam. You have no idea."

Edna had been right. Things had gone much more smoothly when it was taken care of on the front side.

"Tell me when you want to go back out there. You have all the time in the world. They are going to calm down. Fuck, that was way over the top out there, even for my family."

I giggled. "They are wonderful. It took me by surprise. Give me a few minutes to clean up my face."

Mark kissed my forehead. I stood, and Mark followed my movement. Looking in the mirror, my face was tear-streaked and splotchy. I spent a few minutes cleaning up while Mark kept his hand on my lower back.

Finally, I looked halfway presentable. "Let's go."

Before he opened the door, Mark made sure to keep eye contact as he said, "Remember, you and me. Nothing else matters."

This is going to be so awkward.

We both walked back into the living room. It felt like I was going in front of a firing squad. Mark was holding my hand as he walked slightly in front of me. His family all looked up, and their faces appeared absolutely devastated, which made me feel like shit. It looked like Sabrina had been crying a little.

His dad went to speak, but I stepped in front of Mark, wanting to get ahead of this. "If you don't mind, I'd like to say something first."

His dad nodded, and Mark came up behind me, putting his hands on my hips. The gesture spoke volumes, showing how much he supported me.

"I'm sorry for how I reacted earlier. All of you have been so kind and welcoming. I'm not sure what all Mark has told you, but I've never been in a serious relationship before, and this one has been quite the whirlwind." I paused and looked at Mark. "In a good way." I turned back to his family. "I love your son. Just please bear with me as I adjust to all this. I promise, I'm not normally this neurotic."

His mom stood up. "We're so sorry, Sam. I promise, we normally aren't this crazy. We fell in love with you in Colorado, and we have been so excited to get to know you even more. When Mark told us last weekend that he was asking you to move in with him, we were over-the-moon giddy, waiting for it to happen. As a mom, you have no idea what it does for me to see that our son has fallen in love with someone and to hear and see how much you love our son. Mark loves you so much that it's as if you are already a part of the family. I can understand how overwhelming it would be. We are the crazy, neurotic ones. We normally aren't this out of control though, I promise. Would it be okay if I gave you a hug?"

I nodded, fighting back the panicked emotion from letting someone else in so quickly.

She came up to me and took me into a motherly soothing hug while saying, "I promise, we understand. Hell, if David's mom had pulled that on me, I would have passed out."

We all laughed.

She lowered her voice for only me to hear as she said, "Thank you for loving my son."

I squeezed her. "I do with all my heart."

"That's what matters most, Sam—you and him." She let go.

Sabrina stood and hesitantly looked at me, and I walked over to her.

She whispered, "I'm so sorry. I hope you don't change your mind because of me."

"I'm sorry, too. Mark is stuck with me."

She hugged me tight before pulling back. "Good, because he would kill me if I ruined this for him."

I looked over at him, and he was smiling at me. My insides became all gooey from the support. I walked back over to Mark, and everyone else resumed their seats. The tension seemed to be mostly gone.

David was smiling at his family and me. "So, we were thinking that we could all go out to dinner tonight and then see where it leads from there. Keep it a little more low-key and laid-back than what was originally planned."

Mark spoke, squeezing my shoulder, "Sounds good, Dad."

Mark definitely inherited his calmness from his dad. Mark might not look exactly like his dad, but they acted exactly the same.

We eased into conversation from that point forward, and it felt more like it had in Colorado.

Two little knocks sounded at the door as I was finishing putting in my earrings. Mark's family was headed home this afternoon.

Annie's voice came through as she said, "Hey, Sam. Are you in there?"

"Yes, come in."

It was different, staying in Mark's condo with his parents right down the hallway. Last night, when we had gone to bed, I'd felt like I was being naughty, sneaking into his bedroom. Images of him making love to me flashed through my head. It had been erotic, trying to stay quiet as he'd touched that spot inside me just right. He definitely had a few bite marks from when I'd muffled my screams.

I steered my train of thought away from her sex machine of a son as she entered the room.

Annie was wearing some capris and a sleeveless tank. She was fun and had that air about her that made people fall in love with her—at least, with the calm, non-hyper side.

"Hey, they all just left for a run. How does coffee sound?" she asked.

"Like heaven. My phone is almost dead, so let me leave a note for Mark while it's charging. There's a great coffee place right around the corner we can go to, if that works, or we can stay here and make some."

Since the dramatic events of their arrival, everything had been calmer, but at times, I'd sensed they were unsure and timid around me, which was to be expected as we learned about each other. Truth be told, I had been the same with them sometimes when I wasn't sure how my actions would be taken.

Annie gave me a sweet smile. "Let's go out for some fresh air. I'll be waiting in the kitchen."

She disappeared, and I grabbed my sandals from the closet. I had brought them over the night I had gone to the club to find Mark. As I walked in the kitchen, she was cleaning up from breakfast.

I put my phone on Mark's charger. "I'm ready when you are. Thanks for cleaning up. I was going to do that in just a second."

"You're welcome. You cooked it. It was the least I could do. I hope it was okay that I went ahead and cleaned."

There was the awkwardness again. "Of course. Thank you."

We each grabbed our purses, and I quickly scrawled a note telling Mark where we would be.

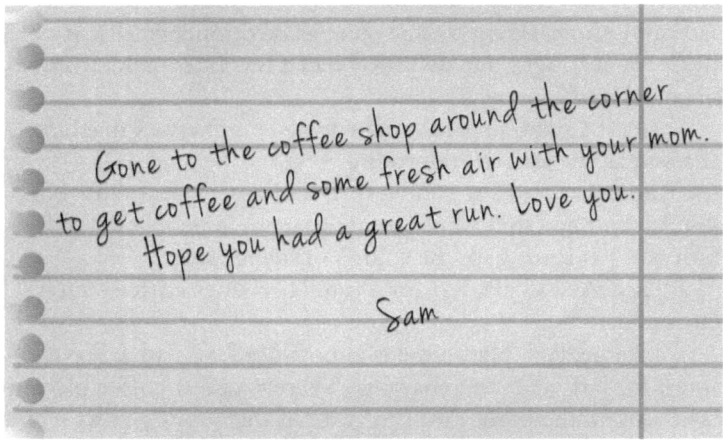

Gone to the coffee shop around the corner with your mom. to get coffee and some fresh air with your mom.
Hope you had a great run. Love you.

Sam

Before we walked out the door, I left the note in the dish where he normally dropped his keys when he came home.

The coffee shop was less than a five-minute walk from the condo. The temperature was perfect with a slight breeze.

Annie spoke up as we arrived, "Do you want to sit outside to enjoy this beautiful weather?"

"Sounds great."

"Okay. I'll get us some pastries. What type of coffee do you drink?"

"Vanilla latte. Thank you. I'll get us a table."

She gave me a sweet expression and went inside to order. Grabbing a table on the veranda, I tried to quiet my mind from reading too much into this alone time. Part of me imagined her going all crazy hyper on me, but I tried to push that event from my mind. As Annie came back outside, the smell of fresh pastries had me salivating. She sat down and gave me a nervous smile, which had my mind trying to race off into fifty different directions.

Why is she more nervous now than at the condo?

Grabbing a pastry, I took a bite. "Thanks, Annie. These look wonderful."

"You're welcome, sweetie."

His mom had something on her mind as she held her coffee cup and stared off into space. While she gathered her thoughts, I people-watched. There was a couple scooted close to each other, sharing morning secrets. I smiled as I wondered if that was how Mark and I looked when we were out and about.

Out of the blue, she started to speak, "Sam, I need to make sure that I haven't broken something between us with our erratic behavior in the beginning."

"No, I swear, we're fine. I'm sorry if I made you feel that way."

It felt good, clearing the air.

"Oh, sweetie, I get it. I promise. It's just…I don't want…" She took a deep breath and moved her body in my direction.

My pulse started to race a little bit, wondering where this was going all of a sudden. *Please don't mention any of the taboo words. I don't think I could handle her planning my future again.*

Annie said, "I don't want to upset you with what I'm about to say, but I feel the need to say it while it's just us."

I wasn't one to normally beat around the bush, but shit, his family was direct. All I managed to say as my mind went through all sorts of crazy things was, "Okay."

What if she tells me I'm not good enough for Mark? What if she asks me to quit dating him? Shit. Shit. Shit. Coffee was a bad idea.

She took a deep breath. "I know we've only known you for a short time, but we really have fallen in love with you. You're perfect for Mark in every way. I've never seen him so alive. He's always been an upbeat person, but the moment you came into his life last year in Vegas, he changed. I knew he had met someone the moment I saw him after the gala. He told me about you when he came home for a few days after Vegas. He was over-the-moon smitten with you. He's finally found the person he would put first before anyone else, and that's how it should be.

"What happened after we first arrived—although I'd rather it not have happened—showed me how he truly loves you. I have a very strong feeling you are going to be a part of his life permanently, which means you'll be a part of ours. I want you to feel comfortable talking to me anytime, especially if I've gone too far. I want us to be close, and I want you to feel like you're my daughter, too."

She stopped and looked at me. My eyes were huge as I took it all in.

She hastily continued on, "I hope I'm not terrifying you to death right now. Mark will kill me if I've overstepped again."

Well, that was a lot better than what my overactive imagination had concocted. I looked down at the steam rising from my coffee, trying to make shapes out of them, while I chose my words wisely and got my wits about me.

Finally, I said, "I'm a little terrified, but it's fine." After blowing the steam and watching it change direction, I continued, "It feels like everyone is putting the cart before the horse. Since going to my parents' house this weekend, the marriage insinuations have been strong…more than strong. It's as though everyone either knows or is seeing something I don't see or I'm not ready to see yet from Mark. I'm taking this one step at a time. I love him, and I want those things, but I'm scared to hope for them. Please don't tell him I said that because I don't want any additional pressure on our relationship. I'm already half-crazy with having zero knowledge of how to do this."

She grabbed my hand, causing me to look at her. "Sweetie, you're perfect for him. Go at the speed you feel comfortable with. I have a feeling that Mark just wants you in his life. I promise to try to keep my enthusiasm in check, but you have no idea how elated I am that he found his true match."

She gave me a wink, and I smiled weakly. I tried to just let her comments be comments, so I wouldn't unleash the fear I was trying to keep at bay.

Her phone beeped. "Oh, looks like they're back from the run, and they are going to meet us here in a few."

"Oh, would you ask Mark to grab my phone off the charger? It should have enough battery to make it through the morning."

She typed out the response, and her phone chimed again with another text. "He said, 'Sure thing.'" As she put away her phone, she asked, "Have you told your parents about the two of you moving in together?"

Blowing out a breath and scrunching my face in horror, I said, "Uh…no. I'm trying to figure out how to best keep Mark and me alive at this point, especially with us going to Atlanta next week for the photo shoot. My parents are not for living in sin, so to speak."

She laughed and looked amused at my bluntness. I felt any tension that had been between us evaporate.

Annie sat back in her chair, seeming more relaxed with me. "My parents were very traditional, too, and they weren't fond of the idea when David and I moved in together right away after we'd started dating."

"Really? Any advice?"

She took a sip of her coffee. "Keep it short and sweet. Tell them over the phone, so they have time to adjust. Then, when they see you next, it's done, and they've had time to process.

That lets the reality of the situation sink in and keeps everyone from saying something they don't mean."

Needing another hit of sugar, I grabbed another pastry. *Telling my parents is going to suck.* Between mouthfuls, I responded, "Thanks. I might require liquid courage before I make that call. My parents are very loving, and they adore Mark, but they're very traditional at the same time. Plus, my dad is still getting used to the fact that I even have a boyfriend."

Her eyes danced with humor. "I think I did three vodka shots prior to calling mine."

I knew from that moment on that everything was going to be fine between us, and the connection we'd had in Colorado felt like it returned. She understood me and knew my feelings. We were laughing as Mark walked up with his family. He looked a little tense, but he was hiding it well while he strode up in confidence, wearing some workout pants and a tank top.

He leaned down and gave me a kiss before taking a seat beside me, not saying a word.

"Hey, did you bring my phone by chance?" I asked him.

"Sorry, I forgot it." His tone was off, and he wasn't making eye contact with me.

Strange.

Both David and Sabrina greeted me, "Hey, Sam."

"Hey, did you guys have a fun run?"

Sabrina came and sat in between his mom and me. "We did. Your boyfriend is getting slow in his old age."

With that, a straw from Mark came flying at her, and I laughed. Mark's hand rested on the back of my chair, proclaiming we were together, but that was it as far as contact went while everyone devoured what was left of the pastries.

Maybe he was stressed, thinking things had turned south again with his mom and me being alone. He would be excited when he learned that everything was fantastic.

"Bye," Mark and I both said in unison.

We were both waving good-bye from the parking lot as his family pulled out and headed to the airport. Things were perfect between them and me again. Mark turned and walked up to the door. He was acting strange again, like he had been when he first came to the coffee shop. Not sure what to say, I went to check my mail at my mailbox to see if there was anything pressing. I was really buying me some time to think about how to approach him. A few bills and junk mail was all that awaited me.

Ugh.

As I came through the door, Mark was not in the main living room area. He obviously needed space, so I went to the kitchen. I was putting up the dishes when Mark emerged with a deep scowl on his face.

I closed the dishwasher as I asked, "Is there something wrong?"

"Who the hell is Adam?" His posture was stiff, and his mouth was set into a grim line.

This was the iciest I had ever heard his voice before.

My mind raced through people, trying to place who would have him riled up like this, but I was coming up blank. "Adam?"

He laid my phone on the counter with a thud, causing me to jump.

"The Adam that wants to taste that sexy ass of yours again."

My mouth dropped open as I picked up my phone and looked at the message blinking across the screen.

> *Adam: Hey, Kitty Cat. When do I get to taste that sexy ass of yours again?*

Holy fucking shit. It was Adam from the sex club I used to go to. *Shit, shit, shit.* I hadn't even thought of Club Envy since Mark and I had gotten together as a couple. Panic clenched my heart as I thought of how I was going to explain this one. We had both agreed that detailing out our sexual history wasn't necessary, but he needed something here. I would need some type of explanation if Mark had received a text like this from a female.

Meeting his gaze, I answered honestly, "He was someone I slept with in the past. I haven't talked to him since we got together. Is this why you didn't bring my phone down to me this morning?"

"Yes."

His mood and him forgetting my phone all made sense now.

"Did he mean anything to you?" The hurt in his voice was clear.

"No, no, no. I promise. No one, and I mean, *no one* meant anything prior to you. You're the only one."

I moved toward him, and he remained where he was, which I thought was a good sign. I snaked my arms around his midsection, and he drew me to him.

He kissed the top of my head. "When was the last time you slept with him?"

"Mark, please don't do this."

The mere thought of talking about this hurt.

"I need to know, Sam. I'm asking for you to tell me."

I swallowed. I didn't want to tell him, but I refused to allow this to come between us. If I refused to tell him, it would become a wedge between us. It would become a cancer that would eat at our relationship. It would set precedence for how this would be handled if something like this happened again.

I gave the answer he had probably feared as I whispered, "The night before I moved up here."

He pulled back, searching my eyes, as he asked the next question, "Did he put those bruises on your hips that I saw in the locker room?"

"Yes." My answer seemed like it echoed through the kitchen, repeating itself over and over again, intensifying the situation.

He released me and began pacing back and forth. "Fucking hell. I want to kill that bastard." He stopped, unleashing those emerald eyes on me, and he grabbed me again. "Did he hurt you?"

"It was all consensual."

Immediately, he let me go and started pacing again, cursing a long list of profanities under his breath. I was trying to let him acclimate to this before I lost my cool, too, since it was in the past. The truck ride home from my parents' house had proven that yelling at each other didn't do us any good.

Instead, I suggested the one thing that seemed to work for us. "I think we should talk in our bed without any barriers."

I began walking back to the bedroom, and I shed my clothes on the way. I crawled under the covers. Hopefully, if he decided to come, this would work and calm him down, reminding him of what we had. Minutes seemed like hours until Mark emerged into our bedroom. He silently removed his clothes and climbed into bed with me. He pulled me to him, and I intertwined my legs with his.

"I know we both have pasts, Sam, but that was a hell of a pill to swallow, seeing someone text you that. Then, I had the image of how he'd touched you. How are you going to respond to his text?"

I pulled back my head, wanting him to see the honesty in my eyes. "With the truth—that I've fallen in love with someone. We were strictly fuck buddies, I swear. He won't care."

There was hurt in his eyes as he responded back, "We started as fuck buddies, Sam. I've seen how these men fall for you, and it scares the shit out of me."

The truth of how I had started our relationship hurt. "I know, but until you, there was no one I wanted. I've been yours all along. I was just fighting it."

He grabbed me with both hands, pulling me flush against him, as he voiced his true fear, "But now that you've opened up your heart, you might change your mind. You might find someone else."

"Never. I have the same fears that you're going to realize how messed-up I really am, and you'll want something simpler and less complicated."

We were clutching each other as if something was going to tear us apart.

He pulled back slightly and stared at me as if he was getting a glimpse into my soul. "Sam, how do I prove to you how special you are to me? You're it for me. One day soon, you're going to be my wife."

My body stiffened in his embrace as he continued on, "I'm not asking this moment, but I definitely want it with you one day."

I was nonresponsive. *What the hell do I say?*

Mark continued to fill the silence that echoed in the room, "Do you see this going in that direction? Remember, I'll take you however I can get you. It's you and me. We decide."

Images of Mark and me at the altar, saying our vows, flashed across my mind. The moment I saw that picture, I knew what the answer was. "Yes. I'm not ready though."

"You've just made me the happiest man in the world. I hope you realize that at the first sign of weakness on your part, you'll be wearing my ring."

His hand trailed down to my ring finger, and he started tracing the line where a potential future ring would sit. It made the thought of being tied to him as his wife start to rise in the back of my mind, but I was doing everything I could to fight it. I was too afraid to admit I was close to being ready.

"You're crazy, you know that?" It was the only thing I could think of to say without showing a crack in my armor at this point.

He gave my lips a grazing kiss. "Crazy about you. While we are getting it all out there, was everything okay this morning with talking to my mom?"

His finger hadn't stopped tracing my ring finger, which was making it hard for me to concentrate.

"Yes, she wanted to make sure we were okay after the chaotic mess. It was good we talked. I told her how much I loved you."

His sigh of contentment against my head made me smile.

"Seeing how people fall for you, it's like you bewitch them."

I shook my head, disagreeing.

"Oh, it's true. After the run this morning, my dad gave me a lecture about treating you right and making sure you knew how special you were to me every day."

"Well, I'd say you have that down each and every time you touch me." I felt him getting harder against my stomach. "I think you should show me how special I am right now."

He had me underneath him in a nanosecond, and my legs opened to him. He slid into me, and I arched at his size, loving the full feeling. As he moved, he kept eye contact with me, pushing deeper inside me, penetrating every pore of my body.

"We're a perfect fit, Sam."

His hands took mine above my head, bringing our bodies closer. Too soon, my body lost control, and the tingling aftereffects of the orgasm rolled through my body. We lay there, motionless, wrapped up in the sensation of each other.

Talking while naked definitely has its advantages when the conversation is over.

The week had been uneventful since his parents left. We were driving back to our place in Atlanta from the airport for the upcoming photo shoot. I thought about the one concern I still had—Adam. There were no feelings there, but he'd responded to my text, and I didn't like him thinking he was right.

He wasn't. That part of my life was over. I had no craving, no need, no desire to go back. I didn't want my past colliding with my future. I had written exactly what I had told Mark as I thought back to that moment.

Walking into our bedroom with my phone, I got underneath the covers, still naked.

Mark rolled over and grabbed me, pulling me to him. "Where did you go?"

"I sent Adam the text. I wanted to make sure that was taken care of immediately."

My phone buzzed, and I closed my eyes, dreading the return text. It was important for Mark to be a part of this, so he knew I wasn't hiding any feelings for Adam.

> Adam: If you need what I've got, I'll be here.
> Good luck, Kitty Cat.

I read it as it flashed across the screen, and Mark motioned to see it. "Fuck. Is he going to be a problem?"

He was starting to sit up, and I pulled him back down and then pressed my body to his.

"No. He was convenient and easy. Anytime I needed a quick lay, I went to him. I know that's not easy to hear, but it's the truth. He's more

of a relationship-phobe than I am. I swear, you don't have to worry about him."

The tension seemed to ebb ever so slightly.

"How are you going to respond?"

I raised my body up and looked at Mark. "I wasn't going to, but I can if you want me to. What will make you feel comfortable? I don't want you to worry about Adam. He isn't worth it. I have no feelings for Adam. I'll even change my number if you want me to."

"Just promise to tell me if he contacts you again."

"Promise."

My mind had battled back and forth about telling Mark about my membership with the sex club, but in the end, I'd decided against it. There was nothing to be gained from telling him since I knew I wouldn't be going back. The thing that consoled me was that I'd always gone to the club in a disguise—a red wig and a kitty-cat mask. No one but Adam and his business partner even knew who I was or what I really looked like. Hopefully, it stayed that way. Mark filled the gap that I used to fill with meaningless controlled sex. It seemed love had been the answer for me all along.

Tonight, we were going to have dinner with Allison and Damien at their place. It seemed like eons since I had seen my best friend. It was amazing how much time it took to fully commit to a relationship.

I drummed my fingers incessantly on the armrest while bouncing my knee. Mark reached across and steadied my knee as I thought about needing to break the news to my parents about my new living arrangement.

"Do you want me to call them for you?"

"No, I'm their blood. They won't disown me. At least, I don't think they will."

I started shaking my foot back and forth since Mark's hand was stopping my knee from moving.

"Hell, Sam, we just moved in with each other. You act as if we committed a felony."

I had ignored Annie's advice and procrastinated in telling my parents. However, my best friend, Allison, had let it slip that we were coming into town for a few days, and of course, my parents wanted to see us again. That would force me to tell them since they wanted to come to my place, and Mark had brought things to move into our place.

"Do you know how mortifying it is for my dad to know that I'm really not a virgin anymore? They honestly think I'm saving myself. I mean, hello? Me moving in with you screams that I'm having sex with you. You don't generally move in with someone to bake cookies."

That earned me a hearty laugh, and I swiped Mark's hand away.

"I'm serious."

"You're so damn precious. You're like a tiger half the time and a sweet little puppy the other half."

I gave him my best growl, which earned me another chuckle.

"Make the damn call, or I'm calling them in five minutes."

Pulling my phone and eyeing it like it had the plague, I watched the minutes tick by. I pulled up their number and stared at my phone. I hated disappointing them, but I wanted to be honest with them about Mark. Mark was the part of my life that felt wholesome and pure. The ugly part I wanted to keep hidden from them forever. When the clock read five minutes later, Mark went for his phone.

I pushed Send and closed my eyes tight, praying it went to voice mail. I had the worst luck. When my mom picked up, I let out a groan.

"Hey, Sam."

"Hey, Mama."

"What's going on? Have you decided when we could meet for dinner? I made you some curtains for your guest bedroom in that purple velvet you like."

I spared a glance in Mark's direction, and he had his eyebrow cocked, which was telling me to get it over with. It was like prolonged agony, slowly ripping a bandage off a wound.

"Um…not yet. I'm waiting on the final schedule. Hey, there's something I need to tell you." My knee was bouncing ninety miles a minute.

"What is it? You sound a little stressed."

Deciding to rip the bandage off quickly to ease the pain of this blow, I blurted out, "Mama, Mark and I have moved in together."

I heard a quick intake of air.

"Did you elope?"

"No, Mama, we didn't elope."

Mark chuckled, and I punched him on the arm.

"We're still just dating, but we are really serious about each other."

"Sam—" Her tone was full of concern and on the verge of being reproachful.

Before something was said that caused hurt feelings, I worked on closing the conversation quickly by saying, "I know you don't necessarily approve, but this is what's right for us. I love you lots. Just think about it before you get too upset, and I'll call you tomorrow. Love you."

"We'll always love you Sam. Please reconsider."

"Bye, mama."

"Bye."

Hanging up the phone, I breathed in a deep sigh of relief. *At least it is out in the open now.* I had my fingers crossed that Annie's advice had worked.

"How did it go?"

I nearly jumped out of my seat and let out a little yelp.

"Shit, Sam. Are you okay?"

"I don't know. I'm dead-bolting the doors just in case. I hate disappointing them, but I won't lie to them about us." I threw my head back against the seat, staring up at the ceiling of the gray interior of the truck.

"Sam, they're not disappointed in you. They still love you. It's not the choice they would have made themselves. They want you to think and feel like they do. It's okay to be different." His calming tone helped soothe my nervous energy that was a ball waiting to explode.

"I know."

Mark's phone started ringing. He fished it out of this pocket. He looked down at the caller ID and said, "It's your dad."

Oh shit. This is bad—really, really, really bad.

"You don't have to answer it. I'll call him. This is not something you should have to be on the front lines for."

"I disagree, if it involves you." He looked at me and pressed Talk before holding the phone up to his ear. "Hey, Dean. Yes, that is correct. It was a joint decision. My intentions have not changed. Yes, my parents know. They were happy for us."

My dad's voice was rising in volume. The words weren't discernable, but the tone was clear. He was pissed off. I started rubbing my hands quickly together, and Mark's hand came out and grabbed mine, giving it a squeeze, as he used his shoulder to hold the phone.

His voice remained calm and even. "Dean, with all due respect, I love your daughter. My priority is and will always be Sam. I understand you might not agree with our decision, but it is our decision to make." He listened a little longer. "I love Sam, and I can't give a timeframe on when that's going to happen. That will depend on when we decide it is right for us. I understand. Hopefully, we'll see you for dinner this week."

He hung up the phone and looked over at me.

I wanted to puke, but I asked, "Was it bad?"

"He's not by any means warm to the idea, but he'll come around. When I talked to my mom earlier this week, she said she went through something similar. Just give them a few days."

I hated feeling at odds with my family.

"Sam, once the shock wears off, it'll be fine. Both our parents will disagree with things we do in our life, but we have to remember that it's our life. Come over here."

I unbuckled and scooted closer, leaning my head on his short-sleeved white polo shirt. "I know. I don't regret moving in with you. I wish it were easier. I knew they were going to have a hard time with it when we decided to do it, but I want to be with you, and I refuse to lie to them or let them dictate our life." I shrugged my shoulders. "Did my dad say anything horrible to you?" I chewed my lip, thinking about having Mark and my dad upset with each other when all I wanted was for them to get along.

He squeezed my shoulder, forcing me out of my spiraling chaotic thoughts. "No, Sam. He was a concerned father. I'd be the same way."

The thought of Mark being a dad had my mind going crazy again with possibilities. First, I would have to wrap my head around the whole marriage thing before I could even begin thinking about the B word.

"Sweetheart, let's go enjoy our dinner with Damien and Allison. Maybe sending your mom a text telling them you love them would help."

I pulled my phone out and typed out a text to my mom.

> *Me: I love you both, and I'm sorry if you're upset.*

A few minutes later, my mama responded.

> *Mama: We love the both of you, too. I promise. It's not what we wanted for you.*

> *Me: Thanks, Mama. I'll call you tomorrow.*

> *Mama: Sounds good. Just know, you'll always be my daughter.*

> *Me: I know. Tell Dad that I love him, too.*

> *Mama: He loves you, too, Sam.*

Leaning up, I kissed Mark's cheek. "Thank you."

I held the phone up, so he could quickly read the messages as he drove.

"See? They just need time. It will all be okay."

Hopefully, they would come around sooner rather than later. There was no telling what my dad had said to Mark during his little rant.

We were pulling into the driveway of Allison and Damien's home. The massive white columns and black shutters created that feeling as if we had stepped back in time to the days of big poufy dresses and horse-drawn carriages. Having been notified by security of our arrival, Allison and Damien were waiting on the front porch by the time we made it to the house. Jumping out of the vehicle, I practically skipped to her and then engulfed her in a hug. There was something different about her.

Pulling back, I noticed it. "Oh my gosh, you finally got a teeny-tiny baby bump."

Damien looked prouder than a cock strutting around in a hen house.

My hand went to her stomach, and I started speaking to the baby, which shocked the hell out of me. "I know you're going to be a girl, and your Aunt Sam is going to spoil you like crazy. Your daddy might end up hanging me by my toes." I looked back up at Allison. "Get to baking that baby. I'm ready to meet my niece."

Allison giggled. "I'm trying, I'm trying. It takes time. Mr. Antsy Pants over here might not make it to January without passing out."

My hand wouldn't leave her stomach as I sent loving vibes to the baby. "When do you find out what you're having?"

"We'll have the option in a few weeks, but we haven't decided if we want to be surprised or not."

I arched my eyebrow at Damien as Allison bumped her shoulder into his.

Damien responded to my questioning look, "I want Allison to decide if we find out. Your mom thinks she's having a boy because of how she picked up the keys she dropped on the floor." He shrugged, clearly confused.

I laughed, thinking about my mama basing the sex of a baby off of that. It also caused that little pain to come to the forefront of my mind, knowing things were rocky between us right now.

Damien continued, "Let's go inside and eat, and then I'm sure the girls are going to want some time to catch up."

We were finishing up dinner, which had been a fabulous roasted tilapia with asparagus and some kind of fruit dish.

As the plates were being cleared, Allison grabbed my hand and pulled me out of the chair. "Do you want to see the beginnings of the nursery? It's a mess, but I've started laying it all out."

Allison's little baby bump under her T-shirt was adorable. It was a wonderful feeling, realizing how far I had come from my initial reaction to her pregnancy. All those old feelings were gone, nowhere to be seen, and I was excited on so many different levels. I felt a bit guilty for being such a shitty friend then.

"Lead the way. Maybe I should get a disco ball to hang from the ceiling for all the dance lessons I'm going to give my little niece."

Giving a little shimmy with my hips, Allison gave me the don't-you-dare look, and Damien paled slightly.

I touched her tummy again, speaking to the baby and trying to aggravate the shit out her daddy. "I'm going to teach you so much about boys. You'll have them eating out of your hand."

That was the trick. Damien was practically choking on his water as I looped my arm through Allison's. I turned, gave a big wink at the daddy-to-be, and marched us out of there.

Mark was watching me, grinning. When we made eye contact, something intimate passed between us as I imagined us having a family. I blinked and focused my attention back on the baby bump as we walked out the room.

"You're going to give Damien a heart attack." Allison could barely get it out because she was so tickled.

"He deserved it. Payback is a bitch."

We both started laughing as we made our way to the nursery. We walked into a room that wasn't far from their master bedroom. The room was a mess with fabrics and paint swatches. In the middle were a bunch of green ones, to the right were pink, and to the left were blue.

"My foot, you're not going to find out. You're tormenting the poor guy."

She gave me a little wink. "We just started talking about it, and I wanted to think it through before I answered since he was leaving it up to me."

I rolled my eyes at her with her never-ending need to think and lay things out as I made my way over to the love seat. It had been pulled to the middle of the room, surrounded by all the decorating stuff. She pulled a stack of pictures off the floor and handed it to me.

"Here's the furniture we're getting."

It was Southern-styled furniture, warm and inviting.

"It's perfect for this room. Love, love, love it," I said.

Allison was beyond excited, and my heart soared, knowing I was here for her and sharing this moment like a true friend should.

She laid the picture back down as she nonchalantly said, "Your mom called not too long before you arrived."

Oh shit. The last thing she needs to deal with is my drama.

Hesitantly, I asked, "About Mark and I moving in together?"

"Yes, they wanted to know if I knew and what I thought about the whole thing."

"And?"

It seemed as if she was taking a millennium to respond as I prepared myself for their bad reaction.

She leaned back, patting her stomach. "I told them I thought it was wonderful that you had found someone you were willing to share your life with even if it wasn't in the order they preferred. I also told them that Damien and I had practically been living together after one week of being together. I had been stubborn about giving my place up, and I'd tried to protect my heart in case he didn't love me. Regardless though, we had technically been living together. Then, I reiterated that you don't do anything you don't want to do and aren't sure of in your heart."

"What did they say?" I held my breath.

She continued to touch her baby. "They asked me to tell you that they still wanted to meet you guys for dinner to talk. They wanted to know if tomorrow worked. It was a shock to them with how fast everything has moved. They didn't want to call you right before you got here and cause a scene or upset anyone."

I practically tackled my best friend on the couch, giving her the biggest bear hug ever. "You are the absolute best friend—ever!" I pulled back.

She returned my hug. "What were they going to do? I'm married and knocked up. Everyone is much nicer to a pregnant woman." She gave the most innocent smile and a shrug that had me smiling.

Hell, she knew exactly what she had done.

"You're getting the biggest kick-ass baby shower this world has known."

"You hear that, baby? Auntie Sam is already throwing you parties."

She picked up a binder and handed it to me. It was full of all sorts of pictures for the baby's room.

Thumbing through them, I sensed Allison thought it was a girl, too, with how much girlie stuff she had set aside.

"Damn straight, lil' baby Wales. You're going to be the most spoiled niece."

Allison continued showing me ideas she had pulled together for the nursery, and it was honestly going to be a fairy-tale room, regardless if they had a boy or a girl.

We were looking at drawings of a play castle she'd had done with the different colors, depending on gender, as she remembered something. "Oh, by the way, I changed the schedule. Tomorrow is only going to be the players, and then the next day, I'll incorporate the cheerleaders. I figured with Missy trying to stir the pot that it'd be easier to deal with the touching only one day versus two. I don't foresee her being a big problem though. Damien runs a pretty tight ship in regard to the team, and she knows if she screws around while working, she'll be gone."

"You didn't have to do that. I'll be fine."

Knowing Mark hadn't had sex with Missy made all the difference in the world.

"Oh, I know you'd be fine. I'm more worried about Missy." She laughed. "Plus, I think I'll be able to get the new guys to focus more without the female distractions."

"Thanks, girl."

We continued looking at different things she had laid out. Getting some girl time felt good and helped balance out all the chaos I'd been feeling.

CHAPTER
23

"Hey, Sam, I'm going to move these boxes in here to make room for some of my gear. Okay?"

Mark had brought a few bags of extra gear, clothes, and toiletries to stock our place here. My drawers were already half-empty with my move to North Carolina, so his move in was fairly seamless.

We had the initial photo shoot with Allison and only the players to go to this afternoon at a warehouse.

I yelled back from the bedroom as I was putting his boxers in the drawer, "Yeah, that's fine."

As I was pushing the drawer in with my knee, Mark came up behind me.

His voice was low and seductive as he said, "I'm thinking this is a definite must for later on or even now."

He put a shoulder-length, bob-styled, fiery red wig in front of my face.

Fucking fantastic. I wanted all this to be in the past. This was part of the costume that I'd used when I went to the club. My stomach instantly knotted, but my brain forced my posture to remain calm and loose. If he sensed any unease, I would have to give him an explanation. There was no way in hell I was putting that on for him and making love to him. *No way.* And I was going to try my damnedest not to talk about it. I wouldn't lie if he asked about it though. Instead, I needed to take the offensive.

Plucking the wig from his hands, I turned in his grasp and threw it behind my head. "Hmm…I was thinking maybe you could tie me up and have your wicked way with me."

Mark flexed his groin into me, showing me how ready he was.

That damn wig turned him on. Shitastic.

Allowing him some control over me was the only thing that had come to mind that would distract him from the collision course I felt we were on. My heart was racing at the thought of being tied up, helpless. I refused to let my nerves surface. This was better than the alternative of explaining the wig.

Mark ran his nose along my jawline. "I like your thought a lot better. Are you sure?"

"Yes, I want this." My pulse hammered in my chest.

He took off toward the closet.

Shit, what else is he going to find in there? That closet was about to get an overhaul even if I had to have Allison throw my sex-toy paraphernalia away for me.

He emerged, completely naked, with two scarves in his hands and a devilish grin on his face. I wanted to run my tongue along that V-muscle near his abdomen. He grabbed his phone, scrolling to what he wanted, and then put it on my docking station. Within seconds, "Sexual Healing" by Marvin Gaye sounded through my room. Without him even asking, I started to strip slowly with the music, swaying my body as the music took over. I focused on the moment to calm myself.

His eyes became hooded as he watched me. Making his way to the bed, he tied the scarves on each side of the wrought-iron headboard. Before he was finished, I started sexily crawling toward him from the bottom of the bed, making sure my breasts bounced. I began kissing up his lean muscular thighs. I moved over to his dick that was jutting out hard as a rock, and I gave it one long lick up his shaft, which earned me a moan of appreciation.

His hands automatically went to my hair, but I continued on and nibbled and kissed all the way up that blessedly delicious V-muscle. His hands came up under my arms and pulled me up to him. He smashed his mouth to mine, trying to alleviate some of the sexual tension that had accumulated between us.

"Sam, lie back, babe, or I'm not going to last or be able to pleasure you like I want to."

"Mark, I want you. I can't wait. I don't want to wait." I pressed myself harder against him, feeling the desire between my thighs intensify.

"Lie back, and I'll ease that ache for you. I won't make you wait, Sam."

I fell back, and my hair fanned out around my face onto my pillow.

"The moment you want to be untied, all you have to do is ask. Understood? I understand how big this gesture is."

I nodded. "I want to be tied up for you. Please."

He tied the scarves around my wrists. It was loose enough that if I needed to, I would be able to free my hands myself, which took care of any anxiety I was feeling. He next positioned himself between my legs and took my clit in his mouth. His tongue drew a figure eight, hitting all the angles, stimulating me beyond belief over and over again. His hands automatically went to my hips, keeping them on the bed, as my hands fought against the restraints. I wanted to feel him and push him harder against my core. He sucked hard, and I was screaming as the orgasm hit me fast.

Sweet relief.

He moved up my body, positioning himself right at my entrance. He began to nuzzle my neck, and I raised my body to him in order to feel as much of his body against mine as possible.

"I'm not keeping you tied up for long. We'll build from this. I never want you to be nervous when we're together." And with that, he pushed in.

One hand went to the side of my body to support his weight, and the other went behind my neck as his mouth took mine. We found our rhythm, and he continued hitting that place that had me tumbling off the edge of desire. My mind was in a euphoric fog as my hands were swiftly untied, and I was pulled to his side. I leaned up and kissed him long and slow, thanking him for what he had just done, strengthening the bond of trust between us. Relinquishing control like that, even if it was for only a few minutes, was a huge step for me.

After, I laid my head on his shoulder and traced a pattern on his chest absentmindedly as I said, "I wish we could stay like this all day long."

"Me, too. We'll have to make sure and get away every chance we get during our downtime. The season will get a little crazy, so it'll be important that we do."

Strangely enough, the season didn't make me nervous since I had traveled some with them last year.

"Mmm...sounds good. We're going to have to start getting ready soon for the shoot."

He pulled me on top of him. "I wish we could call in sick."

I giggled, picturing Allison coming over here in all her fury before dragging us there regardless. He chuckled, too, probably thinking the same thing.

"Are we heading to meet your parents straight after the photo shoot?"

Dread entered my mind again. I had texted my parents on the way back from Allison and Damien's to let them know we would like to see them for dinner.

"Yeah, we're meeting in Macon at Natalia's. It'll take us around an hour and a half to get there. I offered for them to stay here, but they declined. They're going to stay in Macon tonight at a hotel."

This was going to be awkward as my dad was still upset, even after talking with Allison. Although, Mom had told Allison he had calmed down significantly.

Mark pulled me closer to him. "I'm going to give you my credit card during the shoot. Call and prepay for their room. Have them upgraded to a suite. Also, book the private dining room at Natalia's, so you don't have to worry if it gets tough tonight for anyone."

His hand had started tracing something on my elbow. Every time we were together, our bodies naturally migrated to having to touch each other.

I rose and kissed him. "I love you so much. Thank you."

"Your happiness is the most important thing to me. I'll always take care of you."

For some reason, I believed him, and I knew he would put me first. I would do the same for him, too.

⋙⋘⋙⋘⋙⋘⋙⋘⋙⋘⋙⋘

The photo shoot had gone well. The seasoned players had known exactly what to do and listened to Allison's instructions well. Mark and I were almost to Macon, and my phone buzzed with a text. It was from my mom.

> *Mama: We are at the restaurant. They seated us in a private dining area.*
>
> *Me: Great. We'll be there shortly.*

My nerves were shattered, standing on edge, as I thought about how the first meeting with my parents would go since they had learned about Mark and me cohabitating. My mind imagined all sorts of scenarios from my dad punching Mark to them bringing a pastor there to marry us on the spot. It was completely unfounded. I knew that I had exaggerated everything in my mind, but my dad now officially knew that I wasn't a virgin, and I was mortified.

Practically bouncing in my seat, there wasn't a muscle that wasn't moving or tensed up in some way or another. Fidgeting with my phone, checking my email for the millionth time, I never realized Mark had pulled off the highway and onto a side road. He put the truck in park, got out, and came over to my side. He opened my door and the back door simultaneously.

"What are you—"

He pulled me from the vehicle, and his hand wrapped around my back. His cologne was clean and refreshing. His hand moved down my thigh, bunching up my baby doll dress. Whatever he had in mind, I was right there with him, craving it. He gave me a kiss as his fingers pushed aside my panties, and he began fingering me. My insides shook, reveling in the feeling.

"I can't get you too messed-up, Sam, but you need this. It will have to be hard and fast."

I whimpered at his words. He pulled his fingers out and spun me around. I leaned over and heard the zipper of his pants, and the dampness between my legs increased. My thong was then snapped from my body before my dress was lifted, and he pushed in. It was fast, raw, and sensual, and he pushed to the base each and every time. One hand moved to my front and began vigorously rubbing me, which had me flying high in no time. Mark stilled as he emptied himself in me. It had been hard, quick, and dirty. He pulled out, and I lay boneless on the seat. At this point, I felt so good that even if we arrived late, it wouldn't matter. Mark picked me up and put me back in the truck after resituating my dress. Then, he went back to his side.

We smiled dopily at each other as I languidly said, "You knew exactly what I needed."

"What we both needed, Sam. Every time you get nervous at dinner tonight, think back on this and remember what we have. That's all that matters. We support each other, and that's what counts at the end of the day. It's you and me."

We were pulling into the restaurant parking lot less than twenty minutes later. There was only a slight nervousness evading my brain, but as we held hands, I was able to sit still, thinking of how good it had felt having him inside me.

"You seem less edgy," he said.

Leaning my head back, letting the images permeate my thoughts, I responded, "Someone pounded some sense into me."

He choked as he put the truck into park. "You have a way with words sometimes."

I gave a little smirk as we both got out of the vehicle. At the front of the truck, we met and joined hands before we walked in. We were at one of the nicest restaurants in town, Natalia's. It had a semiformal setting, and Mark had reserved one of the private dining rooms. It was done in old world décor.

The waitress, of course, had all eyes for Mark, which he didn't seem to notice, as she escorted us to the back while adding a little extra sway to her hips. My mom and dad were already seated as we entered. They looked as if they hadn't been sleeping well. My heart hurt that my news had probably caused that. They stiffly rose from their chairs. I tried to act as normal as possible, focusing on every part of Mark that was touching me.

He is worth this. We are worth this.

"Hey, Mama. Hey, Dad."

I gave both of them a hug, which they warmly returned. My mom and Mark hugged, and my dad's handshake was on the verge of being semi-unfriendly. Mark remained calm and unaffected.

My mom was the first to break the ice. "Let's order, and then we can talk."

No one really answered as we made our way to the table and took our seats. I grabbed my napkin, so I had something to fiddle with that was out of sight.

My dad decided to cut right to the chase before we could even open our menus. "Have you decided when you two plan on getting married?" His voice sounded like it used to when I had gotten into trouble as a kid.

It felt archaic, how my dad was acting as if Mark had taken my virtue. My temper flared slightly since I was an adult, but I reeled it in, wanting us to come to some kind of understanding, so we could move forward.

"Dad, I get that you're upset and that you disagree with our decision. However, I am an adult and capable of making my own decisions. We love each other and—"

Dad swiped his hand in front of me, instantly causing me to be quiet. "Answer me this then. If you love each other that much, then what's keeping you from getting married? If you're willing to consolidate living spaces and everything else, then why not marry each other? Do you not care what people are going to think or what they will say to your mother when they find out? Have you no respect for how we raised you?"

His words were like acid in my veins. The obvious disappointment hurt me. My mom was stirring uncomfortably beside him, playing with her napkin. She was obviously on the verge of tears. I hated disappointing them. I always had.

How the hell am I going to respond to that?

Mark squeezed my knee slightly before he responded, "Dean, I understand both of your positions on this matter, and we mean no disrespect. However, Sam and I have to do what's right for us, which might not exactly align with everyone's thoughts all the time. Feel free to give my number to everyone who feels like they have a right to discuss our life choices or their opinion of it with you. Sam will always be my priority, and as long as she is happy, that's all I'm concerned with. I hope you both can appreciate the unconditional love your daughter will receive from me. Give us time."

The room was deathly quiet as everyone absorbed Mark's words. His speech was respectful but full of authority.

The waiter chose this moment to come and take our orders. I chose the spaghetti because it was the first thing I'd spotted on the menu. The atmosphere felt like we were at a standstill with no one talking, and I had no idea what anyone else ordered as I tried to process it all.

My dad wore a blank mask, staring at the both of us. It was a little unsettling, thinking about what they would have been like without their talk with Allison yesterday.

The waiter left, and the awkward silence returned. Mark's hand grabbed mine, and his thumb stroked it up and down. I returned his gesture with a squeeze. It felt like we were in some alternate universe where seconds felt like a millennium.

My dad cleared his throat and spoke in a much nicer voice, "Mark, I'll never approve of this because she's my little girl after all. This is not how we believe a proper relationship should be done. I do see and hear how much you love her and are willing to stand by her, which is what Chandra and I have always wanted. We might be considered old-fashioned, but our views won't change on this subject."

Mark went to speak, but my dad held up his hand, continuing on, "With that being said, neither one of us wants the strain on our relationship, and we want to be a part of your lives. For now, we will need to abstain from staying with you guys, and if you stay with us, we will ask you to respect us by sleeping in separate bedrooms."

Mark gave my hand several little squeezes as if each was saying, *I love you*, over and over again, which made this crusade worth the fight.

He responded, "Dean and Chandra, I completely understand. There's no strain. Sam is the way she is today because of who you are and how you raised her. I'm thankful for that. However, this is our relationship. I'll always put Sam first."

That did it, and my mom and I had tears in our eyes. She and I both stood and hugged each other.

My mama whispered, "He loves you so much."

"I love him, too. He's the one."

My body froze as I registered the words that had come out of my mouth. I hadn't meant for it to come out like that. *What the hell did I just do?* Inadvertently admitting that to my mom had shifted everything clearer into focus.

We pulled apart, and I realized that everyone in the room had heard what I had said.

Shit. Shit. Shit.

My dad looked pleased and shell-shocked all at the same time. Mark had a different look about him as he smiled. It was almost calculating. His gaze was burning a hole in me, and I looked away and went to hug my dad.

My dad's demeanor had completely softened, which hopefully meant the worst was behind us.

As I latched on to him, he whispered, "I love you, Boo Bear. It will all be okay."

"I know, Dad."

Our dinner arrived, and it appeared everyone was settling back down. It was a good feeling, knowing that we had been able to work things out with both sides of our families when we had disagreements. I wanted us to all get along and be a loving family. The only thing that was rocking my world at the moment was how I had so outspokenly admitted that Mark was the one. This afternoon, I had told him I was able to see where this was going, but I had laid down the gauntlet and basically declared that I was ready. Hopefully, he was glad we had worked things out with my family, and he hadn't paid attention to my slipup.

I was headed to the second day of the photo shoot, and later tonight, we were going to a formal dinner for everyone who had been brought in from North Carolina, totaling about thirty people. Yesterday had been uneventful with it being a bunch of guys posing this way and that way. The cheerleaders were being added today, which was going to make it a little more interesting. This was part of Mark's life, so I guessed I would see how I was going to deal with the girls hanging on him. I believed I would be okay with it since it was business and not personal.

My car radio was on, and the sunroof was open as I drove to the warehouse for today's shoot. Mark had been picked up earlier per Allison's last-minute request as she needed a few additional shots of him by himself. I had used that time to pay bills.

Pulling in, I jumped out of the car and headed into the warehouse where the shoot had started. I saw Mark in front of a white screen with two girls on each side. He made eye contact with me as if sensing my presence. I gave him a little wave. Missy was off in the corner, and she looked at me and then back toward Mark. Damien was here also. I imagined he'd made his presence known to make sure no one would give Allison any shit.

Different lighting fixtures and silver screened things were everywhere. Several different areas were setup with white screens, intending for those pictures to look like they had been done outside. Allison was going to photoshop in different backgrounds where needed. One area looked like part of the field while the one right next to it was a locker-room setup.

Allison was directing the girls' stances and clicking away. Mark was dressed in full uniform and had a sultry look on his face as he posed with them. Even though I had already had him once today, desire bloomed through me.

I walked up to Allison who was clicking away. "Hey, little mama. Is there anything you need me to do?"

"Not right now. Damien has so many people hired to help adjust lighting and anything else that I need, so I'm good." She knelt down for a different angle and repositioned everyone.

Damien walked up. "Hey, Sam. Make sure Allison doesn't work too hard today."

I gave him my best salute.

He leaned into Allison. "You two take care. Bane and Jeremy are staying here with you. I'll be back before dinner."

She leaned up and kissed him. "Don't worry. We'll be fine."

Damien gave her an endearing smile before walking out the door.

I watched as Missy looked at Mark with lust in her eyes. "How's Missy been acting?"

Allison smirked at me. "She's been fine. She won't act up during the shoot. She knows her ass would be grass if Damien found out."

I knew I loved my brother-in-law for a reason.

Allison paused to get in a different position. She started clicking again as she continued talking, "Did you get Mark's text about bringing his clothes for tonight? We're running behind with all these unplanned and unnecessary makeup touches."

"I did. I also went ahead and brought my dress just in case."

Mark looked uncomfortable with the girls draped on him. I gave him a reassuring smile, and he seemed to relax some. I wondered if he was worried about how I would take all this. It honestly wasn't a problem for me as long as it all stayed professional.

Allison asked, "How did it go with your parents last night?"

I lowered my voice, matching hers, in case prying ears were trying to hear our conversation. "Good. We basically are agreeing to disagree. Thanks for what you told them. I think it would have been a lot more difficult if they hadn't talked to you."

"Anytime. That's what best friends are for. Plus, I know you've covered for me several times with all their questions about Damien and me."

I gave her a wink.

She turned her attention to the group. "Okay, take five, and we are going to move to the stadium set over there."

Allison left to start having the lights and screens adjusted while Mark walked up to me.

He gave me a kiss before saying, "Hey, glad you made it. Did you get my text?"

I pushed myself closer into him. "I did, and your clothes are in the car. How's it going?"

He massaged his forehead with the arm that wasn't holding me, obviously trying to ward off the beginnings of a headache. "It's going. These fucking makeup retouches are slowing us down. We were originally planned to be done two hours prior, but I think it's going to be down to the wire."

Placing my hands on each of his shoulders, I pulled back and looked at him with sarcastic, sympathetic eyes. "Aw, are they having to do a lot of beauty work on you? I did keep you up late last night."

He gave a look of mock horror. "Very funny. I wanted some time alone before we go to the party. I was hoping we could use that wig of yours today."

Shit. That was the quickest way to douse my libido, and all of a sudden, I was thankful for those stupid makeup touches. I'd totally forgotten to throw that stuff out this morning, and I needed to make sure that happened pronto before the evading excuses were gone. However, distraction was my best friend at this point.

Sweetly, I purred, "Well, it'll build the anticipation for after we get back. I might have a red lacy surprise for you this evening."

His uniform pants began to tighten as I felt Robertson Junior harden against me.

"You're going to kill me the rest of this afternoon with my imagination running wild at the possibilities."

Leaning forward, my hips ground into him, and he emitted a low growl. It gave me the distance I needed up top to give him a patronizing small pat on the chest as I pouted my lips.

"I wouldn't want that. Just to ease your pain, it has a garter belt and lace stockings, and the top can be ripped off by your teeth. Mmm...I'm getting wet from thinking about the possibilities."

"Damn it, Sam." He looked around.

Mission accomplished. He wants to take me somewhere.

We were starting to walk away when Allison cut us off at the pass.

"No. No. No. Mark, don't you dare think about it. I'll send Sam away if I have to." She used her no-nonsense voice as she put her hand on her hip.

Mark actually looked like he was contemplating calling her bluff.

I slapped his chest. "I don't think so, Sport. She's not bluffing. Get back to the set. You'll have to wait till later to ravish me, or she'll have me thrown out of here."

"Geez, Sam, I'm standing right here. Mark, march your ass over there now." Allison threw her hand out for emphasis.

Mark walked away, resigned. He even looked back once with those puppy-dog eyes. Allison raised her hand again, telling him to continue on. She gave me a wink as she followed him.

I stuck my tongue out at her in response. "You just cost me a wham-bam-thank-you-ma'am orgasm."

That caused her to cover her ears and continue forward. *Too. Damn. Adorable.*

The shoot was dragging on and on. Overall, it seemed to be going well. I was getting tired of Missy eye-fucking Mark from the sidelines, but other than that, I was fine.

Allison was focused on clicking away as I informed her, "Hey, I'm going to go ahead and get ready. I'll be back shortly."

"Sure thing. We should be done in the next thirty minutes. If they try to break one more time, I'm going to threaten to start adding weight to all of them when I do the edits." She giggled to herself as she went back to work.

I gestured and mouthed to Mark that I was going to go change, and he nodded. He was tired. He dragged a hand down his face as Missy said something in a giggling voice. She wasn't getting out of line, but she was still getting on my nerves.

In the gray cinder block–walled bathroom, I touched up my makeup and pulled my hair back halfway into a gold clip in order to let my dress showcase my shoulders. I slipped my dress over my head and adjusted everything into place. The cut of the dress didn't allow for a bra. For some reason, I liked how the dress looked with a slight outline of my nipples. It was a one-shouldered, spaghetti-strapped red dress that gathered over to the right side. There was a small circular cutout where the fabric came together. The cutout was outlined in a gold clasp that matched my hair clip. The slit started six inches below the cutout and then flowed out, exposing most of my leg. My gold strappy heels were high, which only added to the illusion of how long my tanned legs were. My earrings were simple gold teardrops, and I had a gold bangle on my wrist. After adding a shimmering lip gloss, I stood back and decided that this would definitely get me laid this evening.

I put Mark's clothes near his bag in the men's area, and then I headed back to the photo shoot where they were wrapping up.

Allison was getting one last shot with the guys, and the girls were off to the side. Missy was continuing to eye-fuck Mark, and then she gave me a little I-don't-care-if-you-see-what-I'm-doing look.

We are about to tangle.

The moment I looked back at the stage, Mark's eyes connected with mine, and he actually took a step toward me, leaving his pose.

Allison's voice broke through the connection that was drawing him to me, "Mark, give me ten more minutes, and she's all yours."

That earned him ribbing from the other players. He obviously didn't care about them because he was staring at me until one of them slapped him on the back, breaking into his world. The sexy grin he gave me, telling me he was going to make me scream in pleasure, had my panties nearly combusting on the spot.

I walked up to Allison as she said, rather disgruntled, "Really, Sam? You had to come out here like that before I'm done?"

Giving her my most innocent look, I responded, "What?"

That earned me an eye roll before she focused back on the task. Out of the corner of my eye, I caught Missy heading into the locker room.

It's time that bitch and I had a little talk. "I'll be back in a minute. There's something I need to handle."

I gave Mark a wink, and he looked at me in amusement, his green eyes dancing, before I started to walk off.

Allison looked in the direction I was walking, and I heard her mumble, "Oh hell, be gentle on her."

I waved as I walked toward the locker room. *This little chick is about to receive a reality check.*

Missy was at the counter, still in her cheerleader uniform, combing through her black hair and eyeing her makeup. With how many makeup checks they had done today, she had to have fifty layers on by now. Her short strapless blue sequin dress was hanging from a hook to the side. She saw me in the reflection, and her hazel eyes took me in. She was fit. I had to give the girl that as she turned around in her teeny uniform.

"Hey, Sam, did you have fun today?"

That snarky tone had me wanting to physically knock her block into next week.

I casually walked up, looking at my fingernails as if I had just had them done. "I did. Well, of course, I always have fun, especially when it involves me getting to ogle my boyfriend in his uniform, knowing what's going to come after when we're alone. Hell, he does that uniform justice. How about you?"

Obviously confused by my response, she tentatively said, "I did. I always enjoy the photo shoots."

"Oh, I bet." Walking up to her, I kept about two feet of distance between us. Entering what could be called bitch mode, I continued, my voice turning cold, harsh, and full-on steel, "I'm going to cut right to the chase, Missy. If you pull that shit you did at the bar the other night or continue to eye-fuck my boyfriend inappropriately, I want to warn you that I have no problems airing my grievances in front of everyone, sparing no thought to how it's said. I can't imagine that it would do great things for your cheerleading career. Demerits can be a bitch, I've heard. If Mark had wanted you before, fine, but he obviously doesn't, or he would have tapped you when he had the chance. Don't fuck with me, Missy. I know your game. I have a feeling you're trying to stir up a shitstorm. Cut it the fuck out, or I'll make good on what I said."

Her mouth dropped open, and I turned on my heel and walked out with my head held high. There was nothing she could have said that would have been of any benefit at this point. If she had denied it, it would have been a lie. If she'd explained it, it would have been unfounded. If she'd confirmed it—well, that would have pissed me off even more. She'd known I meant business, and at this point, the ball was in her court. How she played it would determine how I would play.

Maybe it had been a bit bitchy, but I refused to put up with that unnecessary bullshit. My life had too many other things I was working on.

Mark was heading to the locker room with Allison by his side. When they saw me, the relief that flooded both of their faces was almost comical. Mark was probably concerned for me, and Allison was probably concerned for Missy, which made me mentally laugh even harder.

Before the questions started, I put my hands up and said, "Everything is fine. I needed to clear the air on a few things, but I think we came to an understanding."

Mark grabbed me and kissed me before I had a chance to say anything else. Allison was muttering something about bleach as she went into the locker room while I relished in how Mark's tongue felt in my mouth after having to look at each other all day and not really being able to touch. Plus, a man in uniform really did something for me.

Mark was jostled, and it broke our connection.

"You two need a room." It was Gavin, the running back for the team.

Mark grinned.

I pushed him away. "Go get ready, Sport, or we're going to be late."

A few seconds later, Allison emerged in a beautiful black chiffon baby doll evening dress with spaghetti straps. Her natural beauty allowed her to shine without a lot of makeup. I gave Mark a shooing motion, and I walked up to Allison and gave her little baby bump a pat.

"Hey, lil' niece, tell your mama to take a chill pill. Auntie Sam has it all under control."

Allison snorted.

"Oh, shut it, lil' mama. I do."

Missy emerged at that point and gave us both a tentative smile. "Hey, guys. I'll see you at the restaurant."

We both replied, "See you there," at the same time.

I gave a little smirk to Allison, emphasizing my earlier comment. *Things are under control.*

Mark walked out in a custom-fitted black suit with a matching skinny tie. His shirt was dark red, like my dress, and it had a black hue to it. He was absolutely delish, and I wondered if we would make it to the restaurant without a pit stop. I shifted, trying to ease the roaring ache that had been building in between my legs. The motion alerted him to my need, and his eyes zoomed straight to the movement.

Damien walked up in a similar cut suit to Mark's, but Damien's had a titanium color that had black tints to it. His black hair set it off, and he and Allison definitely looked like a power couple tonight.

He kissed Allison. "How did it go today?"

She blew out a breath. "Long, but you're going to have some great promo materials, I think. At least, I hope."

"I have a feeling they'll be the best the team has had. Are you too tired for tonight?" He was looking at her for any signs of distress.

His overprotectiveness used to bother me, but now that I understood love, it made sense.

"No, I'm good."

He eyed her skeptically.

She soothed his doubts. "I promise. Now that I'm not sick twenty-four/seven, I'm not as tired. I'll let you know if I need to go early. It helped having the shoot here versus North Carolina."

"Okay, baby, just let me know." He turned to us and asked, "Do you guys want to ride with us in the limo?"

I looked to Mark to make the decision, silently pleading with him to turn them down. We needed to make a teeny-tiny detour down Orgasm Lane. Hell, I'd even stoop as low to say we had gotten lost if necessary.

Mark politely said, "No, that's okay. Sam and I will meet you there in case you two need to leave early. Then, there's no stress about getting us back to our car."

Best.

Boyfriend.

Ever.

That meant that I was going to have him inside me in no time.

Damien nodded. "Good point, Mark. We can follow each other then, so you guys don't get lost. It's off the beaten path."

I wanted to shake the ever-living shit out of Damien for making that suggestion. Paybacks were a bitch after all the shit I had put him through. If we were to decline, they would know we wanted to sneak off to get some action, and I was already on the outs with Allison on that subject. She'd probably slit my tires to avoid having that mental image in her head.

Cheerily, I responded, "Sounds good, Wales."

Glancing at Mark, I knew he was feeling a similar irritation. It seemed like some days the cards were stacked against me regardless of what I did. We were going to be sexual supernovas by the time this evening was done.

We pulled up to the estate where we were having dinner tonight. It was an old Victorian home that had been remodeled as a private dining establishment. Damien had rented out the entire top level for everyone. There was a string quartet off to the side. Circular round tables framed the dance floor. Everything was done in the team colors of black and blue. The tables had black linens, blue dinnerware, and black napkins with silver accents. I loved the contrast of the colors. The colors gave the ambience a sensual feeling. The smell of silver roses scented the air faintly. I had never seen silver roses before, and they were exquisite. It was hard to believe I was a part of events like this.

Mark and I were talking when Gavin caught my attention from across the room, and he gave me a friendly nonchalant middle finger. When I saw Missy standing right beside him, I laughed out loud, not being able to resist what my little conversation with Missy had probably caused. At least she was moving on to more available pastures. Dramatically, I gasped and acted shocked and appalled, which earned me a second salute from Gavin.

Mark leaned into me. "What's so funny?"

"Seems Missy has set her sights on your friend Gavin now."

I giggled again, thinking about her face in the restroom. She was looking to land herself a player and a Mrs. title. Mark followed my gaze, and he saw what I was talking about. Missy was twirling her hair and had one leg kicked out to the side as she laughed and slapped Gavin's chest. She needed an intervention and lessons on how to be mysterious and make men chase her. Desperate was one of the many words that came to mind.

"It's about time. I suspect you had something to do with it when you went and talked to her after the shoot today."

I shrugged. "Maybe. I just educated her on the fact of what was inappropriate and appropriate when it came to you. Gavin is on his own."

Mark hugged me to him. "I love your spunk."

Pushing my ass into his dick, I responded, "I thought you loved a lot more than that. Should I remind you of what awaits you when we get back?"

He pulled me closer to him, and I could feel his arousal telling me he remembered.

"Good answer, Sport."

He indiscreetly nipped my ear, which had my core pulsing with desire to have his thick rigidness pushing inside me.

"Sam, I plan on tasting every inch of you tonight."

"Mmm...good to know we are on the same page."

Mark's fingers dug into my hip as if he was about to pull us away when a familiar voice called my name.

"Sam, what the hell? You don't call? You don't write? You get a boyfriend, and you disappear on me."

Even though I wanted to punch my friend, I was excited to see him. It had been too long.

Turning, I quipped back, "Martin, what the hell? You don't call? You don't write? You get a girlfriend, and you disappear on me."

He was dressed to the nines in a gray dinner suit. His blond hair had grown long and was pulled back neatly. "Touché, Sam, touché."

I walked up to Martin and gave him a big hug. I ruffled his hair a little to irritate him. He playfully slapped my hand away.

Smoothing his hair back, he said, "Hey, don't mess with perfection. Where's that bastard friend of mine? It's been a while since I've been able to harass him."

Pointing, I showed Martin where Damien stood possessively by Allison's side. Regardless if the world knew she was his, he took every opportunity he could to reiterate the point.

Martin followed the direction of my hand as I said, "He's over there. If you want to get him good tonight, mention how tired Allison looks."

Allison was going to kill me, but it was worth it. Since Martin and I had become friends, we both loved razzing Damien and getting him all riled up. Allison wanted to kill us at times, but Martin brought it out in me. He was the perfect accomplice.

Mark shook Martin's hand. "Hey, man, how are you doing? Where's your girl?"

It seemed like they got along well. Mark had said he enjoyed rafting with Martin in Colorado.

Martin accepted his handshake. "Good to see you. I'm good. She had to go out of town for a photo shoot. I can't stay long, but I was in town, so I wanted to come by for a bit."

Not wanting Mark to think there was anything between Martin and me, I walked back to Mark's side, and he put his arm around my hip. My naturally friendly nature sometimes gave the wrong impression, and Mark hadn't been around Martin and me enough to see that we were like brother and sister.

I gave Martin a big cheesy grin that had him laughing as I said, "Well, before you leave, you owe me a dance. I didn't take those dance lessons with you at Christmas while you were trying to woo your girl for nothing."

Mark seemed relaxed beside me as Martin and I interacted.

Martin gave me a light punch on the shoulder. "Will do, Sam. Mark, it was great seeing you. Take care of her. She's the best and like a sister to me, but I know you already know that. I'll come back as soon as I've said hello and done my best in harassing Wales."

Martin strode toward his target as Mark said to me, "Allison is going to kill you."

Giving a little evil grin and rubbing my hands together, I retorted, "Nope. She's going to kill Martin. We have a pact of not ratting each other out. It allows the ability to irritate Wales the most. You know Martin is like a brother, right?"

"Sam, if I thought he was interested in anything else, he wouldn't be standing right now. However, I want the first dance with you since you're already giving away some of them, brother or not."

Mark led me to the dance floor, and we began to gracefully move around the floor. He was a natural lead, and it made me feel elegant for the first time when it came to ballroom dancing. Martin and I looked like a comedy show when we would dance together.

Mark's arm was strong and firm as he supported me.

"Sport, where did you learn to ballroom dance?"

"No judging."

"Is this worse than singing the part of *Annie* in the school play tryouts?"

Mark's eyes gleamed at me with amusement as he said, "I'm going to kill Brina for telling you that story. She was behind this, too, though. One summer, she needed to learn to ballroom dance. She nagged me until I caved and took lessons with her. It's been stuck with me ever since."

"She's quite the force at times."

"You have no idea."

The look he gave me showed how much he loved her even though he was trying to appear irritated. We continued to dance and laugh, and being with him felt so right.

As the dance ended, he leaned into my ear. His tone was dark and seductive as he said, "Is this evening over yet? I want to take you home."

He didn't have to wait for a response as I started off toward the door to find a secluded place.

Martin crossed paths with us. I had forgotten about dancing with him.

Damn it.

"Hey, Sam, are you ready for that dance? I'm about to head out."

Feeling defeated because Mark and I were not going to get that alone time we needed, I gave Mark a kiss on the cheek and whispered, "Be good. My nipples will be waiting for you."

With the scowl he had on his face, Mark looked like he might punch Martin for interrupting us.

Turning and shaking my finger at Martin, I walked up to him, trying not to think about what I was missing right now. "No stepping on my toes this time. You nearly put me in a cast the last time."

He held up his hands and smirked. "No promises. You're the one who asked for the dance."

Taking my hand, Martin moved us farther onto the dance floor and began doing the rehearsed dance we had learned, which was even less complicated than what Mark had led me through.

Martin chuckled. "By the way, I should warn you that Allison smelled your name all over that. She's gunning for us both now. Watch your back. Damien is about to haul her out of here, and she's about to slap the shit out of him. It's great."

We both started laughing right as I saw Allison giving us the evil eye with a sneer.

Oh, we are in for it for sure now. It is on.

I blew her a kiss, and she smiled. We were still going to get it by the innocent look on her face.

Martin gave a sweet smile toward her as he said to me, "See? I'd start sleeping with one eye open if I were you."

"Shit, we might need to figure out what she's craving right now and then send it to her every day, twice a day."

Giving a little wave her direction did nothing for my cause. We executed our turn, and Martin missed, stepping on my toe.

"Ouch, Martin! Really?"

"Sorry, Sam. I'm fucking terrible at this."

The pain was subsiding a tad as I scrunched up my face and retorted, "No shit, Sherlock."

He was trying not to laugh, and so was I. We were terrible.

"To make it up to you, I'll handle Allison. She'll get a morning treat from you and an afternoon treat from me. Even if it's only crackers, they'll be the best damn crackers money can buy."

We continued to jerkily make our way around the dance floor. I had been so graceful with Mark while Martin and I looked out of sync and awkward. It was how our relationship was, which worked. We were funny together.

Martin looked over at Mark and asked, "So, when is the quarterback going to manage to put a ring on that finger? You seem to really like him."

"Hmm…I don't know. We're living together now, so we'll see how it goes. I'm not in any rush, but I do love him."

Talking with Martin about this was easy because he had no expectations of what my answer should or shouldn't be. We were the type of friends who could pick up right where we'd left off even if it was several weeks between talking. Watching Mark across the room with a wine glass in his hand as he talked with a group of people stirred something in me. It made me want to let the world know that he was mine permanently.

Dustin, one of the players I couldn't stand on Damien's team, was with Mark. He had always given me the creeps. Dustin pulled Mark aside and asked him something. Mark shook his head. Martin was now looking in the direction I was.

Martin asked me, "Who's that?"

"Dustin Marco. He's the wide receiver for the team. He's a sleazeball. Damien has put him on probation for his conduct. Plus, he stepped out of line with Allison a few times."

Martin and I were swaying at this point as we watched the scene unfold. Dustin kept trying to convince Mark of something, or at least it looked that way with how Dustin's hands were moving. Mark was about to walk away when Dustin showed him something on his phone. Whatever was on the screen caused Mark to stop and grab Dustin's phone. Dustin was now smiling and shaking his head excitedly, like he had won the argument, as he was speaking to Mark. Gavin came up from behind and tapped Dustin on the shoulder, which caused him to turn his back to Mark. Mark pulled out his cell phone and took a picture of Dustin's cell phone. Mark then put his phone back in his pocket as Dustin turned back to him.

What the hell is going on?

My scalp prickled as Mark handed Dustin back his phone. Mark gave Dustin a polite smile and shook his head. Dustin shrugged, and it appeared he said the words, *Your loss.* This whole encounter was strange.

I'll have to ask Mark about it later.

Mark's eyes suddenly shifted to mine. So many emotions passed over his face that I couldn't place what he was feeling. Quickly, he turned his back, walked over to where Gavin now stood, and joined the conversation.

What did Dustin show Mark? Maybe Dustin pulled up a picture of a naked girl, and Mark was worried about me looking as he was caught off guard with the pic. But why did he take a picture of it?

Martin voiced my thoughts, "What the hell was that?"

"I have no idea, but I'm going to ask Mark later."

My eyes were still watching Mark's back as Martin said, "Let me know if you need anything."

I nodded to Martin as the song ended. We both did our graceful bows. It was the only part of the dance that we really had down.

"Don't be a stranger, Sam."

"You either. Thanks for the dance."

Martin gave me a kiss on the forehead and then walked off. Mark's back was still to me. He was talking with the guys, so I decided to go talk to Allison and maybe rile up Wales a little.

Making my way over to Allison, who was talking with Damien, I pranced up and gave her a little nudge with my hip. I addressed Damien, "Wales, you always throw a kick-ass party."

"Thanks, Sam. I hear you were harassing one of the cheerleaders today."

I turned to Allison. "Rat."

Just then, someone vying for Damien's attention pulled him away.

Deciding to get her a little worked up for tattling, I asked, "Martin said you looked a little tired. How are you feeling?"

Her eyes narrowed. "I knew it. You two are terrible. You just wait. I'm going to get you both back. If I were you, I'd keep one eye open while you sleep."

"Bring it, sista."

A chime announced it was time for dinner.

"Oh, it's on. Let's go get our seats," she said.

We looped our arms together and made our way to the table. Mark made it to us a few minutes after the salad was delivered, and he was pulled into conversations from other people at the table. Everyone wanted their time with the star player.

Dinner had ended. I was exhausted, sexually frustrated, and ready for some alone time with Mark. Next to Damien, he was the second most popular person at this function. Everyone wanted to run their thoughts by Mark on their game plan or workout schedule. Mark and I had been so wrapped up in each other over these last few weeks that he had in essence been off the radar and unreachable. Allison looked worn out by the end of dinner, and she finally admitted it, which spurred Damien into a hasty departure.

As we were parting ways at the cars, I gave her a hug. "Rest, sweetie. You've had a big day."

She yawned. "Thanks. You guys have a good night."

"We will. Trust me on that."

She muffled her ears as she walked to the car door Damien had already opened.

I yelled after her, "Allison!"

She wouldn't turn my way.

"Oh, Allison…"

"I can't hear you."

She was hilarious. I turned and walked to the car, ready to get to the best part of the night.

Mark was standing at my door, holding it open. I leaned up and gave him a kiss, which he returned, but it was more reserved than normal.

"Is everything okay?"

He gestured for me to get in as he said, "I have a lot on my mind right now. It's been a long evening."

Staring up into his eyes, I tried to figure out what was going on. He looked tired and stressed.

Is this about the incident with Dustin?

"Okay. Don't stress. We're about to get to the fun part of the night. You can leave all this behind and focus on us."

He only nodded as I got in the car.

Strange.

This was the one part of Mark's personality that drove me crazy. When he had something on his mind, he wouldn't talk until he was ready. Everyone deserved to have their time to process, but since the Adam text, I'd found myself more on edge, but I had no idea what this could possibly be about.

I'm probably overreacting.

The drive to my condo was quiet as Mark was lost in thought. I turned the radio on low, preferring that over the silence, and closed my eyes as I listened to the music without listening to the lyrics. I thought about Edna, looking forward to when we would get back to North Carolina. Lots and lots of baking time were definitely in my future before I officially started my job. With Mark's parents in town, I hadn't gotten to see her as much as I normally had. I was ready to share the fact that Mark and I had moved in with each other, my parents' reaction, and my thoughts on marriage. Poor Edna was going to need extra flour for the baking frenzy we would have.

Mark pulled into the garage, and we both got out of the car. The closing doors echoed in the space. With how his mood was, it would appear the fun was over for the evening. As we were climbing the stairs, the silence was about to kill me.

"What is your deal? We were supposed to come back here and have hot monkey sex in the new outfit I got, but you're acting as if someone stole your puppy."

"We need to talk."

Oh shit. Those were the dreaded four words that no one ever wanted to hear. Even being a relationship newbie, I knew this was bad. I was on edge, and I felt myself having all kinds of horrible thoughts about what it could be. *Is he breaking up with me? Has he found someone else? Did he realize how screwed-up I actually am?*

I followed him into the bedroom silently and sat down on my bed. I kicked off my shoes but stayed in my dress. We needed to stay rational. My mind raced, trying to think of what had happened. Nothing clicked. Mark disappeared into the closet and was gone for a few moments before he reemerged in a T-shirt and worn jeans. He was carrying the box from the top of my closet.

Oh fuck. I had forgotten to throw that out today while he was gone. *Shit. Shit. Shit.*

Calmly, I asked, "Are you going somewhere?"

He sat the box on the bed and then went to the corner of the room where I had thrown the red wig. All my senses went on high alert, causing me to stand.

Through gritted teeth, he ignored my question and asked his own, "What was this used for?"

He knows. I didn't know how he knew, but he knew. *I was an anonymous member. How did he find out about it?*

I answered him, hoping that my answer sufficed, "A costume. Why are you asking?"

"Damn it, Sam. Just give it to me straight. Stop fucking around and tell me." He was standing a few feet from me as he held out the wig. He was clearly agitated.

Why didn't I get rid of this stuff? Shit.

This was the part that I had never wanted to reveal about myself. It was the part I wanted to always hide in a deep, dark place.

Looking him straight in the eyes, I said, "You obviously know."

"I want to hear it from you."

If I didn't tell him, our relationship would be forever damaged, and I would lose him. If I did tell him, hopefully, it wouldn't end the relationship, and we would be able to weather through it even if it set us back some. At least, he would still be mine. Regardless, he had asked, and I would never lie to him.

Clearing my throat, I clearly answered him, "When I was a member of a sex club, I wore that wig to hide my identity." My stomach turned as I said the words. I took a few deep breaths, trying to calm down and stay mentally focused on the conversation.

This was about to either break or make us, depending on if we could handle what I had done in my past.

"And this?"

He pulled out my short black leather outfit with the kitty-cat mask.

I wanted to puke at how the sight of those things made me feel. "It went with the wig. How did you find out?"

He still didn't answer my question as he started zinging question after question at me. "Were you hiding this from me on purpose? Is this what Adam meant by calling you Kitty Cat? Is he a club member?" His voice was rising.

That caused me to raise mine, too, as I said, "No, I wasn't hiding this from you on purpose. We both said we didn't need to outline our pasts. Why share if it didn't matter anymore?"

He pressed on. "Is Adam a club member? Is this why he calls you Kitty Cat?"

The emotional distance I felt from Mark hurt. Regardless of what I had done in the past, he had always been there for me, ensuring me of his love. Right now, with how this conversation was going, it felt as if a fissure was opening in my heart.

"Yes. How did you find out?"

He pulled out his phone and loaded a picture. It was a picture of Dustin's cell phone, and on Dustin's cell phone was a picture of me walking down a hall in my red wig, mask, black leather outfit, and whip in hand.

"Some fuckwad went to that club and took your picture. He's fucking selling this picture to horny-ass bastards along with others he's taken. Dustin was asking me if I wanted the site. He didn't recognize you in your costume. Fuck, I wouldn't have recognized you if I hadn't tried to make love to you with the damn thing. Dustin gets a cut of the profits somehow and that's why he was pushing me so hard tonight to take a look at his phone."

I grabbed Mark's phone and looked at it closely. More to myself than anything, I said, "Only Adam and his partner know my real name. Exclusivity is key and a rule he lives by. No one is allowed to have phones in there for that exact reason." I looked up, panicked, thinking Mark was upset that I had potentially slept with that guy at the party. "I've never slept with Dustin."

He took his phone back. "Was Adam the one you went there to fuck?"

His question cut right to the bone. I felt like a whore, having to even answer his questions, admitting to what I had done.

"Yes, from the beginning, I only *fucked* Adam. We were both clear that we wanted no attachments!" My hurt was coming through now as I started to yell my answers, trying to protect my heart as it began to crack.

"What did you do there?" The pain was evident in Mark's voice and eyes.

These questions only added salt to both our wounds. Needing to be closer to him, I took a step forward, and he took a step back, causing me to stop.

I tried to bring reasoning into the situation. *Anything is worth a shot.* "Mark, I don't see how this helps. Do you want to detail every part of your sexual history?"

"If you're going to get pictures shoved in your face, then yes, I would tell you everything you needed to know. I would never want you to see texts or pictures like this." His fists were clenched, and then he tossed the wig on the bed.

Upset and humiliated, I screamed back, "It was supposed to be *exclusive*! How the *hell* would I have known you were going to see a picture of me?"

"Where's the club?"

The chilling tone to his voice had me lowering mine as I responded, "Why are you getting so upset with me? This was part of my past. You knew before you started declaring your undying love for me that I was fucked-up, and now, you're turning it on me. How can you do this to me?"

"Where's the club, Sam?" He stood there, resolute, not budging.

The loving Mark I knew had vacated, and it was ripping me apart. I closed my eyes, wishing we could rewind this whole conversation that had spun out of control. "Why do you want to know?"

"I'll call Dustin and get the site to figure it out if you won't tell me where it is."

Part of me wanted to beg him to let this go and to make love to me. Instead, I started preparing my heart for what I knew was coming. Resigned, I answered, "It's on Briar Cliff Road. It's called Club Envy."

With that, he turned and strode out.

The breath left my body, and my heart broke all at the same time. My past had come back to haunt me. Something that I'd thought was helping me cope with emotions I didn't know how to deal with had cost me the one thing that I now really wanted in life—love.

CHAPTER
26

I sat on my bed, numb and fuzzy. *What just happened?*

The hurt in Mark's eyes had been evident. But the fury—I didn't understand that piece of it. The one thing that I did know was that he was going to the club. My body automatically stood, and I walked to my car barefoot and still in my dress. I needed to see Mark when he left from talking with Adam. That would tell me where Mark stood on everything, and it would at least mentally prepare me for what lay ahead when it came to us.

Zipping through town on autopilot, I parked across the parking lot where I normally had parked when I used to come here. I looked at the old brick building. From the outside, it looked almost abandoned. The bouncers at the front only allowed approved people through the doors, regardless of the time. The front was a club and generally always packed.

If someone wanted to be a part of the sex club half, Adam would put the person through a fairly intensive screening. Each time a member entered, he or she would sign a waiver and acknowledge the rules. The owners, Adam and Brandt, were the only ones who knew the identities of the disguised members who came into the club. After initially meeting Adam and deciding we would be each other's fuck buddies, he had even let me use the employee entrance when I would come. It had been rare that anyone even knew I was there.

Looking back, I realized how dysfunctional my behavior had been, but it had helped me cope. Adam and I had worked well because all he cared about was pleasure, and he let me take control. I controlled the pace and how the sex had happened. Adam had always treated me with respect. Until Mark, I had felt the need to go to the club. I would count down the minutes until I could go again. But the moment I had gone to

North Carolina and slept with Mark again, the desire for this place had vanished. My need for control was still there, but it was more balanced with Mark and I both having equal parts in our relationship.

The picture Mark had shown me was from Halloween a year ago.

The bouncers let me in the side entrance Adam always let me use. I always wore my wig and mask into the club to ensure no one knew who I was. Dressing in his office, I put on my super short black leather outfit and grabbed the whip from my bag. It was Halloween. Adam always called me Kitty Cat, and he thought it would be funny if I had a whip like Catwoman.

Checking Adam's schedule, I knew he would be down the hall, preparing a room for the next group. Leaving the office, I went down the hall and walked through the doors where Adam was standing, giving directions from a clipboard on how to arrange the room. People would come here to fulfill their fantasies with willing participants. They would pay a club fee to be a member, and then as long as they followed the rules, they could fuck whoever they wanted as long as they weren't attached to someone.

Cracking my whip in the room, Adam and the rest of the group turned my way. His tank top showed all his muscles, and he had a body that was fun to use to get me off. Everyone's mouths were hanging open, and I went in for the kill.

"Meow. Kitty wants to play."

Adam handed off his clipboard. "Finish this. I'll be in my office. Don't disturb us."

He gave me a wink, and I followed him out of the room.

"I would have reserved us a room if I had known you were coming."

"Kitty had an itch."

We reached the door, and after we walked through, he turned.

"Oh, I can definitely scratch it for you. Kitty Cat, how rough do you want it tonight?"

My whip cracked through the air. "I want to be sore tomorrow from how hard you fucked me."

He prowled toward me. "So, which one of us is going to be in control tonight, Kitty Cat?"

"Me."

It was always me. I never released control to anyone when it came to sex.

As I relived the memory, I had no recollection of even seeing a cell phone there that night. Looking at the club again, thinking of what I had done, caused my stomach to turn. The things Mark was about to see would probably forever taint his vision of me in his mind. If I had only known where life was going to lead me, I would have held out and made it until Mark entered my life.

Mark came marching out of the club by himself. It had me sitting straight as a board in my seat, holding my breath, as I watched him. His hands were clenched at his side tightly. He looked straight toward his truck. When he got to it, he threw the door open, got inside, and then slammed it shut with so much force that the truck rocked. Since he was in a rental truck, the windows weren't tinted like his personal one, and I could see him from here. He started beating the steering wheel with the palms of his hands. His mouth was moving in what I assumed was a string of profanities that would probably make my ears cringe.

He threw the truck into drive and squealed out of the parking lot. He barely stopped at the entrance before pulling out onto the street in the opposite direction of our condo, his truck fishtailing from the speed.

My heart felt like it was a lead weight, cold and abandoned, as I watched the taillights. It wasn't his fault. I always knew my past might cost me one day. Damn it though, I was mad, too, because he had promised me that it would always be okay and that he loved me.

My phone beeped, and I looked down.

Adam: Come on in, Kitty Cat. I always have what you need. I'll make you feel better if you want to play.

My head snapped up, and I saw Adam standing at the entrance with his hand extended. It was déjà vu. The same thing had happened the night before I left for North Carolina when I was battling myself on whether or not to go in. The moment he had come out and texted me the same thing, it had weakened my resolve, knowing what would be provided behind those doors. Adam was a bigger guy, all muscled and covered in tats. He had a bad-boy persona through and through, but he had always treated me well and never forced anything on me. He was the kind of guy that girls wanted to tame and claim as theirs. I had never had that desire, which was probably why we'd worked so well. He took a step toward me in his ripped blue jeans and white muscle shirt.

I sat there as we stared at each other. The urge never came though. Anything that had linked me to this place was gone. I pulled out my phone and typed a response.

Me: I love Mark. Bye, Adam.

He checked his phone. I put the car in drive and drove off without looking back. I picked up my phone when it beeped.

Adam: Bye, Kitty Cat. You deserve the very best.

Me: You, too. One day, I hope you find what I've found—happiness.

He wasn't going to respond. He would never contact me again. The past was officially in the past. While one weight was completely gone, another pressed on my chest, smothering me, as tears started to build. It was just a matter of time until I lost the self-control I was barely hanging on to. I sucked in a big breath, taming my emotions for a little longer. Mark hadn't tried to reach out to me, and if he had gone back to my place, he would have made it there long ago to find me gone.

I needed to decompress and process. My heart was shattered, and the last thing I wanted was to start another unhealthy habit like I had all those years ago. I had to disappear while I tried to sort out my world, and there was only one person who would keep my location a complete secret—Martin. Allison would try to fix the unfixable problem and try to get Mark to come talk to me. At this point, trying to explain the situation, which included the club, was too much. Martin had had to disappear when he was framed for Damien's sister, Rebecca's, death. I wasn't being framed for murder, but I wanted to hide, and he was the master at hiding.

Picking up my phone and dialing, I called Martin and hoped he'd be able to help me on such short notice.

"Hey, Sam. What's going on?"

"I need a place to stay for a couple of nights. I need to disappear. I'll pay you for it once I get there, but I need to go someplace where no one can find me." My voice broke a few times. Until I got to my destination, I refused to allow myself to have the breakdown that was coming.

Martin picked up on my tone, and the sound of a chair moving came through the phone. "Sam, what the fuck is going on? What happened?" he asked, worried.

"Please, no questions. I'll let Allison know I'm okay, but I need someone who won't tell anyone where I am. Please."

Martin was used to seeing strong and independent Sam, not begging Sam.

"Did Mark do something to you? I'll beat his ass if he hurt you."

I wished Martin could beat what Mark had learned out of him and make him forget forever.

"It's my fault. Please, will you help me?"

My pleading voice had him jumping to my rescue, immediately helping me. "I have a small hotel near Macon. That should get you far enough out of Atlanta that no one will look there. Do you have any clothes or toiletries?"

I wanted to cry at his kindness, but I didn't want to explain what was going on. "No. I'm still in my dress from this evening. I don't even have my shoes on."

Just thinking about Mark looking at me with want when he had first seen me in this dress tonight further stomped on what little remnants of my heart were still together.

"Fuck, Sam. Are you okay?"

"Martin, please. I can't talk about it. I'm barely hanging on."

I heard some shuffling on the other end of the phone.

He said, "I'll have some clothes delivered by the time you get there. I'll put you under Elizabeth Jones. I'm sure you're about to turn off your phone, but you better pick up when I call you at the hotel in a few hours. If not, I'll be forced to come find you myself and make you tell me what the hell is going on."

"I will. I promise."

"We'll talk later. Let me make the arrangements. I'll text you. Are you in your car?" There was clicking in the background, like he was typing something.

"Yes. Thank you." Because of his unconditional friendship, being there for me without question when I needed someone the most, a few tears escaped the jail I had locked them up in.

"I'm here for you, Sam, for whatever you need. Just be careful. I'll be there if you need me, regardless of what I have going on."

There was no telling what he had gone through all by himself while he had been on the run. Martin had refused to talk to me about what he had been through because he didn't want me involved if he ever had to disappear again.

"Thanks, and I will."

I owed him so much for what he was doing for me.

I pulled off the side of the road. I typed out a text to Allison as I felt the tsunami of emotions building. I could only hold it at bay for so long. Soon enough, I was going to be a complete and total mess when I let the realization of what all I had lost hit me.

*Me: I'm going off the grid for a couple of days. My
phone will be off before you have a chance to respond.
It's like what you asked for when you went to Miami.
I love you, and I'm okay. Don't freak out.*

After losing her parents, Allison had gone to Miami just
over a year ago. She had used that time to regroup and find
herself. She had turned off her phone and focused on herself.
It had worked out for her because she had met Damien. Maybe
it would work for me, too.

Next, I entered the address to the hotel into the GPS once
Martin had texted me. Turning off my phone, I started driving
again and focused on watching the yellow lines on the road as
my GPS directed me to Martin's hotel. My brain was chaotic at
this point, and it was difficult to focus on any one thought or
emotion, which was probably good.

I pulled up to the small hotel and opened the car door.

A middle-aged man in black slacks and a red shirt greeted
me at my car door. "Miss Jones, welcome. We will put your car
in our employee parking per the instructions. The things you
have requested have been delivered to your room. Here's your
key. You are in room two twelve. Is there anything else we can
help you with?"

"No, but thank you for everything."

I grabbed the key and walked in. There was no telling what
the front desk thought of my appearance. My eyes were
probably red from the tears, my feet were bare, and my
designer dress was wrinkled. Keeping my head down, I hastily
made it to my room and locked the door behind me. This was
a small hotel, but it was perfect. I wondered what hoops
Martin had made the employees jump through with the
immaculate service I had received so far.

The room had a king-sized bed, a couch, and a two-person
small rectangular table. There were two bags on the bed. I
looked in, and there were several T-shirts and pairs of yoga
pants. The other bag had shampoo, a toothbrush and
toothpaste, deodorant, and a brush. Martin had gone above

and beyond, and it made another tear fall. The table had some kind of meal on it, but there was no way I could stomach food at this point. Just the thought had it roiling.

The phone rang, and even though I didn't want to pick it up, I knew Martin would out me if he wasn't able to verify I was okay. He'd show up at the door, and I needed to be alone.

"Hello?"

Martin breathed a sigh of relief as he said, "Good. You made it."

The staff had probably called him the minute I arrived.

"Are the accommodations okay?"

"They're perfect. Thank you for everything." I knew I sounded like a disconnected robot.

"Take care, Sam. I'll let you be, but you better call me the moment you want to resurface. You stay there as long as you need. The front desk will get you anything you need." His voice was warm, and it reminded me of a voice that I used to find comfort in.

"Thanks, Martin. You're a good friend." I took in a shaky breath.

"So are you, Sam. Take care."

The moment I hung up the phone, I lost it. I knew I was totally by myself now, and there was no chance of someone finding me. My body racked with sobs as I sank to the floor, holding my knees. It felt as though part of my soul had been ripped from me.

Sitting in that parking lot, prior to Mark leaving, I now knew I had been holding out hope that he would come back to me. There was no way he wanted me now. I replayed our conversation from earlier over and over again, trying to find a symbol of hope, but he had been cold and distant.

Slowly, I made my way to the shower and scrubbed myself raw, feeling dirty from all I had done at the club. Images continued to plague me, supporting the reasons Mark had left me.

Crawling into bed, I made myself a promise not to use any vice to cope with what had happened. Every emotion was acute and punched me in the gut repeatedly. After ignoring and subduing them for so many years, they were taking their pound of flesh and then some. I welcomed it. At least I was feeling something and not letting the numbness take over. Pulling the covers over my head, I finally succumbed to a troublesome sleep with visions of what Mark and I would have had if I had done it differently.

Should've.
Could've.
Would've.

CHAPTER
27

It was a rainy, windy day. The weather matched my mood perfectly. I had woken up hours ago prior to the sunrise, and I was staring at the ceiling. It felt as though I was alone in this world, and there was no beauty in it. My tainted past had won.

An idea struck me, and I flung the covers off of me. The clock read after one in the afternoon. After putting on clean yoga pants and a T-shirt, I brushed my teeth and put my hair up into a messy ponytail. I looked like shit. There was no denying that with the dark circles under my bloodshot green eyes.

Picking up the phone, I hit zero for the front desk.

"Good afternoon, Miss Jones. What can we do for you? We can have food brought in from any restaurant you desire."

"Thank you. I need my car. You can let Martin know that I'll be back this evening."

"Yes, Miss Jones. We'll have it ready for you."

"Thanks."

I hung up the phone and went to grab my purse, but then I realized that I hadn't even brought that with me. It was a good thing my dad had always made me keep one hundred dollars as emergency money in my glove box. Making my way to the lobby downstairs, I kept my head toward the ground as it was obvious what the state of my emotions were, and I didn't want to see the pity stares today.

As promised, my car was waiting.

To the hotel employee, I said, "Thank you."

"You're welcome, Miss Jones. Let us know if you need anything."

I nodded and got into the car. My gas tank was full, and muffins were in the passenger seat with coffee in the cup holder. There was a note attached to the muffin bag.

Make sure you eat.
Martin

He was like a brother looking out for me. Forgoing the muffins, I did drink the coffee. It was probably the last thing I needed with no food in my system, but feeding my body only caffeine was soothing nonetheless. I eyed my phone, debating whether or not I should turn it on.

Nope. I was not going to give myself more heartache at this point. I needed to ground myself first. I wasn't sure if it was possible, but I had to try before I was available to the outside world.

The rain was coming down in sheets as I drove. The beating of the water against my car helped drown out what otherwise would be a heartbreaking silence. Before I knew it, I was pulling down the little drive leading to my long-ago-forgotten-by-the-world hidden gem. It was the place where I had confessed my love to Mark, but I drew strength from this place.

As I pulled up and put the car in park, the weather was trying to wreak havoc on the place. The wind blew, the rain poured down, and the thunder threatened it, but my pond stood strong. It withstood any elements that came at it. It wore its scars proudly. I tried to summon the same courage it had.

Hours passed as I watched my safe haven take a beating. I would always mourn the loss of Mark. He had been my true north. Just like my special place, I knew I would survive, even with a permanently broken heart. I was relieved that I didn't feel the need to find a coping mechanism.

Getting out of my car, I tilted my face up into the rain, letting it pelt and soak me. I walked to the front of my car and leaned against it, enjoying the freeing feeling passing over me, as I endured the storm with the place I loved. At one point, the rain was coming down so hard that it stung me, but I stood there, embracing it, finding my inner strength. At least the numbness I normally felt hadn't surfaced. I felt everything acutely.

"Sam?"

I turned at my name being yelled, and there stood Mark to the side of his truck in the same jeans and T-shirt he had worn last night when he left me. It seemed like an illusion, and I wiped the rain from my eyes, wanting to ensure I hadn't become delusional in my tired state.

He jogged up and stopped just short of me. "Thank God you're okay."

The rain was starting to soak him, too. He looked about as bad as I did. He had dark circles under his eyes. Fatigue had clearly claimed his features.

"What are you doing here?" My voice shook, and my body shuddered as I realized how cold I was.

Time had completely stood still while I had been here.

He was completely drenched at this point, but his green eyes continued to penetrate me like they always had. "Damn it, you're freezing. Please come get in the truck, so you can warm up before you get sick."

I simply nodded, and he reached for my hand. Part of me wanted to yell at him for how hurt I was, and the other part wanted to see him one last time before he finished it for good. Putting my hand in his, my body felt that connection, and I longed for it to be forever. I stopped my way of thinking immediately. Dwelling on something that was gone was pointless. He led me to the passenger side of the truck and opened the door for me. I climbed in and felt how chilled to the bone I was as my body started shaking, trying to warm itself. My hair was matted against my face. Mark climbed in and put the heat on full blast. He leaned over the console and reached toward the backseat to grab the duffel bag we had taken to the first day of the photo shoot.

He pulled out a T-shirt and handed it to me. "Here, put this on, so you'll warm up quicker."

"I-I'm o-o-kay." I was so confused as to why he was here, sounding caring and loving like he had prior to finding out about the club.

"Sam, please, I don't want you to get sick."

I reached for the shirt and laid it beside me on the console. He had already seen everything, so it wasn't worth asking him to turn around. It didn't matter at this point. I pulled my shirt over my head and quickly put on his. Not having the freezing fabric clinging to me did feel a hundred times better.

As soon as I finished changing, Mark asked, "Where did you go? I've been half-crazy, looking for you all night."

Staring straight ahead, I reminded myself of the strength this place had. "After what happened, I needed time to process, so I went somewhere and then came here."

"What were you processing?" He sounded sad.

Is he serious? He walked out and left me. Why does he sound hurt?

"Us and what happened. I saw you leave the club," I said, my voice cracking. I closed my eyes while I continued to find my inner strength.

"You went to the club?" His voice sounded disbelieving and hurt, which only added to the confusion in my head.

The rain battered around us as little shivers continued through my body while my teeth lightly chattered.

"Yes, I went to see what happened when you walked out."

"Did you stay?" His voice was low and cautious.

I darted my eyes over to him, and he was looking me over. One hand started to reach for me, but he put it back in his lap.

"Do you mean, did Adam invite me in to fuck me?" My tone had a bit of a bite to it, and the intake of his breath had me regretting it. "Sorry, I'm exhausted. I didn't mean it."

He took a deep breath. "I talked to Adam for a bit. I told him about the picture of you that had been taken and how I came across it. I asked him how that could have happened, considering the club is supposed to be elite and exclusive."

I was beyond baffled as to where this was going. He was ripping this Band-Aid off the slowest way possible, causing the most agony.

He continued, "He was pissed that someone had taken your pic. I forwarded a copy to him. Adam said he would handle it and leave my name out of it in order to protect you. He said you'd never have to worry about it again and that your identity would remain hidden."

Hell was about to rain down on whoever had taken that photo. Adam took his club seriously, and he had always been protective of me. I could only imagine the ass-whipping he would bring. Still, none of this made sense in regard to why Mark had walked out on me, left me, abandoned me.

"I don't understand why you're telling me all this. You don't have to explain to me why it's over between us. I get it. I saw how it affected you."

Mark looked at me like I had grown two heads. "Sam, it's not over between us."

"But…but…you left me. You were cold and distant, and then you left me without any explanation. You came out of the club and beat the shit out of your steering wheel before driving off in the opposite direction of the condo. That clearly defies everything you've told me, that my past didn't bother you and that you'd love me regardless. You left me. You stopped talking to me. You left me…alone." My bottom lip quivered as I relived those painful moments.

His hand came out and grabbed mine. "I'm so sorry, Sam. It's just…" He closed his eyes, taking a deep breath, and then reopened them, focusing intently on me. "When I saw that picture of you and found out where it had been taken, I'll admit that it shocked me. Then, hearing Dustin talk about you sexually nearly had me coming unglued. Knowing I had actually wanted to make love to you in that red wig made me sick. Realizing you had kept that part of yourself from me hurt. I didn't react in the best way.

"When I left I needed to make sure your identity was protected—not for me but for you. You've been through enough in your life. You deserve to have every moment filled with nothing but happiness. I needed something to do, to give me time to process. I was thinking about how I was going to convince you to stay with me, to promise me your love. I should have stayed. I should have stripped you down and talked it out without any barriers, but I panicked, thinking that I wasn't enough for you, that you wanted that free lifestyle over me."

I started rubbing my temples in a clockwise motion, trying to relieve the building pressure. He sounded as if he still wanted me. A person who no longer wanted someone wouldn't say those things.

Thinking back on all of Edna's advice about communicating, I said, "Adam saw me outside the club and texted me, asking me to come in." I heard Mark's teeth mashing together. "I told him bye and drove off. Whatever appeal the club had for me is gone. I hadn't thought about the club at all until Adam texted me while your parents were in town. I wanted the club to stay in the past. I had spent so much time being a prisoner of my past that I wanted to move forward. Any desire for that lifestyle left the minute I became yours. I know I'm not yours anymore, but you deserve to know that you were more than enough for me."

"Hop in the backseat, Sam."

That stopped my temple massaging as I gawked at him. *What in the world is he talking about?*

Lightning flashed across the sky.

"Sam, please get in the backseat. You're not hearing what I'm saying."

Climbing over the console, I got in the backseat on the far right side. He followed and pulled another T-shirt out of his bag before quickly switching his wet one for a dry one.

I miss him.
I miss his touch.
I miss being his.

He looked at me. "Sam, this is not going to work with you over there. We are going to feel each other while we talk."

In one motion, he picked me up and brought me to his lap. Our connection intensified, and my heart started humming underneath my skin. I never thought I'd be in his arms again. His arms came around me and secured me closer to him. Our faces were mere inches apart. The truck smelled of rain. The rain continued to pelt the truck, putting us in our own little bubble.

His finger came up and grazed my cheek as he softly said, "The first thing we need to get out of the way is that we are not over."

"But—"

He cut me off as one hand grabbed my chin, making sure I was looking directly in his eyes. "No buts. I reacted in a shitty way. I'll always be sorry for that. I'll never walk out on you again. I love you, Sam."

The image of his taillights as he had driven away flooded my mind. I felt the heartbreak all over again, trying to protect myself against the hope I was feeling. I tried to move my face, but he firmly held on to it.

Staring into the depths of his green eyes, I told him what I was thinking, "Why did you go the opposite way?"

"I had to get something, and then I drove straight back to our place. When I got there and saw your car was gone, I realized what I had done. I haven't stopped looking for you. I've been up all night, going to every place I could think of where you might be."

His phone rang, and he pulled it out of his wet jeans. He looked at the screen. "Sam, let me answer this. It's Allison. She and Damien have been helping me look for you."

I cringed, thinking about stressing Allison out. Damien was going to have my ass.

Mark answered, "Hey, I found her. Yes, she's fine. I'll let you know as soon as she answers me. Thanks, Allison." He dropped the phone on the floor and focused his attention back on me. "Only Allison and Damien knew you were gone. I didn't call your parents. I drove by there, and Allison called covertly."

I had been so selfish with how I reacted. A broken heart could cause the strangest reactions that didn't necessarily make sense.

"I'm sorry. I didn't mean to worry you. I shouldn't have disappeared like that, but I was devastated, thinking I had lost you forever. I thought you didn't want me anymore." I looked down as I felt the shame of my cowardly actions.

Mark put a finger under my chin to force me to look back at him, intensifying our connection. "Sam, I love you, and I'll love you regardless of what happens. Please tell me I haven't lost you."

My heart leaped, and the ice that had settled started to break free. I might be a little late at grasping what he had been trying to tell me, but it was starting to sink in.

"I love you, too. I'm yours, Mark. My love for you will only grow stronger."

He hugged me to him, nearly squeezing the breath out of me. I felt whole again as my heart reassembled itself.

As Allison's mom had always told us, *Girls, just because it's broken, don't throw it away. Most times, something mended is stronger than it was to begin with.*

Mark looked outside, and I followed his gaze. The rain had dissipated, leaving a clear sky.

He kissed my cheek. "It's about time I broke through that stubborn head of yours. Come with me. There's something I have to do."

Without hesitating, I responded, "Of course."

He opened the back door and slid us out of the backseat. The sky was clear, and I could hear the birds chirping. It was beautiful, peaceful, and perfect. He leaned back in to get something, and then he was back out, pulling me to the edge of the pond.

He turned me toward him. "Sam, you're the one for me. I know our relationship has been fast for you. The moment you came back into my life, I felt as if we were finally going to have our chance. I waited for you because you are worth the wait. When it's right between two people, there's no reason to delay what's meant to be just because of what someone deems is an appropriate amount of time before taking the next step."

He knelt down on one knee and pulled out a black velvet box from behind his back. "This is where I went last night when you saw me going in the opposite direction of our condo. They had called while I was at the party and said it was ready."

He popped open the box. "Sam, would you do me the honor of becoming mine and allowing me to become yours for the rest of our lives? I promise to never leave you and to love you always."

I started exclaiming as I looked into his eyes, "Yes! Yes! Yes! You're all that I want, all that I need."

He stood, and I jumped into his arms before he had a chance to put the ring on my finger. Our lips smashed together, and my body never felt more alive. I now knew that we would be together forever, and we'd be able to overcome anything. He knew the worst of me and still loved me. Like this place, our relationship had weathered the storm and had come out more beautiful than ever.

After sitting me down, he slipped the ring on my finger. It was a beautiful square-cut diamond in a platinum band.

I gasped. "It's beautiful. I love it."

He pulled me back to him. "I had it made especially for you."

I looked at my hand and watched the diamond sparkle.

His thumb came up and caressed my cheek. "Can we go to where you are staying? I want to spend some time with my fiancée without any barriers. I'll have someone pick up your car and deliver it back to our place."

The word *our* had me elated beyond belief. "Yes."

Stopping at my car, I got my cell phone and locked the vehicle up.

As we got into the truck, he said, "I need to call Allison."

"Okay. Tell her that I'm sorry."

He pulled out his phone and dialed her number. "Hey, Allison. She said yes."

He pulled the phone away from his ear, and I could hear the squeals coming from the other end.

"Yes, she's right here. Hold on."

He handed me the phone.

"Hello?"

"Oh geez, Sam, you had us so worried. Congratulations, sweetie. You deserve this happiness more than anyone."

A few happy tears fell down my face. "Thank you. I'm so sorry."

"Oh, we'll talk about your stunt later. For now, let's enjoy this happy moment."

"Love you, bestie."

"Love you, too. He's a keeper."

I looked over at Mark, who seemed so happy, even in our tired state. "I know. We'll come by and see you guys before we head out of town."

"Sounds good."

After handing the phone back to Mark, I lifted the console and scooted closer to him. *This feels perfect.* I had one more person I needed to let know that I was okay. I turned on my phone and ignored the new texts and voice mails that had come in during that sad time.

Quickly, I sent Martin a text.

> Me: *I'm okay. Mark found me. It was a misunderstanding on my part. He proposed, and I accepted.*
>
> Martin: *I'm glad, sweetheart. You women make things so much harder on us guys—which supports my theory on males being the smarter gender.*
>
> Me: *Thank you for everything. You're the best. I'm making you an appointment to have your head examined. You men make us women crazy.*

> *Martin: You'd be there for me, too. Call me this*
> *week. I feel a bet coming on. We'll discuss the terms*
> *later. Prepare to lose.*

> *Me: Will do. Oh, I'm preparing my victory dance. See*
> *ya later.*

> *Martin: Later.*

After I put my phone beside me on the seat, Mark asked, "Who were you texting?"

"Martin."

He didn't say anything as he brought me to him. He kissed the top of my head, and I stared at my ring.

The happiness in my heart was spilling over. "I love being engaged to you."

"You have no idea how happy you've made me."

This was going to be our forever.

∞∞∞∞∞∞∞∞∞∞∞∞∞∞∞∞

Back in the hotel room, we were lying together in a tangled mess of sheets with my head on his chest.

I can't believe it! I'm engaged! My mind was yelling it over and over again in excitement.

As I was thinking about how happy I was, Mark asked, "Hey, Sam, did Martin know where you were?"

I raised my head. "Yes."

Something passed over his features.

"What's wrong? I thought you had left me. I didn't know where to go. I needed to disappear, so I could deal. The last thing I wanted to do was try to cope with a broken heart in a negative way, like I had all those years ago. Martin had no idea what was going on. He still has no idea, but he now knows that you found me, and we're engaged."

He closed his eyes. "I was terrified when I couldn't find you. We couldn't reach Martin, and that was probably why." He opened his eyes. "You have to promise me that you'll never run away like that even if you think it's over. We have to talk it out, Sam. I was scared shitless, thinking something had happened to you. We are going to be together forever, Sam. We work it out together as one. It's you and me."

I kissed his cheek. "You and me. I promise, I'll never do that again. Don't leave me like that again."

He relaxed and pulled me to him. "I won't, I promise. I was thinking that we should purchase your little hidden gem, have it fixed up, and get married there."

I sat up in bed with the sheet pooling around my waist. "Are you serious?"

He rose, too. "Yes. It consoled you all those years. It's where you first told me you loved me, where I got you back, and where you agreed to be my wife. I'd like to get married there. Eventually, we can build a house out there."

"Yes. I want a Christmas wedding. Do you think that's doable?" I moved to straddle him.

He started grinning. "Yes."

I started bouncing on his lap, and immediately, I felt him get harder underneath me.

He smiled. "Christmas it is."

And with that, I raised myself and slid onto him.

He is my forever.

CHAPTER
28

Early December

"Sam, hold still."

I was practically bouncing as Allison and my mom were trying to lace up the back of my wedding dress. Allison's warning didn't help as I continued bouncing, not being able to help it.

"I'm trying. You guys haven't let me see or talk to Mark since yesterday evening after the rehearsal dinner."

My mom, wearing a red dress, was the next to pipe in, "Calm down. You'll be down that aisle in no time. I'm going to go check to make sure your dad is getting ready. He was chomping at the bit to get you two married, and now that the day has come, I think he'd rather you live in sin."

That caused all three of us to laugh.

"Poor Dad. You might need to slip him a shot or two. I know I could use one."

"Sam…"

I loved razzing my mom into using that motherly tone. However, I really could use a shot or two.

As she was leaving, she stopped and put her finger in the air. "On second thought, you might have a point."

We all laughed as she left the room.

I was anxious to get to Mark.

"Don't even think about it. You're not seeing him until it's time." Allison rocked back on her heels with her little tummy, putting her finger to her chin.

She was, I thought, even more adorable at eight months pregnant. She was all belly and walked with a slight waddle. I loved the plum baby doll dress we had chosen together for her bridesmaid dress.

"Oh, I remember something similar happening to me, and all I received was an evil little cackle when I complained."

Thinking back to Allison's wedding day, I had been a tad obnoxious. I would never admit it to her though.

"Not funny, Allison." It was amazing how much my perception had changed on everything. "And you won't tell me where Mark is taking me on our honeymoon? You're supposed to have my back." My voice had officially gone whiny. I deserved to be slapped.

I'd had total control over the wedding, and Mark had asked to plan our honeymoon as his wedding gift to me.

"Whoa, you were the one who agreed to let him surprise you. That's not my fault. Oh, I should tell you this one thing he's doing. It's so romantic." Allison put her hands up to her heart, all dreamlike.

We had spent three days here in preparation for the wedding, and we would be on our honeymoon for five days. Mark had seven days between games, and the next game was pretty much a guaranteed win for their team, so Damien had given permission for Mark to be gone.

I love my brother-in-law.

I chewed on my lip, wagering with the devil on one shoulder and the angel on the other, both telling me why I should or shouldn't find out the secret Allison was keeping from me. The devil won. "Tell me. Tell me. Tell me." I was an absolute basket case as I grabbed her shoulders and gave her a slight shake.

Then, she started trying to imitate my cackle from her wedding day.

Oh shit, she is playing me.

"I don't think I will. I remember all the little things you and Martin did to harass Damien. You can suffer." She gave me a little squeeze before she went to get my veil.

"You're evil."

I stuck my tongue out at her, and Allison laughed as she returned to my side.

I started patting her tummy, and I was rewarded with a kick from the baby. "How's my little niece doing today?"

I was still giving my mama a hard time about her wrong prediction. I might have done a victory dance around the living room when we'd found out at the reveal party.

Allison rubbed her tummy. "She's still cooking and getting bigger and bigger. She's an active one. Her daddy has gone a bit overboard in the safety department." She paused, smiling, and then refocused on the task at hand. "Let's finish getting you ready. It's almost time to go."

I jumped up and down in excitement.

"Sam, be still, or you'll be late to your own wedding."

I stopped, and she giggled as she attached my veil.

"You just want to go straight to the honeymoon."

"You bet your ass I want to get to the honeymoon. I'm excited to ravish him over and over again."

Allison raised one eyebrow. "You know your niece has ears."

I gave her a little salute, and there was a knock at the door.

One of my favorite voices came through the door. "Your mom said you were upstairs, and I wanted to come give my little baker a hug."

I practically skipped to the door as Edna walked in. She was wearing a little green dress suit with a red flower. Allison gave me a little hug before she left.

"I'm so glad you're here," I said to Edna. I gave her the biggest hug.

It meant so much to Mark and me, having her be a part of our intimate ceremony.

"Oh, I wouldn't have missed it for the world. Just know that even though you'll be married, your tokus better be in my kitchen every chance you get. You're like a granddaughter to me, Sam."

My lip started to quiver.

"Oh, don't you dare. You're about to go meet that fine man, and we are not arriving as blubbering messes."

I nodded, afraid to speak.

"You look beautiful. Are you ready?" she asked.

"Do you have any parting advice before I become Mrs. Robertson?" I took a deep breath, letting the realization all set in, but there wasn't a nervous bone in my body.

Edna grabbed my shoulders and gave me a loving smile. "Freeze this moment in time in your mind. When the difficult times come, think back on this day, and you'll be able to find your way."

I gave her one final hug. "Thank you. Thank you for everything. You gave me so much strength as I found myself." My body started fidgeting again as I felt the moment getting closer.

"Let's go get you married before we have to sedate you," Edna teased.

I nodded in agreement as I was practically jumping as we walked down the steps. My mom was at the bottom of the stairs, and I saw two white limos waiting outside the front window. Edna continued on to the front door to join Allison, and they walked toward the front limo. That only left my mama and me in the entryway.

Mom followed my gaze and answered my silent query. "Mark wanted you and your dad to ride to the ceremony together. Allison, Edna, and I will be in the front one."

I had to start fanning my face to keep the tears at bay.

She leaned toward the side table and grabbed a small white box. "I have something for you. When you were born, your grandmother bought you your own bride's Bible to carry with you. She wanted it to be kept a surprise until your wedding day. In it is an inscription for you and Mark to read in private prior to the ceremony. It's your something old."

I started fanning my face again. *This is too much.*

She reached again, picked up a blue box that was on the table, and handed it to me. "Second is your something new.

Allison got this for you, but she wanted me to give it to you during our time together."

Mama opened the blue velvet box. Within the box, there was a diamond pendant on a white gold chain. Three intricate diamond hearts were connected in the most amazing way. The pendant sparkled magnificently.

She took it out, and I turned around, so she could put it on my neck.

"She had one made for me and another for her. The three hearts represent how the three of us are linked for life as mother, daughters, and sisters."

Allison was so much like Damien when it came to this romantic shit. I grabbed a magazine from the table and began fanning my face to keep any moisture from seeping out of my eyes.

How much is a girl expected to take?

From her wrist, Mama took off the bracelet that she wore to every special occasion. "Third is your something borrowed. This is the diamond bracelet I wore on my wedding day. It was given to me by my mother as my something new."

She clasped the bracelet on my wrist. I was afraid to speak because I was barely hanging on with my heart being in my throat.

Next, she picked up a book from the table. "Edna got you something to have also. It's not to take to the wedding, but it is old, borrowed, new, and blue."

Mama handed it to me, and I saw it was a cookbook. The title read, *Bake with Love*.

When I opened it, there was a note on the front page.

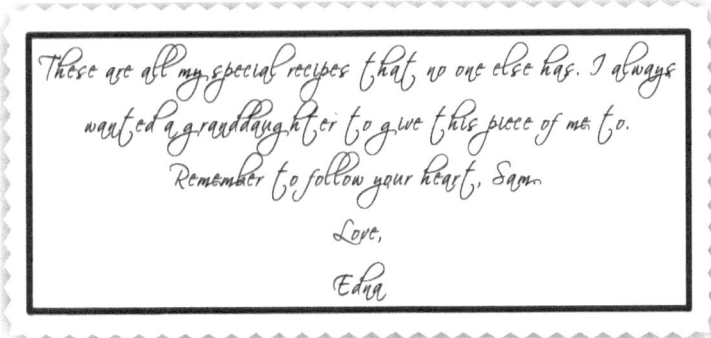

These are all my special recipes that no one else has. I always wanted a granddaughter to give this piece of me to. Remember to follow your heart, Sam.

Love,

Edna

I handed it back to my mom, and I started fanning myself again.

Are they all trying to get me to bawl my eyes out before I get married?

That small saying from Edna meant more to me than she would ever know. The lessons and friendship that had been formed through baking helped me open myself up to the promise of love.

My mom continued on, "Sam, before we go out there, I want you to know that you are the most precious gift I've ever received. Having you in my life made it complete. You have a remarkable man waiting for you, and I'm so thankful you found each other."

I gave her a hug as I took deep breaths, and I whispered, "Thank you, Mama. I love you so much."

"Now, Allison knew we were probably going to be a crying mess, so she wanted me to give you this after we had our moment for your something blue to take down the aisle."

My mom wiped away a few tears from her face. She handed me a box, and I opened it and started laughing. Allison was always there in the exact capacity I needed her. In the box was a garter that had the same design as my dress with a delicate blue ribbon woven into the white. At the front of it dangled the letters *P* and *V* in silver.

My mom clearly didn't get the inside joke. "You two have always been like peas in a pod. She said you would get it, and it would help keep the tears away. Are you ready to get married, my sweet daughter?"

"Yes, Mama. I'm ready for all the promises that love brings."

Walking hand in hand with my mom, we went to the second limo. I slid in next to my ever-anxious dad in his tux, and my mom helped put my wedding gown train in the car. The door closed behind me.

"Looking good there, Dad."

He was a jittery mess, too. It was evident where I had gotten the whole knee-shaking, muscle-moving nervous habit.

"Boo Bear, you're beautiful. Mark is a lucky man."

"We're both lucky, Dad."

I reached for his hand as the limo started driving to the ceremony location. I had been involved in all the planning to refurbish my little gem, but I'd wanted to see it for the first time on my wedding day. This was the first day of my new life. It felt right after all that this place and I had endured together.

My dad started rubbing the bridge of his nose as his foot bounced and then stopped. "You know, in the beginning, I wanted to march you to the justice of the peace, and now that you are actually getting married, I want to rewind back to when I used to push you on the swings with you in your pigtails as you giggled, thinking I was the strongest man in the world."

His voice cracked, which was almost my undoing.

One tear seeped out of my eye as I responded, "Dad, I'll always be your little girl. I love you. You set the bar on the type of guy I would marry."

"Well, Boo Bear, I think you found the perfect man."

"Me, too, Daddy." I leaned over and gave him a hug with a kiss on the cheek.

"Shit, I need a shot. Is there alcohol in here?"

That had me laughing. *Mama should have listened to me.*

"Check the mini bar."

He scooted over and poured himself a shot. He took another one, which caused me to laugh again.

"Not a word to your mother. Desperate times call for desperate measures."

I sealed my lips, crossed my heart, and threw away the key. Dad chuckled at me.

The limo pulled to a stop, and it was almost twilight. Looking out the window, I gasped. It was more beautiful than I'd imagined as I saw twinkle lights in the distance. This pond had comforted me, this pond had witnessed my confession of love to Mark, and this pond had witnessed the proposal, sealing Mark and me together forever.

My mouth dropped open at the sight I saw down the lane. The dream I designed was a reality. The little pathway that had been full of underbrush was mowed. We had a small dock and arbor built for the wedding, but it would become a part of my special place. For the wedding, lights had been added all around the area. I looked over at my dad, and he smiled. My mom and Allison were at the limo door, and they opened it and helped me get out. I started walking toward the twinkling lights, drawn to them, knowing who was waiting for me there.

When planning, I had found these beautiful fire pits that now surrounded the area where the ceremony was taking place. The sales staff had sworn that it would keep the chill off our guests. Thank goodness it was in the mid-sixties. It was as I had imagined and planned. It was stunning with the lights and fire.

I could sense Mark was here, and I longed to be in his arms again. Allison though was right there, pulling me off to the side, cutting off my view.

"Hold on there, Sam. It's not time yet."

"But—"

She grabbed my shoulders, forcing me to look away from the lane I wanted to go down. "Just five minutes, and you'll be with him. He wants it to be perfect for you."

"Well hell, what am I supposed to say to that? By the way, thank you for the necklace and the garter. The garter was definitely needed."

She gave me a wink. Allison had known I would be on the brink of losing it emotionally, and I wouldn't want a tear-streaked face the first time I saw Mark. Damien, David, Sabrina's husband, and Martin came out from the path, all dressed in tuxes. Annie, Sabrina, and Nina followed them, wearing elegant dresses. This was the entire guest list.

Martin gave me a wink and blew me a kiss, which I caught and held to my heart. He was like a brother to me, and we would always be a part of each other's lives.

The pastor followed right after.

Everyone was stunning. Mark's parents were looking at the limos and then looked my way, realizing I was already out. Everyone stared. His mom and Sabrina blew kisses and mouthed they loved me. Then, they walked off in the other direction.

Damien remained in the part leading to where my love was.

Allison whispered, "They're acting under Mark's orders. He doesn't want their spazziness, as he put it, to act up right before one of the most important times in your life."

I gave her a horrified look. "I hope he didn't say it to them like that."

They were spastic, but I loved them for that exact same reason. Hell, half the time, *I* didn't know if I was coming or going.

"No, he actually said that he wanted to be the first one to talk to you, outside of the people who were at your house. Then we'll start the ceremony and your dad will walk you down the aisle."

Damien turned to Allison and gave her a nod.

"It's time to go see your future husband."

I started walking toward the opening. A slight chill ran over my skin until the heat from the fire pits made me feel comfortable. I stepped into the clearing and saw Mark standing at the other end, wearing a black tux. His blond hair was tousled stylishly, and his green eyes glowed. He was the most gorgeous guy I had ever seen. His smile was triumphant and loving, and it made my heart soar.

We were about to be united.

My mind went back to the day we'd found the dress.

I walked out of the dressing room in a vintage wedding shop in Atlanta. When I saw myself in the mirror, I knew this was the dress. My mama was tearing up behind me. It was an off-the-shoulder A-line gown with intricate beading framing the top. The beading trailed along the right side of my body where the fabric gathered and then flowed out gracefully. From there, the beading was placed all over the gown and then became heavy again at the end.

My mama came up behind me and squeezed my shoulders. "Sam, this is the one."

"I know, Mama. I love it. This is the dress I'm going to become Mrs. Robertson in."

My hair was done on top of my head in big loose curls in order to showcase all of the intricate beading on the back. When Mark took one step to me, I lost all composure and started jogging his way. When I made it to him, he grabbed me by the waist and swung me around in a circle, kissing me the entire time.

"I've missed you, Sport."

"You have no idea. Come, I want to show you something. Close your eyes."

I obeyed, and he put me down. He grabbed my hand and then started walking.

We had taken a few steps when he stopped us. I was about to say something when he said, "I can't believe I forgot to tell you. Your beauty has me flustered, and what I'm about to do has my brain scattered in excitement, but you look absolutely stunning, Sam. Every time I see you, it knocks the breath out of me."

His voice was a warm caress to my ears.

"Mark, I love you."

It was an amazing feeling that I could penetrate that calm outer shell he had. He pulled on my hand again, and we started on our way. The grass gave way to wood as Mark helped me with my footing, ensuring I didn't trip. I already knew what everything should look like in theory since I had planned it, but I had refused to see it as it was being constructed. Allison had checked on it for me to ensure it was exactly what I'd wanted.

Pressure from his hands turned me, and then his arms came around me.

"Open your eyes."

Our pond had been completely transformed. It was just as I had imagined. My long-lost gem had finally been loved as it deserved. The pond and I had weathered the worst of things and come out stronger in the end. I felt forever tied to this place. The trees had been shaped, the underbrush had been removed, and the water had been cleaned. Off to the side sat benches, which was where the wedding guests would sit after Mark and I had a few moments to ourselves. Mark and I had decided to keep the wedding small and intimate since this place was ours, and we didn't want to share it with the masses.

"It's beautiful. It's perfect."

"I hope so. You're about to make me the happiest man in the world by becoming my wife. The promise of having you forever is more than I could ever hope for. I'm going to cherish your promise, Sam. I'm getting the only thing I ever wanted out of life—happiness with the woman of my dreams."

I stared up into his crystal green eyes as he said some of the most beautiful words I had ever heard.

"I never thought I deserved to be happy, but your patient love showed me otherwise. Thank you for believing in us enough to wait for me." I bit my lip as I smiled. I was beyond blissfully happy in this moment.

Mark leaned down and gave me a kiss. "Your mom said she gave you a bridal Bible from your grandmother and that we should read the inscription together prior to the ceremony."

I had forgotten about Mama giving me that. I fished it out of my small purse. Mark looked on as I opened up the bridal

Bible. His hands went to my hips. On the inside flap was a note written in my grandmother's writing. I ran my fingers over it before I read it out loud.

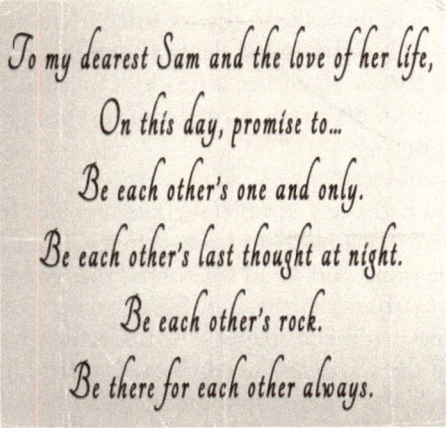

To my dearest Sam and the love of her life,

On this day, promise to...

Be each other's one and only.

Be each other's last thought at night.

Be each other's rock.

Be there for each other always.

Mark hugged me closer as he said, "I promise, Sam."

"I promise you, too."

He kissed my cheek as I continued to run my fingers over my grandmother's soothing words. After a few moments passed, Mark pointed to the top of the gazebo. The gazebo was a permanent fixture that was staying here after the wedding, so we could have it as a part of our lives forever and always. At the top, there was a skylight with two interlocking rings in it that was part of the design.

Mark answered my silent query, "I added this skylight after we finalized the plans. It's a symbol of our never-ending promise to love and cherish each other. Our wedding rings also have the symbol engraved on the inside of them."

"Oh, Mark." I turned in his embrace. "Promise me, I'm not dreaming."

"This is forever, Sam. You and me. I promise."

Epilogue

December—One Year Later

It was two days after Christmas, and we were headed in Mark's truck to Allison and Damien's home to celebrate the holiday. Mark and I had just celebrated our one-year wedding anniversary. As we drove from our place in Atlanta, I looked over at Mark, and he gave me a sly smile as he spoke on the phone to his agent. They wanted to do some shots of us for promo material to release. Allison had asked, and I had agreed. Mark was informing his agent of his plans. As he talked, I thought about our honeymoon and how wonderful it had been. He was taking me back to Barbados as soon as the season was over. It was one of my Christmas presents. I closed my eyes and let the memory engulf me.

When I got out of the shower, Mark was nowhere to be seen. Since touching down in Barbados, two days ago, he had hardly let me out of his sight. We had barely left our villa. I was saddened that we would be leaving soon. Mark had promised to bring me back to explore the islands. As I was walking through our bedroom, a white dress lying on the pale green duvet cover caught my attention. There was a note on pale pink paper lying on top of the white dress. I picked up the note and smiled as I read it.

> **I HAVE A SURPRISE WAITING FOR MY BRIDE OUTSIDE.**
>
> **PLEASE COME JOIN ME.**

I bit my lip in excitement as I dropped my towel and put on the strapless sundress. I slid it on, went to the mirror, and clipped my wet hair up. My eyes danced with excitement. I had never been this happy in my life. I walked out into the dark night from our villa onto the deck, and I stopped in my tracks as Mark stood there with a single white flower. He was wearing white linen pants with a white linen shirt that was only partially buttoned. I practically ran into his arms, and he took me into his embrace.

"Miss me?"

I nuzzled into him, memorizing his scent. "Yes. I don't want to go back to reality."

"Me either. I want to show you something."

We left the deck and stepped into the soft sand. As soon as we turned left, I stopped in my tracks. On the beach were lots of luminaries giving off a romantic glow as the Caribbean Sea sparkled from the reflection of the moon.

"Mark, I don't know what to say."

I was stunned into silence at the sheer beauty. Mark continued to walk me through the sporadically laid lanterns to the center where a blanket was spread across the sand. The ocean sounded in the distance. We sat down on the blanket and soaked in every part of this moment.

"It's beautiful. Thank you."

He pulled me onto his lap into a straddling position. I leaned down and kissed his lips barely. As I pulled back, Mark's eyes made contact with mine, and the rest of the world slipped away.

"Sam, I promise to treasure you forever."

My heart burst from the love emanating from him.

I needed him. "Make love to me."

At my words, he switched places with me, and I was now beneath him. His hands started to travel up my thigh in a slow, sensual movement. His fingers caressed my skin as they continued to push up my sundress. Mark's head came down as my stomach was exposed, and he pressed his lips softly to my skin. He adored my body at an excruciatingly unhurried pace, and I reveled in it, absorbed it, and memorized it.

He kissed up to my neck, leaving tingly trails all over my body. I used my hands to push down his pants low enough to free him. Mark hovered over me as he took my mouth in a deliciously seductive kiss. His erection nudged at my entrance, and I moaned, knowing I was about to have the love of my life inside me again. Mark began to move inside me, and my body zinged at the sensation. It was the slowest build I had ever had, but the orgasm shook me to the core as he emptied himself inside me.

"Sam?"

Mark startled me, and I jumped, looking like I had been caught doing something I wasn't supposed to be doing. I giggled.

He raised his eyebrow. "I was saying that everything is cleared with my agent. We can do the photo shoot whenever Allison is ready as long as you're feeling up to it. What were you thinking about?"

I laid my head against the headrest, admiring my husband's profile, as he continued to drive. I loved how much he loved me.

I sighed. "I was thinking about that night in Barbados when you surprised me with the luminaries on the beach behind our private villa and how you made love to me under the Caribbean sky."

Mark gave me a devilish grin. "I cannot wait to get you back there."

"Me either."

We had spent Christmas this year with his family, and Mark had given me a trip back to Barbados to go on after the football season ended. His family was still a tad obnoxious at times, but I had adjusted. I felt like I was truly part of the family. They were still fans of the group-texting craze, but I would respond when I could without feeling any pressure. If they needed to get a hold of me, they would call.

My dad and Mark got along great. They had truly buried the hatchet. Mark had even flown my parents to a few games, which they loved.

I let out a sigh of contentment as Mark's hand drifted to my stomach. His hand stroked my stomach lovingly.

"How's our baby?"

I responded, "I'd say he's percolating."

We were a little over two months pregnant. It had been planned. Over the summer, I'd started having the desire. We had been having one of our no-barrier talks when I had mentioned wanting to try for a baby. Needless to say, babymaking had commenced that evening. It had taken a few months to get pregnant.

In the beginning, I'd been scared that my previous lifestyle had broken something in me. The moment I'd stopped worrying, we had created a life together. The only other people who knew were Allison and Edna. I had told Allison as I wanted her to be a part of it from the very beginning. Edna had figured it out one afternoon while we were baking.

Hell, she probably knew the moment we conceived our baby with how that woman's intuition worked.

I used the cookbook Edna had given me all the time and not only for cooking. When I had looked closer at her wedding gift, each recipe had a life lesson to go with it. Anytime I needed her guiding words, I would go to it and randomly open a page. It was always exactly what I needed.

"He?"

"Yes. I don't know why I think it's a boy, but I do. I feel it."

Mark left his hand on my stomach. "I can't wait to find out. You're going to be an incredible mother."

With my screwed-up past, I was still worried that I wouldn't be a good mother. But with Mark by my side, we could do anything.

I put my hand on top of his, looking at our oneness. "I can't wait either. I can't wait to tell everyone. Once we tell our parents, we can start telling everyone." It was only the millionth time I had said that.

I was nervous letting the proverbial cat out of the bag with all the possibilities of what could go wrong. The doctors had assured me I was having a healthy pregnancy, but I was still a nervous wreck. I now knew why poor Wales had acted the way he had.

This was also one of the reasons the photo shoot was being rushed. They weren't planning on using the shots until the summer prior to the start of the new season, but I would be very pregnant then as my due date was in July. Big preggers lady with a football player wouldn't scream hotness.

Allison and Damien's baby girl, Kendall Marie Rebecca Wales, was about to celebrate her one-year birthday. They had named her after Allison's mother, Kendall, and my middle name, Marie. From the moment I'd held her, my internal baby clock had started ticking for one of my own. Just thinking about the day had tears welling in my eyes.

I had flown in from North Carolina the moment Allison had gone into labor. I walked into the room while Damien was standing proudly next to his wife. He was looking at her and his baby with love and affection. Allison was holding their little girl, who was swaddled in pink.

My heart soared for them. "Hey, little mama. How are you doing?"

Allison grinned at me. "Perfect, now that I have this little miracle in my arms. She's our dream come true."

Damien's answering grin as his fingers touched his child's cheek was one of the tenderest moments I had witnessed.

Allison asked, "Would you like to hold her?"

"Yes! Oh, yes. I've been dying to meet my little niece. Mark is coming in on the next available flight. You just had to go into labor the night before game day."

I knew Allison had wanted some alone time with Damien and the baby, so I had waited to come until after her new family had time together. I pulled up a chair right next to the bed.

Allison handed over baby Kendall.

All of a sudden, I was a nervous wreck. Panicked, I looked up at Allison. "Please tell me if I do something wrong. I don't know what I'm doing."

"You'll be fine, Sam."

The moment she was in my arms, a connection formed between Kendall and me. I loved her fiercely. I was surprised, but then again, she was a part of my best friend. She was perfect with her little scrunched-up face as she slept.

I broke out of my trance as Allison said, "We named her Kendall Marie Rebecca Wales—Kendall from my mom, Marie from you, and Rebecca from Damien's sister. I wanted her to share the names of the most important women in both our lives. I hope she has your strength, tenacity, and love for life."

That caused the dam to break as a few tears slowly slid down my cheeks while I held little Kendall Marie to me. The fact that Allison had named her after me meant that Allison hadn't thought about my past or the things I had done. Allison loved me for who I was even after knowing everything.

I softly said, "She's perfect. It's amazing how much I love her already." Looking up, Allison had tears in her eyes as I continued, "Thank you. I love you, Allison."

She nodded as I stared back at Kendall Marie. I spoke to her, "I'm going to be the best auntie ever. We are going to play dress-up, go on outside adventures, get sundaes, go to the movies, and shop. You and I are going to have so much fun. I might even teach you how to give your daddy a really hard time."

Looking up, I saw Damien and Allison watching their baby adoringly.

Damien came over and got his little girl from me before sitting back down next to Allison. "Don't listen to your Auntie Sam on that last part."

Mark's voice brought me back from my thoughts. "Are you excited to see Kendall?"

"Yes. I haven't seen her in over two weeks. She's probably already forgotten who her Auntie Sam is."

He chuckled at the serious note of distress in my voice.

Every time I'd called Allison, I would make her hold the phone up to Kendall, so I could talk to her. Kendall would squeal in delight as I spoke to her with excitement.

Mark's phone rang, and he connected the call via Bluetooth. "Hey, Mom."

I chimed in, "Hey, Mom."

Annie said happily, "We had such a wonderful time at Christmas. We can't wait to see you again. Are you guys going to see that precious niece of yours?"

I answered, "Yes, but your son is driving like a grandpa. We should have been there ten minutes ago."

Annie laughed. "Give that baby a hug for me. I sure hope it gives you the baby fever, Sam."

I mashed my lips together.

Mark said with a warning tone, "Mom…"

She gasped. "Oh my gosh! You're pregnant, aren't you? Oh my gosh! I knew it. I knew it from the moment you walked into the house at Christmas."

My eyes bulged. *How the hell did she figure it out?*

Mark was stunned, too, and he muted the phone. "Sam, I swear, I didn't tell her. I swear."

"I know. What do we say?"

He shrugged, looking as dumbfounded as I felt, while we whispered back and forth to each other.

How did these women know?

She knew, so there was no reason to lie to her now just to turn around and call her this evening to tell her that we were pregnant.

"Go ahead and tell her," I said.

He nodded, grinning.

Thinking about my parents, I clarified, "But they can't say anything. My parents still don't know. I don't want them to feel left out."

A ginormous smile spread across his face. I loved seeing Mark this happy, knowing I had something to do with it.

He unmuted the phone. "Mom?"

"I have you on speakerphone, and I conferenced in Brina," she said.

I started laughing. This was a typical Robertson family moment, all out there and in the open.

Mark continued in a warning voice, "You guys cannot say anything because Sam's family doesn't know yet. So, no posting on any of your social media sites until you get the go-ahead. Yes, Sam and I are having a baby."

The other end of the line went loud with cheers and clapping.

Annie broke through all the noise and said, "Oh, Mark and Sam, we promise, we promise, we promise! We wouldn't want to ruin this for you guys. Congratulations. I'm going to be a grandma! Can we come see you next week? When are you due? Sam, how are you feeling?"

Mark looked at me and grabbed my hand, and then I brought our hands to my stomach. I embraced their craziness. If it ever got to be too much, I knew I could talk to them, and they would back off.

Mark answered his mom, "We'd love to have you guys. Sam is doing great. She's a little over two months along, which puts her due date in July."

There was more clapping and screaming, and it caused me to start laughing.

Mark was trying to talk through all the chaos. "Mom, Mom, Mom."

They weren't paying attention as they were all planning showers and the baby's first Christmas. I loved each and every one of them.

Pulling up to Allison's place, it looked like we were the first ones to arrive.

Mark continued to try to penetrate the Robertson chaos barrier, "Hey, guys. We are here. Remember, not a word of this to anyone. Sam's parents need to be the next to find out. I want to make sure we're at our place when it hits the media. The news of our wedding caused a lot of pandemonium, and I want to be prepared this time if it's the same. I'll text you when you can start going crazy with the announcements."

When pictures had been released of our wedding right before the playoffs, the press had swarmed us for weeks. We had almost gotten security.

That sobered up his mom. "Mark, I promise. We won't say a word. We will respect you and Sam. This is your baby."

"Thanks, you guys. We'll call you this evening to plan your visit."

His mom was so excited as she responded, "Love all three of you guys. Take care. Mark, you keep driving like a grandpa. That's my grandbaby in there with you."

"Will do, Mom. We love you, too." He hung up the phone as he put the truck in park and then stared at my stomach. "I'm sorry that didn't go as planned. I know you wanted to tell your parents first."

I scoffed and smiled. *This is how it's supposed to be.*

"When does it ever go as planned for us? Edna knew the moment I walked in. She's the reason we took the test to begin with."

"True. I have no idea how these women know." He stopped and swallowed, and then he penetrated me with those deep green eyes. "Thanks for giving me this, Sam. Thanks for giving me you and our child."

I bit my lip as my hand went back to my stomach. "Thank you for giving me you. I'd never have this happiness if it wasn't for your unconditional love."

He leaned over and grabbed my face to kiss me.

Pulling back, I smiled, and then I remembered that my precious niece was beyond those doors. "Will you grab Kendall's gifts? I have to get to my niece."

"Sure thing."

With that, I opened up the truck door and practically jogged to the house.

Mark called after me, "Sam, slow down. You're going to trip."

I turned and gave him a salute as I giggled. Trying to slow down a little, I continued on, and I went through the front door to the noise coming from the massive family room. Allison and Damien were on the floor, playing with my niece. She was a crawling machine. My knees would never recover from all the crawling I had done with her.

My target was my niece as I dropped to the floor. "Hey, you guys." I held out my hands. "Come here, sweetie. Auntie Sam has missed you so much."

Kendall squealed as she crawled toward me. She was in a red ruffled dress. I scooped her up, and her hands went to my hair. We looked at each other as I hugged her to me.

"You've gotten so big. You must be eating your Wheaties."

Allison laughed while Kendall grabbed my hair. "Tell me about it. She eats and eats and eats and eats."

I put my fingers underneath Kendall's little chin to look at her. "You're a growing baby girl. Yes, you are. Your Auntie Sam missed you so much. Yes, she did."

She made the most adorable face, and then the most wretched smell came from her. Mark walked into the room and laid the gifts by the tree before sitting down next to me. He smelled it, too, and the look on his face caused me to laugh.

I held Kendall to me. "Whoa, whoa, whoa. How does that come out of this cute little princess?"

That had everyone laughing at me as Damien came around. "I'll change my sweet baby girl."

Before handing her over, I gave her one last kiss. "Wales, I want her back."

He began sauntering out of the room, cooing to his baby.

"Wales, I'm serious. I get her back."

He didn't say a word.

Bastard. By the look on his face, I knew he was thinking that we would have our own little bundle of joy in a few months.

Allison cleared her throat. "Martin should be here in a few minutes. So, are you still telling everyone this evening? Your parents are going to be so excited. Are you feeling okay?"

I was perfectly content among the baby toys as we sat on the floor. It was amazing how much my life had changed.

"Yes, Mark's family guessed while we were on the phone with them on the way here. We'll tell my parents when we start opening presents."

She moved over to me and gave me a hug. "Your mom is going to be ecstatic. She comes to see Kendall once every other week when we are in town."

It was sad that Damien's mom never plugged in. She lived in her own little world and had only wanted Kendall when it suited her social circle needs. Damien refused to let his daughter be used, so his mother had only seen her a couple of times.

When Damien walked back in the room, I gave him my best puppy-dog face. He brought me Kendall as Martin walked in with his girlfriend, Nina. He was proposing to her on New Year's Eve. He had rented a yacht and planned to do it while the fireworks lit up the coast of the Atlantic Ocean.

Kendall was happy to be back with me as she started kicking and trying to speak.

I always talked to her like I knew what she was talking about. "I know. I know. I missed you, too. I can't wait to see everything Santa brought you."

Mark leaned over and gave Kendall a pat as I said, "Can you say hi to your Uncle Mark? He told me he wanted to play dress-up with you. All you have to do is say pretty please, and he'll give you anything you want. If he doesn't, you come find Auntie Sam."

She was squealing as she reached for Mark, and he took her.

I looked over to my husband. "I'm loaning her to you. Martin and I have something we need to give to Wales before my parents get here."

Mark didn't answer me as he started pretending to zoom Kendall around like an airplane.

Bastard. I will get Kendall back.

Martin gave me a wink as I got up.

I grabbed one of the gifts from the pile Mark had left by the tree, and I handed it to my brother-in-law. "Wales, this is from me and my partner in crime. You're welcome."

Damien proceeded with caution as I walked over and gave Martin a high five. I was glad his girlfriend seemed completely okay with Martin and me being friends.

Damien opened his present and peered inside as if it were radioactive.

He's smart.

He opened the tissue paper and laughed. He held up the book titled, *How Not to Be an Overbearing Dad*. Everyone broke out in laughter. He looked at it closer and then laughed even harder. Martin and I had written him a guide on things he shouldn't do, and we had it printed in hardback. Mark set Kendall down as she was now more consumed with what her dad was doing.

He opened it up and read aloud, "Rule number one: Pretending to be a princess and looking for Prince Charming is not a declaration of her getting married. Stow the gun, Wales."

Allison was laughing, which caused Kendall to crawl to her mom and laugh. Allison scooped her up and said to her daughter, "I love you."

I turned my attention back to Damien and noticed when he saw the other book in the box. He pulled it out and showed it to everyone. It was another book Martin and I had written. It was titled, *How to Drive Your Daddy Nuts*.

Damien opened it and read the inscription aloud.

> **To: Kendall**
> As soon as you can read, this present is for you.
> Martin and I have become pros at how to
> drive your dad a little nuts with lots of practice.
> We are bestowing this knowledge
> to the next generation.
> Lots of love,
> Auntie Sam
> Uncle Martin

Everyone was in tears as Damien read the first page, "Guideline number one: Tell your daddy about every boy you meet every single day."

Allison looked at me. "You're so bad. You wait."

I moved my finger in a come-here motion and said, "Bring it, sista."

Smiling, Damien put the gift away. "Just so you know, Kendall is going to be a nun."

I retorted, "Uh-huh, if you say so."

My parents walked in the room, and everyone greeted them. Kendall began crawling over to my parents. Seeing my mama's face light up made me want to tell them immediately.

I looked at Mark, silently asking if it was okay, and he kissed me on the cheek.

He whispered, "Go ahead. I can't wait either."

I sprang up, went to the tree, and got the joint gift for my parents. I was jumping up and down as I walked over to them with Kendall now in Mama's arms.

I held out the gift. "Mama, Dad, we want you guys to go ahead and open up one of your gifts."

My parents looked confused as my dad took the gift, and they walked over to the couch. Once seated, Dad took Kendall and gave Mama the gift. She opened and gasped as my dad looked, and their eyes shot to me and Mark, who was now standing behind me with his hands on my stomach. Their present was a picture frame that had the word *Grandkid* written on the top. In it was an ultrasound picture we had done just for this moment.

I said, "Congrats, Gram and Gramps."

My parents got up, and Mama handed Kendall to Allison. Then, with tears in their eyes, they hugged us.

Almost two years ago, what had started out as a vacation when Allison went to Miami had turned out to be the catalyst for my best friend and me to find true love. If she hadn't gone on that trip by herself, she probably wouldn't have met Damien, which meant I would never have met Mark. It was amazing how interconnected life was at times.

My world was complete in a way I never knew possible.

Allison had gotten a family she never thought she would have, and I had gotten a love that I never thought I deserved.

It was all built on the foundation of...

Trust.

Love.

And a promise.

On the following pages
are two scenes written in
Mark's point of view.
Hope you enjoy getting
a little piece of Mark.

Sam and Mark's night in Vegas in *Trust Me*.

This was their first night together.

The night was coming to an end. I had met an incredible woman here tonight. Sam Matthews was beautiful, sexy, and funny as hell. We had been flirting all night, and there seemed to be an irresistible spark between us. We'd kept finding each other the entire night, and I wasn't able to take my eyes off her. Her green depths made me want her. There was something special about her. Whatever was going on was more than a one-night stand. I wanted to take her out on a few dates and get to know her.

I started making my way toward her. She bit her lip and gave me a sly smile from a few feet away as some asshole was talking to her. Not wanting to chance her leaving with him, I walked up to them. Sam looked at me again and gave me the most gorgeous smile as her eyes lit up. The other guy stopped speaking, realizing he had now become the third wheel.

This night is shaping up.

She linked her arm in mine. "Hey, Sport, are you ready?"

My cock jumped to life at her seductive tone. *She has a body made for worshiping.*

"Never thought the night would come to an end." I gave her a wink, and we both laughed.

We started walking. I loved having her on my arm.

It was time to start laying the foundation to get to know her. "There's a coffee shop in the lobby." I sounded like a pussy, but I wanted to get to know her before we got into bed together.

The sexual tension between us was high, and it was only a matter of time before we were together.

She stopped and looked at me as a million different emotions flashed across that beautiful face of hers. She glanced toward the exit and then toward the elevators as if she were torn. Almost as quick as it had happened, she masked her emotions.

She came closer to me and stood up on her tiptoes as she sexily whispered in my ear, "Mark, I think you know what I want, and it's not a cup of coffee."

Fuck me, she is direct.

Normally, when I slept with a girl, there was a connection of some sort. I wanted to see where it would go. It was like a get-to-know-you period. But Sam wanted to have sex.

If I push for coffee, she might bolt.

The thought of having coffee seemed to scare her for some reason, but she seemed undecided, like maybe a piece of her wanted more.

I kissed the part right below her ear. "I'm in room four fifteen."

"Good choice." She gave a little whimper before stepping back, and then she sassily walked toward the elevators.

I followed Sam into the elevator. After I pushed the button, I started to speak, wanting to try to use any chance I had to strengthen the connection, but she put her index finger on my lips.

"Don't ruin this, Sport. Just be in the moment."

Most women wanted to talk to me. Sam wanted to fuck me. I had a feeling that she'd walk if I pressed the limits too far. I knew I had seen something earlier, but her defenses were up, like an impenetrable force. We rode up in silence as we stared at each other.

Maybe if I give her what she wants she'll have breakfast with me?

The elevator door pinged, and we walked out into the corridor. We made it to my door. I slipped in the key card and turned the doorknob.

As I was about to push it open, Sam's hand came down on mine. "Mark, before we do this, I need to know if you're clean."

I stopped and turned to face her. "Sam, I would never sleep with someone if I wasn't clean. I'm tested regularly."

There was something else that passed over her face.

She softened. "I didn't mean that you would."

"Sam, it's fine. You call the shots and the speed of how this moves."

She nodded and seemed relieved. She released a slow breath that most wouldn't notice, and she seemed to minutely relax around me. Sam then opened the door. As she turned back, she crooked her finger at me. The no-nonsense, confident Sam returned and beckoned me farther into my room.

I normally didn't do this with women. If a woman only wanted my dick, I walked.

But Sam was different.

Letting the moment take over, I walked toward her and put my mouth on hers. She moaned and started going for my jacket.

This is going too fast.

I tried to slow down, but she went straight for my pants next, working on the buttons. I found the zipper on her ball gown, and I was unzipping it as she was working on my shirt.

When her hands made contact with my chest, I lost it, and I had her out of her clothes in seconds.

Round two can be done more slowly.

She broke the kiss, stepped back, and let her dress drop. She was in a black lace bra, matching panties, and garters.

The words, "Fuck me," slipped out of my mouth before I had a chance to rein them in.

She walked seductively to me. "Oh, I am about to do just that."

My dick won, and I kissed her again as I started walking us to the bed. She wrapped her legs around me. I was about to step back and go down on her when she bit my earlobe.

"Rip off my underwear. I need to be fucked right now."

I paused for a second too long as she grabbed my hand and put it on her heat.

She repeated, "Rip them off, Sport. I need you, hard and fast." Sam's tone was impatient.

Her panties were sheer, and I tore through them with no problem. She lay back on the edge of the bed, and I was about to thrust in when she stopped me.

Breathlessly, she said, "Don't forget to use a condom."

"Shit. I can't believe I almost forgot."

I went to my wallet where I always kept one. It had been a while since I had been with someone. Rolling the condom on, I walked toward the bed again. *I can't believe I almost forgot. I never forget.*

She spread her legs open, and I sank into her.

She is perfect.

I started moving in and out, building her slowly, and she moaned. She seemed to be enjoying herself.

Suddenly, her eyes snapped to mine. She stiffened, and as if she was torn on what to do, she said, "Stop playing fucking patty-cake with me. Hard and fast!"

What the hell? All the women I had slept with always wanted to be primed.

Each time it had seemed like we were having a tender moment, she would stop it and switch gears on me.

What is she scared of? What caused her to react like this?

I pushed into her hard, and I received an ecstatic moan. I started doing as she'd asked. I fucked her hard and fast as I held her legs up. She was getting tighter, and I knew it was about time for her to orgasm. I increased my speed and received a satisfactory response as she clutched the sheets. I refused to go this quick. I wanted her in my room for as long as I could keep her here. I needed to make this last. She arched her back as she let the orgasm take over. Her eyes fluttered as she pinched her nipples. Holding back was the hardest fucking thing I had done in a long time.

As her orgasm began to ebb, she relaxed into the bed, and I pulled out. She looked down and noticed I was still hard as a rock. Sam's green eyes danced with lust as she grinned. She stood up and brought her mouth to mine. I grabbed her, pulling her closer to me, and then she pulled back, exposing her neck. I kissed up it slowly, and she leaned back further, allowing me more access.

Sam then tensed slightly before saying, "I think it's my turn to ride."

What did I do wrong? I had been trying to appreciate her body and make love to her this time.

"You think you've got enough in you to handle the ride, Sport?"

She put her hands on my chest to turn me, and I complied.

Before pushing me back, Sam whispered, "I'm about to give you the ride of your life."

I fell back as my dick jumped. She crawled over me and positioned herself right above my erection. She slid onto me and bit her lip at the sensation.

"Mark, I want you to squeeze my nipples hard as I ride you. Don't stop until we both go."

Hell, she is beyond direct. I liked it. I leaned up and started massaging her perky breasts. *Fuck, they are amazing.*

"Harder, Mark. Squeeze them harder."

I did as she'd asked, and she rewarded me with that sexy moan of hers as she started moving up and down, increasing her pace. She was riding me fast and hard. I was sweating as I gritted my teeth, holding off on letting go. Perspiration started to coat her skin as I continued to squeeze her nipples hard. The torture continued as she rode me frantically, hard and fast.

Sam snapped her eyes to mine, and then her core squeezed my dick in a massaging motion. I lost it as I released myself into her.

It felt fucking amazing as she kept up her pace and screamed, "Yes! Yes! Yes!"

She took us both over the edge before collapsing onto my chest. My hands went to her back, and I trailed my fingertips down her spine.

"Sam, that was incredible."

She lifted her head. "You're not too bad yourself, Sport."

She froze and then rolled off me. We were both still breathless. I wanted to bring her to me and stroke my fingers against her soft skin again, but I knew she wouldn't want that. There was something about the close contact that terrified her.

How the hell am I going to convince her to give us a try? We were good together, like two puzzle pieces that fit perfectly.

Her eyes began to close, and I took that as a good sign.

"Night, Sport."

"Night, Sam."

She'll be here in the morning, and then we can talk about seeing each other again. My eyes slowly drifted close as I thought about how this woman had come into my life and rocked my world.

I stirred and looked at the clock. It was after four in the morning. I instinctively reached for Sam and found the bed cold and abandoned. I rose and ran into the bathroom, praying she was in there. I flipped on the light, and it was just like the bed—empty. I ran my hand through my hair.

She left.

No note.

No number.

Just…gone.

This was not the last Sam Matthews is going to see of me.

Sam and Mark's night together in North Carolina in *Love Me*.

This was their second time together.

It had been *months* since I had seen Sam. She hadn't been to any other team events with Allison, Damien Wales's wife.

But my luck had changed. Sam had been offered a job on the team, and she was meeting with the kicker tonight at a local hotel. From talking with Frank, I knew that their meeting would be over within the next twenty minutes. I drove over to the restaurant at the hotel. My goal was to run into Sam and hopefully rekindle what we had that night in Vegas.

I knew it had been more than a fuck that night. Since then, I had gone on a couple of dates, but my thoughts had *always* gone straight back to Sam. For some reason, Sam was different, and I didn't think I could forget her even if I tried. I remembered seeing something in her eyes that had told me she wanted more.

I parked my truck and went into the hotel lobby. I headed straight for the restaurant. It was dark, and as I quickly searched it, my heart sank. *Maybe I missed her?* Saying a silent prayer that I hadn't, I went to the bar and stopped in my tracks when I saw the black-haired, green-eyed goddess sitting on the stool.

Sam was sipping on a drink as she looked around. I walked over to the seat next to her. She was methodically looking over the area. Moving the stool out, I sat down beside her. The bartender came up to me and nodded, silently asking what I wanted.

"Bourbon."

"Yes, Mr. Robertson."

Living here and being the starting quarterback for Wales's team caused a lot of people to recognize me.

Sam stiffened at the name and then turned slowly toward me. When our eyes connected, those same sparks we'd had in

Vegas started to fly. I felt the connection, the heat, the want, and I knew she felt it, too. She shifted toward me, and for a moment, a look of wanting more passed across her face. Her green eyes sparkled, and she smiled at me.

Sam was more beautiful than I remembered.

"Hey there, Sport. It's been a while." Her voice was confident, but her right hand was tapping the counter.

It must be a nervous habit.

I shook my head with a smile playing on my lips. She seemed to be more at ease when I stayed relaxed.

"I was beginning to think you weren't up for another round," I teased.

Sam took a drink and winked at me. "Oh, I have another round in me. Question is, can you survive another round with me?"

That is the question of the day. The last few months, I had barely gone a day without thinking about her.

I wanted to spend more time with her. I knew she'd probably take me to her hotel room immediately. Her eyes were all excited as her tongue swiped her bottom lip a few times.

Trying to postpone us sleeping together, so I could get to know her more, I asked, "Would you like some dinner?"

Sam swallowed hard, and the same look that had passed over her face in Vegas reappeared for a split second. Then, it was gone. As if to mask her real emotions, she turned more seductive as she moved her leg closer to mine. She gave me a serious look as her hand went to the inside of my leg.

"Mark, I don't do attachments, but I do want to have some fun, if you're up for it."

Fuck. I wanted her. I wanted her badly, but she wanted to sleep with me and then leave again.

I had to keep trying, keeping pushing through, but for now, I would give her what she wanted. "What floor is your room on?"

I literally wanted to kick my own ass for not pushing dinner, but I knew she would walk if I had.

She got off the stool, and I went to follow when her hands went to my shoulders.

"Stay there, Sport. I'll be right back."

She grabbed her clutch but left her phone on the bar as she left. I then picked up her phone and quickly sent myself a text, so I would at least have her number now. It might be a little creepy, but she was tough with those walls she had surrounding her heart. I set the phone back on the counter and waited.

A few minutes later, she waved a room key in front of my face. "Room two twelve. Let's go."

I handed Sam her phone, and she took it. As we walked toward the elevator, I knew I had a limited amount of time to find out more about her.

Trying to be as casual and nonchalant as possible, I said, "So, I hear you're going to be working for the team."

I pushed the elevator button as she responded, "Yes, Wales wants me to help with contract negotiations at this point. The job will be more defined as I get closer to graduation."

The doors to the elevator opened and we walked in. I pushed the button for the second floor and the doors closed.

"When are you graduating?"

This damn elevator is going too fast.

The doors were already opening for the second floor. We walked out of the elevator.

Sam was in a tight red number that hugged her delicious body. My dick couldn't wait to be buried in her, but my heart wanted more than just her body. For now, I wanted to be given the chance to get to know her. I wanted the opportunity to see if we would be as great together as I thought we would be.

"I graduate this spring, and then I'll be moving up here." She slipped the key card in, and the door clicked.

As I was about to speak, she leaned toward me and said, "I can't wait for you to fuck me against the wall."

Her voice caused my dick to press against my pants. She did things to me. She caused something to stir deep from within.

I wouldn't make the mistake of falling asleep again tonight. I would stay up and hopefully talk her into breakfast.

We walked through the door, and Sam was on me. She wrapped her right leg around my waist. I turned, putting her against the wall. I wasn't going to deny her. My hands went to her skirt as her lips devoured my mouth. Sam's hands went to my pants and unzipped them, and then she rolled a condom on me before I knew it. She wanted it quick and dirty against the wall. Only lust was involved, but I wanted more.

"Against the wall, Mark. Don't wait."

She ground into me, and I inched up her skirt. Even though it had been months since I had slept with Sam, my body remembered how wonderful it was.

"Whatever you want, Sam, it's yours."

With that, I eased in, and I enjoyed the sensation of her tight heat around my dick. My mind wanted my body to slow down to enjoy this. It had been too fucking long since we had been together.

"Faster, Mark. Harder. I need this."

That was my undoing, hearing her say that I had something she needed.

I moved into her faster. She was moaning, and her tight heat began to squeeze me. The moment I felt her orgasm, I released. It was better than I remembered, and we hadn't even made it to the bed yet. Sam sagged against the wall as I pulled out of her. I was craving intimacy with her, but she still felt distant.

We both tried to slow our breathing down. She gave me a satisfied sexy smile and leaned her head back, exposing her skin. I kissed her neck tenderly, and she moaned. Finally, I was making some headway with her. Before I knew it, she stiffened as if realizing the same thing herself. She barely pushed against my chest, and then she pulled down her dress. She was obviously nervous now.

Fuck, I shouldn't have kissed her like that.

I wanted to hold and savor her.

I backed away and discarded my condom in the nearby wastebasket. I zipped up my pants. *Calm. Remain calm.* I needed to make her feel comfortable. I took a step back and walked toward the bedroom, removing my sports jacket.

When I turned around, Sam was unzipping her dress and letting it fall to the floor.

"Sport, I hope you have round two in you."

At least she isn't leaving. It felt like a small victory.

"I'm always ready for you."

Sam gave me a seductive grin as she started walking toward me.

She owns me—completely.

All I want is her.

It was after one in the morning. Sam lay motionless, her breathing shallow, on the other side of the bed, not touching me. I refused to fall asleep. If I stayed awake all night, maybe there would be a chance to go to breakfast together.

I slipped out of bed to use the restroom. I was quiet to ensure that I didn't disturb my sleeping beauty. She was beautiful, and I craved an intimate connection with her.

I returned back to the bedroom to find the hall light on and Sam gone.

Double fuck.

She was gone—again.

There was still hope. Sam was moving to North Carolina.

There is only so long that woman can run and hide from me.

RECIPES FROM
EDNA

Swedish Heirloom Cookies

Remember, a relationship requires many different ingredients—
love, trust, openness, and forgiveness.
Without one of the ingredients, the recipe becomes ruined.

Yield = Four Dozen

Ingredients:
½ cup shortening
½ cup butter or margarine
1 cup sifted powdered sugar
½ teaspoon salt
2 cups all-purpose flour
1 tablespoon water
1 tablespoon vanilla extract
1 ¼ cups ground almonds
1 cup powdered sugar
Additional powder sugar for coating

Directions:
Cream shortening and butter at medium speed
with an electric mixer until light and fluffy.
Add powdered sugar and salt.
Mix well. Stir in flour. Add water, vanilla, and almonds.
Stir well. Shape dough into one-inch balls.
Place on ungreased cookie sheet and flatten.
Bake at 325 degrees for 12 minutes or until done.
Dredge warm cookies in powdered sugar.

Chocolate Pie

Regardless of the outside, each person has a soft center.
Respect and protect your other half so that they have
a safe place to be when all else is falling apart.

Ingredients:

1 baked pie shell

Pie:
¼ cup plain flour
¼ cup powdered cocoa
¼ teaspoon salt
1 cup sugar
½ cup milk
1 large can evaporated milk
2 egg yolks
1 ½ teaspoon vanilla
1 tablespoon butter

Meringue:
2 egg whites
4 tablespoons sugar

Directions:
Whisk together flour, cocoa, salt, and sugar until smooth.
Add evaporated milk and egg yolks. Whisk until mixture is
smooth. Cook for 2 minutes in the microwave. Take out and
whisk. Cook another 3 minutes in microwave, take out, and
whisk. Repeat last step. Continue this process while decreasing
your time until you have a pudding-like consistency.
Add vanilla and butter. Whisk until smooth. Pour into baked pie shell.

Meringue: Beat 2 egg whites until stiff. Gently add
4 tablespoons of sugar and continue to beat until smooth.
Pour on top of pie and bake 8 to 10 minutes at 400 degrees or until brown.

Strawberries on a Cloud
Sometimes, a proper cooling-off time allows
each person to become levelheaded.

Ingredients:

Crust:
3 egg whites
½ teaspoon cream of tartar
¾ cup sugar

Filling:
1 (eight oz.) package cream cheese
1 cup sugar
1 teaspoon vanilla
1 large carton Cool Whip
6 cups whole strawberries
2 cups sliced strawberries
1 large package of strawberry Jell-O
2 cups of boiling water

Directions:
Heat oven to 275 degrees. Beat egg whites with cream of
tartar until foamy. Add sugar a little at a time until soft peaks
form. Spread on brown paper on a cookie sheet to make crust.
Bake for 1 ½ hours. Turn off oven and leave meringue shell
in oven to cool.
Blend cream cheese, sugar, and vanilla. Fold in Cool Whip
and spread over meringue shell. Dissolve Jell-O in water.
Chill until it begins to set. Stir in strawberries enough to coat.
Pile strawberries high on cream-cheese filling. Chill.

SNEAK PEEK OF
ripple Effect

BOOK ONE OF
The Effect Series

COMING OCTOBER 2014

CHAPTER ONE
Adam

I had a major fucking problem to deal with. Someone was taking pictures of members at my club and then selling them online. Earlier this evening, I had been informed of the leak when Mark Robertson brought me a picture he had seen of his girlfriend, Sam, on his football teammate's cell phone. There were supposedly other pictures of other members being sold on this exclusive site. The wide-receiver prick, Dustin Marco, was getting a piece of the profits from what Mark had said.

I stared at the pic of my old fuck buddy, Sam, in the cat mask, red wig, and black leather outfit Mark had given me from Dustin's cell phone. Sam was now going to live the life of merry commitment and fucking white picket fences with Mark. I was glad she had found someone. She deserved to be happy. Mark seemed like a decent guy. When Sam and I had been together, we had both known the score—no attachments, just sex. *It worked for us, and we both knew our arrangement would end one day.*

My phone rang. It was my partner and best friend, Brandt.

I answered, "Did you pull the footage from last Halloween?"

"Yeah, I've got it all cued up, and I'm reviewing it. We'll catch this asshole, Adam. I'll keep you posted. All else looks good in both areas of the club."

"Thanks. I'm going to make my rounds. Let me know when you find something."

"Will do."

We both hung up the phone.

Brandt and I had been friends since we were kids. After our first year in college, we'd decided college life wasn't for us, and we'd opened up a dance club. We called it Club Envy. In the beginning, it had started as a regular dance club that had a band, bar, and a dance floor.

After a year, we were smashed after turning a decent profit for the bar and came up with the idea to expand and add an exclusive sex club in the back that would be part of Club Envy. We hadn't given the sex club a different name since we didn't want to draw attention to it. Those that participated in the sex-club scene knew about us, and that was all I cared about.

Walking out of my office to make my rounds while Brandt looked at the footage, I looked around. The crowd was sparse tonight, as expected, since it was the middle of the week.

I went to the bouncer, Trigger, who guarded the side entrance to the club for employees and VIPs only. The main entrance was across the club. There was more security on that side, and paperwork was needed each time you entered. Trigger was about twenty-two with brown eyes and messy blond hair. Hell, he was stacked and could throw a punch. The girls seemed to like him, and on his nights off, he took pleasure in what the club had to offer. Trigger was what we called a free lover. He wouldn't do the exclusivity thing. He just wanted to float from girl to girl.

Trigger gave me a nod as I walked up.

"All's good, Adam. The new girl you just cleared came in with Nora, and she's at the bar. Snake is currently with her, like you requested."

Normally, either Brandt or I met any new member who wanted exclusive membership at the door, but Nora and Ainsley had signed the necessary paperwork for Nora to bring her inside.

"Thanks, Trigger. Let me know if anything comes up."

Trigger gave me a nod, and I walked off toward the bar of the sex-club. Each side of Club Envy had a bar area. This side of the club was completely different than the bar-club side. The sex-club side was retro in style with frosted glass tables and different-colored lights of red, green, purple, yellow, and blue that illuminated and gave the room a sexy glow. Odd-shaped chairs sat around the tables. There were high tables, low tables, lounge areas, and the bar area. The bar of the sex club was all done in the same frosted glass with the same colors lighting the separate boxed sections. Behind the bar area, there were rooms where different scenes could take place, depending on a member's desires. If all the rooms were booked, there was a communal or exhibitionism room anyone could use.

Unless members were in one of the rooms, we required them to be dressed. We didn't mind the main area getting a little hot and heavy, but discretion needed to be used. All the members who were here tonight were seasoned patrons and generally abided by the rules.

As I approached the bar, a bright pink wig caught my attention. It had to be Ainsley Pearson, Nora's friend, the potential new member. Her back was to me, but she was laughing and talking with Nora, the bartender.

Ainsley's questionnaire had intrigued me. She wasn't the typical person who sought membership at my club. From the picture I had of her, she was beautiful with long chestnut hair and pale blue eyes. Nora had asked for a favor to fast-track Ainsley on the visitor list. It normally took longer than two weeks to get a visitation night. We didn't want any riffraffs from the street coming into our establishment, and I needed time to complete the screenings. When Nora had shown me Ainsley's picture, I had wanted to meet her myself for some reason. Generally, I always went with my gut instinct on those types of decisions.

I walked up slowly and nodded to Snake, another security guard, who was standing about four feet away from Ainsley. He had short spikey black hair with a snake tattoo that wound up his neck. With the tip of my head, I gave him the signal that I had Ainsley for a bit.

As Snake walked off, I saw him take his walkie-talkie from his back pocket. He was probably talking to Brandt to see where he needed to go next. I hated those damn walkie-talkies that Brandt had insisted we get for all the personnel. I never carried mine. If there were a problem, security would find me.

If I had to get involved, whoever was causing the problem would wish like hell that he or she hadn't started anything.

Next, I checked Ainsley's wrist to make sure she had on the black bracelet. Nonmembers weren't allowed to engage in sex in the club. Membership fees weren't cheap, and I needed to make sure they were serious before they started benefiting from the pleasures the club could offer. Per the reports I had received, Ainsley didn't have much money in her account, and she worked at the university's library part-time. Sometimes, the fees were waived if a member became mine or Brandt's partner. I hoped that Ainsley was on the same page as me in what she wanted to get out of this experience.

I leaned up against the bar. "Hey, Nora. How about a beer?"

Nora gave me an endearing smile and went to get my standard brand of beer, Guinness. From the corner of my eye, I could see I had Ainsley's attention. She was watching me with her head cocked slightly as if she was trying to figure me out. I wasn't ready to look at her yet. Nora popped the cap off my Guinness and handed it to me. I took a swig of beer and turned toward Ainsley. Nora had said that she and Ainsley had become good friends during their sophomore year of college. They were seniors now.

Ainsley was even more beautiful than her picture. Her chestnut hair was hidden underneath her bright pink wig. Her makeup seemed heavier than the more natural shot I had of her in my office. She gave me a sly smile, and I was instantly hard. She had the perfect mouth, and I wanted those lips wrapped around my cock. The moment our eyes connected, my dick wanted inside her.

I looked around, making sure no one could hear me. I wanted to see how she reacted. The one thing that hadn't been clear on her questionnaire was why she wanted to join a sex club. Her answer was vague, which in this case, only intrigued me more. Normally, if I wasn't able to get a clear picture from the paperwork, a visitor pass was not issued.

I tipped my beer her way. "Ainsley, right?"

Her smile dropped, and her eyes darted around the bar. She looked surprised as she said, "Do I know you?"

I extended my hand. "I'm Adam, owner of Club Envy."

Her features relaxed as she extended her hand. "Nice to meet you. Thanks for letting me visit tonight. Are you the person I talk to about becoming a member?"

She was direct. I liked a woman who didn't beat around the bush.

I took a swig. "Let me show you around, and then we can talk."

Ainsley glanced toward Nora, who nodded.

So, little Miss Pink Wig is the cautious type.

Most women who came here would go off with the first dick that approached them. I liked that she wasn't like that.

Ainsley slid off the stool. Her tight skirt went up slightly, and I had to stop myself from wanting to run my hands along her inner thigh.

"Sounds good. Lead the way, Adam."

Her head came to the top of my shoulders. I was just over six foot, so she had to be five-five or five-six. She was a petite little thing. She adjusted her skirt back in place. She was insanely gorgeous, and as her dress clung to her, I assumed she had a very toned body.

We started walking, and her perfume had me wanting to fuck her against the first available surface, club rules be damned.

Fuck me. She's hot. Shit, I need to beat my pansy-ass for not being able to control my dick right now.

She asked, "So, how does one get into the sex-club business?"

My eyes went to hers. In the four years I had been doing this, no other female had ever asked me that. She seemed genuinely curious as she continued to look around at everything, absorbing the atmosphere.

She must have sensed my surprise as she clarified, "I'm a student at the University of Georgia, and I was just curious.

I'm taking a summer course on marketing, and my mind was thinking about how, in your case, sex really does sell."

I laughed as we approached the private rooms people had to reserve to use. I took another swig of my Guinness as I thought about how to answer.

"Well, my partner and I started the dance club five years ago. One night, we got drunk and started talking about fuck pads. From there, we came up with this." I shrugged.

We stopped in front of one of the doors. A slight blush crept across Ainsley's cheeks as she looked at the door. There were signs on each of the doors. This particular one said:

AFTERBURN

Since the place was swankier, Brandt and I had gone with the names of the shots we had taken that night as we schemed up our new adventure together.

Ainsley looked at it and murmured, "Afterburn?"

I replied, "Shot names."

"That makes sense, and it goes with the atmosphere. So, Adam, what lies behind the Afterburn door?"

I gave her my standard speech. "As you might have noticed, the main bar area requires clothes. All members can have a tab, but the balance is due on a weekly basis. This is where the private rooms are. There are six total. The other side has two separate rooms. One is a communal room, and the other is set up for those who like exhibitionism. Since it's the middle of the week, two of the rooms aren't booked tonight, so I'm able to show you what one looks like. Each room is styled differently, but the apparatus and toys are all the same. After each room is used, everything is sterilized and cleaned prior to the next usage. Generally, rooms are booked for full evenings. Any questions so far?"

She was calmly taking it all in. I was having a hard time figuring her out. One minute, she would blush, and the next, she would ask business questions, but she wasn't trying to fuck the first thing with two legs that walked her way. She was a puzzle to me, and I was drawn to her.

What is she after?

She shook her head. "No questions right now. Show away."

I opened the door, and she walked in, looking around from floor to ceiling.

There was a bed, some sex chairs, a dresser full of toys, and a few other pieces of furniture that made for some fan-fucking-tastic sex. We had two rooms that were BDSM-centered, and they were equipped with whips, chains, shackles, and the like. That wasn't my style, but I had tried it a few times.

Ainsley walked farther into the room. Her tall heels helped emphasize her toned calves. She turned back my way. "This is different but intriguing. What does someone do to find a partner, if interested?"

Ainsley cocked her head to the side as she looked at me. I thought she was trying to read me as much as I was trying to read her. She wasn't going to let me get away with shit.

I like it.

I took another swig of my beer. "I'd wager that you won't have any problems finding someone, if you're interested. Once that black bracelet comes off, it's like dating. People approach you, and you either agree or don't agree to take the next step. Just because you come to a room with someone doesn't mean that you have to follow through. You can leave at any time. If you ever run into a problem, you can come find me, if I'm not already around."

I planned to be the one exclusively with her.

She bit her lip and looked down. Thinking about her in this room with all the ways I could pleasure her, my cock got so hard that it was turning to stone. I knew my body, and it had never reacted this fucking fast to someone. I needed to get her out of here to make sure she understood how this worked before I made a move. She wasn't ready for that step. If

Ainsley was looking for a happy ending, I wasn't her guy. I hoped to be the in-between guy who worshiped her body in the way it deserved to be touched.

I started walking backward toward the door. "Why don't we go to my office and talk some more? We can see what your thoughts are and go from there."

She started walking my way as she said, "Sure, I'd like that. I have some questions, if you don't mind answering when we get to your office."

"Not at all."

I motioned for her to step out of the room, and I followed. Music from the club surrounded us. Ainsley paused, and I took the lead as we started walking toward my office. I generally found that people got nervous next to a guy like me when I was quiet. They would start chatting up a storm and divulge information I wasn't able to tell from the questionnaire—but not Ainsley. She was taking everything in. Her wheels seemed to be constantly churning in that beautiful head of hers.

We walked into my office where the swanky decorations continued. I had a glass desk, black leather desk chair, and two black leather chairs in front of the desk. In between the two chairs was a funky vase that sat on a glass Z table.

Ainsley's eyes drifted to the door in the back. That door led to my private quarters for when I needed to stay the night at the club. No girl had ever been back there. She took a seat in a chair, and I went to my desk chair.

She looked at me again with those inquisitively sharp eyes. "How would I stay anonymous if I was able to afford the monthly fees?"

"You'd continue to wear wigs or whatever you wanted, and we'd give you another name to use when you check in. If you wear a wig, keep it on, even in the rooms. Otherwise, people will be able to spot you in public."

Ainsley's fingers went to her pink wig, and she played with the strands. "How many members do you have?"

I took the last sip of my Guinness. "Currently, we have around fifty members, only about twenty-eight are regular attendees. There are twenty people on the waiting list to get in. I like to slowly introduce new members to the club in order to maintain control and balance of the atmosphere."

"How did I get in so fast?"

It was more out of mere innocent curiosity.

Ainsley seemed confident and collected. From the questionnaire she had been given, she had confirmed she wasn't a virgin. Virgins were a no-go for the club. Nora had mentioned that, until recently, Ainsley had had a steady boyfriend through college. I figured the breakup was a part of what was driving her to try this scene. However, from what Nora had shared, Ainsley seemed like she'd had a normal healthy relationship in her day-to-day activities. This was the part of Ainsley that I'd found most intriguing about her wanting to visit the club. It was the swaying factor in moving her ahead on the waiting list. She didn't seem to have some fucked-up part in her that I saw in a lot of people who came here. Most of our members were unable to have relationships outside of the sex-clubs walls. It seemed the majority of the members used sex to escape some reality they needed to face.

Hell, I should know.

Leaning forward in my chair, I thought about the best way to respond. There was something about her that I craved to taste. I wanted to take her off the market before the sharks out in the club could have a chance to feel her, touch her, pleasure her.

My heart started beating faster. I had never responded to someone like this, and I needed to get my proposal out in the open. If she rejected me, I wasn't sure what I was going to do. I hadn't feared rejection in years, and the thought was unnerving. *Stop being a pussy and just put it out there.*

In the extended silence, she didn't begin to fidget. She calmly sat there as if she embraced the silence. She was taking me by surprise. I found it best to always turn the question back on the person until I knew what they wanted. Years of deceit had taught me that. After being burned by my own fucking brother in the worst possible way, I protected myself.

"Why do you ask?"

Ainsley's delicate fingers grazed the vase. "From what I can tell, you run your business on stringent rules and guidelines. Everything seems to have order and a procedure. To move me ahead on the visitor list after being here tonight surprises me. You know from the background check you did on me, I don't have a substantial bank account. I'm a simple college student with scholarships and a part-time job. When Nora told me I should try Club Envy, I put the thought aside for several weeks before applying. When I did apply, I thought it would take months. Then to fast-track my application when you know I wouldn't be the most profitable business decision surprised me."

She was good, really good. I wasn't ready to start answering her questions without having a little more information about her. Her questionnaire only said she was a business student. Normally, I rejected vague questionnaires, but I'd had to meet her.

"What's your major, Ainsley?"

Her pale blue eyes met mine again. "I think it's only fair you answer my question before I answer yours. How'd I get in so fast?"

She held her ground, and it turned me on even more.

Putting my hands behind my head, I responded, "Fair enough. I'm intrigued by you, Ainsley. From the moment I saw your picture, I wanted to meet you."

The reflection from the light danced off the silver tinsel sporadically placed through her wig. Interlacing her fingers, she responded, "My major is business analysis."

That explained her observations of the finer details of everything.

Not giving her time to ask anything else, I went right to the heart of the matter. "Why do you want to be a member at Club Envy?"

She sat straighter in her chair. Her eyes became slightly sad. "I want to do something with no strings attached. I want to live, be a little rebellious, and be in the moment. Nora and I were talking, and she suggested this place. I've never done anything like this before."

Her eyes flickered to the left slightly, and I knew she wasn't telling me everything. Years of watching people had allowed me to read people better than most. I continued to watch her as she penetrated me with her pale blue gaze. I wondered if she'd really meant it when she said she wanted no strings. I was able to do no strings. However, a lot of people said they were able to do it, but in reality, they were trying to tame the wild part that refused to settle down.

My dick was aching to be in her, but I wouldn't go there if I thought it was going to end up with fucking hearts being drawn around our names. Hearts and love were overrated. I should know since mine had been ripped out...gruesomely.

We sat there in silence. She never tried to fill the uncomfortable gaps with conversation. Hell, at this point, it seemed like she could outlast me with the silence.

"What type of guy are you looking for?"

She crossed her legs, and my eyes were again drawn to how toned they were.

"Before we get to that, I think we should discuss the membership fees and any additional rules or information that didn't come with the visitation packet. I don't want to waste your time if I can't afford it. In fact, after seeing the place tonight, I know I can't afford it."

Normally, the first questions from potential members were all related to sex. Besides the money aspect, the rest of the shit didn't make a difference to them. She was definitely different.

If she did join, she'd be one of the younger women here, and fuck, she would get a lot of attention. I needed to think about how I wanted to handle this. The thought of her walking out of Club Envy and wrapping her legs around someone else pissed me off.

From the moment I approved her visitation, I had doubted she was going to be able to afford the fees, but I didn't care. The only possibility I had wondered about was that she might have had a trust fund of some sort or an allowance from her parents.

Leaning forward, I thought about how to best approach Ainsley with becoming my new fuck buddy. From what I could sense, she wouldn't take handouts. My last partner, Sam, hadn't been able to afford this place, and I had waived her membership fee for her exclusivity. I never shared partners. They were mine, and I was theirs until we parted ways.

I want Ainsley bad. The worst thing she could say at this point is no. Shit, I want her to say yes.

"Ainsley, I want to propose something. The rules are the same as the packet you received. The confidentiality agreements that you signed will still apply. All of the STD tests you took will be put in your permanent file. If there's no new information to add to the questionnaire, I can use the same one you already filled out." I paused, and Ainsley nodded.

"The reason I ask what kind of guy you are looking for is because I want to be your partner while you're a member here. Some members want multiple partners, but that's not how I do it. We can discuss fees later, but it will be something within your budget. I don't want you to feel demeaned by my offer, but I think you and I can give each other what we need."

She played with a ring on her right index finger. She turned it over and over again while watching me. She crossed her legs in the other direction. By the slight squirm, I knew she was attracted to me. She was doing a damn fine job of masking it though. I sat there with no emotion on my face even though my dick was jumping for joy at the thought that she wanted me inside her.

She cocked her head to one side. "I'm not a submissive. I don't know the ins and outs of all of that, but I know that's not for me."

She was all business, and I liked that about her. She wasn't doing all that lovey-dovey giggly shit.

I relaxed my posture in my seat since she hadn't said no. "I'm not asking for a submissive. We'll both give each other what we need on equal ground. We'll never do anything you are uncomfortable with."

She let my words absorb. My eyes kept going to her top. It was a low-scoop green silk shirt. The club was cold, and as she shifted, I could make out the faint outline of her nipples.

Ainsley relaxed her posture slightly like me as she leaned back in the chair. "And what do you need, Adam?"

"To fuck you hard, countless times, to be buried so deep inside you while you scream in pleasure—that's what I want out of this, Ainsley. Lust and sex—that's it."

I heard her intake of breath, and her eyes became clouded. She was looking me over—for what, I had no idea. She started twirling her ring again. Her breathing was a tad quicker. To the normal observer, she would still appear unaffected.

"So, how does that work? Do we make appointments to have sex?"

I let out a small breath. I was making ground and could feel the deal was about to be closed. I would have to kiss her tonight before she left. I was going to have to stick my finger inside her. And if I was lucky, I was going to fuck her against the office wall.

Keeping my voice calm, I responded, "More or less. We work out times to give each other pleasure, and then we return to our normal lives. There are no strings, no complications. It's just sexual gratification. What do you think?"

She stood, tall and confident. Without wavering, she said, "Yes."

THANK YOU

To Paul—You are my everything. Each and every day you show me trust, love, and promise to be my forever. Thank you for always being there for me and supporting me through this journey. I love you infinity factorial.

To Makaela—I love you! I love you more! I love you the most! That is one of my favorite moments of the day when we each say those three lines to each other after being apart. You are such a blessing to my life, and I will love you forever and always.

To my parents: Kathy, Tim, Gehrig, and Janet—It's not often that a gal is blessed with four wonderful parents. Your love, unconditional support, and being there for me mean so much. I hope I'm always there for Makaela as you have been there for me.

To Sarah Harper—Well, Harper, can you believe the Trust Series is finally published? I can't. It seems like just yesterday when I sent you the first five chapters of *Trust Me*, and this incredible journey started. You're the peas in my vegetable medley. Or am I the peas? I can't remember. Ha-ha! Thanks for always being there for me. I heart you, girl.

To Kelly Elliott—Girl, are you picking up what I'm putting down? You know what I'm talking about. Um…um…um…what would I do without you? Seriously, what would I do? Your friendship means so much to me, and I don't think my chickler or chortle box has ever gotten such a good workout. I love you, the NWVK!

To Jovana Shirley—Bibbidi-bobbidi-boo! Poof! All I have to say are those words, and my Fairy Edit Godmother appears. You're brilliant and amazing in your editing skills! Thank you *so* much for everything. Xoxo!

To Heather Davenport—Girl, I don't know how you do it, but you are a woman of many, many talents. Thank you for everything you have done with arranging the release and blog tour for *Promise Me* through your company Book Plug Promotions.

To My Beta Readers:

> Maren—I miss you! I can't wait to come visit you this next year, but thank goodness for FaceTime. It's amazing that what started off as a common love for touring as much as we could in Mexico turned into an amazing family with kiddos the same age. Thank you for everything and for being such a wonderful beta reader. You are such a special and dear friend to me.

> Nikola (Again, you never shall be called Nikki from me.)—You are one of the most sincere people I know. I'm so thankful that my job many moons ago brought us together. We had some good times and built a friendship that will last forever. Thank you for being the last set of eyes to read my books!

> Brandy—As always, thank you so much for taking the time to read with your hectic schedule. Thank you for all your feedback. It's amazing what a little chat can turn into. Oh, and P.S., thank you for putting more Slater in this last book.

> Heather—You are one of the fastest readers I know! I love seeing messages from you in my inbox asking when I'm sending the next bit of my book to you. I promise, I'm hurrying. I've enjoyed getting to know you and becoming friends. Thank you!

To Chris Chandler and Eddie Smith at Chandler Graphics— Thank you for yet again another beautiful cover! You do such incredible work.

To April Park at April Park Photography—Your photos are incredible. I have loved shooting the Trust Series with you. Thank you for sharing your talents.

To Damien's Darkside Divas—Ladies, ladies, ladies! Your diva attacks are epically out of this world. Thank you for all your love, support, and for bringing a smile to my face daily. I will treasure these memories forever. I'm still trying to figure out how in the world I'm going to get a pass into Diva Land! I heart you guys so much!

To the Trust Series Discussion Board—As I sit here and type this, my little notification sound is going off, and it appears that I'm being guilt tripped to consult my Magic 8-Ball to give you guys some kind of hint as to who Mr. XXX is. Hehehe! I remain strong in the fact that I am a hint-giver and information provider, not a teaser. And now that it is printed in a book, I think that makes it official!

To Karen Wilcox (Thelma), Kelly Wheeler (Louise), Jennifer Isaacs (Picture Fairy), Lori Peixoto (PS), Mary Kornegay (Movie Director), Amy Hapner (Lucy Lover), Lisa Waugh (BFQ), Cynde Eller, Shawna Tremoulis—Thank you for everything! You guys have done so much for me, and I am so grateful for everything you do. It's amazing the friendships that have formed. Thank you for the laughs, thank you for the support, but above all, thank you for the friendship. I heart you guys so much!

To Readers—Thank you for all your support through this journey. You have made every step in this journey completely worth it. Thank you for everything. You will never know how much all your messages mean to me each and every day. I hope you enjoyed Sam's story, the extra scenes from Mark's point of view, and the sneak peek at *Ripple Effect*, the first book in the Effect Series.

www.ingramcontent.com/pod-product-compliance
Lightning Source LLC
Chambersburg PA
CBHW020237200626
46816CB00001BA/11